PAPER GHOSTS

*To Zach —
Thanks for
your help!
Best Jesse*

JESSE KALFEL

Fulton Books
Meadville, PA

Published by Fulton Books 2023

ISBN 978-1-63985-900-9 (paperback)
ISBN 978-1-63985-901-6 (digital)

Printed in the United States of America

For my wife from whom I ask advice on virtually everything and my daughter who makes me so proud to be her dad.

He was naked running through the woods, heading to the waterfalls, which were steps away. His body was bloody, his flesh dangling in shreds, torn apart by the man who chased him. He stopped when he reached the edge. The man caught up to him. He opened his mouth, shoving the thing inside that the man so desperately wanted. Before the man could reach him, he stepped backward, knowing he would die. As he fell, he remembered the image of the 9/11 falling man, and a peaceful sensation he had not experienced for most of his life flowed through him. That was his last conscious thought as his head and neck smashed against a rocky outcrop. Looking like a rag doll with limbs akimbo, he plunged into a pool of swirling water. He drifted into the middle like a man enjoying the relaxing buoyancy of floating in water.

PROLOGUE

SWAN SONG, ITHACA, NEW YORK

Pink was troubled. It was New Year's Eve. He was throwing a grand party, a goodbye to his movie-making days. Goodbye, 1925. Hello, 1926. But the coming New Year didn't seem like an occasion to celebrate. Not at all. Probably more trouble would fall upon the people he knew like a shit storm raining down hard from the movie gods.

Over the past five years, he had seen too many scandals, too many deaths, and too much change take over the world he inhabited. Pink's good pal, Fatty Arbuckle, was accused of rape and murder. The tabloids said he ravaged Virginia Rappe, a bit actress, with a champagne bottle at a wild party. He knew his friend. He was funny and, yes, fat. But he wasn't capable of doing any of the horrible things the newspapers said he did. This whole business with Fatty was a rotten business. It was show business, everyone said. But he knew it was really a place called hell dressed up with pixie dust.

Then there was his friend Olive Thomas, whom they called the Ideal American Girl, an up-and-coming actress who was Jack Pickford's adoring girlfriend. She committed suicide, or so they said, swallowing a bottle of mercuric chloride that Jack, the wandering dick, was taking to treat his syphilis. William Desmond Taylor, a well-known director at Paramount, was found murdered in his bungalow apartment. Wally Reid had died in a padded cell while kicking his morphine addiction.

The list of tragedies went on. The movie business seemed glamorous to the public but was a living hell for too many of the people who worked in front and behind the cameras.

On this particular night, the last night in December, Pink should have been happy, but he felt cheerless. It was a party for his boys and the people whom he had worked with. A gorgeous dame, hung on his arm, kept pressing her bosom into his side. She was slim and pretty and wore a flapper outfit that all the gals were wearing these days. It was a shimmering number, tiered and sparkly, a sequin-trimmed neckline scooped low to show off her ample cleavage.

She was an extra on the last movie his studio shot who believed that *schtupping* him would pay off getting her better roles. But there would be no better roles. No more pictures. He was closing down DimaDozen Studios forever. She would probably think she was flim-flammed when she found out but that's the way it worked. Men and women alike had an "open for business" sign for fucking if it helped get them what they wanted.

"See that little girl over there?" Pink asked, pointing to a cute child wearing a sailor's dress outfit with gold nautical buttons, a white bow attached on the front.

The aspiring starlet looked over to where he pointed. "She looks kinda lost."

"Make friends with her. See how she's doing."

"Happy to, sweetie." As she left, she bent over, showing him her ladies.

Pink then moved past the long table with plates of cold shrimp, caviar, and oysters trucked in from the Chesapeake Bay. He was sipping top-shelf bootlegged brandy and smoking a good Cuban, the rewards of having been a successful player in the motion picture business. He had just bought a brand-new Packard Roadster the week before along with a house in town. This part of his life was coming to a close; the rollercoaster life he had lived over the past thirteen years was now ending like the last scene of one of his cliffhangers.

He looked around the ballroom he had rented at the Clinton House, a stately hotel built in the Greek Revival style back in 1828. Everyone was there—all of his stars: Irene Castle, Milton Sills, Pearl White, Lionel Barrymore, and many others as well. And then there were his boys, the people audiences never saw on the screen but made everything work behind it. Delmar Gilmore, Ollie Gustafson, and

Marcus Ellwell. They gave one another nicknames when Pink first put together his production company back in April of 1913—a sign of his boys' affection for one another and a way to build camaraderie in a business that was cut-throat. Needles Gilmore was his costume man who could handle a Singer sewing machine like the best French tailor. Crank Gustafson was his ace cameraman, his moniker created because of the way he could smoothly hand-crank his Cinegraph camera. Loci Ellwell was his location scout who could find the best place to shoot any scene he needed. Pink had given himself his own nickname. He was Percy Maxwell to the public but known among friends as Pink. Why he chose *Pink* no one knew.

Irene Castle came up to him and patted his ass. "Nice party. We're going to miss you."

"Likewise."

She held the hand of a monkey dressed in a tuxedo. "Say hello to Jennie Lynn."

Pink smiled at the creature and then at Castle. "Seems you like collecting these little apes. Funny kinda hobby," he teased.

"Capuchin monkeys, darling. Can you give me a light?" Irene asked as she held out a cigarette holder.

Pink gave her a light.

"I just had to get her. Saw Jennie dancing around an organ grinder in the Bowery. Gave the guinea fifty clams. Handed her over faster than a colored boy flying past a Klan picnic."

The bosomy actress returned, sashaying across the hall, and sidled over to Pink, once again slipping her arm through his. In her free hand, she held the little girl's hand.

"My little friend here has a question for you," said the woman. Pink looked down into the girl's eyes and smiled.

"Can I have a Dr. Pepper, Uncle Pink?"

"Sure thing, Suzy," he said sweetly then removed the woman who had reattached herself to his arm. "Can you take the kid over to the dessert table and get her a soda?"

"And some cake too," the girl said, more like a plea than a demand.

"And cake," Pink said to the woman.

"Be happy to." She led the kid away, exaggerating the swing of her derriere for all to admire.

"Nice tush on your *shiksa*," Castle commented.

"I like to keep my options open."

"Pretty though. She a keeper?"

Pink shrugged. "Depends if the magic she imagines we have is still there after I tell her I'm done with DimaDozen."

"Magic's what we put into movies. Not in between the sheets."

"Some of the women I bed say my bedroom technique is magical."

"Well, of course they would say that, you idiot."

Pink grinned.

"So who's the little girlie?"

"My half-sister. Susan. She calls me Uncle. Less complicated."

"She lives with you?"

"Her grand folks. Next town over from here. Gotta farm. Good people. I promised to take her to my party tonight."

"You staying in this hick town or fleeing westward with all the other full-of-shit picture folks?"

"Gonna pitch my tent here. It's not that bad from May till October. Pretty countryside and you can't beat the fresh air. I bought a little place down in Key West to go to when my nuts start turning blue from the frost."

"Key West, huh? You must like mosquitoes," Castle joked then turned and looked at all the people who came to Pink's party. "You were liked. Nice turnout."

"Free food and giggle water will do that."

"Hard to give you a compliment," she said playfully then gave him a kiss on his cheek. "So you're really retiring from the life."

"I did the dance, had some chuckles, made some dough, and came out alive. Not hooked on dope. Still fairly sane. I'd say I had a pretty good run. Besides, our world is going to change."

Castle's raised eyebrows signaled Pink to explain.

"Talkies."

"You think that's going to catch on."

"One of the reasons I'm shutting down my studio. My actors know how to mug to the camera. But think about it, Irene. Mugging for the camera makes people look comical with over exaggerated gestures. But with words, you don't need all that chest beating, all those put-on facial expressions like your monkeys make."

Castle smiled and then pantomimed a woman in distress, her mouth forming a wide *O*, the back of her hand pressed against her forehead.

"Worse than that, most actors have terrible voices. Squeaky, gravelly, stutterers, lispy."

"And those Brooklyn accents," she added. "Geez Louise."

"You mean like our friend Clara over there," he said, pointing to Clara Bow, Brooklyn-born and now being lauded as the *it girl*.

"What do you think of my voice?"

"Perfect," said Pink. "Not sure about Jennie Lynn's." Pink looked around, taking in the crowd then turned back to her. "You going to keep acting?"

"Not sure if I want to," she replied. "It's a tough crowd. You read that *Photoplay Magazine* thing on me? They said I painfully reminded them of a dressmaker's mannequin. Not even sure what that meant, but I'm guessing it was not a compliment."

"It gets tougher every year," he said.

"And now we got Will Hays censoring our scripts, setting himself up as the motion picture morality czar like whether we see titties showing through flimsy fabric. The man needs to get laid more."

"Never a dull moment for us."

"Dull doesn't sound so bad." Castle took out a white handkerchief and pressed her lips to it. She slipped it into Pink's breast pocket. "Remember me, toots." She walked away, turned back to Pink, and blew him a kiss.

The aspiring starlet came back, reattaching herself to Pink's arm. "Your girl sure likes her sweets. Just like you liking me." She fluttered her best bedroom eyes look at him and bent forward, showing him what was in store later that night.

A heavyset guy in a black suit came over to Pink. He was Theo Mazer. The party hat he wore was pushed back so that his forehead showed, with small strands of greasy hair sticking below the brim. "How's it going, chum?" Mazer asked, slapping Pink on his back.

"It's going."

"You gotta minute to yak?" he asked.

"What about?"

"Shake the dame loose," Mazer said, a rubbery smile stretched across his lips like a Halloween mask. "I got your pals in the back room. Just some chitchat is all. You're gonna love what I have in mind."

Mazer waited while Pink peeled the woman off his arm. "I'll catch up with you later." He patted her rear as she walked away.

She gave him a sultry look, wiggling her hips as she strode in the direction of Warner Oland, a friend of Pink's and an actor who was frequently being typecast playing evil Asian types.

"Fucking dames," Mazer said, shaking his head. "Can't live without 'em and ya can't shoot 'em…except in the movies." He belly-laughed at his own joke.

Pink followed Mazer across the floor of the ballroom into a back room. His boys were sitting on chairs around at a table, a bottle of champagne and fluted glasses in the center. They were all wearing party hats. Two of the men had young women attired in sleeveless flapper dresses showing some leg, sitting on the men's laps, their faces heavy with makeup, and all smoking thin cigars. The third man had a too-handsome young man trying to look like Valentino sitting close giving him a gooey-eyed stare. A photographer stood in front of the little gathering and took a picture, the flash bulb popping a bright white flare into their faces.

As soon as Pink and Mazer entered, the latter gave the women a death stare, and the two young ladies and the Valentino lookalike exited as if on cue.

"Seems your guys like them, Dumb Doras," Mazer said to two of the men eying the women as they left. "Except you," Mazer addressed Loci, "no offense. Gotta admit, you *faygalas* got a good eye for snaring pretty men."

"Did you drag me back here so you can give the boys a lesson on choosing a better class of floozies?"

Mazer waved a dismissive hand at Pink. "Nah. Forget what I said. I wanna talk about the future. Your future. My future. Our future."

This time, Mazer swept his hand, indicating his pronouncement concerned all the men gathered around the table.

"Didn't think you had crystal balls, Mazer," Crank said. His floppy newsboy cap faced backward—a habit he had from being behind the camera. "The ones in your pants are too small to see anything beyond your last shit."

The men laughed, but Pink didn't join them. He knew Mazer. The guy was a wheeler-dealer. Always looking for an angle, fast-talking some kind of business deal. He waited for the pitch.

"Our world is changing," Mazer continued, dismissing the men's wisecracks. "Nickelodeons are being replaced by movie theaters. Investors know movies are where the money will be. People love 'em, like moths drawn to candlelight. We got new money folks who wanna invest and they ain't just off the boat. They ain't wops and kikes. Their ancestors landed on Plymouth Rock. Got rid of the Indians, built railroads, and own banks."

"Sounds like a fun bunch," Needles said.

"Here's the thing," Mazer said. "All the studios are pulling up stakes, mine included. Not just here in Ithaca but everywhere. Willy Fox is leaving Jersey City, and Louie Mayer is gettin' outta Fort Lee. You know why? The fucking weather. Right? The winters are killing us. We can't make movies half the year. We can't do anything but hold our frozen pricks till spring. Investors want us to pump more of our shit out to the paying public. And so do the schnooks who want to escape from their miserable lives for a couple hours."

Pink knew Mazer was right. People wanted more movies, and they wanted them made faster. His actors hated this place as soon as the frost hit. By November, Pearl would hit the hooch; Barrymore would go cokey again. And if you didn't finish a serial that kept people coming back week after week, the audiences would spend their nickels elsewhere.

"Yeah, we all know this," Pink said. "That's why I invited you here tonight. You mighta guessed it's my going-away party."

"I did."

"So what's with you having this chitchat?"

"You're closing down DimaDozen," Mazer said, confirming what Pink had just told him.

"Yup."

"What about California?"

Pink shook his head. "Not the life I want anymore."

"Me, I like the life. It's the American Dream, right? Well, the rest of us are moving out West. Great weather all year round. You can build indoor studios cheap and also shoot outdoors when you want. You got mountains, snow if you want it, the ocean. It's fucking movie-making Valhalla."

"Send me a crate of oranges when you get there."

"What about your boys?" Mazer asked, looking at Pink's inner circle, the men who were the stalwarts of his production studio.

Needles spoke first. "Me and Crank are going to the Polacks."

"The Warner Brothers," Mazer clarified. "Always wondered how you go from Wonskolaser to fucking Warner."

"We are the other. The funny-looking, with funny food and funny names. That's how you go from Wonskolaser to Warner," Pink explained.

Mazer knew that. His family's language was the language of newly landed immigrants that appalled the Mayflower arrivals. The great melting pot had never really melted, and so Moskowitz had become Mazer. He scrubbed off the language and stink of his parents' Polish ghetto, replaced by a lower East Side tough-guy burr. He didn't follow his father into the garment business but made something of himself. Whatever nickels and dimes he made, he always spent on movies. They were his way to fantasize about a world he wanted to be a part of. But he had to deal with the Mayflowers, and they were as threatening as the black-hundredits that drove his parents from Bialystok after most of their family had been slaughtered. There was no way he'd be slaughtered. Fear was for the spineless, and he had the chutzpah of a hundred Samsons.

Mazer's eyes landed on Loci. "And you?" he asked.

"I'm done too. Great time with Pink, but I got a job with my father-in-law selling stock."

"Stock, huh. Kinda like shooting craps," Mazer said.

"Yeah. Like you moving to the West Coast and hoping you make it."

The guys laughed, and Mazer gave them a fat lips pout.

"So you got Needles and Crank heading to Warners, and Loci is headed to Wall Street," Mazer summed up.

"That's about it," Pink agreed.

Mazer walked around the table. "So I got this idea for you."

Pink knew this was coming. The Mazer spiel. Some deal he wanted to make. He figured Mazer had more to say now that he had a good idea of where DimaDozen's key employees were headed.

"Here's the thing," Mazer started to elaborate. "I'm moving my production studio out West. I grabbed an old warehouse in Burbank. I'm setting up my new company there. HocusFocus." He beamed a glittering smile at Pink, sweeping his hands outward like the Pope blessing the crowds.

"You going into the magician acts?"

"*Hocus Focus*. Not Hocus Pocus."

"Cute name," Pink said. "So what do you need?"

"Need, shmeed," Mazer exclaimed, looking hurt. "I am here to give, not take."

"What do you need?" Pink repeated.

"Okay, you're closing down, right?"

"We established that as soon as you showed up tonight and started drinking my good booze and guzzling oysters. I'm staying right here in Ithaca."

"What and be a farmer?"

"You never know. Sell my equipment and find a nice place and maybe a terrific dame who doesn't wanna be a star."

"And that's where I can help," Mazer quickly added. "Not the finding, the dame part. Look, you got equipment. Cameras, sets, lights, costumes. All that stuff you won't be using anymore. I want to *relieve* you of those things so you don't have to worry about disposing of them. I can do this quickly instead of you tracking down buyers."

"Very charitable," said Pink, knowing this wasn't Mazer being charitable. It wasn't in his nature. "But isn't *relieve* kinda like taking?"

"Semantics."

"Okay, cut the bull and give me the bottom line. What do you want?"

Mazer took a deep breath. "I want everything I said before."

"I planned on selling the whole lot and splitting the profits with my fellas."

"You could do that and miss an incredible opportunity."

"Incredible opportunity?" Pink said in a blank tone. "I haven't heard anything that resembles an opportunity except you wanting my stuff."

"I'm getting to that. See, I got some damn good writers waiting for me out there. I have Gish, Alma Rubens, and maybe even Chaplin interested."

"Sounds swell." Pink rubbed his chin, trying to figure out Mazer's angle. "So you want to *acquire* my inventory. I can give you a good price."

Mazer gestured with both hands again, this time pantomiming as if he were pushing a piece of dusty furniture away from him. "Pink, Pink, Pink," he appealed. "I'd like to suggest another option."

"I wouldn't have expected anything less," Pink said, knowing that the quick-talking dealmaker would have a different deal in mind.

"Truth be told, my investors are tapped out," Mazer admitted. "Whatever dough I got I need for salaries, rent, and expenses."

"So I should give you all my equipment for free?" Pink said, shaking his head.

"No, no, no," Mazer objected. "Not free."

"So what then?"

"I'll give you fifty grand and shares in my new outfit," he said, extending his arms wide to show how big an offer this would be.

"Shares of what?" Pink questioned.

"Fifteen percent of my company split between your boys."

"Fifteen percent of nothing is still nothing," Pink maintained.

"Maybe now," Mazer agreed, "but in two years, my company will be worth a couple of million. Maybe more. You guys cash out and live like kings…or a queen."

Loci shook his head.

"There goes them crystal balls again," Crank said. "Maybe I should take you to the track."

"You know I can hustle," Mazer said confidently. "I started with three Nickelodeons back in '03 and by 1912 owned one hundred and forty eight. From Manhattan, to Chicago, and even in Topeka, where they still think Hebs have horns and tails."

"You mean you don't?" Loci said trying to look serious.

"How about you pull down my pants, *Mr. Faygala*, and kiss my *tuchas* so you can get a real good look?"

"I'll pass, although it's an exciting offer."

"So you want me to gamble on your hustling skills?" Pink said, getting back to Mazer's proposal.

"I got a good track record."

"Maybe," Pink said. "So I make money how?"

"If my company is worth two million in a year, I'll buy back all of you guys' shares. That's three hundred thousand dollars. Maybe a year later, it's four million and you make even more."

Mazer took out five sheets of paper and handed them to Pink. The papers were contracts with a distinct and very large HocusFocus logo at the top, a cameraman aiming a lens straight ahead.

Pink read one of the contracts and frowned. "What if you're bought? Zukor is swallowing up companies like it was a fire sale. So are the others."

He thought back to several years before. In 1916, Adolph Zukor merged his movie production with the Jesse Lasky's outfit to form Famous Players. The combined studio then bought Paramount Pictures. In 1924, Marcus Loew gained control of Metro Pictures, Goldwyn Pictures, and Louis B. Mayer Pictures. The result: MGM.

Mazer's hopeful smile faded. "I'm getting an uncomfortable feeling in my stomach like I just ate one of my Aunt Ida's matzo balls. You gotta an issue with my terms?"

"If we go for the deal, what kind of guarantee do we have about these shares' value if you get bought?"

"Ain't gonna happen." Mazer waited then asked, "So what do you want? More dough?"

"Nope. I want you to amend the agreement." Pink explained the new language he wanted added.

Mazer turned the idea over for a few minutes. "Why not? I'm sure my *gonif* lawyers can take care of that. But just letting you know I ain't going to get swallowed except by one of your floozies."

Pink turned to his men. "What do you guys think?"

Loci shrugged. "You're the brains in the outfit. Whatever you decide is fine with me." The other men nodded.

"Okay," Pink said. "Draw up new contracts. Life's a crap shoot, right, boys?"

"I'll send you all a new version to sign tomorrow with the new clause," Mazer whispered into Pink's ear. "What name are you going to put on your copy? *Pinchas Moskowitz* or *Percy Maxwell,* the *goyish* one you made up?"

"Maxwell will do. I only use my *shtetl* name for special things."

"So what, this ain't special?"

"You make us money and I'll send you a thank-you card."

Mazer went around the table slapping each man's back. "Let's toast with the bubbly," he cheered, pouring champagne into all the glasses.

Then he called out for the cameraman, who stumbled back into the room. "Hey, schmuck, take a picture of us and then skedaddle."

Pink, Mazer, and the guys sat. The man held up the camera, and the flash of the bulb lit the seated men's unsmiling faces.

"What a way to start the New Year," Mazer exclaimed a bit too cheerily. "This will be the first good thing you all did in 1926. We're all gonna make a fortune."

"Sure," Pink said without much enthusiasm.

"Hey, this is a killer deal where no one gets killed," Mazer joked. "That only happens in the pictures, right?"

"Sure," Pink said through a tight-lipped smile.

CHAPTER 1

EVERYBODY'S GOTTA PIMP TO PLEASE

She would be my last hooker, number six. One hooker each day this past week. Each woman had been different. And now Fiona, a white girl from Staten Island, whose story I would hear. Six hookers. Six different stories. Stories about why they did what they did. Some told their stories truthfully, some with lies, but all of them said it was about money.

As I left my apartment in Chelsea, I scouted the street for the Uber I had requested. The summer in the city was stifling with its hairdryer-hot blasts of air funneling down the avenues. Fiona had agreed to meet me at a bar in Manhattan's old Meatpacking District. She would be sitting in a booth in the back by a pool table at the Black Rose on Hudson Street. She said she was a redhead and drop-dead gorgeous.

I had met most of these ladies at hotels by answering ads I found on the Internet. The Web had become a cyber pimp. Google *escorts* and you'd find scores of sites to meet working girls.

When I met these ladies, I told them I just wanted to talk. "Whatever you want, just pay me for the hour," they'd say. I told them about my editor, whom I needed to keep happy for this story.

"Whatever," would be a standard response.

Some of my subjects convinced me without much effort to taste their delights for authenticity's sake. *A journalist must do what he must do*, I'd rationalize; my professional ethics were unreliable when offered the tasty pleasures of the flesh. Not a good thing when you had a girlfriend who wanted to know all about your work.

Before I entered, I found a darkened doorway next to the bar. I ducked in and pulled a vape pen out of my pocket. I looked around to make sure that no member of New York's finest was in sight. No need to be hassled. Lighting up in public was still illegal. This I knew, having had a brief stint as a rookie cop in a former life. I said *former* because I flunked out of the academy when my blood test showed traces of sativa. In my way of thinking, I thought weed gave me enhanced insights working a crime scene. The po po didn't go for that. But that was another story, another life.

I took a couple of hits and entered the bar, ready for my lady-of-the-night encounter. The Black Rose had seen better days, but it had the charm that the newer yuppified watering holes couldn't match. It had a worn look like an old but comfortable pair of shoes—a neighborhood place, people at the bar chatting with each other in a familiar, jocular way. It was places like this that made me love my fucking city so much.

I headed toward a pool table and had no trouble spotting her. She saw me coming and looked up, giving me a practiced smile that said I was the most special thing she had met in a long time. If I needed a shot of self-confidence, that smile was worth the cost of a therapy session.

"Hi," I greeted, "you Fiona?"

"Have a seat, honey." Her full lips looked like Angelina Jolie sucking on a sour ball.

I slid into the booth opposite her. She had a drink in front of her, something sweet-looking with a pallid cherry floating on top like a crimson corpse in a milky swimming pool.

I had a hard time not looking at her breasts, the weed directing my focus away from the muses and toward her ta-tas. Her dyed-red hair was cut in a Rod Stewart jagged style. She was pretty in a hard way as if the hooker life she was leading wasn't giving her any breaks. I guessed she was about twenty-five, but she could have been younger. She wore a thin cotton top—braless, her nipples hard, pressing against the delicate fabric—and my eyes betrayed me.

"You like my tits," she said, matter-of-factly.

I smiled like a boy caught reading a *Playboy* under the covers by his mom.

"They are quite nice."

"But you don't want to play with them, right? Or with me. Just talk."

"I would love to, but yeah, just talk."

"You sure? You really don't wanna tap this?" She stood up, slapped her butt, and twirled around, showing me a very round and pert ass tightly packed into a pair of black yoga pants. A few men at the bar came alive and shouted catcalls.

"Still saying no?"

And then it happened—that thing I sometimes did that I couldn't always control. I began to sing...if you want to call it that.

> Shake that booty
> It's so fine
> Shake that booty
> Till I lose my mind

"What the fuck?" she said. The people at the bar agreed as they turned to me with their own what-the-fuck looks.

The words had flown out of my mouth, and I grimaced. I tried to explain. "Sometimes I just say these things. Kinda fucked up the way my brain is wired."

"Seriously fucked," she agreed.

I have a mild case of coprolalia, which is an involuntary outburst of socially inappropriate remarks, sounds, or verbal gobbledygook. Sometimes it's creative, sometimes obscene, many times inappropriate.

"You're no Florence Nightingale with those pipes, just friggin' weird."

I didn't correct her Nightingale reference. "That's the rumor."

She stared at me for a while, trying to make sense out of what I had just done. "Get you in trouble? This uncontrolled thingamajig you do?"

"Sometimes."

Fiona smiled, shaking her head. "But that thingamajig tells me you like my booty. You wanna go somewhere for a taste?"

"Alas, I must pass on your ass," I sang.

"You did it again."

I smiled.

"Either you have a girlfriend, are a monk, or gay."

"Yes, no, and no."

"Girlfriend, huh? My johns, most are married. They take their ring off, but I see the tan line."

"And so they come to you…?" I left my question hanging in the air for her to fill in, starting my interview.

"To *cum* in me," was her reply, and she laughed.

I waited for more. She saw that on my face.

"Who knows? Like, I'm not a shrink, right?"

Fiona opened up her palms, implying she couldn't read minds or intentions. She was not a shrink. However, my mother, Selma, was, and I'd been her long-term work in progress, which according to her was making no progress.

"You got an hour minus the last five minutes."

"Right."

"I usually ask if you are a cop, but we aren't in a hotel room with me ready to take you in my mouth."

She looked at me, waiting.

"Cash," she said, moving the four fingers on her right hand in a "gimme" gesture.

I took out an envelope with four hundred dollars inside. She opened her shoulder bag and slipped the envelope into it, giving me an "Okay, buddy, let's get going" look.

The trick of a good interview is to appear interested but not in a way that shows too much eagerness. You also have to share something about yourself, a good listener that does not judge. You can't be the guy wearing a bathing suit on a nude beach.

I took out my pocket tape recorder. "So, Fiona, you fine with this?"

"Sure. And my real name ain't Fiona, and nobody would give a fuck about this anyways."

4

She said this matter-of-factly, but I heard a thread of sorrow that told me somebody might've cared about her once upon a time.

"This going to be printed, my story and all?" she asked.

"Assuming my boss likes what I write."

"Everybody's gotta pimp and someone to please."

I'd never thought of Stan, the publisher of the magazine I worked for, as a pimp, but maybe I was just a different kind of whore—a freelance writer that wrote for a paycheck.

"The meter is running," she said, reminding me we were on the clock.

"Right."

"Fire away, Shakespeare." She smoothed her shirt tightly over her breasts, and I began.

My questions had been the same with all the women I interviewed. When did they get into their profession? What were their clients like? Did they ever get into a situation where they feared for their life? I used the word *profession* since it sounded better than "Why did you choose to become a hooker?"

She saw herself as a tradesperson and said, "You gotta a dick, and I gotta a pussy. I make money 'cause they fit together."

She went on about her rules, the dos and don'ts. Her profession was loaded with acronyms: DFK (deep French kiss)—nope; BBBJ (bareback blow job)—yup; CIM (cum in mouth)—pay extra. I was getting the full tutorial.

"But as a rule, I don't kiss or go Greek. If I do, it's extra."

She saw a clueless look from me since this one was not listed in my glossary of terms I'd learned so far.

"Anal."

"Right," I said. I wondered if Greeks were offended by the association of anal sex and being Greek.

"You try that with your girlfriend?"

I shook my head. Lilly, my girlfriend, was fairly clear when it came to her own set of rules of what orifice could be entered.

"Greek. That hurt?"

"Nah. For me at least. Others, maybe. I ain't no gynecologist. Men think it gives them power. Some domo shit. Let 'em think that as long as they pay the extra fare."

I wasn't sure a gynecologist covered that piece of anatomy, so I let it slide next to Florence.

"What's up with the 'no kissing' rule for you?" I asked.

"Too personal—it fucks up your head like they're thinking they're real boyfriends or something. You get naked and fuck, but that doesn't mean nothing. I do my moaning-oh-god show, and they're happy. If they go down on my cha-cha, that's okay if they know what they're doing."

I assumed her cha-cha was her vagina. I liked the term. It was musical. I had never thought of Lilly's as musical, although if I worked it the right way, she might make sounds that approached singing.

"You still got time on the clock."

"Yeah." I waited a couple of seconds. "You ever want to leave the life?"

"And do what?"

I didn't have a ready answer.

She suddenly got up and slid over next to me in the booth. Her hand had magically found its way to my crotch, and she found it hard. "You all excited about all the shit I told you?"

"I guess so." I was a bit rattled as she rubbed my junk. "What are you doing?"

She whispered in my ear, "I'm going to the little girl's room. I think you should order another drink for me and you and then go to the head like you were needing to pee."

Before I could reply, she got up, and I watched her walk away, her fine-looking booty moving in a rhythm that was saying "Don't be shy and give it a try." I ordered two drinks and headed to the head. I wasn't sure what she had in mind, but once again, sometimes research is a requirement for authenticity.

The door to the ladies' room was slightly ajar. "Come on in, sailor boy. Let me give you a lesson you won't forget."

I did. She locked the door and went over to the sink. She leaned over, pulled down her yoga pants, and revealed a bare ass.

She felt me hesitate.

"Second thoughts?"

I was silent.

"I'm going to take you to Greece. This trip is on me."

Ten minutes later, I completed the mission. Or emission, I should say.

"I bet our drinks are waiting for us."

She left first. It was different, but not something I'd pay extra for if I was a hobbyist. *I guess I'm really a cha-cha man. I wondered if Lilly would like taking a trip to Greece.* I had a hunch what the answer would be.

CHAPTER 2

PANTS DOWN LOW

Returning to the booth, I sat across from Fiona, and she smiled.

"Nice, right?"

"Different," I said. I had a good feeling about my sex workers' stories. It was titillating but showed the human side of what my subjects thought about what they did. It was right up Stan's alley.

Fiona's smile disappeared, and that was when I felt a heavy hand grip my trapezius muscle.

I flinched and looked up at a brawny white guy who was doing his best to impersonate a ghetto gangsta. He wore a cap on his shaved head backward, a heavy gold chain dangling over a nylon jacket with embroidered letters spelling out *Represent*. His blue jeans hung down low, showing off a pair of red-and-white-striped boxer shorts. The pants-down-low look that lots of guys adopted was a fashion statement which they were totally clueless about.

"This is Ronny," Fiona told me with a hitch in her voice, "my manager."

Ah, her manager, aka her pimp.

"Whatchu doing wit' dis guy?"

He said this, still gripping my muscle. His language was as ripped off as his gangsta look, a student, no doubt, of the Lil Yachty school of diction.

"Nothin', Ronny. He's nobody," she said, almost pleading.

He lowered his free hand and placed it under his crotch, hoisting his package up. Another rapper move that I didn't understand.

8

Was he checking that his junk was still in place? Did he think someone had stolen it?

"Cool threads," I said, scrutinizing his outfit.

Ronny sneered at me. "You dissing my look?"

"This thing about that pants-down-low thing you got going," I began.

"Whatta 'bout it?"

"You know who started that look?"

His beady eyes went blank, showing he had no clue.

"In prison," I said.

His sneer turned into a slanted smile. He must've thought his prison look added to his badass badness. Then I broke the news with a 411.

"These baggy pants showing off underwear thing started as prison code."

I had his attention. He was waiting for the badass secret code to be revealed.

I went on. "The man wearing them down low was advertising his availability to be the bitch for some other inmate if you get my drift."

He squeezed my muscle tighter. "You callin' me a faggot?"

"Not at all. Just educating you about some fashion history. Besides, a gay man would never dress like you except maybe on Halloween."

Fiona shook her head as a warning. Ronny was not to be messed with.

"Now how about taking your hand off of me."

"Fuck you, you fuck." Ronny turned his attention to Fiona. "You bankin' on the side, bitch?"

"Just talkin'," Fiona said.

He kept his hand on my shoulder muscle. "You should be fuckin', not chattin' it up with dis mofo." Ronny eyed Fiona's bag and, with his free hand no longer clutching his crotch, pulled out the envelope I had given her.

"Hey," she protested, and he slapped her.

A gash appeared on her cheek, a trickle of blood running down.

She gasped, touching her cheek. "Just talkin' is all."

Ronny spotted the tape recorder on the table and let go of my shoulder. He picked it up.

"That's mine," I said.

"Not no mo', nigga." His eyes moved from me to the recorder and then to Fiona.

A cracker calling another cracker a nigga. We had slipped into a cultural wormhole.

"Nobody no how talks to no one 'bout what she do."

I also was about to point out his ill use of double negatives when Ronny slapped Fiona again. Tears flowed freely down her face, and he pocketed my recorder. The bartender was about to say something to Ronny, then thought better about it, not wanting trouble.

"That's mine, friend," I said again, firmly now.

"I'm gonna fuck your white ass up."

Ronny snarled at me, showing a row of teeth with a band of golden metal weaved across them, a hip-hop grill look borrowed from the Lil Wayne rapper accessories catalog.

I had all my interviews on my recorder and needed it back. When I tried to get up, Ronny's fingers returned and dug into my shoulder again. My belly button signaled that that moron was not someone I could reason with. It was not unusual for me to get into uncomfortable situations when I did my work. Her pimp gave me no choice.

In one quick movement, I jabbed my elbow into Ronny's groin. He let out a "Oh, fuck" groan and released his fingers, which usually works when someone has his nut sack whacked hard.

I got up quickly while Ronny was holding his scrotum underneath his pants-down-low pants. I stepped close and retrieved my recorder. I turned back to the booth and looked at Fiona.

"You okay?"

She held a cocktail napkin against her cheek and didn't answer, tears running along her nose.

"You can leave the life and that jerk off."

Her eyes were glassy but widened suddenly as she saw something behind me.

"Motherfucker," screamed Ronny, apparently recovered from my jab. He held a very large switchblade in his right hand and came at me. I darted to my left as he swung the blade toward my neck. He lashed out again, and I jumped back and backpedaled until my ass bumped against the pool table.

Two guys who were playing pool watched slack-jawed as Ronny tried to cut me. The guy closest to me was holding a pool stick, and I grabbed it from him. I blocked what would have been a nasty slice to my face with the stick. Ronny came at me again, and I blocked another slashing move.

I was growing tired of using the pool stick to thwart that clown's attempt to open up my arteries. I raised the stick up and brought it down over my knee, breaking about five inches off the tip. The stick now had a jagged point.

Ronny's eyebrows came together in a what-the-fuck look as I moved my feet into offensive stance.

"You some kinda Zorro?"

"Better." I went into a Filipino stick fighting position called *Ritriada*.

He challenged me, moving his knife from one hand to another. I had seen that move in gang face-off movies. Cool on the screen but, in reality, dim-witted.

His blade came at me, and I thrust my makeshift weapon into his pectoral muscle. He dropped his switchblade and yelped. I pulled the broken tip of the stick out of his chest, and he yelped again, grabbing his wound. My next move was a blow to the side of his head, which sent him to the floor.

I stood over Ronny and placed the broken end of the pool stick an inch away from his jugular. His eyes grew wide with fear.

"You touch Fiona again, and I'll find you and hurt you."

Ronny nodded.

By now, Fiona had slid out of the booth and stood watching me. "You can leave this asshole, you know," I said, repeating my advice.

Fiona didn't say a word. She looked at me and then at the creep on the floor. I raised my eyebrows and shrugged.

"It's your life, sweetie."

I tossed the broken pool stick on the floor and headed to the door. When I turned around, Fiona was on her knees next to Ronny, holding his hand. Go figure. A victim of her own choosing.

When I got back to my place, I felt good about what I would write. This Ronny run-in would be an added bonus. It had all the signs of a winner. I'd send it to Stan that weekend, and he'd call on Monday as he always did to make sure the writing Muses had made contact. Minerva, my cat, gave me a bemused smile as I entered my apartment. I knew she could read my mind, which was okay since she had yet to master the English language and drop a dime on me when Lilly asked me about how my assignment went.

CHAPTER 3

APHRODITE FOR SALE

He stared at the woman's face. She was beautiful in a classical way. Her eyes were almond-shaped, her lips full with a hint of a smile. Her hair was styled with precise waves that wrapped around her head into a bob tied in the back above her long neck. A draped robe hung loosely over her shoulder, exposing a full but youthful breast.

He stepped closer to examine her torso, which was fully exposed. Her nakedness excited him, but it was the overall exquisiteness and perfect proportions that he treasured the most. He felt a tingling sensation begin in his groin. This wasn't the first time artwork excited him in this way.

Marvin Brinks knew exactly where she would be placed in his house. The bedroom would be too obvious and crass. She should be seen by everyone who came to his home, although that was a select number. His living room had the right lighting for her. She would stand next to the mahogany Hepplewhite hall table with its serpentine-shaped top and burled mahogany front panel.

"She's quite attractive," said a well-dressed man, who held an iPad. He wore an Armani suit; his cologne was mild but pleasing. Gray hair along his temples gave him a self-important look. Brinks knew this guy was a dilettante that dressed the part of an art aficionado.

"Very," Brinks agreed. He was also well-dressed but lacked the mannered appearance of the gentleman standing next to him. Brinks was neat and had a well-groomed look about him—clean shaven and physically fit but someone whom you might pass on the street without taking notice of.

The man with the iPad noted that Brinks was the kind of customer he liked since he smelled of money without giving off a stink of the *nouveau riche*.

"A statue depicting Aphrodite, after the style of the sculptor Alexandros of Antioch," the gentleman said in a slight English accent, his nose pointing more up than down. He held out his free hand and introduced himself. "Tremont Bradshaw. I manage estate auctions for Hammerstein."

"Marvin Brinks," he said, shaking the man's hand. "Third-century BC I believe. Typical Hellenistic style." Brinks confidently inserted his own observation. He too could play the *I am so cultured one-upmanship* game.

"Exactly," Bradshaw agreed. "I see you know your art history."

"I try," Brinks replied.

Brinks had been looking at the sculpture for nearly half an hour. He roamed the rooms with more than twenty other interested parties at the private on-site estate auction hosted by Hammerstein auctioneers. It was being held in August when most moneyed people were on vacation. That meant less bids and less competition.

The estimated price was just under a quarter of a million dollars. If his bid won, he might also be able to shave a bit of money off if Hammerstein took less of a commission which was not unheard-of.

Brinks felt his pulse quickening. That was the thrill of an auction. The adrenaline rush escalating as the bidding began. He loved the suspense since it felt like gambling. And of course, there was the thrill of winning.

"Perhaps it would be a good time to take your information, register you for our auction. Assuming you'll bid on this stunning statue."

Brinks nodded. The Hammerstein man led him to another room in the estate's mansion, which had been turned into a temporary office. He offered Brinks a seat before he took his own behind a desk.

Bradshaw handed Brinks a form. "Please confirm your bank's transfer number and your contact information."

Brinks took his fountain pen from the inside of his suit pocket—an eighteen-carat gold Conway Stewart. He remembered buying this one at another estate sale, which was a bargain, paying half of what it was worth. He filled in the form and handed it back to the auctioneer along with his business card.

The Hammerstein man glanced at the business card. "Glowball Productions. You're in the movie business."

"Isn't everyone?"

"Many are hopeful."

"Or hopeless."

Bradshaw grinned. "So true."

Brinks left the office and walked to the statue, once again taking in her beauty, walking around her, admiring it at every angle.

In the office, the Hammerstein man began typing on his laptop. He entered Brinks's information. A few seconds went by. The man frowned. He picked up the telephone on his desk and made a call. After a brief conversation, he got up from the desk and went back to the showroom. He approached Brinks, his face a bit grim.

"Something wrong?" Brinks asked.

"The bank seems to have issued a credit freeze. Something about you exceeding your line of credit."

Brinks's heart started to beat rapidly, anticipating the next few words that the Hammerstein man would say.

"Perhaps you can talk to your bank and straighten this matter out."

"Of course. Must be some mistake." He walked to a nearby chair and sat down, feeling dizzy. Bradshaw followed him to the chair.

"If the statue doesn't meet the reserve today, you may still be its proud owner. The people whose estate we represent are willing to negotiate fair offers for items that don't get sold."

He gave Brinks a beneficent look and held up the business card he had been given. "In the meantime, I took the liberty to put a call into your company to verify your employment status. I can see you must be very important there." He waved the card.

Color drained from Brinks' face. "You called my office?"

"Yes. I spoke to a very pleasant woman there. She works for you and a Mr. Wolfe. A Miss Brandy Vicks. She confirmed your employment. I believe she said you are one of their top managers at Glowball Productions."

He vacantly nodded. "Did you mention my intention to acquire this sculpture?"

"Just the possibility that you might. She was very inquisitive. Said she never had the pleasure of going to one of our auctions. Out of her price range. She giggled when she said that."

"Did you happen to mention the reserve price?"

"Not the exact amount. It is an auction after all. One never knows how things turn out, *n'est pas.*"

"What *not exact* amount did you tell her?" An icy feeling began to slide down his spine.

Bradshaw smiled a toothy smile again and added a wink, implying discretion. "I said it could be in the six figures. High six maybe. She was impressed even though my reply was rather vague."

Brinks closed his eyes, thinking to himself that the man was a self-inflated buffoon, and his answer was not even close to vague. A burning pit formed in his stomach. This would be like starting a line of dominoes to tip over. Brandy was the first tile.

He imagined Brandy chewing the fat at the water cooler. She would retell her conversation with the Hammerstein man to her office chums. The second tile tipping would be the amount of money he *vaguely* mentioned.

The third tile was a time bomb because sooner than later, his boss, James Burton Wolfe, CFO of Glowball, would get wind of it. It would be natural for his boss to wonder about the considerable money involved. How could Brinks, at his salary level, afford something like that?

Brinks's chest grew tight as if steel bands were being wrapped around his ribs. More than likely, Wolfe would become suspicious and start looking more closely at how he managed the company's money.

The Hammerstein man remained silent as he watched Brinks's color come back to his face. "Are you feeling all right, sir?"

"I'm fine. I'll call you after the bank matter is resolved," he said then started to walk out of the showroom.

As he gave the statue an admiring glance, his heart sank. He couldn't call the bank and *straighten things out* any time soon. In fact, the bank asked him to come in to talk about late payments on his equity loans. Maybe he should consider selling some of his assets, the bank suggested. The idea of getting rid of any part of his collection would be like nailing a spike into his heart.

He headed to his car, thinking he would never willingly sell his assets. They were the things that made his life livable. His career goal was never about gaining wealth or power in the movie business. It was never about making money for money's sake. It was just a means to an end. He would do almost anything to protect what he had come so far to acquire.

He started his car and had a feeling of foreboding, like an ill wind blowing through the shutters he had carefully erected to make his life invisible to others. The reality of what he had been doing for so long might finally have caught up with him, how he manipulated Glowball money to support his passion.

He thought through what might trigger an internal audit and what would happen. Brinks needed to identify his bookkeeping weak spots, where the vulnerabilities were, what could expose him, etc. He could conceal the bogus transfer of funds to the phony companies he set up, the fictitious transactions to bank accounts that were so offshore they weren't even on a map. Brinks also had his paid-off bag-men and women who helped launder his money. If he went down, so would his willing coconspirators. They'd keep their mouths shut. He knew that.

Reaching home, Brinks parked his car in the driveway, walked to the front door, punched in the alarm code, and entered his house. He needed a drink. He went straight to his bar and mixed himself a vodka and soda. Taking the drink to his sofa, he studied the artwork on his walls, the rare books on their shelves, and the vitrine that displayed his more delicate objects d'art.

He had come far since his hardscrabble days as a kid in Maine. His mother was a bookkeeper, his father a lobsterman. A yard with chickens and a caged pen with rabbits. Fried chicken and rabbit stew were regular meals along with potatoes and anything else that a meager garden provided.

Back then, his life was dull. The dullness tore at him. The only excitement he had was when his mother asked him to bring in a chicken or rabbit. He'd go outside and pick one, something plump, and then wring its neck. He did this without remorse.

His home had been without artwork—walls as stimulating as a prison cell. No one understood how the dullness affected him; his attraction to things that were beautiful in ways that escaped them. Beautiful things are faithful in their consistency. People disappoint you. You could love an artwork and it didn't have to love you back, so there was never a broken heart or a rejection unless you couldn't acquire it. He loved every object he had collected even more than a shark loves fresh blood. He could care less about people. Especially in LA, where real friendships didn't exist. People were always figuring out an angle to get something from you.

His love of art had morphed into a relentless obsession. It had become a drug. His passion, no matter how harmless he thought it was, had him by the balls.

What wasn't dull now was how his possessions validated his life. His gaze wandered to the three framed original movie posters that hung on a wall next to the vitrine, all of them in mint condition. They were posters from silent movies, a period he prized. Charlie Chaplin in *The Tramp*, Irene Castle in *The Whirl of Life*, and Mary Pickford in *Tess of the Storm Country*. They had been celebrities from a bygone era and now were celebrated ghosts with an illustrious past.

As he studied each poster, a notion crossed his mind. Maybe it was nothing. Or maybe it was something. The idea began to grow. Ghosts. He knew what he knew about his own ledger book prestidigitations. He also knew that he didn't know things—the nameless things from Glowball's past that could pop up like specters concealed in a jack-in-a-box. That could be a problem.

Right now, he had to focus on the present. He would take a fine-toothed comb to his books and ledgers, and go back five years to the time he started playing hard and fast with the company's money.

He felt confident that he could erase any links to what he had been doing. He'd start tomorrow.

Brinks finished his drink. He needed to take his mind off his situation. Taking out his cell phone, he dialed.

"Is Fantasia available tonight?" He waited while the booking agent looked through her schedule of her ladies' availability.

"Great," Brinks replied, hearing the answer. "Send her over at seven. And have her wear the Black Widow outfit."

The outfit seemed right for tonight.

CHAPTER 4

AS KOSHER AS A BALLROOM OF DANCING RABBIS

Monday was *clean his shit up* day. Camouflage the shell games. He needed to hide things even more than they had already been. He needed to erase cash out fingerprints, digital breadcrumbs, and anything that smacked of embezzling.

Brinks paced around his office, thinking, ruminating about his ledgers, deciding what he needed to do first to cover his tracks. His laptop was on, the glow of a spreadsheet filled with numbers casting a dim light onto his desk. The Hammerstein unpleasantness would pop up sooner than later. He could deal with his boss and any of the knuckleheaded Glowball accountants if Wolfe decided to have them peek under the hood.

As it had been every day since the estate sale, Brinks's mind kept returning to his life and what could happen if the shit hit the fan. He cherished his life and would do almost anything to keep it.

He stopped pacing and stood by his wall-to-ceiling office window. He gazed at the incredible view of Santa Monica Boulevard and beyond. He should be thrilled with how far he had gotten—the things he owned, the women he took on his getaway weekends, the restaurants that always had an open table for him whenever he called.

His thoughts were interrupted when his telephone rang. He answered it, hoping it wasn't the man from Hammerstein again who asked him if he had cleared up the little credit issue since the Aphrodite had not sold. The call wasn't from him. Instead, it was his secretary.

"I've got Mr. Wolfe on the line," Brandy said.

He took a breath. Brinks figured the cat was out of the bag.

"Put him through." He heard a click and then Wolfe came on the line. "Wolfman," he said.

"Marvin," Wolfe answered, his voice deadpan. "We got a problem. I need to talk to you in my office. Now."

Brinks wondered if the first tile of the dominoes had fallen. "I'll come right over."

He walked into Wolfe's office five minutes later. "What's up?"

"I've been hearing some rumors."

"Rumors," Brinks repeated, knowing what they would be. "What kind?"

"Something about buying a sculpture. A piece in the high six figures."

"Oh that," Brinks said as coolly as possible, adding a slight smirk.

"So give me the lowdown, Marv." Wolfe's fingers did a nervous tap dance on his desk.

"I went to an estate sale last week to poke around. Sometimes you can pick up a nice print for a steal."

"And that statue?" Wolfe asked.

"You know me, the *let's make a deal* guy. I've collected a few nice pieces. Come on, you should know that that rumor has no legs with my salary."

"So why am I hearing this office buzz?"

"Simple. I went to that estate sale. I asked this Hammerstein douche bag about a sculpture of Aphrodite, probably Hellenistic…"

"I don't want an art history lesson," Wolfe interrupted.

"The fact of the matter is that I said I *might* be interested, but it was just something to say to the guy who was hounding me like a hard-up used car salesman. I had to say something to get him off my ass was all."

"And he called here…"

"Because I gave the schmuck my business card. Big mistake, I admit. You know how aggressive these sales guys can be. He probably figured a studio exec could buy anything he wanted to. He was checking me out to see if I was real."

"You were kicking tires."

"More like kicking Carrara marble. Did you know that Michelangelo—"

"Enough with the fucking art lectures," Wolfe said, cutting Brinks short to change the subject. "One more thing."

"Sure."

"You know that kung-fu movie remake we're doing?" Wolfe was referring to the 1970s TV show starring David Carradine as Kwai Chang Caine.

"Yeah, we start filming next month in Hong Kong."

"Brenner is looking for investors over there."

"News to me."

"We have a possible bankroller from China who may want to invest. Hong Kong Capital."

"That's good, right?"

Wolfe leaned forward, putting both palms on his desk. He took in an unsteady breath. "He's thinking of putting in about five mil and wants to see how we operate, check out our production costs, see how we handle our accounting. That means we need to show him our books."

Brinks held back any visible reaction, seeing that this was clearly bad news.

"He's going to send over a few of his number geeks from Hong Kong."

As he said this, Wolfe felt his chest with his left hand and closed his eyes as a shooting pain came and went.

"You okay?" Brinks asked.

He reached inside his desk drawer and took out a vial. He shook out a small white pill and placed it under his tongue.

"I'll be fine. My angina acts up when I'm stressed. Keeping track of our bookkeeping minutiae is not in my wheelhouse, and that's what these guys will want to tear into."

"Makes sense," Brinks agreed, feeling his own stress well up.

"Brenner is all over me. Wants to make sure our books smell like roses when the bean counters get here."

"Of course."

"These guys can spot a speck of fly shit a mile away. We don't need any distractions when they arrive."

"Of course."

"The books need to be kosher, and that's on you."

"They'll be as kosher as a ballroom full of dancing rabbis."

"I have no idea what that means." Wolfe paused a moment, wiping sweat from his upper lip. "In any case, you and I need to go over all your books, what our expenses have been over the last twenty-four months before the Chinese arrive. I want them to know we run a tight ship."

"Sure thing," Brinks said, knowing this was not a sure thing at all.

"Have what we need by the end of the week," Wolfe continued. "That should give you enough time to get everything together for us to review. I'll have Brandy set up a meeting early Friday morning. The investors' people are coming in two weeks."

The pill Wolfe took seemed to work, and he took in a deep breath. "I'm glad this little mix-up with the statue is off the radar."

"Miscommunication is all," Brinks assured as he made his way out of Wolfe's office and returned to his own.

He thought Wolfe was a putz. He was not just his boss but also the CFO of Glowball Productions. James Wolfe was fifty-five and came to the job using his uncle's connections, who happened to be on the board of directors at Glowball. With one phone call to Walter Brenner, the head of the studio, he had a job he had no right to have. The guy was a pure Hollywood flake and as deep as a dried-up creek, overweight and bearing a resemblance to the Pillsbury doughboy. His attempts to make himself appear hip were obvious—mismatched clothes like wearing Zega silk jackets, Jimmy Choo shoes with corduroy pants. The hair plugs didn't help either.

He also had a new wife. Her name was Morgan. She was at least twenty years his junior. A bit player from one of Glowball's movies. Brinks doubted if Morgan was attracted to Wolfe's charm or good looks since the man had neither. But he had beaucoup bucks. He wondered how Wolfe handled her. She radiated sensual devastation. How could this putz keep up with her since he was as exciting as a baked potato? No doubt her acting skills could make their way to the boudoir.

He began pacing around his office. The sculpture mess was chicken shit compared to any serious number crunchers scrutinizing his work, diving into his books, and being fastidious. He didn't need fastidious right now.

Paranoia started to creep inside of him. He looked into the distant LA skyline. He wondered if Wolfe might see through his smoke-and-mirrors accounting methods that were as genuine as a zircon diamond. If Wolfe uncovered his shenanigans, Brinks's next living quarters would be an eight-by-ten cell decorated with prison graffiti and not Picasso's.

He sat down and pressed his palms into his face. Only four days to scrub all the accounting data. That would be tough. He realized he had to have more time to cover his tracks, but how?

His mind churned, and suddenly, an idea emerged. What if he could take Wolfe out of the equation for a while? Postpone any scrutiny on his part with enough time to hide what needed to be hid from the abacus guys? He needed a ploy to do that, something to put Wolfe out of commission for a while. All he had to do was think of how to take advantage of Wolfe's stressed-out state of mind. Some shock and awe to get the Wolfman unhinged.

CHAPTER 5

FUCK-IT LIST

Monday morning felt like Judgment Day. I had sent my piece about "women in the life" to Stan over the weekend. I was waiting for praise, although it would be faint praise knowing Stan. I could live without the praise as long as I continued to get assignments to support my hand-to-mouth lifestyle. This story was a sure shot as far as I was concerned. Salaciousness sells. That's what Stan always said, and I delivered.

My apartment was in Chelsea. It was one level above a hovel, but a hovel in Manhattan is what people will sell their grandmother's souls to the devil for. My one-bedroom studio apartment had a gritty view of a street lined with stores owned by Koreans that sold wholesale plants and handbags. The handbags didn't come with the plants.

Lilly, my most recent girlfriend, was in my bed asleep. I moved quietly out of the bedroom to the kitchen, where I stopped in front of my silverware drawer. This was where I kept my various blends of sativa and indica. I didn't see myself as a stoner. Selma might have disagreed if she had known about the frequency of my imbibing. I had explained that that was my way of clearing away the blockage to my inner muse. She said that was bullshit and called it my medicine to avoid reality. Her suggestion was therapy and Xanax as needed.

Stan was late to call, and I became fidgety. A couple of tokes of Special Queen and my first cup of coffee had put me in a better place to face him. I looked around my crib that reflected my temperament. A comfortable confinement. The kitchen, dining, and living area were in one room. I had a desk next to a window to watch the passing parade below. All the walls were covered with story ideas pinned to corkboards, which upset Lilly's *Better Homes and Gardens* sensibilities. She would prefer framed art prints. Her décor way of thinking scored an F on my "Why I should not be with Lilly" fuck-it list. She didn't get how I worked or thought. To me, a wall was not a place to put artwork but a place to put ideas.

I had often found myself in this predicament with the women I dated. Women liked me at first because I was entertaining, had an interesting gig, and told stories about my assignments that impressed them along with their friends when they risked having me meet them. I also had a look they liked. A few had even told me I looked like Bob Dylan on the cover of his *Hard Rain* album. That worked for me.

I knew why I did this list thing with the women I dated. Some people have their life's bucket list, but I had my fuck-it list. Like "*Why the fuck was I with that person?*" list. It was about a relationship's shelf life. Predictably, the honeymoon daze morphs into what we really are when we are not trying to be pleasing and loveable. I was sure the women I had dated had their own fuck-it list of complaints about me. I just created mine faster so that I could, as Paul Simon says, find fifty ways to leave my lover. I know I don't score well on the maturity and commitment Geiger counter.

Lilly had not stirred. I walked to the nearest corkboard and looked over the sticky notes and newspaper clippings I had push-pinned. These were ideas for articles I could write.

I studied a note to myself about eccentric ladies who fed alley cats and another note about nose-less clubs. I focused on the clubs. In the middle of the nineteenth century, syphilis was raging in New York City. Many who were afflicted had lost their noses to the disease. This deformity was so common among those suffering from it that "no nose clubs" sprung up. Prosthetic noses were worn by members who found a place where they could drink and dine and find partners to have sex with since there was nothing more to lose except their lives.

I heard Lilly stirring, and she called me in a sleepy voice from the bed.

"What are you doing?"

"Looking at some ideas."

"Oh, your scrap wall." She said that where *scrap* sounded more like *crap*.

I added another bad letter grade to her list.

"Can you bring me a cup of coffee, please?" Her tone was now sweet.

"Half and half, one sugar."

"You remembered."

I had only been seeing Lilly for a few months and began to get the hang of what she liked and disliked. It helped when a relationship hit the rough patches and needed smoothing over, a rough patch I could count on coming based on my history.

"I have a really important question," she said.

"I'm all ears."

"Which is better? Pilates or yoga? I think my tummy needs some work. Make it tighter." She pushed the bedsheet down so I could view her perfect stomach along with her perfect breasts.

"Your tummy looks just fine to me." I was seeing that this was an obsession of Lilly's, tracking her body-to-fat ratio on a weekly basis. Another adverse check mark.

While I prepared her coffee, I heard a familiar tapping sound. Like clockwork, upon arising, Lilly reached for her cell phone to check messages. Heaven help us if someone had texted while she slept and asked her what she was doing and why she hadn't immediately responded. Did her peeps think she had died on a date with me?

She tapped away like a woodpecker. Lilly was encouraging the death of conversation, replacing it with texting OMG ripostes. The bad grades were adding up today.

I brought her a cup. She blew the steam off the top. Despite my judgment about her and texting and her interior decoration predilections, I loved the way her lips formed over the coffee cup like a kiss you blow to a child. As she moved the cup to her lips, I stared at her breasts. *Nicer than Fiona's*, I thought. She caught me and, with her free hand, pulled the sheet down to the top of her pubis. I raised my eyebrows, my eyes widening in appreciation.

"You like mister, mister?"

I noticed something that I hadn't detected before. She had trimmed her pubes into what looked like a heart shape. I wondered why she'd performed this topiary trimming. The ladies I interviewed went all out bald down below or were trimmed like a landing strip. Was Lilly following a trend for women who were not porn stars? Or was it a new aesthetic? Maybe a subject for another article.

She put the coffee cup down on the night table. With her index finger, she gestured for me to come back to bed. I shed my boxer shorts, not missing a beat.

"You have a very nice ass," she commented.

"Thank you," I said, "as do you."

"So how was your last hooker?"

Lilly knew the story I was writing. My bathroom visit to Greece immediately came to mind.

"Interesting," I said straight-faced. "I met her pimp."

"That go okay?"

"Not really. Gave him some fashion tips which he didn't like."

Lilly squinted, not sure what I was saying. "I have a question."

"Sure."

"These women."

"Yeah?"

"You ever want to do it with them?"

"Of course," I said, knowing that denying it would raise Lilly's "liar liar, pants on fire" alarm. "But when you do the kind of work I do, doing that would compromise the relationship I try to establish. You know, trust. They would treat me like any other john."

"Like a doctor-patient, lawyer-client thingy."

"Exactly."

I should have felt bad about the bullshit I had just shoveled, but I didn't. To be honest, but not with Lilly, I had the ability to compartmentalize, so me fucking them was put into neat boxes that didn't interfere with whatever was going on with Lilly. Having flexible moral principles, an oxymoron I acknowledge, worked for me. It was the kind of justification I told myself to stave off the idea that I was a dickwad. I was woke, a self-aware cad.

I slid into bed, and she pulled the sheet aside.

Lying next to her, I admired her body. No doubt, it was near perfect. Long, shapely legs. Firm. No fat. A body that went to a gym on a regular basis. Victoria's Secret breasts that if I were a bra, I would be honored to hold them in place. She had the looks of an extremely sexy model or candidate for the *Sports Illustrated* swimsuit issue. She was a junior high school teacher. The pubescent boys in her classes must have had countless in-class boners.

I moved to her neck and kissed her smooth skin that still smelled of sleep. I whispered in her ear.

"Oh God, I am not going to do that."

Travel plans to Greece were nixed. Lilly saw my disappointment. She, in turn, whispered something in my ear.

"That would be different," I said.

She smiled and moved her body down, past my knees. She used her mouth and tongue in an area she had visited before and in ways I had known before. But then she did something new with her tongue in a place she hadn't explored before. Her tongue rimmed around my Athens airport, and I happily groaned.

Seeing I had been pleasured in a new way, she resurfaced.

"I liked that," I said. I gave her an A-plus.

"Maybe try it with me."

I started my journey. My hand traveled down to her stomach, and I made circular strokes. When I reached her garden of earthly delights, she spread her legs to let my fingers explore her. I moved down, and my mouth went over her cha-cha, and I hoped to make her sing. I also let my tongue explore the same area she had visited with me.

Her *hmmm* vibrated along her slender throat, and then an elongated *ah* was what she sang.

Reciprocal sexcapades, quid pro quo.

A throaty moan now. "Come inside me now," she said. I closed my eyes and entered her, my mind drifting away from her for a minute, her face and body replaced by a previous girlfriend who had grown tired of my commitment phobia. Lilly dug her nails into my back, and my attention returned to her. After ten minutes of enthusiastic thrusting—but who was counting?—I felt her body quiver. My job below was completed. Climax accomplished. But my girlfriend drifting bothered me. At least I didn't conjure up Mamie Eisenhower.

"That was nice," she said, a bit out of breath.

"Very."

She didn't wait long to ask me about our dinner plans for tomorrow.

"Mom and Dad will be so happy to meet you at last. Are you as anxious as I am?"

I thought I'd rather have nails hammered into my eyes than meet them. And so I sidestepped Lilly's question for the moment. Having had a wonderfully depleting orgasm, I was vulnerable. I bet Lilly was aware of my weakened mental state when she asked me this. A first dinner with her parents or any parents of the woman I happened to be dating sent up warning flares. This kind of sit-down, face-to-face, breaking-bread repast was really a beauty contest where the 'rents got to see whom their prized only daughter had been shagging. It was their chance to check out the goods, ask the obvious questions about what I did for a living, what my parents did for a living, college degrees, and other personal resume items.

They'd think I was an okay young man, a little odd but interesting. Lying next to Lilly, my anxiety began to rise. I started to sing.

> On review
> Half a Jew
> A li'l bit strange
> But not deranged.

"Fenn," she groaned, "you can't do that when you come to my folks' house."

"I know," I said.

"I find it charming. Sort of. But…"

"I get it."

"We need to be in Scarsdale at six," she said. "I'll come by tomorrow around five-ish."

"Right."

"I'm going to shower," Lilly announced as she strolled toward the bathroom.

I watched her, admiring her amazing body, and she felt my eyes on her. She turned, giving me a full frontal, then curtseyed and walked into the bathroom. For that, a previous bad letter grade got erased.

Twenty minutes later, she was freshly dressed and heading out.

"I'll pick you up at five," she reminded me.

She wanted to make sure I was dressed appropriately, wearing the Brooks Brothers pants and shirt she purchased that week that I would never have bought. Not my style. Not on my budget. But I acquiesced.

I kissed her, and she left.

I went back to my corkboard and scanned my idea archives, hoping that something would jump out at me for my next story.

CHAPTER 6

BUBBLE BURSTING

After Lilly left, I did one of my martial art exercises called *Kalarippayattu.* It originated in southern India using a complex series of leaps with a fighting stick, a different version of what I used on Fiona's pimp. My downstairs neighbors loved that one. When I heard them bang on their radiator steam pipe, I stopped.

As soon as I put away my fighting stick, my cell phone played "Reveille," a ringtone I assigned to Stan Blanker, my boss. He always called at eleven to go over whatever I'd sent him.

"Hope I didn't wake you."

My reply was as smooth as a baby's ass. "Stanley, I've been up for hours just waiting for a round of applause."

"Ass licking doesn't work unless I'm dating you, and you're not my type." He paused then said, "You sound out of breath."

"Just finished my workout."

"At your kung fu thingy place this early?"

"It's not a thingy. It's a martial arts dojo. And no, I did a little workout in my crib."

"Why don't you go to a normal gym? Use a treadmill, firm up your butt with an elliptical."

"I'm not going for the Arnold look. More like Bruce Lee."

"And you realize he's dead?"

"Spirit connection," I replied.

"Fenn the Zen."

I liked my new nickname. But I was getting impatient with his banter, wanting to hear what he thought of my submission.

32

"So did you call me to make fun of my lifestyle?" I asked. "Or were you about to lavish me with praise on my *Life of a Call Girl* article I sent you?"

"Actually, we're going to hold off on this one."

I felt an "Oh, shit" moment coming. "Okay, what's up?"

"You know I really dig your writing," Stan started. "I liked your stories on the PTSD firemen who need that adrenaline rush, most of them returning vets from Afghanistan."

"Thanks." My belly button alarm button went off, which I liked to think of as my navel intelligence, sensing bad news coming.

"And that homeless piece. Like on any given night, there are a couple thousand people sleeping on the streets in the city. Most of them mentally ill."

I said thanks again but knew he was leading up to something. Start with praise and then let the hammer down.

"I know you have that quality of getting people to open up to you."

I felt a *but* coming.

"But your story." Stan paused a beat. "Come on, Fenn. Our women readers will think they're having a date with Harvey Weinstein. This is not, and I repeat not, *Me Too* friendly."

I was taken aback. "I thought this piece was actually good. Different. Authentic."

Stan chuckled. "Authentic as in you bonked all of them?"

I said nothing.

"Let's look at what and how you write."

I made a noise that was a reluctant go-ahead grunt.

"You've been freelancing for us for almost a year now, and frankly, I'm seeing a pattern develop."

Having your publisher see a pattern can't be a good thing. Patterns are good for wallpaper, dresses, and diagnosing mental illnesses.

"And I have to be honest," Stan said.

When people say that, you know what's coming next won't be good.

"That piece didn't have the *oomph* that I know I can get from you."

"Oomph meaning what?"

"Grab-me-by-the-balls oomph. A story with a wow factor. Your piece felt like you were reporting about what these women do. I can get that from the *New York Post* or the *Daily News*."

His take on my story was a huge let-down.

"I took a gamble when I hired you. I want to be a believer again."

His loss of faith in me was unsettling.

"Okay, you want more depth and more wow. No problem." I said this with enthusiasm, hoping to impress Stan that I got his message loud and clear, although I knew my article was way more superior than those newsprint rags.

"There is another thing. What is one thing all your stories have in common?"

I had to mull this over for a minute. They had provocative subject matter that Stan liked, so it must be something else. I drew a nervous blank.

"Your silence tells me you have no clue," Stan said. "Then I will tell you. All your stories take place where?"

I shrugged even though it was hard to convey that on a telephone.

"In New York City. It's like you live in this bubble. This urban cocoon. You and your stories never leave the asphalt jungle. You live under a dome."

"It's a story-rich dome," I said, defending my turf. "It has more material than anyone could ever cover."

"The center of the universe is not Manhattan. Have you ever left the city for a story or for anything else?"

"I've been to Florida several times."

"Vacations with your grandparents in Century Village don't count. God forbid you cross over the George Washington Bridge."

"Okay, Stan, cut to the case," I said, showing my irritation.

"This magazine needs to reach beyond our city. We need stories with a national appeal. Does a nurse in Boise give a fuck about crazy ladies who feed alley cats in the Bronx?"

Well, there went one of my corkboard story ideas.

"You need to find enticing subjects out there that people will care about and read about, things they never knew."

Clearly, Stan's *out there* was not my usual stomping grounds.

"Can I explain my take on you in a different way?" Stan offered.

Did I have an option to say no?

"I'm seeing this lady. She speaks six languages. Lovely tits and long, slender legs."

"Lovely breasts and long legs are very fine qualities," I agreed.

"She speaks Mandarin, which is a big plus for me."

"A big plus?" I wondered where he was going with this.

"Sure. Better service when we dine in Chinatown. We can order off menu, not the tourist goop you get. Had some great Chou Dofu last night along with duck tongue."

Chou Dofu, Stan explained, was also known as stinky tofu. "Take a little brine made with shrimp, vegetables, and some salt, ferment it for a few months, soak a chunk of tofu in it, and you have a dish famous for its overpowering odor."

"I'll pass."

"That's my point exactly."

"I guess I'm not seeing your point."

"You must challenge yourself like my experience with Chou Dofu."

I shook my head, bemused by Stan equating my seemingly cuisine wimpiness to my approach to writing.

"You know what the Chinese say."

"They say many things," I said.

"About food, I mean. There's an old Chinese saying. It says they will eat anything with legs that's not a table and anything that flies that's not an airplane."

I carried my coffee mug and cell phone to the kitchen, where I poured another cup. "I get what you're saying. You want me to leave my dome, write about something and somewhere different."

"Exactly." Stan waited a few seconds. "You can imagine that I have a bunch of good writers that are begging me for work," he said, the not-so-subtle hint of a threat hanging over me with this remark. "Your next story needs to hit the ball out of the park."

I knew well enough that there were tons of hungry writers out there barely making ends meet, taking shitty jobs to make the rent. If I lost this gig, I might have to go back to subbing English at high schools with ADD kids that thought good literature was tweeting. Lilly would probably like that.

"And I am very grateful for the opportunities you have given me," I said, trying to sound as grateful and humble as possible without sounding like I was groveling.

"Then I am done with my life lesson for you."

I was on the verge of making a wisecrack, but you don't crack wise when you're given the last seat on a lifeboat.

"You know what you need to do," Stan finished.

"Yes," I said, not knowing what the hell my next story would be about but knew it was a make-or-break deal.

Stan saved me from trying to pull an idea out of my ass.

"I have what could be a compelling idea for your next article," he said. "It's in line with your interest in doing stories from Bizarro-land. You nail this the way we talked about, and we'll be good again…" Stan's words trailed off, his warning not needing to be uttered in a complete sentence.

"I'm all ears," I said, wondering what Bizarro-land idea he had in mind.

"This idea goes back to a childhood fantasy that a lot of us had." He paused for drama. "Running away with the circus."

I thought about that fantasy. I was sure I never had that one. My childhood fantasies had more to do with having Superman's powers and x-ray vision so I could beat up the tough guys that bullied me and see through girls' dresses.

"One more detail you should know," Stan continued. "And it's a truly sad thing."

"Which is…?"

"The big time, three-ring circus is dying. Look what happened to Barnum and Bailey. They were at it for one hundred forty-six years.

Now the fucking Greatest Show on Earth is gone forever. So what's left? The small one ringers with carnival rides and the midway."

"Gone like drive-in theaters and Walkmans."

"My point exactly. I'm thinking you should do something about the people that work on one of the remaining traveling circuses with its carnival rides," Stan went on. "A nostalgia piece. Specifically a piece on the midway."

"So you're thinking bearded ladies, midgets, and human oddities. What their lives must be like, that kind of angle?"

"Basically," Stan answered, "but with compassion. How they view the world that views them as not really normal."

"Whatever normal is," I muttered under my breath, questioning what a standard-issue humanoid was.

"Live with these folks for a while. Gain their trust. Walk a mile in their moccasins sort of thing."

Since this was Stan's fantasy, I assumed he had put some thought into this assignment. "You have any leads, seeing as this is your idea?"

"Funny you should ask. I was hoping you'd be open to our little chat, so I did a bit of digging around. There's the Kelley Miller Traveling Circus. That's in the Oklahoma area. But I found one that travels around upstate New York—the Giambolvo Brothers. Gets you out of the city but not that far so that your comfort level about leaving your bubble won't be traumatic."

If needed, I had my vape to assuage any trauma with regard to departing my bubble.

"They're in Ithaca for a couple of weeks. Cornell country."

"Cornell as in the college," I said to confirm where I was going and began to hum "Hit the Road Jack" by Ray Charles.

"Fenn, you're doing that weird thing you do."

I stopped.

"You're going to put on your big-boy traveling pants. Of course you'll be on a deadline since we shit-canned your hooker piece."

He put that last sentence out there, knowing I'd have to deliver or else.

"I expect a draft three weeks from tomorrow, assuming you'll leave tomorrow."

"Sure thing," I said, trying to sound all in. "Doing a story on citizens of the midway compared to South Bronx gangbangers should be a walk in the park."

"I called the Giambolvo Brothers. Told them about you writing an article about them. Said we wanted to focus on the midway folks. The more interesting, the better. They kind of chuckled and said they had a couple working their midway acts that would be perfect. They'll introduce you. Ask for Eddy when you get there."

"Okay."

"We'll rent a car for you," he said. "You have a license I hope."

"I do," I said, realizing it must be stashed away in some dark desk drawer.

"Call my assistant. He'll make sure the car has a GPS so you can find your way out of Manhattan. Keep in touch."

"Like Stevie Wonder working with Braille."

"Think positive, my boy. Just bat your baby blues and give them that winning smile."

"My eyes are brown."

"Whatever," Stan replied. "And don't charm them so much that you'll be asking me to be best man at your wedding with the four-breasted, fish-scaled woman."

"There you go again with the titties."

"I was never breastfed," he explained, and with that, he hung up.

CHAPTER 7

EXPECTATIONS

Another call came right after Stan's. I knew who it was before I looked at the caller ID.

"So?" a familiar voice said when answered.

Selma Cooper, my mother, usually started her telephone calls to me with *so*. *So* was usually a prelude to questions that centered on why I was basically a fuck up, although that would not be the term my mother would ever have passed through her lips.

In Selma's eyes, I had a job that was the equivalent of a traveling salesman. Think Willy Loman as a scrivener. The bigger sin for Selma was the fact that I was still single. That meant no grandchildren in the near future—or maybe never. I lived in a small rent-controlled apartment that couldn't fit a table big enough to invite people over for a proper meal. My mother judged stability on how much food was in your frig.

"So," I said back.

"So are you coming over for dinner next week?"

Selma, who was Jewish, was also a native-born Texan from Abilene. As a result, her language of guilt was delivered in a drawl sounding like a Yiddish version of Tammy Wynette in a disappointed mood. My dad, Marco, was an Italian Catholic and was a homicide detective raised in Brooklyn. He sounded like a cast member from *The Sopranos*. Like me but for different circumstances, he left the cop world to get a degree in psychology. He was done with murder scenes, wife beatings, and finding dead junkies in hallways. The psychology degree was probably to have arguments with Selma on more equal footing.

"Sorry, Ma. I'm off on a job."

My mother's silence hung in the telephonic air like a stalled zeppelin. I heard a sigh that was meant to be heard.

"So how's Lilly?" she asked, knowing that this was a delicate subject.

Selma thought Lilly and I could be destined to be together if I just got my act together. Lilly would probably agree.

"I was just thinking about calling her," I answered, having to cancel my dinner date with her creators.

"She's very nice from what I can tell."

My mom had met her just once but probably had some kind of extrasensory insight into the women I dated. In her mind, Lilly would be a good match. Hope and grandchildren spring eternal.

"Yes, she is." Any woman that I might be dating was nice in my mother's eyes as long as she had no facial piercings and no tattoos unless they were small and confined to locations that were covered most of the year. Lilly had most of the right qualifications: She had a steady job, a college degree, and a pelvis meant for child bearing.

"I was hoping for a visit so we could have a talk about some other things."

Ah, the ubiquitous other things that had no specificity other than the never-ending self-improvement lecture.

"Lilly is a sweetheart…" I said, keeping Selma focused on someone else.

"I need to tell you something," Selma interrupted, with her usual concern for my well-being.

"Of course you do." A call to my mother without scrutinizing my psyche would be like serving guacamole without avocado.

"Women and your work. There has to be a balance."

I made a small sound that let her know I was listening to her.

"With the ladies, you are ADD. With work, you are a bit OCD. Little sustained focus with the women. With work, you dive in and it's all focus."

"Interesting perspective," I replied, thinking there was some truth to her analysis.

She added, "No medication for that, I'm afraid. But a bit of therapy might help."

"Why would I need theirs when I have you?" I said.

"Always quick with the wisecracks."

"What? You want me to learn how to stutter," I replied, using a line from Bogie's *Maltese Falcon*.

"Again, a funny man."

"I'm leaving town tomorrow," I said, cutting off another chance for a complaint. Having been editorially waterboarded by Stan a few minutes before, I didn't need any additional battering of my self-confidence.

"Out of town?"

"Out of town," I repeated.

Another *oh*.

"Upstate New York."

"Upstate? Not in the city? Someone died?" Selma assumed leaving town could only be accounted for by a funeral.

"No. An assignment. I'm on a deadline."

I took her silence as an inability to deal with what I had just said. "Put Dad on," I quickly requested to end the possibility of her continuing her grilling.

I heard Selma call for my father. "Marco, it's your son." She yelled *your son* like it was his fault, whatever that fault might be.

"Don't mind her," my father started as soon as he got on the phone. "I was listening. All the disappointment is really about wanting you to be happy."

"I know," I said, "but she has to stop thinking of me as her work in progress. I have already been launched."

My dad's voice dropped to a whisper. "But it's overrated."

"What is?"

"Happy. Your mother deals with depressed people all day. She strives to show them how they can be happier. Me, I'd settle for thirty percent happy. For you, she wants a hundred percent. Maybe more. She's a mother. What can I say?"

"But I am happy. Not all the time like you said. But I like what I do. I like my life."

"And that's what counts," my father agreed.

"She still sees me as a kid."

"And you will always be that. It's hard to stop being a parent."

"I guess," I said, not knowing the feeling. Still single. No kiddies. Ah, the life of the vagabond scribbler.

"Life is a journey, not a destination." My father was a fan of Ralph Waldo Emerson.

I said, "For Mom, life should be made up of pit stops. Land a steady job, get a wife, pop out some kids, and retire somewhere warm."

"When the time is right, maybe you'll do just that." He paused a moment. "Or not. What will be, will be."

"I have to go." I explained where and why.

"Good luck," he said. "Be safe and call if you need anything."

"I will," I said, and we both hung up.

Lying on my well-worn Salvation Army sofa, I decided that I could use a different perspective on the last hours of my city life. I imbibed another self-prescribed amount of Special Queen into my biosystem.

It didn't take long after I exhaled my second hit that my thoughts drifted back to Stan. My reaction to his slam on my writing had rattled me. It was not like I didn't know what he was talking about. I was a pretty solid writer as a journalist but not of the Breslin ilk. I could weave a story, throw in provocative insights, and have a fair amount of similes and metaphors to make my pieces come alive. But I didn't have any illusions about becoming a literary force.

I was a world watcher. A people watcher. A New York City watcher. Why did Stan think there was more there out there? The city really was the center of the universe. Everywhere else was just noise.

I relied on what people did and said. Anais Nin said that the role of a writer is not to say what we all can say but what we are unable to say. Whatever my doubts or misgivings, I recognized that I loved the process.

I closed my eyes, and Descartes entered my head. The dead sometimes will do that without my permission. "I think, therefore I am," he said. *I am, I am… I'm Popeye the Sailor Man.* Then Socrates arrived. Another great dead philosopher. According to him, the unexamined life is not worth living—strong advice from a Greek who was sentenced to death by drinking hemlock. *How much of his life did he have to examine?* I wondered.

I took one more toke and tried to see that Stan's assignment was not a test but an opportunity. This could be an adventure. Maybe it was something I needed. I just had to give myself a chance.

I returned to my laptop and confirmed that the Giambolvo Brothers would be in Ithaca, New York, for two weeks before heading west to Buffalo. I made a list of what I needed to pack, never having had to pack except for summer camp a million years before.

My cat wandered over and hopped onto my lap. She purred and blinked her yellow, citrine-colored eyes. I thought she could read my thoughts, but I never seemed to know what she was thinking. I wondered if cats and dogs had a sense of humor. What seemed funny to them, if anything? Did they laugh when we were not watching?

It suddenly struck me that my cat and plants' reliance on me for food and water to sustain their lives would be an issue when I left. I liked them since they didn't judge me and had very low relationship expectations. I called Lilly and knew my favor would not go down well.

"Hi, sweetie," I started off with a honeyed greeting.

"Miss me already?"

"Of course." I hesitated and said, "I need you to feed Minerva and water the plants."

"Why?" She was confused.

"Change of plan," I started. "Can't meet your folks tomorrow."

"Why?" This time, her question came over the phone like razor wire. She had been counting on that meet, greet, and eat event.

I explained my new assignment.

"It can't wait?"

I told her about Stan's threat and that my job was on the line.

"Maybe that's good."

She said that because of my erratic freelance assignments that had no guarantee of stability. A stable job in her eyes meant a stable relationship.

"In what way?"

"A career change," she happily explained.

"And do what?"

"Something else." A vague answer with undefined options. Not helpful right now.

"How about we can talk about that when I get back?"

"Go fuck yourself."

"I take that as a no," I said, referring to the care and feeding of my pet and plants.

"I love the way you can read between the lines." Lilly's response was piqued, for which I couldn't blame her. She paused, and I could tell she had more on her mind about *us*.

"The trouble with you, Fenn, is that you don't think our relationship has any problems. You don't even consider that you might be the problem. You think I'm Shirley Temple and our relationship is the Good Ship Lollypop. On a happy, no-strings-attached cruise. We go out, hear music, have dinners, and like to fuck. You never talk to me about the future. *Our* future."

I loved the Shirley metaphor. But I had a preference for a *Titanic* comparison. The *Titanic* seemed more fitting, given my dating history. The band playing while the ship went down.

"You're a teenager pretending to be an adult."

That one sank in. "I don't disagree," I responded to her accusation. Most arguments with my girlfriends would stop when I agreed that I had flaws. Another good reply was saying, "I'm an idiot." Maybe I should try this next.

"I'm an idiot, but Minerva needs you. She will die if you don't come over and feed her." I hoped that cat guilt would work and defuse Lilly's ire. "She mumbles your name in her sleep when you stay over."

I got a tiny laugh out of her. Progress.

"And your plants? Do they whisper my name when I pass by them?"

"More of a sighing sound," I said.

"I hate you, you know."

"*Hate* is a strong word."

"We have a great thing going," Lilly said, "then out of the blue, you withdraw. No reason given."

"My job," I countered.

"Bullshit. You're breaking my heart, Fenn. What's up with that?"

"I'll make it up to you. I would love to meet your parents. It really is about this assignment. My paycheck. Come on…please."

"You're a charming bastard," Lilly said after a long a moment. "Charming, but still a bastard."

"Thanks," I said. "I will take you out for fabulous dinner anywhere you want when I get back. And talk about our future." I said that but knew the topic was way out of my comfort zone.

"Dinner in Paris?" she suggested.

Going to France was more frightening than my trip to Ithaca. "No, but I see Manhattan in your future, and we could do Le Bernardin," I explained.

"Bribes work," she said, softening.

"And good, sizzling sex?"

"We'll see, big man."

I thanked her. Maybe the upstate fresh air would also give me a chance to sort out my relationship with Lilly. I was a self-aware cad, an oxymoron description of my personality I recognized.

I would leave for Ithaca in the morning. Three weeks to write a wowie zowie piece about the denizens of the midway. They say sitting on a ticking bomb can give you a whole new perspective about life. I just hoped the bomb didn't blow up before I could finish examining my unexamined life.

CHAPTER 8

CLEANUP

Marvin Brinks woke Tuesday morning with a very troubling feeling. In the hypnopompic state that lingered as his dream receded, he remembered and thought of himself as a junkie. Not heroin. Not crack. It was a jones for buying expensive things, an unquenchable need to possess exquisite items that drew him like the sea nymphs of Persephone luring sailors to their death.

The dream also reminded him of the bigger problems he would be facing, coming at him faster than a Himalayan avalanche. His money problems could not be ignored anymore. The bank calls. His overdrawn credit limit. Now the auction fiasco and his wary boss.

He got out of bed and made himself a cup of strong coffee. He sat on a stool at his kitchen counter, thinking about his life at work. Brinks didn't get to his position at Glowball Productions the easy way. He worked hard, but he was also cunning. He wasn't born with a silver spoon up his butt like his boss. His time growing up was dull and pitiable. Escape was needed. Movies transported him from his dreary life. He liked the ones with happy endings and decided that he should work for companies that made them.

After college with a degree in business, he moved to LA. He started working at small-budget production companies and eventually moved to ones with more money, bigger stars, and better reputations. Ten years later, he wound up at Glowball, hired to work in their accounting office, starting on the bottom rung.

He was smarter than his associates. He saw angles that cut costs, knew about tax loopholes that increased the bottom line, and wrote contracts with vendors where Glowball wouldn't be screwed with padded invoices or inventing services never delivered because nobody paid attention to the details.

In a weird way, the vendors' shifty practices became his training ground by learning from their slippery antics. He didn't need a Wharton MBA where the essential techniques about fleecing were never taught.

Brinks had a second cup of coffee; his ideas for a plan to take Wolfe's attention off him kicked around his head. The man was recently divorced, his wife having run off with a scriptwriter from a movie that Glowball had produced. However, her leaving him was a wakeup call, and he reinvented himself. James became Jimmy.

He bought a zoomy sports car, got designer eyeglasses, had his teeth whitened, and stumbled upon a much younger and very attractive woman who worked in Glowball's makeup department. She had put the squeeze on Wolfe—and not just figuratively—at a holiday party. And quicker than a hot knife slicing butter, she soon became the new Mrs. Wolfe. What Wolfe didn't hear was his trophy wife's straying antics whispered around the corridors at Glowball. Brinks guessed that Morgan was way too hot for the new Wolfman and was trolling for more excitement than hubby could provide. Brinks stored this bit of info into his mental Rolodex.

"Good morning," Brandy said, the secretary he shared with his boss as he walked to his office. Her voice always had a chirpy quality to it, like the Walt Disney bluebird singing to Cinderella.

Brinks smiled at her. "Mail come yet?"

"On your desk," Brandy said shortly then eyed him for a moment and asked, "Busy weekend?"

"Not really."

"You check out any more auctions?"

Brinks's stomach twisted, but he forced a chuckle. "Nothing in my price range."

"Yeah," she agreed as if she was a regular bargain hunter at auctions. "I can grab you a coffee."

"Thanks.

Brinks worked all day pulling up spreadsheets for expenditures over the last twenty-four months. He knew which line items he had pushed with charges for things that were never delivered or services not rendered. He had a list of altered agreements, murky ledger entries, and mischaracterized expenses. He had set up several phony, in-name-only company LLCs where checks for these bogus invoices were sent. Once he nailed down a record of these payments, he would have a starting point as to what needed to be reconstructed. He calmed his apprehension by reminding himself to focus on solving his numbers problem one line item at a time.

At six o'clock, he noticed the sky had reddened, the LA sunset lighting up the haze that hung over the city. It was time to go home.

Brandy popped into his office to say good night.

"See you tomorrow," Brinks said.

He left soon after and knew he would do the same ledger scrubbing tomorrow. Walking down the corridor, his thoughts returned to Wolfe, and he wondered how he could effectively sidetrack the man's attention to give him more time for his cleanup activities.

CHAPTER 9

EASY-PEASY

Tuesday morning and the sound of two pigeons fucking outside of my window woke me. The male was furiously flapping his wings to keep himself from falling off the window ledge. I wondered if that was an omen but couldn't figure out what kind. Alexander the Great's death was predicted by several omens, including ravens falling dead at his feet as he approached Babylon. I didn't know what two pigeons fucking predicted.

I was packed. I had a cup of coffee with Minerva on my lap. If a cat could have a worried look, then she had one.

"I'll be fine," I reassured her. "Lilly will take care of you. When you see her, make happy purring sounds. She'll like that."

I left my place and picked up the rental with the GPS app. It had a woman's voice. Sort of soothing but firm at the same time as she gave instructions when to turn in so many feet or miles.

The drive out of the city was an adventure of sorts. Going through the Lincoln Tunnel was like being born; a perverse metaphor, I would agree, if that tunnel with exhaust fumes and jazzed-up Uber drivers could be compared to going through the birth canal. But that was how my mind worked. The tunnel funnel popped me out into Weehawken, New Jersey. Weehawken was where Alexander Hamilton and Aaron Burr had their famous duel over Hamilton's journalistic defamation of Burr's character. Hence, let's praise the resolve of journalists, although sadly, Hamilton was mortally wounded—a fate I hoped to avoid as I entered the hinterlands.

I kept driving. Stan would be proud that I actually went through a large piece of New Jersey, although from what I saw on their license plates, I was confused as to why it was called the Garden State. Gardens I did not see. I drove through Pennsylvania next, the Keystone State, a nickname that once again made no sense.

Another one and a half hours went by, and I passed by Scranton. The radio blasted Springsteen's "Death to My Hometown." I sang a couple of lines that I recalled, bobbing my head and doing a car seat dance.

A car passed me as I did my car seat boogie, and a teenage girl stared at me through the backseat window. She flashed a peace sign. I imagined that she thought I was way cooler than her dad up front who drove. I peace-signed her back.

Three hours later, I was near Binghamton, New York. I passed by farms and cornfields and actual cows that mooed at me when I slowed down to gawk. They must have sensed I was not from around there.

"Thanks for the half and half," I said to them.

After Binghamton, houses in the countryside looked weathered and worn, like pairs of old shoes that people had given up on mending. Twenty miles later, I reached Whitney Point. Main Street was populated by gas stations, convenience stores, and fast food joints. One thing caught my eye: an old army tank sitting out on an athletic field. Its turret and 75mm gun was pointed across the main drag at the local Dunkin' Donuts. I wondered if that was a warning to coronary-prone customers who should be snacking on low-fat fiber bars instead of glazed jelly doughnuts and Coffee Coolattas.

On Route 79, I passed through invisible towns like Richford and Slaterville Springs, which had names but nothing else to indicate a town was there. Not much longer and I rolled into Ithaca. The trip took me about four and a half hours with two pee stops as my GPS guided me to the Super 8 motel off Route 13 just outside downtown Ithaca.

Checking into the motel was easy. There was a continental breakfast, I was told by the reception lady, and free Internet. Continental sounded so very European and classy, but in reality, she explained, it was buffet-style trough of breads, cereal, and generic scrambled eggs.

I was learning new foodie things, having been sheltered from the motel cuisine experience.

In my room, I unpacked and retrieved my vape, blowing Sativa mist out of the window. There were no Korean stores or pigeons fucking from my ground-floor view. Trucks swung past the motel, and the parking lot was peppered with what I imagined were other rental cars carrying a different crew of Willy Lomans.

I sighed. I was a stranger in a strange land. The absence of city noise and smells and anthill activity threw off my inner gyroscope. I resisted a panicky feeling by taking a few deep breaths and exhaling them with a few *oms*. This was just new, I told myself. That was what an adventure felt like. I felt better. Sort of.

Predictably, the munchies arrived, and I thought about dinner. At the motel reception desk, a new welcomer was on duty, a young man who was trying to do his best fighting acne.

"Can you recommend any places to eat?" I asked.

"We got the Slate diner," he said.

He could tell I was not a diner kinda guy.

"Or ethnic."

"Other than Chinese?"

He scratched his cheek, disrupting a facial blemish. "You okay with Vietnamese?"

"Sounds great."

"Saigon Kitchen on West State. Got real Vietnamese cooks."

I imagined that was a good sign instead of having some white folks trying to emulate ethnic food they learned on the Cooking Channel.

Back in my car, I thought about tomorrow and the sideshow people I would meet. I decided on a plan. Just stroll around the grounds and absorb the vibe. Look. Watch. Observe. Record. Like I usually did when I went after a story. I would find the Giambolvo Brothers. Stan had told me they would introduce me to two of their more unusual and interesting midway people. Not sure what *unusual* meant since I assumed all midway people were a bit unusual. The assignment should go smoothly, I assured myself. *Just bat my baby blues as Stan instructed me. Easy-peasy.*

CHAPTER 10

AS TRUSTWORTHY AS A FORTUNE COOKIE

The guy seemed creepy. She was used to most people's looks, but often it was men who gave her a variety of lingering, too-long stares. She saw the gawking stares, the lewd ones, the sympathetic ones, the embarrassed ones. Of course, she knew that it was partly due to what she did for a living being a carnie fortune-teller but she knew it was her size. This guy was looking intently at her as if he were puzzling her out. No ogling, not gawking, a different kind of observation.

The midway was where people strolled and watched the entertainers if that was what they were, what she was. The Giambolvo Brothers had a sword swallower, the kid who painted portraits with a brush jammed between his toes because he had no arms, the knife-throwing couple, the five-hundred-pound man, a contortionist, a tattooed lady, and a sword swallower. Classic sideshow curiosities the paying public expected.

Being billed as a fortune-teller by itself wasn't such a big deal. But being three and a half feet tall in a grown woman's body was. She looked at herself in the mirror mounted on a door inside her trailer then dropped her robe to the floor and studied her body. Zena turned to her right side and gazed at her profile. She ran her hands down her rib cage and then over her ass and thighs. She was perfect, she told herself. Sexy. And like Alice who tumbled into Wonderland, her DNA took a swig of the "Drink Me" potion. But unlike Alice, there was no "Eat Me" cake to make her grow taller.

She knew she wasn't perfect according to *them*. Other than her height, she had the physical attributes of a dwarf. The shape of her face, the pug nose and high forehead, short arms and bowed legs. In a land of dwarves, she would be just right and the *others* would be the freaks.

She looked more closely at her reflection in the mirror, held her breasts, then ran her fingers over a flat stomach. Even though she was not living amongst dwarves in a little-people world, she told herself, she was one hot little bitch.

The guy came back into her thoughts. He had been hanging around the midway all day. He was scoping out all the acts, talking into a recorder on his phone and taking pictures of the acts.

At first, Zena wondered if she should have one of the brothers' muscle heads roust him until he actually sat down in the chair at her booth with Big Eddy behind him. As it turned out, he was a freelance writer wanting to do a story about the midway, about people, and specifically about her and her best friend. Eddy Giambolvo, one of the two blimp-sized brothers that ran the circus and midway, introduced this guy. Told her to cooperate. Be good for business.

He wasn't the first person to try and wrangle a story out of her. She had blown all the other interlopers off. They pulled out the stops with their make-believe smiles, dripping with honey come-ons, and she always told them to fuck off. She didn't do that with that guy, and didn't know why.

In any case, the Giambolvo Brothers didn't give her much choice. She agreed to listen to his pitch. He didn't come across like those other dudes. She had a feeling about him. He seemed sincere enough. But she also sensed desperation. Like getting this story had more to it than just getting a story. In the end, she told him that she and her friend would join him for a late lunch the next day.

She billed herself as "Zena: The World's Smallest Fortune-Teller," but that was just the midway tagline to get people into her booth. Her fortune-telling was about as trustworthy as a fortune cookie. But what she had was a special gift, an uncanny ability to read people and their body language, a sixth sense about what they were going through when they came into her booth. And there was another thing that she had going—a special vibe she emitted that made people trust her and relax enough to share things that they wouldn't or couldn't with other people.

Zena went to her closet and picked out a *go to lunch with this dude* outfit. This felt a little bit like a going on a date, although going out on a date was something that never happened to her. If a guy came on to her, it was usually all about wanting novelty sex that had nothing to do with her. She would be a good fuck story to tell his buddies. When she was really horny, slightly drunk, or incredibly lonely, she might take a man on then throw him out of her trailer as soon as she climaxed. Wham, bam, thank you, bigger-than-me-man.

She thought about the writer guy and picked out an outfit that would make a statement, not like she needed to. She decided to show off her breasts with a tight T-shirt and then wondered why she wanted to do that. She hadn't flirted with a man in ages. Maybe never.

CHAPTER 11

PLAY THE FREAK

My two lunchtime companions would be waiting for our luncheon date. Once in my car, I headed back to where the Giambolvo Brothers Circus had set up on the Tompkins County Fairgrounds. As before, the GPS found the location, and I didn't wind up in Biloxi. It amazed me how my parents ever got to wherever they were supposed to go with handwritten directions and unwieldy AAA maps.

My lunch mates were standing at the front gate next to the ticket booth. As I pulled up, I tried not to stare at them since under normal circumstances, these two people would be worthy of more than a stare. I had met the little lady the day before, but her friend elicited some serious gaping.

"Thanks for coming," I said, unlocking the passenger and back-seat doors. Simultaneous grunts were their responses as my passengers took the back seat of the car.

Hoping to break the ice, I said, "Pretty exciting for me. Getting a behind-the-scenes view of your circus and the midway."

"Exciting. Sure." This came from the pint-sized woman that I could barely see glancing into the rearview mirror. I drove out of the fairgrounds heading to Ithaca, stealing glances at them while they stared at the passing scenery.

"I know my invitation to grab a meal when I saw you yesterday must've seemed pretty much out of the blue."

"Not really—the brothers strongly suggested we talk to you. Hard to refuse when your boss insists," the little lady explained.

I felt the same way about my all-or-nothing assignment that Stan had compelled me to agree to. "Better to be the boss than bossed," I said, trying to show I was on their side.

"Fuck 'em...all," said my other passenger, who went by the name of Holey John, which was made up, probably like the little lady's alongside him. She had been introduced as Zena, and I had been watching her the day before from a safe distance along with the other midway attractions. Her size as advertised made me wonder if she was a midget or a dwarf. *I'd have to ask her in a polite way*, I thought, knowing that the little folks had issues about what they were called. And minding what came out of my mouth was always a risk.

I didn't realize whom her interesting friend might be as described by Eddy. I had seen him do his sideshow act, standing on an oriental throw rug with only his Speedo on, getting his flesh lanced by his audience for five bucks a pop with pins and jewelry they picked out of a fishbowl, which, truth be told, made my skin crawl like when a dentist performs a root canal with an old drill.

"I'm Fenn," I said, introducing myself.

"Fern? Like the...plant?" the jewelry-bedecked passenger asked.

"No." I spelled my name out.

"Weird," he said to Zena, who in turn nodded.

"I was hoping we could talk a bit during our meal. Away from here. It'll give me a chance to get to know you better. And likewise, you guys to know me."

"Circus food tent slop or lunch in Ithaca," Zena suggested. "Easy choice."

We drove in silence. Conversationalists they were not. As a journalist that needed a good story, this was not a great sign. Her wry rejoinder was also a danger sign. My belly button's navel intelligence indicated that this was not going to be easy peasy.

I found a public parking lot on Green Street, and we all got out of the car.

It must have looked odd, the three of us walking together. People stared at us, some taking double takes, others sneaking sidelong glances, a few breaking out in wide smiles.

There were a few good reasons to take Zena in. I guessed she was less than four feet tall and maybe thirty years old. She wore yoga pants with a leopard-skin pattern, pink sneakers, and a tight-fitting T-shirt with "Betty Boop" printed on the front giving the finger. If she was going to get gawked at, she seemed to want to make the most of it.

Then there was Holey John. Unlike Zena, he was over six feet tall, the lines around his deeply etched eyes placed him in his late sixties, but his body was still youthful and sinewy like a high school wrestler that had won most of his matches. He was bald except for a ponytail with streaks of gray running through it. He wore a blue denim work shirt with rolled-up sleeves, the shirt tucked in a pair of blue jeans and a beat-up knapsack slung over one shoulder, its contents heavy, making the bag sag.

What made him stand out in the afternoon sun was his face, which looked like a shimmering chandelier, the rays of light bouncing off over fifty silver studs and plugs that pierced his cheeks, lips, ears, and any other piece of face flesh that could be used for his flesh-piercing real estate. Sure, I had seen punk rockers like Slash from Guns n' Roses, Tommy Lee from Motley Crue, and Dave Navarro from Jane's Addiction with their cheeks, lips, noses, and nipples pierced, but Holey John brought piercing to a new level.

I invited my new acquaintances to a brunch at Maxie's Supper Club on West State Street. I did a Yelp search and found that the restaurant was a funky New Orleans-style fish house that also offered slow-smoked barbecue. I figured that my guests would fit in quite nicely. Funky places with funky patrons can do that.

We made a left onto Seneca Street. Two teenage girls dressed in the latest Goth wear stared at Holey John while squinting at the same time, hoping they wouldn't go totally blind.

One had a tattoo of barbed wire inked around her neck. The other had so much black mascara around her eyes that she looked like a raccoon. They winked at him.

He flashed a peace sign.

"Cool," they both said.

"How far is this place?" Zena complained.

"Close," I answered.

"I am so starving. I think I could eat a fucking horse."

I chuckled and caught her glaring up at me.

"What's so funny?" she asked annoyingly. "You're taking me literally, right? You see this little person swallowing a horse and it strikes you as funny. I get it."

I didn't reply, although I did have that thought. Could she read minds as well as fortunes? Selma, the therapist of the emotionally wounded, would love to have that skill.

"If we are going to get along, you're going to have to stop seeing me only as a little person. There's more to me than that. Same with Holey John."

"Of course." Another rule of an interview: Agree with the person you want to interview.

"We may play the freak, but that's because the world sees us that way and we use that to survive."

"You'd never…survive," Holey John added.

I gave him a quizzical look.

"You're nothing…special. Even if you recited poems…in shiny undies," he elaborated.

This was the first complete sentence that Holey John had uttered. I couldn't help notice that his words were halting, punctuated with long pauses. I glanced at the scar on the side of his head and wondered if it had anything to do with his speech. I'd have to ask later, once I gained his confidence. And hers.

"I have a question," Zena started.

"Shoot."

"You picked me and Holey John. Why?"

"I didn't. The Giambolvos said you two were interesting."

"Assholes," Holey John muttered under his breath.

"You do any midway research, you being a top-notch journalist?" she said this with obvious sarcasm.

"I Googled the different types of the sideshow schticks people see."

Holey John turned to Zena. "What's…*schticks*?"

"It means your act or gimmick, what you do. If you watched more Woody Allen flicks, you'd know shtick."

"Yeah, like that's ever going to…happen."

"So you watched us and we stood tall compared to our other friends," she teased, making another size-related pun for my benefit.

"Basically," I replied and looked at Holey John. "I watched your act several times yesterday. *Unique* is what I came away with."

"I never heard me described…that way," Holey John said. "Crazy and a sick fuck are usually whispered…loud enough for me to hear."

I sensed hurt feelings. The man who got his skin lanced was not impervious to pain when it came to his emotions.

Holey John billed himself as the "Human Pin Cushion." I saw that he had chosen his name, and consequently, he must have a sense of its irony, a bit noir but maybe the kind of sarcasm you needed to get by.

I was intrigued by his act but even more curious that there were enough flesh-piercing sadists out there to give this guy a decent day's takings. When I'd watched him the day before, he seemed unaffected by pain, a vacant look entering his eyes when a spectator paid for the privilege to lance him.

"And me?" Zena questioned. "You watched me too. My ravishing beauty was like a babe magnet for your literary libido, right?"

My eyes quickly danced over her body. She had several attractive features, but I didn't check her out like I would've if she were more like Lilly, who was definitely a babe. I caught myself thinking this and realized I was guilty of dismissing her, probably like most of the full-sized world did. And like most men.

"Can I be honest?" I said.

"Make me go all goosebumpy if you do."

"I stood in the back of the crowds watching you," I said, "for quite a while."

"Writer as stalker."

"I'd rather call it observing."

"And you observed what?"

"I was actually looking at the people that came into your booth. What I saw were people grasping your hands in thanks, some having tears run down their cheeks, others nodding like you were saying stuff that resonated with them."

I couldn't say why I was particularly fascinated by Zena and Holey John compared to the other acts except that they stood out in a singular way. A man into pain that showed no reaction to what people did to him and a diminutive woman giving people fairgrounds advice. Lucy from Peanuts goes professional.

As we neared Maxie's, the aroma of good food wafted our way, and I took in a deep breath. It wasn't because I wasn't savoring the food that awaited us. My breath was a way to tamp down the apprehension of sharing a meal with my distrustful eating companions and getting them to love me. Actually, I'd settle for *like*. Or just put up with me for now. This was one assignment I could have done without.

Thank you, Stan. Fuck you, Stan.

CHAPTER 12

IN THE LAND OF LILLIPUTIANS

The three of us reached Maxie's. It was just before the lunch crowd had hit, so the place was practically empty. If the hostess was shocked by her new arrivals, she didn't show it. She sat us at a table, gave out menus, and told us that our server would be over to take drink orders.

Maxie's was a two-floor eating establishment with a wrought-iron balcony on the second floor that gave the place an old French Quarters look. There were curtained windows surrounding the first floor with a crowned fish logo painted on the front door's window. I glanced around as I sat waiting for our server and spotted an antique mahogany bar stretched across the back wall with carved stars and half-moons along the trim. A dusky mirror that looked like it could be over one hundred years old faced a few patrons, the local old Harley and hippie crowd amicably interacting at the bar.

I waited for my guests to start a conversation but was met with blank stares.

The server came over and took our drink order. Zena asked for Genesee Cream ale, Holey John wanted a rum and Coke, and I ordered a ginger ale.

"Ginger ale?" Zena questioned. "Aren't writers supposed to be heavy drinkers? Hemingway, Cheever, Dylan Thomas, Kerouac."

"You know your boozy writers."

"I have a lot of time on my hands, and so I read. My social life with the Brothers has its...*shortcomings*."

I smiled. "Can I quote you?"

Zena gave me a look that said she'd be interviewing me before she would consider me interviewing her, much less quoting anything she said.

The drinks came a few minutes later. "See those two people at the bar," our server said. "Your drinks are on them. The lady said she saw you last night."

I looked over at the bar. A young couple stared intently at Zena and Holey John. The young woman smiled and waved at Zena. The man with the woman did not. He glowered.

"Wow, celebrities. I'm impressed," I said.

"One of the perks of being a pint-sized fortune teller hanging with a bejeweled man."

I glanced around the restaurant and saw more people trickling in for brunch. A few people spotted us as they found tables and tilted their heads in our direction.

Zena watched me watch the dining crowd and shrugged. "We get a lot of that too. You get used to it."

"Fuck 'em," Holey John said.

Our drinks came, and we gave the server our food order. Holey John went for the Maxie's Mighty-Mighty Gumbo made with chicken, andouille, and crawfish served over rice. Zena asked for their pulled pork sandwich, and I had the Blackened Catfish Creole with red beans and rice. I felt gastronomic joy reminiscent of my hometown heading my way.

"So what did you find out about circuses and midway life?" Zena started. "I figured you did some research, being a top-notch writer." The smile she offered was a sardonic stab at my credibility.

I waited a moment before answering, studying Zena's face more intently than I had before. She had dark-brown eyes, almost black in the right light, and a tangled mane of curly black hair falling past her shoulders. Her mouth with its full lips seemed extremely sensual.

A thought immediately hit me as I looked at her. I recalled that I hadn't checked her out like I did with most women I met for the first time as possible beddable candidates. She reminded me of a young Sophia Loren but transfigured into a really small person by a spell like you read in a fairy tale.

I caught myself staring, so I started. "I read some circus history," I began. "The Romans and Greeks had circuses with chariot races, staged battles, and exotic animals."

"You're a regular *Wikipedia*," Zena teased.

"Fast forward two thousand years and the circus came to America. I understand George Washington attended one of the first in Philadelphia."

"So you must have read about P. T. Barnum. His menagerie of human oddities. Exhibits of the physically deformed."

"His freak show."

At the mention of the term *freak show*, Zena and Holey John exchanged looks and then looked hard at me.

"I didn't invent that term," I quickly defended myself.

"You know what P. T. Barnum's last words were before he was covered with a dirt blanket?" she quizzed, changing the subject.

"There's a sucker born every minute?"

She shook her head. "'How were the receipts today?' He also said, 'Every *crowd* has a silver lining.' The man had money on his mind until his last breath."

Holey John cracked a grin. "I like...money from the...crowds. Maybe buy a house one day...lead a regular life. Have a family."

"There won't ever be anything regular about you, honey," Zena said and patted his hand.

"I still gotta...dream."

I wondered about what kind of family Holey John imagined beyond the midway. If I got that far, I would ask him.

A skinny man in a T-shirt with a *Life Isn't So Good* logo came over and asked for an autograph. He held a circus program, and Zena signed it.

"Maybe you can give me a stock tip." He left chuckling at his own joke.

"Fortune-teller as money manager," she said. "You have to wonder about fans like that who collect our autographs."

"What about them?"

"Usually a fan wants an autograph from an actor, a rock singer, or someone famous."

"You are a celebrity of sorts," I said.

"Of sorts," Zena repeated. "We are oddities to most of the world, like what they see at *Ripley's Believe or Not*. Actors are remembered for their acting. Somebody famous did something memorable. But we haven't done anything special except that God or Nature or something that scrambled our genetic code made us different from the rest of you so-called normal people."

"Normal people aren't always that normal."

"Sure, but look at my size and entrancing physique. I'm off the bell curve of your normal normals world. However, to your point about normal, in the land of the Lilliputians, you would be like me. An anomaly."

"Point taken."

"Our fans don't see us as people. We are *things*. He could be collecting stamps. Instead, he collects ephemera about us."

"The price of fame," I said, trying to lighten the conversation up.

"And isn't that fucking great?" Zena flipped me the finger again.

Maybe I was beginning to get on her good side.

CHAPTER 13

DIVERSION

Wednesday morning came but not soon enough for Brinks. Another day taking a fine-toothed comb to his bookkeeping shell game. Around noon, he took his eyes off his computer screen. Rubbing them, he got up from his chair, needing a break. He would get a sandwich from the studio's commissary.

"I'm going to lunch," he said to Brandy.

A few minutes later, he walked into the executive commissary. That's when he spotted Wolfe's hottie wife. Wolfe, he noticed, was not with her. Most times his boss was busy when she showed up and she'd pout all the way down here. Brinks assumed this was another cancelled lunch date by his boss.

Brinks ordered a turkey club and Caesar salad to go. While he waited, he noticed that Morgan wasn't eating. Her eyes darted around the room like a nervous squirrel. She was obviously looking for someone. Her cell phone chimed, and her expression brightened and she hurried off to an exit. Brinks wondered if Wolfe had come down to join her and take her to the Pampas Grill, the Brazilian place close by.

On a hunch, Brinks trailed behind her at a safe distance and saw her step quickly across the parking lot. To his surprise, he saw her head to a car, and it wasn't Wolfe's. It belonged to an actor he had seen before, a good-looking guy that had been cast in a movie called *Roach Man* which Brinks remembered as a box office flop. He witnessed a quick smooch, and the couple ducked safely inside the car.

Brinks watched as they drove off and smiled all the way back to his office. The idea that was just a whisper of a plan yesterday started to take shape. He knew exactly what his next steps would be.

"Freddy, it's me," Brinks said, back in his office with his door closed.

"Marv, what the haps?"

"We need to talk."

Freddy was a man he had met a few years back who dealt in questionably obtained artworks that he fenced. On a tight budget before he had more disposable cash courtesy of Glowball, Brinks bought affordable pieces from this guy, mostly signed prints or pilfered antiquities that would be hard to track down.

After work, he met Freddy at a west LA bar in a neighborhood that did not attract tourists on the prowl for stars.

"What's up?" Freddy asked as he sat down at a booth.

"I need someone who can follow a woman, take some compromising photos."

"Sounds juicy."

Brinks hunched over the table toward Freddy and, in a whispered voice, said, "My boss's wife. She's playing rubba-dub-dub with one of Glowball's actors."

"Really juicy." Freddy's lips curled into a leering smile. He was shaved bald as a cue ball, his body angular, with shuttered eyelids that hid his pupils. He liked to wear light silk sports jackets, pressed jeans with loose white shirts that were never tucked in. As always, Freddy sported the obligatory diamond stud in his right ear, the middle-aged man's attempt at having people think he was still real cool. He also adorned his upper lip with a pencil moustache à la David Niven.

"So how about it?" Brinks asked.

"You doing it for him? Nail the cheating wife to get a divorce?"

"Nah. It's for me?"

"Now that's interesting."

Brinks didn't answer.

"I gotta guy. You want him to rough the actor up? He'd do it for free. He likes that stuff. A real nose buster."

"Just need the pix," Brinks said shortly. He wanted to keep the actor intact so that Wolfe could recognize the guy in the flesh on the lot. Brinks gave Freddy an 8 × 10 head shot of the actor he'd downloaded from Glowball's casting book.

"Leon does good work," Freddy said.

"Leon?"

"Yeah. Leon Schitke."

"*Schitke*. You're kidding me."

"Spelled with an 'e' at the end."

"Still."

"Yeah, I know. Has ideas about becoming an actor."

"He'd better change his name." Brinks pushed another photo to Freddy. This one showed Morgan and Wolfe as the happy couple at a fundraiser. "That's his wife."

"Consider it done," Freddy said. He got up and took the photographs. "Cost ya five Franklins for Leon and two for me for the introduction." He looked down at Brinks and gave him a radiant smile. "This is what I love about this town. When the sun goes down, that's when bad girls and boys have their nasty fun."

"Hornywood," Brinks agreed. If he needed Wolfe to be distracted, then what could be better than a cheating wife caught *in flagrante* on video? Shock and awe.

CHAPTER 14

WITH FANS LIKE THESE

The food arrived. As we started eating, I felt a presence standing next to us. I looked up to see the young couple from the bar.

"You were right," the young woman said, giving Zena a cheerful smile. "You said I should do the test, and the strip came out blue. I'm so thrilled!"

Zena looked at the woman's stony companion.

"I wasn't thrilled, in case you wanna know," the man added.

"Now, Wally, it ain't so bad. You'll see."

"Your fortune cookie crap is giving her some wrong-headed ideas about me wanting to be a daddy," Wally said, spittle framing his words. A blood vessel on his neck pounded, the pulsating jugular vein making his death skull tattoo throb as if it were alive.

He pointed an accusing finger at Zena and continued his rant. "She thinks havin' a kid is gonna make us a fucking family now. You put those ideas in her head, you midget bitch."

Holey John started to get up, but Zena patted his arm. She stared deeply into the angry man's eyes.

"What are you looking at?" he said, practically yelling.

"You name is Walter, right?" Zena started.

"So?" he said annoyed.

"But everyone calls you Wally. Not Walt, which sounds better. More manly. You hated the nickname. Wall-eee. Sounds like a wimpy cartoon character from a kid's show."

Wally suddenly looked confused. I could see his expression say, *What the hell is she doing?*

Zena continued, "You are short, not like me of course. You think of yourself as a pit bull and never shy away from a scrap. You even look for them. A few beers and anyone giving you the hairy eyeball would regret it."

He stared at Zena, his beady eyes like peppercorns drilling holes into her head as she unveiled him in public.

"You doin' some circus I see-through-you crap on me? Just cause my girlfriend paid you, you little cunt, and you gave her your *looking into the future* bullshit that's ruining my fucking life doesn't mean you're gonna do your mind-bender shit on me."

Zena stayed calm and kept her eyes on him.

"Some people can see this as a good thing, Walt," Zena said agreeably.

"Yeah, happy as stepping in dog shit without shoes."

Wally took a threatening step toward Zena with his index finger thrust at her like a bayonet. "You're nothing but a scamming carnival midget!" Wally raised his right hand and balled it into a threatening fist.

I got up to block Wally's hand, but Holey John jumped to his feet and quickly grabbed the guy by his shirt and lifted him up, his feet dangling a few inches off the floor. "You better apologize... friend. She doesn't like being called...a midget."

Wally spit into Holey John's face, and with his right arm, he reached into his boot and pulled out a switchblade. He pressed a button and the blade flicked out. Wally took a swipe at Holey John's face, leaving a thin cut that began to bleed.

Holey John grabbed Wally's wrist that held the knife. He squeezed it, and a cracking sound could be heard. The guy turned white and yelled in pain, dropping the knife, his left arm waving around weakly like a wounded bird.

He dropped Wally to the ground while most of the restaurant watched this incident unfold.

"Apologize...now."

"Screw you, freak. I'm gonna fuck you up real bad."

Wally picked up his knife and quick-stepped away holding his wrist.

"Let him leave, Holey John. Too many idiots out there to worry about shit like this."

Holey John watched Wally scramble to the door. He turned to Holey John. "You better watch your back, fuck wad."

Wally left, but his girlfriend stayed a moment. "Sorry about him."

Zena squeezed the girl's hand. "He may come around."

"I hope so," she said and made her way to the door.

The waitress came over, having seen the drama unfold at our table. "You guys okay? You want us to call the police?"

"We're good," Zena assured.

"You want another round?" the waitress asked. "On the house."

"I'll have another Genny," Zena said.

"Nothing for me," Holey John said dismissively.

"Ginger ale," I said. The waitress smiled and walked away. "I guess the fortune-teller biz has its risks."

Zena shrugged.

"Your fan base is unpredictable."

"Like life."

"How did you do that?" I asked. "All that stuff about Wally."

"It's just observation. Looking at a person's physicality and having studied a lot of people. He comes over and I see he's pissed. I see a short guy rough around the edges and assume he hates being short. So he has to project himself as the tough guy. Walking over to our table, he glared at the bikers at the bar. I considered his body language and created a little story around him."

"Psychic radar?" I put out.

"My gift. I pick up on people's energy. Sounds a bit woo-woo, I know, but I have this knack. I would say I nailed it pretty close."

"Too close," I admitted. "I guess not all fortunes have happy endings."

"Just like life," she said again as if these three words explained all you needed to know about life's roulette wheel.

I decided to change the subject. "You know something? You remind me of my mother."

"She's a little person?" Zena asked with an ironic smile.

I chuckled. "No. A psychologist. No bullshit, just unfiltered straight talk. Tough love and all that. That's what you seem to do aside from whatever special ability you claim to have. You're a midway therapist for the rubes."

"There you go again. They are not rubes. And like *midget*, the term is offensive. Most of these folks are just plain old working folks looking for a little hope."

I regretted my comment and saw that hanging out with Zena would be a life lesson on how not to judge people and filter my already runaway mouth.

"What's your angle?" Zena asked. She said this in a pointed way, her dark eyes challenging me. "This nice lunch at this swell place a bribe? To make us like you?"

"Probably," I answered honestly. I knew better than to try to pull the wool over Zena's eyes by now.

"Good answer," she said.

"I'm not the enemy. I could be a friend at some point."

"We are not at the friend's level by any means," Zena said straightforwardly and paused. "And what's up with your name? Fenn?"

"My full name is Fennimore Cooper, like the writer."

"*The Last of the Mohicans*. Liked the movie, not the book so much."

My petite companion was a reader as she had said before. I gave her a score on my just-created Zena Fuck-It List. Like Lilly's but Zena's first entry was an A-plus.

I continued with some personal history. "My father's family came over from Naples. They were Cupertino. On Ellis Island, they became Cooper. Being the literary type, Dad liked Fennimore since it went with our last name."

"Still sounds like…a plant," said Holey John.

I turned to Zena. "Since we are talking about names, *Zena* is what?"

"My name."

She knew what I wanted. Like where did her name come from? Was it made up? I could see she wasn't going to give me the pleasure of knowing that. At least for now.

"What about yours?" I asked Holey John.

He didn't answer as if he were struggling to remember it.

"Here's a piece of reality when it comes to our people and what handles we use." Zena said this in a tone that clearly implied she didn't care to share anything about her family.

I gave her my best "I'm very interested in anything you share with me" look, the look I used to prime the revelatory conversation pump. A journalist technique I'd perfected. It also worked really well on first dates. But maybe not with her, I was feeling.

"Most carnies and roustabouts get hold of fake social security cards and bogus papers to invent a new identity. We are citizens that exist beyond the fringes of society, some of us one step away from living in a refrigerator box under a bridge or a step away from the law."

I said nothing, taking everything in. Fodder for my article.

"It's not hard to figure out that our life here is an alternative for folks who don't fit comfortably into your so-called normal world. Then there are those who are running away from something because standing still is too terrifying and would make them face their demons."

I caught Holey John's body stiffen, hearing Zena's last description. Another mental note.

"The exceptions to this gritty social stratum are the celebrity performers like the acrobats, the horse riders, and the guy who handles the big cats."

"A caste system?" I said.

"Like the fuckin'…Romanians," Holey John explained. "They look down on us."

"I can tell you're going to try to figure out what my name is all about," she said.

"Your name has a bunch of meanings."

"Really." She gave me the withering look of someone who didn't want her life unearthed.

"Zena means stranger in Greek mythology. It can be spelled differently with an X instead of Z. Like that old TV series *Xena: Warrior Princess.*"

"Warrior princess. Friggin' knew...you were," Holey John grinned.

"Then there is xenophobia. It means intense fear or dislike of strangers."

"You got that right. You are a stranger to us. You show up here. You want to pull back the curtains and see the real us. Like in that scene from *The Wizard of Oz.* Just like that." She snapped her fingers. "Like you're entitled to invade our world."

"I'm not invading. I'm here trying to understand your world. That's what a journalist does. You show me what you want. You control the curtain."

Zena eyed me, weighing what I said to her. "I need a bio break. All this truthiness is doing a number on my bladder."

She got down from her chair and headed to the bathroom.

I could see I was off to a bad start.

CHAPTER 15

LIKE CATS IN HEAT

The car Leon had followed pulled into a parking lot. The motel was a low-priced, one story affair. He circled around the motel, seeing that most of the windows in the rooms were dark. He glanced at his passenger seat. The digital camcorder sat there. He checked the battery and turned on the shotgun microphone so he could capture voices if his subjects decided to talk before, during, or after their hookup.

Leon watched as the driver got out of the car and opened the door where the woman sat. A light from the parking lot's lamp post illuminated the car. Her long legs came out first, followed by an ass packed into tight jeans you could hold on to. As she emerged, she shook her long, blond hair as if she had just come out of a shower, throwing her head back. The driver stepped in close to the woman and pulled her to him. She wrapped her hands around his neck, and their mouths locked onto each other like suction cups. The kiss lingered for a while, and then they finally broke for air.

Leon looked at his watch. He guessed it would be no more than five minutes before the lights in one of the rooms came on. This was not the kind of job Leon liked. It paid okay, but as far as the work he did, it was bottom-feeder shit, a *Peeping Tom* job for someone who probably needed to dig up dirt for blackmail.

Freddy had called him for this gig earlier in the day. He had connections to a better breed of Hollywood scum. Leon wondered if he would help him one day make a connection to someone in the movie biz. So he decided he would do this creeper caper, hoping good shit would fall his way. Sometimes he'd play a creepy creeper game for fun. Walk down a crowded street. Pick out someone. Follow them. Stay out of sight the whole time. And then he would see a spot where the person passed by. Secluded. An alley. A doorway. A nearby dumpster. And he thought this was where he could kill them. Knowing that he could kill them if he wanted gave him a rush. He could kill anyone if he chose. That was real power. Not Hollywood BS power.

This was something he'd done before. Taking people out. It had been the real deal. Totally legal and lethal. *Thank you, Uncle Sam.*

As he waited for a room light to come on, he thought about his past, how he wound up working for Uncle Sam.

Leon enlisted when the Boston Municipal Court judge gave him a choice after he assaulted a cop at Fenway. Leon had kicked the shit out of a Yankee fan. When the cop tried to intervene, he broke his nose. This wasn't the first time he had been arrested for assault. He had broken the jaw of a classmate at Exeter Prep who called him a fag because of his peculiar speech flaw. The judge said he had two options. Jail time or army time. He chose the military.

Standard procedure after induction was taking the Armed Services Vocational Aptitude Battery. Leon took a series of tests that identified what his strengths were to determine which army jobs were best suited for him. He took more tests, and they showed he had an innate capacity for killing. To hurt people without remorse.

He had his father to thank for that. Even though his father was highly educated, a history teacher at Exeter Prep where Leon attended based on the fact his father was faculty, the man's wiring had a short circuit problem. Without warning, the man would explode, screaming about how he was a victim, how he deserved to be department chair. His ranting seemed to come out of the blue. He'd say they were out to get him, and when Leon gave him a sideways look not comprehending what made his father so enraged, his father made him the target of his fury and ravings.

When Leon said he was going to be a theater major if he went to college, his father called him a pansy, and the belt came out and he chased him around the house until he caught him. For Leon, getting hit so often made pain and abuse look and feel normal. He would just go to another place inside his head while Pops whipped his ass.

The Army assigned Leon to special group of men much like himself, inured to what they would do; all of them were delegated predator operators. His new posse was virtual drone drivers that swept over targets to gather recon and take out bad guys without seeing their faces as Hellfire missiles vaporized them. It was like sitting around playing video war games. Anonymous X-box killing.

Leon was stationed at Creech Air Force Base outside Las Vegas. This was ground zero for America's drone operations. He spent hours sitting in unlit rooms 7,500 miles from Afghanistan, where he remotely controlled MQ-9 Reapers, his drone of choice. Beside him, Jabo Jabowaski was his sensor operator who controlled TV and infrared spotting cameras.

Leon spent long hours staring at digital displays of video feeds from battle zones. And when he got the command, he squeezed a joystick trigger and a Hellfire missile blew up a single person or maybe a bunch of people half a world away. He could tell what was inside a house when the missile hit. Gray dust for an empty building; assorted colors for a warehouse full of whatever, and gray mixed with pink for a building where people inside were pulverized.

Death from above was his officially sanctioned job he did day after day. Until he sent an unauthorized Hellfire into a house full of noncoms. He did it once just to know he could.

He remembered what Jabo had said: "*What the fuck, dude?*" and that was when he got discharged from the military. An *Other Than Honorable Discharge* was what he received—no charges that would show up as dishonorable since that would be real bad PR for his commanding officer. Just one of those things that happen over there, his senior officer explained. Unfortunate collateral damage. It happens. War is messy. That was the spin.

They sent him to a shrink. The shrink at the VA said he had become desensitized. He lacked empathy. Take these meds. Come to group sessions and talk about it. In his first session, he said that what he did was too anonymous. Not hands-on enough. He really wanted to see the anguish of death up close. The fear in a vic's face. The rapid breath. The pleas. Watch life leave their eyes.

The group went silent, and the shrink shook his head. "You seem to think this fantasy is okay. I'm afraid you might take it somewhere that's not healthy someday." Leon walked out after his first session.

Lights went on in a room. He grabbed his camcorder and mic, got out of the car, and moved toward the first floor window. He saw that the woman had not pulled the curtains completely together, leaving about a three-inch space with a clear view of the bed.

He turned the camera on just as the couple stepped into view. Either they were in a rush or they liked the sex a little bit rough. The man practically tore away the woman's shirt, leaving her standing in a sheer bra. Her jeans came off next, showing her thong panties. She had a killer body, and Leon adjusted the camera to get the full length of her into the frame. She quickly dropped to her knees and unzipped the man's pants, reached in, and put him into her mouth. Leon zoomed in on her skilled pneumatic application of mouth-to-organ thrusting.

The man pulled the blonde's head away, and they moved to the bed. They finished undressing and collapsed onto the bed. The man spread his body over hers. He worked his head down between her thighs, and their stalker moved his camera to catch the expression on the woman's face. It was clear she liked whatever this guy was doing. Sounds came from the room, faint through the window, but the shotgun mic would pick it up nicely. When he came up for air, he drove his penis inside her, lifting her ass up to get a deeper rhythm going. Then he flipped her over, and they were doing it doggy style.

The show went on for close to half an hour. The couple could have been paid porn stars if this was actually being shot for that. They knew all the moves as if they were making an instructional tape for some "joy of sex" video. He could see the sweaty sheen of the sex-capade on their bodies. When Leon thought the man was spent, she moved down between his legs and took him in her mouth, and the show began again. Leon decided one installment was enough.

He shut off his camera. He felt his groin had grown warm, his penis hard after watching the couple. Except for a few encounters with random women he met at bars, he'd never had any sort of extended relationships with women. It was much easier to literally take charge of his sexual urges into his own hands, masturbating to porn or his own fantasies. It was quick and efficient.

Leon quickly stepped back to this car and drove off, stopping a mile away in front of a coffee shop. He got out of the car and went inside. The waitress came over, and he ordered pancakes and coffee. While he waited, he took out his cell phone.

"Academy Award performance. Like stray cats in heat."

"Bring it over," Freddy said. "We can watch it on my wide screen. Beer and popcorn on me."

CHAPTER 16

PAIN HAS ITS USES

We sat there in silence after Zena went off to pee. Silence hung over our table like a stalled cloud on a windless day. I knew zip about Holey John, so I decided to start with a few softball questions.

"You and Zena seem pretty tight," I began.

Holey John didn't look at me, his eyes going somewhere that only he seemed to know. Finally he said, "Yeah, she's good...people."

"So, Holey John, nice play on words," I commended. "Clever."

"That's me...all right. Clever."

My attempt at a compliment went flat. "I guess stage names have to be catchy," I continued, trying to keep the exchange going.

"Catchy," he agreed.

"So what do people call you when you're not doing your midway act?" I asked, being one sneaky bastard of a journalist, trying once more to get his real name.

"Holey John."

"I meant your real name."

"You don't listen too...good," he answered with gravel in his voice.

"Guilty as charged. My persistence is not an admired quality when my write-a-great-story meter is running."

"Meter huh? You a...taxi driver?"

I gave him a wide smile.

My chat with Holey John was not going swimmingly. "So how about this question? An easy one."

He shrugged.

"How long have you been with the Giambolvo Brothers?" I figured this one wouldn't wind him up. But he closed his eyes as if the question was buried deep and he had to work hard to dig it up.

"A while," was all he said.

He looked directly into my face, daring me to figure him out.

"Your act or whatever you call it. Does it hurt when they pierce you?"

"I deal with it."

"How?"

"Mind over fucking…matter."

I wanted to hold back my next question, but I couldn't. "Do you enjoy the pain?"

I got another hard stare from Holey John, and I was suddenly afraid that my question hit too close to the bone.

"It has its uses," he said impatiently.

"As in pain as a prop?" I suggested.

He rubbed the side of his head, where a vein stood out like a line on a map. "It has its uses," he repeated, unwilling to reveal more details. "Brings the crowds…in. Like people who watch…cage fighting. They wanna see…blood. Not their own. And they think I'm the…weird one."

"So you're okay with what you do?" I asked for confirmation.

He shrugged.

"You know there's a term for people who like to inflict pain on themselves?"

"Yeah and go fuck yourself…Dr. Phil," he spat out. "You don't know shit…about shit, trying to…figure me out?"

"Just trying to write a story."

"I don't even want *me*…to figure *me*…out."

That reply threw me off. What did he *not* want to figure out?

"Just trying to write a story," I said directly.

"Yeah, well, this thing you want to write…about Zena…and me. Forget about the part about…me. I don't like your…questions or you."

It didn't take a genius to see that Holey John had a Pandora's Box that was best not opened. Unfortunately, I had and now paid the consequences.

Zena came back to the table and saw that the atmosphere had changed like a bad smell coming from a manhole cover.

"You okay, honey?" she asked Holey John, seeing he was troubled.

"Just fine."

He got up from the table. "I need to take a…walk."

"Good idea," Zena said while giving me the death stare.

Holey John pushed the chair away from our table and walked out of the restaurant. I watched him as he left. Through the large plate glass window, I saw him turn his head one way then another as if he was trying to make up his mind as to which way to go.

"What the hell happened? I take a pee and you send my friend into a bad funk."

"Just asked him questions," I defended.

"Like what?"

"Why he does the piercing stuff."

"He answer you?"

"Cryptically. He said that pain has its uses."

Zena looked sad, her eyes cast down, looking at her hands.

"He ever tell you about his life?" I asked, hoping to have more insight into the man who had blown me off.

"No."

"You ever ask him?"

"I don't probe. You, however, do that for a living. I, on the other hand, let people tell me what they want, when they want."

"I was just doing what I do," I said plainly.

"And you crossed the line. *His* line," she insisted.

"Yup. Told me basically to fuck off," I replied, disappointed.

"Find another colorful character, Fenn. He clearly doesn't want to tell you whatever it is you want to know."

Losing him was like losing my left nut. My story would have no balls. *Goodbye, paycheck.*

I waited a beat then asked, "Just for curiosity's sake, where did he go? He seemed determined."

"Walking calms him down," Zena explained.

"As in walk it off?"

She nodded. "When there's a break at the midway, he likes to roam the streets." She thought for a moment. "But it's different here."

"How?"

"I asked him once where he goes here. 'A special place' was all he said."

"Special, huh?"

She looked at me, her face softening a bit, getting over being mad at me for pissing her friend off. "You have a special place?"

"Katz's deli on Houston Street. Best pastrami sandwich in the world."

"You are some kind of weird."

"I hear that a lot."

"Isn't that where Sally faked her orgasm with Billy Crystal?"

"Yup. They have a sign hanging over the table where that scene was shot."

"Take me there one day, and I'll give you my rendition," she said with an impish glint in her eyes.

That look was new.

"If my publisher likes my story, I'll treat you."

"Assuming you write the story now that Holey John is off the menu."

"Point taken."

"Point given."

"You better find another subject."

"You already said that."

"Just making sure you heard."

"If your friend isn't an option, maybe you could point me to other people."

"As interesting as us?" she said with a smirk.

I nodded.

"Now that would be a challenge, wouldn't it?" Her smirk morphed into a smile.

"Any help would be appreciated," I said, looking at my former prickly subject's empty chair.

"And so he asks for a little help from a little person. Gee, my own charity case."

CHAPTER 17

A MAN OF FEW MEMORIES

It was all bullshit. People were bullshit. The people looking for auto-graphs. The punk who badmouthed Zena. And now this writer ass-hole. He pushed the door to the café open and was hit by the summer heat and the bright light of the afternoon. He felt the sun warm him, hitting the silver and gold body jewelry covering his face and fore-arms. He exhaled a sigh of relief getting away from that writer creep.

Holey John turned right on Cayuga and walked with a deter-mined spring in his step, shifting his knapsack to his left shoulder. Whenever he landed in Ithaca, it was as if a map appeared inside his head, and like a car on automatic pilot, he knew exactly where he was going but didn't know why.

A few people shot glances at him like every other town he wan-dered through. Some folks smiled and nodded. Others turned away guiltily as if they were intruding by staring at a man unlike any other they had seen. The younger people weren't shy and openly gawked, usually giving him a fist bump and a "Hey, dude" acknowledgment.

He turned on Green Street and passed a few landmarks that were familiar. He slowed his pace and stopped in front of a statue of a Union soldier mounted high on a granite plinth. The man's face was young but expressionless. He showed no fear or excitement or the intensity of a man charging into battle not knowing what the next moment would bring. The statue was created as the perfection of the resolute warrior. But Holey John knew a face of fear would be more realistic.

The glory of war was never glorious. He knew that from experience. He had been over there; witnessed battles won and lost. But a nagging feeling followed him for decades—that he had been part of something horrific he must've done. It had to be since he had buried it so deep that even he could not unearth it. Perhaps it was the only way he could live with himself. Keep the memory buried never to be dug up. Stumbling through life where one day flowed into another so that years had no meaning.

He backed away from the Civil War monument and continued walking. There was something else, which he couldn't explain. He had an old photograph of a woman and a kid but didn't know who they were and why he kept it. Soulful eyes peered out of the photo as if directly looking into his soul. He wondered who she and the child were and if there was a reason why he could not remember them.

He worked his way to State Street, made a left onto Mitchell, and then made another left onto College Avenue. Holey John noticed trash cans as he walked toward the place he was always drawn to. Next to the cans was recycling, bundles of newspapers and magazines. He started to examine them as he was in need of a fresh supply, and this seemed like a gift. There were few gifts in his life. The only good one was Zena. He knew he'd be lost without her.

It was the magazines that he liked best. Holey John bent down and picked up a stack. He sorted through them. These were good ones. Flipping through the pages, he saw what he needed. Full page photographs with faces that filled them. And there were plenty of eyes staring out from the pages. Eyes. He always needed more eyes. Taking his knapsack off, he put the magazines inside it.

He lifted the knapsack and flung it over his shoulder. A few minutes later, he stopped. He inhaled a deep breath, and felt an odd emotion move through him. It was across the street, right in front of him now. The house. The one on College Avenue. It was like a magnet, drawing him here again. There was a familiar feeling about it. As Holey John studied the house some more, he noticed a sign. It was hanging from wooden stake planted in the small patch of lawn that fronted the house. He squinted but couldn't make it out.

He looked both ways, saw that no cars were coming and crossed the street. He stepped up to the sign. His forehead creased into hard lines as he read the words on the sign: *For Sale*. He read the sign a second time, and a swirl of feelings suddenly spun inside him. The muscles that ran down his neck and shoulders bound up like a sailor's knot, making him feel dizzy. He took a deep breath to steady himself, not understanding why this was happening to him.

An old man stood on the porch of the house and studied Holey John.

"You lost, fella?"

He shook his head.

"Inspecting my house, then? It's on the market."

"Just looking…at it."

"I know you?" the old man asked.

"From the…midway…maybe. The circus that's in town."

The old man shook his head. "I haven't been to a circus in a while."

Holey John lifted his shoulders and then let them drop. "I walk around…your town a lot. Maybe you saw me…pass by your place."

"Maybe so."

A shadow passed next to Holey John, and he looked around. It was Wally driving by in a shit box truck.

"Hey pin head," he shouted from the rolled-down passenger window and then made a gesture with his index finger slashing across his throat before motoring on.

"You know that guy?" the old guy asked.

"A jerk is…all."

"He must have a hair across his ass about you."

Holey John grunted.

The old man started toward the front door. "Need my cat nap. I can show you the house if you're interested. Get one of them flyers hanging on the For Sale sign and call the real estate lady. She'll set up a time."

Holey John's eyebrow arched, a bit stunned by the offer.

"Okay," he said, and as he said, that he felt like a long journey was about to end and a new one to start.

CHAPTER 18

A MUNCHKIN WITH BRAINS

"You worry about him?" I asked after Holey John left Maxie's.

"He'll be all right," Zena said. "He's suffered fools worse than you."

"You flatter me." I decided to continue my Q and A crap shoot with her. "So what's the deal with you two?"

I could see she was struggling with how much she wanted to say to me. She swallowed some beer and then took a deep breath, coming to a decision.

"He's like a big brother to me. My protector. If some yahoo at the midway gives me trouble, Holey John seems to appear out of nowhere. And I try to be the big sister when he drifts off into the dark places he tends to go."

"He looks as if he's led a tough life," I said.

"You can say the same thing about most of the people that wind up here."

"What about family? Does he have any?"

Zena shrugged. "No clue. What about you?" She turned the interview table on me, and I went along.

"I told you about Selma, the interminable psychologist, when it comes to me. And Dad is a retired cop. No sibs."

"Ah, a spoiled only lonely child."

"That would be me."

"Girlfriend?"

I hesitated for a moment. "Yup."

Zena sensed the hesitation. "A rough patch with her?"

"Relationships have their ups and downs," I said, trying to avoid any particulars.

"Like a pogo stick in a mine field," she said wryly.

I assumed she was making a comment about relationships in general, although I wondered what ones she might have had.

The server came over and cleared our plates. "You want another Genny?" she asked Zena.

"Sure."

"I'm still good," I said, covering my half-full glass of ginger ale with my hand. "So how many months are you on the road?"

The waitress went off, and Zena looked at me. "You've started."

"What?"

"You're starting the thing you do. Asking me softball questions before you throw the hard ones."

Man, was she sharp.

"Your assignment feels like you using us so you can pay your bills."

I looked straight at her. "You're right and you're wrong about what I'm doing."

"What about that vibe of desperation I get?"

Another unexpected insight—that was creepy.

"It's true that I need to write this story. But I am drawn to you because you are—"

"Interesting. Tony gave us up as subject matter."

"There's that."

"Fenn, the practiced smooth talker."

I ignored her insult.

"Since Holey John ghosted me, I'll try to find other people on the midway who seem interesting. Our readers like to read about things that are different from their normal, predictable lives."

She turned her head up at me and glared. "*Things?*"

"Jesus, you know what I mean."

"I know exactly what you mean and what most of the world means. They look at Holey John and me and they don't see people— they see *things!*"

The anger was back. Every word I spoke was an opportunity for her to be offended.

I tried once more. "Look. We are all different. Even what you call normal people feel that they're different; that they don't fit in. Be black in a white world. Poor in a rich world. Unattractive in a beautiful people, TV commercials world."

She shook her head. "Here's what you don't get. No one looks sideways if you are black, rich, or homely like they look at me."

I was about to point out that black, poor, and the homely do get looks, but she was on a roll that could inform me of what she had gone through as a little person, so I didn't argue.

She went on. "But you so-called normal people still look at me and think I look wrong. It wasn't that long ago that *defectives* were sterilized. Just over twenty years ago, most states in the good old US of A forbid mentally challenged couples from getting married. The Nazis threw people like me into the camps along with the Jews and Gypsies." She took a deep breath. "You see a little people product line coming out from Barbie land? Mattel high-five themselves cause they covered all the races. Now they got the plus-size, big-ass girl. Got the tall girlie and petite chick but not the really petite like me."

"I never said you were defective or wrong," I said, in an attempt to calm her down.

"But I bet you think that way." She threw a look at me and fired a question that pulled my head back. "Have you thought of having sex with me?"

My silence was my answer.

"But if I looked like a hottie babe out of the SI swimsuit issue, you would have thought about fucking me more than once since we met. The way that you normals deal with people like me is to make you feel better about yourself. You pity us with 'Oh, you dear things' or 'How brave you must be to live as you do.' Pity removes you from having a real relationship with us."

I took this all in and realized Zena was probably right. Whenever I saw someone who looked mentally challenged or severely handicapped, I thought of them differently. I wasn't repulsed, but I didn't go out of my way to engage them. Zena was certainly not mentally challenged. Nor was she physically handicapped, but maybe, unconsciously, I placed her in the *not normal* category.

She finished her third beer and called the server over, ordering another one. She then got up and said, "Don't worry. I have to pee again and wouldn't want to miss what you are going to say to me when I get back."

When she walked off, I thought about what she was about to do. The peeing part. Most public restroom toilets, sinks, and paper towel dispensers were not designed for people of Zena's stature.

She came back five minutes later. "So any revelations? We can come back to the sex stuff later."

I looked at her straight on. "You're right about everything you've said. I do put you in a different category. Holey John may look more like what you call a normal, but clearly he isn't. So I put him into a category too."

"The veil is lifting from your eyes."

"See, that's what I'm getting at. I want to write about you and your friend but from your point of view. Not mine. Not Fenn as the reporter. Give me your view of the world. Like everything you just said. How you see it and how you think it sees you. If I am ignorant, then you can educate me. Educate my readers."

"I am not sure I want to be the one to raise your consciousness. Or your readers'. Maybe you should find someone else."

My gut tightened, thinking that she too might abandon my storyland ship.

"I could try and do that," I said, trying to hide any tint of panic. "Find other people. But what's cool about you is that you are really articulate and don't bullshit."

"Oh, how he doth flatter," she said, shaking her head.

I went on. "You tell me what you think without candy-coating it. I want to make other people understand what you are all about and how they—we, me—pigeonhole other people."

"Give her a few beers and she talks real swell. You found a Munchkin with brains."

I smiled. "Can I use that in my piece? A Munchkin with brains."

Zena balled up a paper napkin and threw it at me.

"You're smart. This can be a story that goes beyond the people I usually write about. It can challenge their belief systems."

"Wow. Belief systems. You trying to be the Martin Luther of journalism?"

"I have one last appeal."

"Give it your best shot, honey."

"When I do write about people, I use their words and try not to misrepresent their views. My subject matter may be provocative, but I am not. I'm straightforward about whom and what I write about."

She closed her eyes for a moment. When she opened them, she said, "I know that."

"You do?" I said, wondering what she meant.

"I read that article you wrote a while back. The one about baby dumping."

"You read that? My *New Yorker* piece?" It was a piece about parents abandoning their children in a public or private place with the purpose of disposing them without ever wanting them back.

"You sound astonished. Yeah. The Munchkin with brains actually reads the *New Yorker*…and not just for their way-too-clever cartoons."

I continued to feel like an idiot, wondering how many feet I could put into my mouth during a simple lunch.

"I could relate to it," Zena almost whispered. Her eyes grew moist, but she quickly blinked away her tears.

"Really?" I asked, having no idea what she meant.

"Yeah." She went silent and stared past me, not focusing on anything or anyone in the restaurant. A few moments later, her eyes returned and met mine. "I was baby-dumped."

CHAPTER 19

DEVIL FALLS

Holey John watched as the old man went inside. When he heard the door close, he walked to the sign post. He glanced around. Wally was no longer circling the block.

The *For Sale* sign for the house on College Avenue stirred something inside him, but he couldn't put his finger on what it was. There was a rack attached to the signpost with flyers inside. He took one and read the sheet. It described the house, the number of rooms, square footage, and asking price along with the realty company and an agent's name. Holey John slipped it into his backpack.

He rubbed the side of his skull as he walked down the block, feeling the ridge of where the surgeons had opened up his head to remove the shattered metal shrapnel from his helmet that a bullet had caused. It was a miracle that it didn't kill him. The two things he vaguely remembered were being airlifted to a medevac and the captain from his company saying he was a hero. What he said after that was something he couldn't recall. He was told that his platoon had stumbled into a village full of NVA regulars and that he laid down covering fire for his men to retreat taking a bullet himself. His corporal recalled what had happened to the captain when they arrived at the Mobile Army Surgical Hospital where the MASH surgeons were able to save him.

The docs removed more than just a few pieces of metal. They had removed his memories. Too many of them. What was left came and went like uninvited guests with bad manners, arriving without notice and then disappearing just as quickly as they came.

He saw it was well after noon. He was MIA from the Giambolvo Brothers, and they would give him shit for that. There was lots of daylight left, and he started walking again, retracing his steps back to the restaurant. Maybe Zena and that shit bag writer guy would still be there. He would go back with her to the midway and resume his act, shutting himself off to the flesh-piercing pain. If this was atonement, he had no idea for what.

Holey John passed a sign on East Street and stopped, walking back to read it. *Taughannock State Park*. The name was familiar. Taughannock. That name nipped some brain cells loose. It sounded like an Indian name. Could be that, but then he heard a distant whisper in his head telling him something else. He had a similar feeling like he'd had at the old man's house.

He saw where the sign was pointing and decided to head in that direction. Fuck the Giambolvos. He was already in deep shit today.

More signs pointed the way as he trekked on. Two miles later, he was on Danby Road then on Prospect. The sun was beating down on him, and cars honked as they passed him. Windows went down and a flurry of words came at him, mostly in the *way cool* category.

He reached Route 89 north of Ithaca and walked for a long time, following the road along the western bank of Cayuga Lake. He smelled the air coming off the lake and breezes blowing gently through the trees.

One vehicle seemed to slow in the distance. As it got closer, Holey John saw that it was a pickup truck. He kept his eye on it, an old blue Ford F150, which sped up when it was about fifty yards away from him. He expected the usual shouts regarding his looks. Instead, the truck swerved, the tires coming off the asphalt road hitting the gravel on the shoulder of the road, spitting up rocks and dirt. He froze as the truck aimed its front end at him. He dived into the bushes off to the side of the road just in time to see the raging face of Wally shouting obscenities at him.

He lay on his back, a few cuts on his elbows and road dirt smearing his clothes. His head ached where the part of his skull with the scar hit a rock. When he felt his head, he saw a smudge of blood on his fingers. He lifted his head as Wally floored the Ford away.

Holey John got up and brushed himself off. He watched Wally's truck disappear over the rise on the road before he started to walk again.

A car slowed and came to a stop. The window came down, and one of the girls he had passed earlier on his way to eat, the one with the barbed-wire tattoo around her neck, gave him a big wave.

"Dude!" she yelled. "You all right?"

He nodded.

"Where you goin'?"

He pointed down the highway. "State park."

"Commune with nature, huh?"

"Try to."

"I saw that pickup. Tried to run you over. Not cool, man. I got his license plate. You wanna call the cops?"

Holey John shook his head.

"You know him?" the girl asked.

"Some jerk-off I pissed…off."

"World is full of jerk-offs, right?"

"Amen to…that."

"Wanna a lift?"

"Nah. I'm…good."

"Cool," she said. "See ya around, right?"

He gave her a thumbs-up, and the car started off.

Soon, he saw signs to the state park. More cars zoomed past him, more horns beeping at him, more shouts as passengers saw the glint shimmering off the dazzling walking man.

He reached the entrance to the park and headed in. The air was cool and fresh, a scent of pine filling the air. He went past a parking area with several cars in it. Holey John had the same feeling he'd experienced when he left Zena after his meal and walked to the house on College Avenue. He was on automatic pilot again, crossing a wooden bridge and finding a certain trail that snaked upwards through the woods. He followed the path that was marked Rim Trail. It took him to the edge of Taughannock Falls, set in the back of a wide canyon before abruptly ending. He stepped cautiously to a rocky edge and looked down at the plunging walls of the waterfall, the jutting rocks shiny with the spray of tumbling water.

Holey John backed away and looked at the surrounding area. The sun was getting lower in the sky, and the air became cooler. He walked slowly along the rim, sticking to the beaten paths that hikers had made. He stopped by a stand of trees. Another familiar feeling. He turned toward the other side of the falls. One rock jutted out from the sheer wall that formed the boundaries of the falls. The rock had a face. A prominent chin and hooked nose stuck out. Two outcrops seemed to protrude from what could be seen as the face's forehead. Horns? A devil?

Holey John stared at the face. An eerie feeling crawled through him, making him believe he had stood there before in exactly the same spot. He was with a man, an older man with kind eyes who held his hand and pointed to the face and told him how you could stare at rocks and clouds and imagine all kinds of forms, like animals and faces. "Devil Falls," he muttered, the name floating belly up from somewhere in his head.

"Crazy shit," he said, quietly dismissing the thought and the image of the old man disappeared. There were trees to his left and right and several behind him. He lay on the ground, and watched a few clouds drift by through pine boughs that undulated as puffs of breezes touched the treetops.

He knew Zena would worry, and he sat up and took one last look at the falls and the head of Lucifer embedded in the rock. When he stood, he turned to find the path he had taken there when a singular tree caught his eye. It was an old oak tree with burls protruding from its trunk. There was a hollow about four feet up the tree. Like a magnet pulling at a piece of metal, Holey John stepped toward the dark cavity. Some gut feeling drew him to inspect the tree hollow, and he cautiously stuck his hand inside the opening moving his fingers around like a blind man feeling his way in the dark. He touched something and pulled it out. It was an acorn hidden away by squirrels.

He stuck his hand deeper inside and probed again, and this time, his fingers found something round and cool. He gripped it and pulled it out. It was a smooth, round stone the size of a golf ball. He probed again and lifted half a dozen of the same type of small rounded rocks, which he laid out on the ground. The last rock had something crusty stuck to it. It was thin and fell off to his touch.

A long-forgotten detail popped into his head. He studied the flaking material that had been wrapped around one of the rocks. It had faded stains weathered by time and moisture. He thought for a few minutes. This was not part of the rock; it was paper that had been wrapped around the rock.

He closed his eyes, forcing himself to think. The old man appeared again, the man holding his hand. The hollow in the tree. A boy holding a pencil and writing on a piece of paper. A rock with the paper wrapped around it. A boy dropping the rock with his wish written on the paper into the magic mailbox inside the tree.

He went back to the hollow one last time, probing again. Maybe there would be more rocks with paper wishes—wishes that had not deteriorated in the decades that they had been sheltered inside the oaken mailbox. He wondered what the wishes may have contained.

There were no more rocks. He picked one up, putting the one that once was wrapped with a piece of paper in his knapsack.

He thought about starting back, retracing his trek through the woods. It would be a long walk back to the midway. He would miss his time on stage, and he knew he would pay dearly later. They were sure to give him hell, maybe even rough him up. But it was worth it. This had been a day where several pieces of his broken memories seemed to fit together, although how well he didn't know.

He found a spot where a layer of pine needles had fallen. He pushed them together with his foot and lay down. He thought about his day. So much had happened. The punk who tried to run him over. The house and the old man. And now the waterfalls, the devil's face, and this tree.

He felt tired. Darkness began to set in over the park, and the sky was turning inky black, speckled stars poking through that shimmered like luminescent fireflies. He stared straight up at the sky, waiting for sleep to come to him. It was always an uneasy sleep where reoccurring nightmares intruded like ghost walkers. Always the same nightmares. They came at night and briefly lingered in the morning just as he awoke and then vanished as if an ill wind whisked them away.

CHAPTER 20

IT'S ABOUT TRUST

"You were dumped," I said as if I didn't hear her correctly. I was shocked into silence for a moment and gave Zena an uncomprehending look.

"The man of many words has nothing to say," she teased.

"You screwing with me, right?"

"You think I'd be making this shit up?" she shot back.

"You just took me by surprise." I gathered my thoughts. "How old were you?"

"An infant."

I watched her closely, trying to see if this was another attempt to play me. Her face remained serious, and I saw she wasn't fucking with me.

"Okay, so you're not trying to screw with my head?"

"I have much better ways to screw you." She waited a minute then gave me a devilish smile.

This took me by surprise as well. I crossed my arms and leaned back against my chair, waiting for her to tell me more.

"I have to assume my parents didn't want me," Zena said without any emotion. "Saw I was not going to be a typical, full-sized child. They could have left me anywhere, like in a shopping cart at Walmart."

"Did they?"

"Nope. Left me on the steps of a church. What a cliché."

"How did you feel?"

She gave me a withering look. "That's a stupid question. I was maybe a year old. I have feelings now, like what the fuck was up with them?"

I saw that Zena's life on the midway would be interesting enough to write about, but being abandoned to boot made her story even more compelling. I wondered how she navigated the white water challenges of her life with this added trauma, what the emotional and psychological damage of being dumped coupled with being a dwarf in a world of tall people did to her. She was a survivor. I could see that. I also couldn't help think that that story could be beyond amazing if I could get Zena to open up her proverbial kimono even more. I felt uneasy, wondering if I was writing a human interest story or just a story to keep my job.

I really didn't know what to say next as Zena downed the last of her beer. She seemed to be thinking seriously about something as she stared intently at me, the smile now gone.

"Give me your hands," she ordered. "Put them into mine."

I leaned forward and placed my hands palm down into hers. I felt an unusual warmth flowing into mine. She tightened her fingers around my hands and closed her eyes. I watched her face. Her eyes fluttered behind her eyelids.

"Okay," she finally said and opened her eyes. She kept my hands in hers.

"Okay, what?"

"I'll talk to you about what happened," she said.

"What changed?"

"I got a vibe."

This was entering woo-woo land, but I just accepted what she said.

"I'll talk to you about my life because despite you being a jerk, you also have a perceptive side that shows compassion. I sensed that in that story you wrote. It wasn't tabloid shit, which it could easily have been."

I was taken aback by what seemed a sudden change of heart.

"Besides, I'm feeling desperation. That you need to write something or else—whatever the *or else* is I don't know."

My eyes widened. Her sixth sense again about my Stan situation bordered on spooky.

"I'll decide how much I'll reveal. Maybe as you argued that educating you will educate others, but I won't hold my breath."

"Okay."

"It's about trust. Me trusting you."

"I still have a question about why you are helping me now."

She thought for a while. "Maybe this story can help me put into words what I've experienced mostly in my head. If so, I want people to know me the way I know me." Another pause. "I don't want to disappear."

Her last reason shook me. Did she feel her diminutive stature made her seem invisible to the world?

"One thing. My terms," she said quite firmly. "I get to read what you write before I say you can print it."

I stiffened at first with this condition, then I knew I'd write honestly without sensational tabloid spew, so I relaxed and nodded.

"When can we start?" I asked.

"Tonight, after we close down," she replied. "No ginger ale in my trailer, but I've got a good bottle of single-malt Scotch. Let's continue what I assume will be your very penetrating questions there. I like penetration."

I smiled at her knack for the double entendre, but it made me wonder about her last remark. There was the sexual insinuation popping up again.

"Come to my trailer around eleven, and I'll give you all the gory details. Drinks and appetizers included. My trailer is the one with pink flamingos around the front. They will be lit up. A guiding beacon to my humble abode. Let's see if we can have a Kumbaya moment."

"Flamingoes, drinks, appetizers, and a gory story. How can a man like me refuse?"

"You can't."

CHAPTER 21

HAUNTED

The dream that always came arrived. It started with the faces of children, mothers, and old men looking into his face. Confused and terrified eyes. His nightmares always played the same movie. He wasn't watching it like someone in the audience; he was in the movie, one of the actors, and it always started the same way.

He was with other men on patrol with his platoon. He always was on point heading his men through the jungle. He didn't trust anyone else to do this. Even though he was alert as a prowling cat, fear gripped him whenever he went out. He felt trapped on the trails like being on a road with no off ramp. He told his men not to talk—no smoking, nothing that would drift through the jungle to give them away.

They had cut through a bamboo forest and stumbled upon a small village called Hoang Lien. The people were cooking on open pit fires, washing clothes, tending pigs and chickens. When the men entered, the villagers froze seeing soldiers. His men stood nervously and spread out. A villager came out of a hut and startled the soldiers. The man held something—a rake maybe. Someone from the platoon shot the villager, the man hurled backward, the rake falling to the ground.

Holey John shouted to the platoon to stand down, hold their fire. The people screamed and scattered. The men in his platoon were spooked, and then one of his men panicked, seeing the villagers running in all directions. It was that corporal with the itchy trigger finger, always talking about killing gooks. He raised his M-14 and began shooting, and then all hell broke loose. One after another the soldiers shot wildly. And suddenly, it was over. Over twenty people lay on the ground, their bodies torn apart by the bullets. A baby still held in its mother's arms, the mother and child lifeless like ragdolls.

Holey John smelled their blood in his nostrils in his dream. He saw the same images like a loop of film that kept going from beginning to end, villagers' bodies flailing as the bullets danced them around like convulsive puppets. He walked around their still bodies and stared down at their faces as they lay on the ground with eyes open, not blinking, open or half-shut with no life left in them. The eyes…always the eyes looking at him.

The men in the platoon were silent after that. A few wore faces of disbelief. Others had the misshapen smiles of Halloween masks.

"They were Cong," Corporal Stinger said, breaking the silence, the hair-trigger grunt. "I saw a rifle. That man from the hooch."

Another man nodded.

"I saw it too. Had to be," Private Duffy confirmed too quickly.

"It was a rake," Holey John corrected flatly, having walked over to the dead villager, kicking the wooden handle with his boot.

But no one bothered to search for weapons, and they all started to back away from the tiny village and the bodies splayed on the ground.

"We have to report this," Holey John was saying to Stinger. He didn't like him. Didn't like his attitude—the cruel product of an entitled prep school, ROTC hothead. Holey John heard Stinger talk about having big plans for himself once he served his time.

The other men stared at him, shifting uncomfortably where they stood.

"Not a good idea," muttered Corporal Stinger who fired the first shot. He looked at Duffy and exchanged squinty-eyed, conspiring CYA looks.

The latter gave Stinger a slight nod. "Okay, guys," Stinger said, "let's head back to base camp. Let the sarge do whatever he needs to."

The platoon turned and headed away from the village except for Stinger who watched him go to each person lying motionless on the ground. He wasn't going to let his sergeant ruin his life.

A teenage boy whose mother had fallen on top on him, keeping him safe from the carnage, gave Holey John a pleading look. He was looking at the kid who had a deep cut across his forehead and was about to help him up when Stinger suddenly yelled, "Look, over there! At three. Charlie with an *AK*!"

Holey John turned to where Stinger pointed and saw no one. He started to turn toward him and saw his rifle raised at him, and the last thing he remembered was severe pain, like a spike had been driven into his skull. And then blackness.

The blackness lifted in the dream, and his nightmare always ended with one other face. Not a dead villager but a young woman with almond-shaped eyes and long, black hair. Her face was sad as she looked directly into his, her slender fingers always caressing his cheek. She would reach out to him, throwing a lifeline so he would not drown. Holey John murmured "*Linh*," and watched as the woman with the almond eyes drift away behind his shuttered eyes.

When he woke in the morning, the memory of the dream was gone as always except for a terrible feeling he was left with of something dreadful that had best be forgotten and the woman who tried to save him.

CHAPTER 22

BE YOURSELF, EVERYONE ELSE IS ALREADY TAKEN

The fairground lights had been turned down. The cacophony of sounds from carny barkers and the rumble of twirling carnival rides went silent as the day's visitors left. I was stopped by a very large man at the gate, who had a neck the size of a ham hock.

"Here to speak with Zena."

I told him my name, and he looked me up on a clipboard then let me pass, having been told by the Giambolvos who I was.

There were clutches of people, folks who worked there sitting on crates having a smoke, laughing. Some bottles were passed. Some joints changed hands. I passed by the cook tent, and other people were gathered there drinking coffee and jawing. As I went into the field where the caravans and trailers were parked, I saw small camp-fires with people seated in lawn chairs chewing the fat. One big, happy, but not quite ordinary family, but then again, what family was?

I spotted the pink flamingoes blinking their lights around a trailer and looked at my watch. I had arrived at her trailer at 11:00 p.m. on the dot. Before I knocked on the door, I took a quick hit from my vape then pocketed it. I was clearly nervous to be granted a private audience with Zena.

Zena opened it a half-minute later. She was dressed in a kimono with her hair up in a bun with a pair of chopsticks keeping it in place.

"A man on time. I like that. Better than a man who comes too soon."

The Queen of the Double Entendre was at it again.

"I like taking my time," I said. "No sense rushing certain things." I could verbally parry with this bittersweet petite.

I stepped inside her living quarters, and she nodded toward a love seat. I noticed that the loveseat's fabric was decorated with pink flamingoes.

She gave me a smile with a hint of slyness glinting from her wide eyes. I sat while she took a bottle of Glenfiddich from a cabinet and grabbed two glasses. She poured the Scotch into the glasses and handed one to me.

"No ice," she announced.

"Of course."

"This puppy is twenty-one years old." She took a sip and smacked her lips then rolled her tongue over them. "Yummy."

I raised the glass to my nose, closed my eyes, and inhaled the brown liquid's aroma. "Ah yes. Smoky, with a hint of peat bog, coffee grounds, and a light splintering of oak barrel."

"Funny man," Zena said with a smile that crinkled her nose. "You're describing wine, not good Scotch."

Zena had dimmed the lights in her trailer with a scattering of candles. I sipped my Scotch and took in the trailer's décor. She seemed to favor kitsch when it came to interior design.

I stared at the wall behind her. On it hung an array of movie posters: *The Wizard of Oz, Freaks, The Tin Drum, Snow White and the Seven Dwarfs, Austin Powers with Mini Me,* and *The Attack of the 50-Foot Woman.* Obviously, she had a size theme going on here. My eyes were drawn to a small library across from the loveseat. I squinted to read titles. *In the Little World, The Science of Mind and Behavior,* and Freud's *The Psychology of Love* caught my eye.

Zena stared at me as I eyeballed her living quarters. It was more than a simple observation of me taking in her digs. She was checking me out, her eyes rolling over me. Her checking me out felt funny for some reason—not expected. Different now. Not like, *Is this a guy I can trust to write about me and my world?* Something else, a kind of inspection.

"You can tell a lot about people from their looks before trying to get into their heads."

"What can you tell about me?" I wondered if she could nail me like other women had since my time with her had been fairly short, no pun intended.

She looked more closely at me. "You worry too much."

"And you know that how?"

"You bite your nails," she said flatly.

"True," I agreed, looking down at them. "What else?"

"You favor your right arm. Your biceps are bigger on your right arm. You are probably good in a fight," she added.

"Really?"

"When that guy Wally came at me in the restaurant, you started to get up, but John beat you to the punch. You sort of jumped forward like you were going to attack him. Maybe you have some training. Like fencing or something."

"Something."

"Not fencing?"

"Nope, but you got the training right."

She smiled provocatively and said, "Then no lunging experience."

I smiled, but her implied continuing suggestive repartee was curious.

"You think highly of yourself," she continued, "but I'd say you have room for improvement."

Her last remark could be said for about anyone. That said, people like Lilly would like some improvements.

"So you're not a fortune-teller like your sign says."

"I'm not. Telling people about their future is a problem when the future doesn't see it your way. What I do is read people. Not credentials I can frame on a wall. I read body language like I said before. People have all sorts of tells."

"Like in poker games."

"When someone sits down across from me, I don't present myself as a fortune-teller but more of a safe person to talk to. I don't judge. I am like a stranger on a train. Someone who you may never meet again. You can spill your guts and never see them again." Zena paused briefly and sipped her drink. "Most of the time, that's all they need. Just someone to talk to. Hopefully they get something from me, and I always get something from them," she finished.

I wondered if it was the same with the people I interviewed.

"Everyone needs something they don't have," she said.

"Like fame and fortune."

"Some do. Not everyone. They want other things."

"Like…?"

"Peace of mind."

I thought of Holey John.

"Some want bad things," I added.

"Yes. Where there is love, there is hate. Where there is fortune, there is misfortune."

I was drinking Scotch with Zena *the philosopher*.

"The one thing I always do is remind people they have choices no matter what their situation is. Most people feel life takes away their power. I try to make them see that there are always choices."

I wondered why she had made her choice as a sideshow act with the Giambolvo Brothers.

"What is the something you want?" she asked directly. "Aside from that story of yours."

I thought a few moments, deciding to answer candidly. "Being appreciated. Respected. Understood and not judged."

"By whom?"

"Everybody."

Zena considered this. "Oscar Wilde said, 'Be yourself, everyone else is already taken.'"

I gave her another A-plus. "What about you?"

"Maybe by the time you leave and go back to your happy home, you'll know."

I decided to change the subject. I had come back to her trailer so she could tell me about her being abandoned and, hopefully, about her life with the Giambolvo Brothers. I had to admit her remark that she was actually baby-dumped was gnawing at my journalist's curiosity. And I knew that Stan would hang on to this part of her story like a cheap suit.

"So what about what you said before?"

"You mean about being left at a church?"

"Yeah, that."

She stood and refilled our glasses then shook her head. "You being a writer drooling for a juicy story will love my little tale." She patted her ass. "I don't mean this one…for now."

I knitted my brow. Her out-of-nowhere flirtations were becoming more frequent. By now, I realized that Zena liked to tease. But these repeated sexual innuendos were confusing. Was it the booze talking, or was she feeling comfortable enough to make me think she was obtainable? And did I even want to pursue her? Or did she think I wanted to?

My ethical rules as a journalist having sex with a subject were foggy as demonstrated by having recently put my P in the Vs of six paid-for-pleasure ladies. But there was this bigger issue at hand. Ignore the bigger adjective. I had never made love to a woman of her stature. Just thinking about this made my mind twirl like a dizzying top. I quickly erased an image I conjured up of Zena without clothes and returned my focus on her, sitting there on the flamingo-patterned loveseat about to reveal a side of her that she assumed not many people knew. Maybe I was just imagining things, that her flirtations were just a way to play with me, take control.

"Where did you just go?" she asked, noticing that my thoughts had left the room.

"Just thinking about what it must be like," I lied. "The fact you were cast off."

"Yeah, just like baby Moses." She squinted that scrutinizing look at me again then spoke. "Okay, so I begin this tear jerker about the bonds of parenting, love, and kindness that will absolutely warm the cockles of your heart."

There was something in her delivery that made me feel the exact opposite would be true. I also wondered what the hell a cockle was. I would have to Google that later. My list of things to look up was growing.

She emptied her glass and looked at mine. "Drink up."

CHAPTER 23

HANKY-PANKY

On Wednesday, a day after Brinks met with Freddy, he got a call on his cell phone at work.

"I got a present for you," Freddy started.

"The thing I wanted?" Brinks's question was said in a low voice, seeing his door was open.

"Meet me when you get off from work. Same place as last time."

Brinks walked into the bar and saw Freddy in a booth in the back. He sat across from him as a waitress arrived.

"I'll have a double Chivas straight up, on his tab," Freddy said, jerking his thumb at Brinks.

"We only got the Dewars and Old Smuggler," she said with a shrug.

"Dewars with a twist," Freddy said.

"What about you?" she asked Brinks.

"Tequila with a splash of OJ," he said. "Don Julio will do."

"We got Cuervo," the waitress suggested. Brinks reluctantly nodded, and she wiggled her way to the bar.

"How's it hanging, chief?" Freddy asked.

"It's hanging."

"We keep meeting here, people will think we're dating."

Brinks forced a smile.

"You still trying to put out your work fires?"

"Yeah."

"This should help." She passed a DVD case across the table.

"That was fast."

"We aim to please."

"What's on it?"

"What you wanted."

Brinks eyed the disc.

"Very wild, hanky-panky video of your boss's missus."

"You look at it?"

"Gave me a woody." Freddy took both of his index fingers and put them on the sides of his eyes, stretching the skin to make him look Asian. "Me so horny. Me love you long time."

"Not PC," Brinks scolded.

"When this town gets PC, I'll suck my own dick."

He took out an envelope and handed Freddy the five hundred dollars he had promised. He had the salacious evidence that he would deliver to Wolfe. It should give the guy a mother humper of a shock—enough to devastate the man psychologically, distracting him so much that he couldn't focus on doing his job, especially with what Brinks had been doing.

"You have an idea of how you're going to drop this bomb?" Freddy asked. "Open to ideas if you have any."

"He use a laptop?"

"We all do at work."

"They have DVD players?"

"Most do."

"Then just figure out a way to slip it into his DVD drive. The media player will auto-boot when the laptop boots up."

"Auto-boot?"

"Yeah. It'll start to run as soon as his laptop finishes its startup routine. The DVD will play right off the bat, and he'll get quite a show. Not sure he'd get a boner. More like a bummer. You should take peek."

They finished their drinks, and Brinks threw cash on the table for the waitress.

"Let me know how the matinee goes," Freddy said with a mischievous grin as the two men left the bar.

Brinks got into his car, wondering what Wolfe's reaction would be seeing his newly acquired bride in the throes of action passion with another guy. He smiled. You never know how an audience is going to react on opening night.

CHAPTER 24

HOW YOU GUYS TREAT US

Zena refilled our glasses. She took a sip of her Scotch and moved a strand of hair that had fallen across her forehead.

"I pieced most of what I am telling you together. Bottom line, my folks did not win any prizes for being warm and tender parents."

"No doubt."

"Left no forwarding address." She took a moment. "What gets me is I see parents who hold hands with their kids that have Down Syndrome. I'm sure they're going to have a challenging life, but I see love. They don't run."

Zena smirked and emptied her Scotch then poured two more fingers into her glass. The lady must have hollow legs.

"They did one thing, though."

"What?"

"Left a note. One word. *Sorry.*"

"So no contact all these years?"

"Not in person," she said enigmatically.

I didn't pursue this sidestepped answer.

"Anyway, I was handed over to social services who put me into foster care. The Baker Springs Home for Children. The people that ran the place were real nice. I got a good education, a bed, and warm meals. People would come there every week looking for children that they would consider adopting. No surprise. I was never picked."

"And you stayed there…"

"Till I was eighteen," Zena finished my sentence. "They said I was real smart and should go to college. I got a scholarship to go to a small liberal arts university, started as a psych major. But I had a feeling that this would not be my life's work."

"My mother is a therapist," I reminded her.

"So you said."

"She says she first studied psychology as a safe way to understand what made her tick."

Zena thought about that for a few moments. "I did the same thing except I wanted to understand more than that. I needed to learn survival skills to handle the world that would always see me as different. I had to learn how to keep my shit together dealing with you guys."

I grumbled at her *you guys* remark. "So the little people in the world are never cruel."

"Actually, we can be crueler. It's usually a reaction to how *you guys* treat us."

I gave her a half-nod. I knew that the world was an equal opportunity distributor of cruelty to people who were seen as different from them. My journalistic forays into the world showed me both the good, the bad, and the ugly no matter what or who a person was.

"You have more power when you know what people are about," Zena elaborated. "Some people never find their power. Something gets broken in them because life can be messy. Some people can work through it. I have."

I believed she did but with a whole lot of emotional armor.

"But others never do." I hesitated. "I mean look at your friend. Doesn't he give up his power to the people who pierce him like a voodoo doll?"

"My sixth-sense secret sauce doesn't work with him."

"Do you think he even knows why he does what he does?"

She shook her head again, this time with her eyes closed.

"I think it's time for a snack," she said, changing the subject.

CHAPTER 25

TABOO LAND ISN'T A CARNIVAL RIDE

Zena got up and brought back a plate with crackers and cheese. The Scotch was giving me a slight buzz, so the crackers were a welcome treat to help me listen and not break out into song.

"What happened at college?" I asked, trying to keep the conversation going.

"A few people tried to make me feel like I was like anyone else, but I still got the looks and the stares. The jocks and frat boys would hit on me, trying to win some bet that they could screw me. Novelty sex. Fuck the dwarf. I got along with the geeks okay. But they just reinforced my feelings of being an outcast."

"The geeks and freaks club." It slipped out of my mouth, but Zena held her glass up and tipped it to me in agreement.

"So I graduated. And doing the psych thing for work seemed like a possibility. My next step was being an intern. I lasted one day. My first client came in and saw me in a chair that swallowed me up, my legs dangling over the edge, my feet not even close to the floor. She took one look at me and asked if I was waiting for my mommy. When I told her I would be counseling her, she smiled and said she didn't think so and left. My next three clients basically had the same reaction. A person of my stature couldn't possibly deal with their *big* problems. I wasn't taken seriously."

"So you gave up your budding career as a psychotherapist."

"There wasn't a big demand for a shrink whom they saw as shrunken."

I smiled but saw that Zena had been deeply hurt by her experience. I waited, got rid of my smile and said, "Of course my next question is—"

"How I wound up with the Giambolvo Brothers." Zena's eyes sparkled as her mind rolled back her memory tapes. "Life has a way of presenting you with unexpected opportunities."

I noticed that she had a way of talking where she carried on conversations with a saying that Yoda might say.

"The Brothers were passing through my college town where I was doing the intern thing. They had these colorful posters advertising their big tent show with amazing animal acts, acrobats, and clowns." She sighed pleasantly and added, "This was a good fifteen years ago."

"Fifteen, huh?" That was a long time to live under her carnie dome, but who was I to judge since, according to Stan, I was an adamant dome dweller?

"What caught my eye back then was a family of performers called the Tom Thumbers. It was a troupe of little people. Since you said you did some research on circus history, you should remember General Tom Thumb."

"I do."

"P. T. Barnum discovered him when he was only five. Turned him into one of the most famous circus acts in history."

I remembered Charles Stratton, a.k.a. Tom Thumb, who toured America singing and dancing and doing comedy routines. He eventually reached three feet in height and married another midget. When the general died of a stroke at the age of forty-five, over ten thousand people came to his funeral.

Zena picked her story up again. "I never had contact with other people like me, little people I mean. So I went to the first show on opening day, got there early, and sat in the front row. When the Tom Thumbers came out and started doing their routine, I just gawked at them like people had gawked at me all my life. Pepe, the oldest member of the troupe, noticed me staring at him and smiled. I smiled back. They were great. When their act was over, he came over to me and whispered into my ear, telling me to come to their trailer after the show."

"And off you went," I said.

"Of course. I spent the next three days with them. Hanging out with these people was comfortable and familiar."

I didn't have to be a whiz kid to see why she was drawn to them, finally finding her lost tribe.

"It was on the last day of the show. They said I should join their act just for fun for the last performance before they went onto the next town. I said what the hell, and they dressed me up in a belly dancer outfit and all I had to do was gyrate my hips standing on Pepe's shoulders."

I tried to imagine her doing that. For some reason I couldn't understand, I liked the thought of seeing her do the gyrating thing. *Okay, Fenn, keep that thought to yourself.*

"So 'Bleed Beldame' came over the sound system. You know, by Mezdeke."

I kind of nodded, having no idea what she was talking about; my knowledge of belly dancing's top forty hits was more than a bit rusty. Nonexistent actually.

"I was Bettina, the Beauty of the Nile, and the crowd went nuts over me. For the first time in my life, I was a gorgeous, sexy chick that got the kind of stares from guys the way I wanted."

"Bettina and not Zena," I said reflectively.

"A temporary stage name for that evening."

"I take it that you had a great night."

"I did. Tony G. was in the big tent and saw me. Straight out asked me if I was interested in joining the show. I didn't hesitate for a second. Packed my bags that night. I worked with the Thumbers there for a few years then struck out on my own with my own act."

"Funny how life throws you a curve ball that changes everything," I said, this assignment being my curve ball.

"When I joined the G brothers, I could reinvent myself. What a rush. And *voila*. Zena, the World's Smallest Fortune-Teller."

"Are the Thumbers still here?" I asked.

"Pepe died a couple of years ago. Some little folks don't have the life expectancy you have. Especially dwarves. His wife, Bella, is alive, and we still have Ethel and Larry. They are too old for the act. Ethel sells admission tickets, and Larry has a concession stand selling stuffed animals and the toys you couldn't win at the fixed carnie games. Bella looks after them. The other Thumbers retired."

A question came up for me, and Zena could tell I was struggling with it.

"What is the technical difference between—"

"A dwarf and a midget and just a small person," she said, once again completing my thought. "A dwarf is a person of an uncommonly small stature, usually with a body whose proportions are not normal as in your world. Most dwarves have oversized heads in relation to their body. Stubby fingers. Bowed legs. Some have even more challenging physical problems. On the other hand, a midget—and I can say that and you can't—is also a person of an unusually small size but whose body is physically well-proportioned. I am a well-proportioned dwarf by medical standards, what is called a physiologic dwarf." Zena finished.

I hoped I could remember all of this since the Scotch was making my brain mushy.

"In any case, I am exceptionally well-proportioned as you can see." She thrust her chest out to display the outline of her well-endowed and proportional portions.

My eyes surveyed her body, and I smiled. "That belly dancing outfit. You still have it?"

It was meant as a joke to lighten up what had been a very dark telling. She giggled and got up. I noticed that talking about the Thumbers had changed her mood for the better after reliving what was certainly a heavy past.

Zena walked to the back of the trailer where her bedroom was located. She stopped at the door and turned, giving me a come-hither look, then went inside the room, closing the door. I thought she was trying to flatter me with that look. Like I was desirable. I wasn't sure that I wanted to be.

I sat there with my Scotch, the remnants of some weed still in my biosystem and my imagination staring at her bedroom door. Of course, I wondered what she was up to.

I heard the slight tinkle of bells and her soft voice singing. My belly button was telling me she was changing into her old costume, having taken my question literally to heart. I thought of her undressing, and my mind ping-ponged with very graphic images. Imagining a naked Zena seemed more off limits than my time with the ladies of the night. If I was heading to Taboo Land, I knew it wouldn't be a carnival ride.

CHAPTER 26

SURVIVAL

That night, Marvin Brinks wished he was Jimmy Wolfe. Not exactly the man himself but the man who could bed his wife. He sat at his laptop and watched the video half a dozen times. The woman was sizzling hot, and Brinks felt aroused watching her do things to the actor that he wished one of his on-call ladies would do to him. He watched her unabashed enthusiasm appreciative of the kind of things she could do with her tongue, hands, and ass.

He burned a backup copy and put the original away in the safe where he kept records of all the faux companies he had created, the transactions made, his offshore accounts, and what they held. When he went to bed, he dreamed of Wolfe's wife.

In the morning, Brinks took a shower and repeated in his head the steps he would carry out when he got to work. He didn't feel hungry for breakfast, so he nibbled on a corn muffin, washing it down with orange juice. His case of the nerves wasn't surprising since today was also the day that his boss wanted to meet, go over the books, and take a closer look at all the expenditures for which Brinks was in charge. He went to the living room and slipped the DVD inside his briefcase.

Forty-five minutes later, he was at his desk. Brandy, his admin, brought him his usual morning coffee.

"By the way, Mr. Wolfe left you a copy of an invoice you paid. I put it in your tray."

His secretary left his office and closed the door. He looked in his desk tray and found a copy of the invoice. "Shit," he muttered. The invoice had a big question mark written on it. Brinks felt a moment of uneasiness. It was an invoice from one of his sham companies he used to bill Glowball. One of his conspirators would bank the check and then transfer Bitcoins to Brinks's digital money account minus their cut.

Wolfe would be back in thirty minutes, returning from his usual weekly morning round of golf with his buddies. No doubt he would bring up the invoice. He wondered how the invoice wound up in his boss's hands.

Brinks took a last sip of his coffee. He took a calming breath and stretched his hands out in front of him and studied them. Steady as a rock. It was time to get started.

"Brandy," Brinks said when she picked up her desk phone.

"Yes, Mr. Brinks."

"Please go down to the mail room. See if there's an overnight package from Vanguard. I'm expecting a signed contract and need it for my morning meeting."

Brandy said sure as Brinks sent her off on a wild goose chase to buy needed time since there was no contract and no Vanguard. He waited a minute and opened his briefcase, taking out the DVD.

No one was outside his office when he opened the door. He headed to the corner office where Wolfe was situated. Brinks opened the door and quickly entered, closing the door behind him. He saw Wolfe's laptop sitting on the desk. Brinks didn't need to get past the firewall to access his boss's software. He only needed to open the DVD disc drive. He inserted the DVD and closed the drive. Wolfe's lightning bolt from the blue was waiting to strike as soon as he turned on his computer.

Glancing around, the scene was set. He opened the office door and saw that Brandy was chatting with another woman a few cubicles away, her back turned away from Brinks. His heart raced as he slipped out of the office. He headed to Brandy before she could see where he came from.

Brandy saw him as she turned and shook her head. "Not there."

"No problem. It'll show up in the afternoon mail."

The timing couldn't have been better. Brinks spotted Wolfe walking down the hall.

"How did you hit 'em?" Brinks asked as if he cared.

"Killed a lot of worms." Wolfe didn't look like a happy camper. "You ready for our meeting?"

"Give me ten so I can get everything I need."

"And we need to talk about an invoice you paid. Someone from finance red-flagged it."

Brinks held down a spasm of alarm and set off to his office as he heard Wolfe's door open and close. He went to the window that faced the Hollywood skyline. He stared into the distance and knew the next five minutes would steer his life in one of two directions, a cell in San Quentin or time enough to tighten up his mischief. He waited as the next seconds ticked away, hanging heavy in the atmosphere like foul Peking air.

Wolfe went to his desk and powered on his computer. As it ran through the cycles of booting up, the DVD player kicked in and whirled. He watched the log-in screen that was asking him for his user name and password. He typed in both, when the DVD booted up and a movie began to play.

"What the hell!" he said out loud, unsure of what was going on.

At first, he was confused by the bodies wrestling on the sheets of a bed. Moaning sounds became louder. The angle of the camera changed, and the lens zoomed closer. He squinted through his contacts and gasped. Then he saw and heard his wife clearly. "Fuck me harder! Harder!"

She flipped over on her back, and Wolfe saw the man's face. He recognized the bastard, a guy with a bit role in one of their movies. The actor drove his pelvis into his wife like a jackhammer and she continued to scream "Harder!"

"God! Oh my fucking God!" Wolfe choked on his own words. Tears began to run down his cheeks as he grasped what he was watching. Convulsively, his hand swept a row of framed photographs of his wife off his desk along with a flurry of papers which floated to the floor. As they crashed to the floor, he grabbed his chest.

Brinks heard the sound of breaking glass. His first impulse was to leave his own office, but he drew himself back and waited. Timing had to be just right.

Wolfe saw a new angle focus on the copulating couple. The woman was moving her head down the actor's stomach, her tongue flicking like a snake as she got closer to his groin and put his penis into her mouth.

"Goddamn bitch!" This time, he let out a tortured scream that might have escaped the shrieking man's mouth in that Edvard Munch painting. He grabbed his chest again and threw his body back against his chair, the chair tipping over, spilling Wolfe onto the floor.

Brinks went to his door now. Brandy was standing at her desk then ran to Wolfe's door and jerked it open. At that moment, she cried out.

Brinks quick-stepped to Wolfe's office. Brandy was on her knees hovering over Wolfe. He was gasping for air like a fish out of water, vomit running down his cheeks, a gagging sound plugging his airway. She seemed clueless as what to do or what had happened. Brinks moved her aside and felt the pulse on Wolfe's neck. His heart beat was rapid and breathing more labored.

"Heart!" moaned Wolfe. "My pills." He pointed to his desk drawer.

Brinks nodded. Brandy was no longer looking at Wolfe but was staring slack-jawed at the movie of the copulating couple.

"Call 911," Brinks commanded.

She jumped up and ran for her desk.

"That bitch," Wolfe spit. "She's dead meat."

This was not the words of man who had been thrown into a disabled state of mind. This was a pissed-off man set on revenge.

Brinks fast-forwarded his plan. The clips of his wife did not have the planned effect. It rapidly dawned on him that this scene was not unfolding in the way he had imagined. Wolfe could recover, and Brinks quickly saw a new scenario take place. The EMTs would get there and revive the betrayed husband and get him to a hospital. He'd be back at his desk in no time at all, his lawyers lined up to file for a divorce.

He heard sirens below on the street, meaning that the paramedics would come up any minute now.

He had to think fast. He looked into Wolfe's eyes. They were rolling around like crazy marbles. His skin was getting a bluish tint, and his breaths were getting shorter. Brinks saw more vomit dribble from Wolfe's gasping mouth. His reaction to his wife's sexual acrobatics produced a physical, not mental, reaction.

"Pills!" Wolfe sputtered again.

Brandy was nowhere in sight. He was alone with Wolfe but would only have seconds before the office would fill with people.

Wolfe saw Brinks eye the invoice that had landed on the floor with a sticky note attached. His boss had scribbled "This isn't right! Talk to Brinks!"

Brinks picked it up and shoved it into his pocket.

Wolfe choked and then pointed to the invoice that Brinks had confiscated. A split second of clarity came back into his eyes. "You're fucking with the books!" he said accusingly, his condemnation barely audible as he gagged.

Brinks said nothing.

"You did this," Wolfe choked, pointing with a quivering finger at the computer screen. He stared back at Brinks. "Why?" he gagged.

A dark survival impulse drove him to act. No way was he going to give up all he had worked for. He pinched Wolfe's nose, squeezing his boss's nostrils tight. Wolfe was forced to breathe through his mouth, but his mouth and throat were full of the regurgitated contents of what must have been a filling breakfast.

Sheer panic filled his face. He tried to move his hands, but Brinks swatted them away. He quickly looked around. Brandy was still yelling something into her phone about letting the ambulance guys up to her floor.

Brinks moved his hand over the mouth of Glowball's CFO. Wolfe made gagging sounds and his body shuddered, his bulging eyes of disbelief losing their light. The convulsions stopped as did his breathing, and he was suddenly as still as window glass. Brinks wiped the hand that had vomit on the palm on Wolfe's shirt and then felt Wolfe's throat. No pulse.

He remembered one thing that he hadn't planned for: Brandy seeing the movie of a copulating couple. He wondered if Brandy had enough time to figure out who the woman was. Brinks made another quick decision. He found Wolfe's zipper and pulled it down. Reaching inside the dead man's pants, he took hold of Wolfe's penis and slipped it out through the zipper.

He got up and removed the disc from the DVD drive and shut off the media player. Brinks quickly found Wolfe's link to his Internet browser, searched for porn sites. He found a link to a nubile teen giving head to one man while another penetrated her from behind. He nodded to himself satisfied and left it on the screen. Next, he took out the vial of pills of the drawer, putting them in the dead man's hand.

He heard noise in the hallway and put the disc inside his jacket pocket. No damaging evidence, the job done.

By then, a crowd of workers had gathered down the hall.

"We need you to go back to your desks," Brinks ordered as he stepped out of Wolfe's office. He thought of what would follow. He had to nail down what had happened when asked. The police might be called in. His story needed corroboration. The EMTs would help seeing Wolfe with his vial of nitro pills in his hand. He needed one more person to back up what went down.

Brinks stood in the hallway. "Brandy," he said with obvious seriousness.

She looked up from the crowd around her desk. Brinks gestured for her to come. At Wolfe's door to his office, he patted her on both shoulders.

"We need to keep Mr. Wolfe's dignity intact," he practically whispered.

Brandy looked puzzled.

"What he was looking at on his computer."

She looked at the computer with the people on the porn site having an active threesome and then at Wolfe, his penis in full view, and nodded that she understood.

"I want you to keep this to yourself. Then call Mr. Brenner. Can you do that?"

The secretary nodded, still in shock, and left the office. Quickly, he put Wolfe's member back in his pants and deleted the porn site. He took the vial of nitro pills from his desk and put it in the dead man's hand, wiping his own fingerprints off.

People cleared a path for the EMTs, and Brinks felt like he was already in charge. He would talk to Walt Brenner, the head of Glowball Productions. *Sad news, Mr. Brenner. But I think we have things under control.* It wasn't the outcome he had planned for, but the end results were the same. He had waylaid Wolfe—permanently.

As his adrenaline rush faded from his actions, he waited for some conscience recognition of what he had done. He had killed Wolfe. He waited for guilt and remorse to crash over him like a chilling wave. But none came. He had done something unthinkable, and all he felt was nothing. Like breaking the necks of rabbits in the backyard of his parents' house. He knew he had been left with only one option. He had made a choice. It was a matter of survival.

Back at his desk, he pulled the DVD out of his pocket and put it safely back inside his briefcase.

His phone rang. It was Brandy.

"I have Mr. Brenner on the line."

He thanked her and heard her sobbing.

CHAPTER 27

I AM YOUR NEW WORLD

I waited while my imagination spun like a Tilt-a-Whirl. When the door opened, Zena the Fortune-Teller was now Bettina, the Beauty of the Nile. From where I sat, I stared at her standing at the threshold of her bedroom. The flicker of candles shimmered against the walls of the darkened room. Her bare feet were placed on a small rug that had caught my eye, a rug decorated with brightly colored rose petals and white unicorns. My eyes traveled up. She wore a gold beaded bra with coins that dangled from the bottom, which held her ample breasts. Her harem pants were black, a light fabric, and very sheer. The panties underneath were black as well and hugged her private parts, making clear the anatomical lay of the land one would discover if ever removed.

"Yowzer, bowzer, in my trousers," I blurted, my coprolalia kicking in.

She raised her eyebrows.

I wasn't sure that was what I should have said. I caught myself gawking, feeling like a naughty kid sneaking into a peep show.

"I assume your *yowzer bowzer* is a form of a weird appreciation," Zena said, reminding me of similar words that Lilly had recently uttered, her "You like, mister?" response to seeing her pubic topiary.

This was a memory that added confusion to what was taking place. A song came drifting out of her bedroom like a soundtrack from *One Thousand and One Nights*, and Lilly and her manicured pubes floated out of my mind.

She smiled and started to sway her hips and do that in-and-out stomach muscle thing that belly dancers do. She gyrated her way toward me and stopped at the sofa. The next few minutes had me spellbound like a deer caught in the headlights of a semi. As petite as Zena was, sensuality steamed off her skin as she danced. My eyes roamed over her body, focusing on her breasts that jiggled one moment, then her undulating tummy, then to her firm and sequins-covered derriere.

I was mesmerized, but before long, my peep show goggling suddenly became evident, and I felt self-conscious.

She stopped dancing and looked deep into my eyes. Her hand took mine, and she tried pulling me off the sofa, wanting to lead me to the bedroom. I felt my heartbeat increasing. Trepidation followed. The little voice in my head told me that this wasn't a good thing to do. And then there was this muddled idea of having sex not with Zena but with a dwarf; Zena was no longer a person but a concept. Whatever was happening in my head was turning into a mind fuck about fucking.

"Maybe I should head back to my motel and we can call it a day," I halfheartedly offered, sensing this would be a unique adventure but one I shouldn't take. "There would be major boundary issues for me, for us, if this is headed where I believe this is headed. Shrinks don't sleep with patients, teachers with students…"

"You're killing my mood," she said playfully. "Up you go, big fella."

Zena and the Scotch and the weed and my curiosity and my quickly disappearing reasons of why this wasn't a good idea helped get me off the sofa. I followed her dumbly as her bells jingled, following my Arabian Nights Tinker Bell into the bedroom.

As I sat on her bed, I looked around. She had lit candles, and mellow music played in the background, replacing the *One Hundred and One Nights* tune.

"*Watercolors*. Pat Metheny," she said, naming the album as she slowly began removing her clothes. I watched her and felt a new mixture of excitement, arousal, enthrallment, and confusion. Most of the time, any woman who undressed in front of me would cause me to simply be excited and aroused. The curiosity part here was about what a naked little person looked like, not having had the pleasure of that experience before. My thoughts continued to bounce around like a careening pin ball. Lilly came into focus again but went out just as fast as Zena unhooked her jingling bra. The harem pants and thong went next.

"Voilà," she said with a sultry smile when the last piece of her costume had fallen to the floor. "As said, a perfect and delicious body."

Delicious, yes. But perfect in what I was used to, no. She was not flawlessly proportioned. At least not compared to most of the women I had bedded. The baked-in image of Lilly lying naked in my bed just a few days before intruded again. She had the perfect body in my world. Long, shapely legs. A firm butt shaped like a cantaloupe. Natural breasts that a plastic surgeon would envy. Of course, I was using the normal scale of proportions. Zena hated the word *normal*. But that's what it ever was as David Byrne had sung.

"I am just littler than the women you have shagged," she said, sensing my hesitation.

Once again, my eyes traveled over her body. Her legs were slightly bowed, her head a bit larger in comparison to the body it was attached to. Aside from that, she was petite, but her body was that of a woman, just a lot smaller as she said. And despite my contrasting her to the standard-issue ladies I had slept with, I found Zena strangely desirable, which made me feel even stranger, and I didn't know why.

I kept staring but made no move nor comment.

Zena picked up on my drifting attention again. "I am standing here in the buff, offering myself to you, and you look like a man contemplating the meaning of life and how gravity works."

I refocused and looked her straight in the eyes. "You are very pretty, lovely in fact. I was distracted by your beauty," I said, whisking away thoughts of porn movies I had seen in college with dwarves and midget women screwing not little people men.

"That's a start," she said, coming closer to me.

"But..."

"But what? You never made love to a little person. I get that. But all my parts are in perfect working order, I assure you."

I smiled at that, but I still hung back. What was this all about? Clearly, the Scotch was making any of her inhibitions go away. Ditto for myself. A few hours ago, she had hardly trusted me, wondered if I was using her, and now she was ready to hop into the sack? Did opening up to me with her past crack that amour she so assiduously erected? However, I hadn't thought seriously about venturing into the land of sexual possibilities with her before. She had asked me about whether I had ever thought about having sex with someone like her when we were at Maxie's. I never answered her question. I was thinking about the question now.

"There you go again, falling into the rabbit hole of 'Do I or don't I?' indecision," Zena said, bringing my head back to the moment.

She saw by my tell that she was right.

"Let me dispel some little people's sex myths," she started.

"Okay."

"You, no doubt, have an average-sized penis. I assure you it will fit into my little person's vag. Your man tool is not going to reach my lungs, puncture my heart, and if it makes me gag, I won't bitch."

"I feel better already," I said with a halting smile.

"Now let's talk logistics."

"Why not?"

"All that matters is that our parts line up. I like being on top, but that doesn't mean you should spin me around like a Dreidel. There is, however, one position that may be a problem."

"Oh."

"Sixty-nine. My torso is too short to plant my butt on your face while I try to reach your manhood."

I pictured what she said and saw that it would indeed pose a problem.

"However, when it comes to giving head, I'm the perfect height because you can stand, and I can just walk right up to your pocket rocket."

I could not contain a chuckle.

She sat next to me and began to rub my thighs as I sat on her bed. She saw I was getting aroused. "I know you like this. Your friend down there talks to me while you worry about whatever you are wor-rying about. Another tell of yours."

"Hubba, hubba," I eventually replied like an idiot, a bit sur-prised that my penis seemed to agree with her remark, but I still sat there, not moving.

"Hubba, hubba. Now that's a romantic response. Better that *yowzer* I guess."

I smiled a sloppy, intoxicated grin and shrugged.

"We are both adults," Zena said as if she were lecturing some-one who was legally dim-witted. "As you likely guessed, the Scotch has worked its socialization magic. Maybe I will eventually like you, but that still remains to be seen. What I do know is that I am as horny as hell and haven't been with a man in a while. I don't expect an engagement ring. This is a nice way to become intimate for a few hours, but it's my 'just for a one night' version of that. Tomorrow will be like any other day with you. I told you a story before that only a few people have heard so that in itself is a plus for you. But you don't have to worry about this being the start of a relationship. And for your information, I don't have relationship issues. I just don't like them. Relationships, I mean. And I bet you can guess why."

I took all this in. Zena was giving me a free pass. It was the reverse version of a man giving a woman the 'no-strings-attached' speech. I had used those lines myself. My brain may have been a bit fermented, but one thing I didn't buy was her not having relationship issues. My take was that everyone has them. I decided not to argue about that.

"Your turn, big boy," she challenged.

"You know I have a girlfriend," I uttered, my last reason for not proceeding with what might not be the best choice for me to make.

"She's not here."

I saw my resolve slipping away again as she rubbed my thigh, her hand brushing against my penis. I was a man that was easily seduced. A sexy woman and some flattering words was all it took. Mata Hari unclothed would have had me blabbing state secrets in a nanosecond. No waterboarding needed, Mr. Cheney.

I stood, slipped off my shoes and socks, and unbuttoned my shirt.

"Atta boy," she said and worked on my belt and pants.

Once I was undressed, she stepped away and looked me over.

"Not bad for a journalist. Looks like you do more than sit at a computer and write all day."

Zena pushed me onto her bed. She moved quickly and slid her body over mine, her head above me. She looked down on me with an alluring smile. I tried to kiss her, and she pushed me away. Instead, she kissed my neck and then my chest. Her lips were soft and warm. When I tried to kiss her lips again, she moved her head but continued kissing my body. I wondered why her lips were off limits. The working girls I interviewed had "no kissing" rules as well. Too intimate. Maybe the same for Zena.

I put my hands on her back and moved my fingers down, exploring her like a blind man touching something new for the first time.

She raised herself up, and I touched her breasts. She closed her eyes as I continued my journeying, taking my time.

"You like?" she asked.

"Hmm."

"Different?"

"Yes, but in a good way."

I watched her closely as I caressed her body. As her eyes closed, small sounds of pleasure came from her. I turned her over on her back and began kissing her body. My mouth traveled over her, tasting her neck, her nipples which went hard, and her stomach muscles which quivered. I kept my explorations going for quite a while, this being a new and exciting territory for me.

Zena's eyes flickered open, and she came close to my face and spoke softly into my ear. "Okay, Columbus," she voiced tenderly. "I am your New World. It's time to explore my Southern Hemisphere."

I got the message and smiled, heading down south to her cha-cha and the promised land. I saw no heart-shaped bush. The woman was *au naturel*.

CHAPTER 28

THE CHINESE WILL BE FINE

Walt Brenner shook his head. His silver-gray hair did not move as if every strand knew it would be punished if it did. He had multipurpose penetrating blue eyes that could be threatening when he needed to manage a cranky director, pacify a truculent actor, or soothe investors for over-the-budget movies.

His tan was even, skin taut to give the impression of youth. He was sixty, looked forty-five, and successfully headed Glowball Productions due to winning a mix of puerile buddy road trip moneymakers and the occasional art house movie that was supposed to make critics believe he could cinematically ponder the meaning of things profound. It also prevented these same critics from writing him off as a complete hack.

Right now his eyes were fixed on Marvin Brinks, squinting slightly as he tried to make sense of what had happened to James Burton Wolfe just a few hours before.

"So Jimmy's dick was out, flapping in the wind," Brenner said, cutting to the chase.

"No flapping, but yes, sir, it was out," Brinks replied.

"And he had porn on his laptop?"

Brinks nodded. "Afraid so."

"Who saw it?"

"I did. Our secretary too."

"What the fuck was he thinking?" he asked, his upper lip tight against the top row of pearl-white teeth.

Brinks turned his palms up. "Stress. Boredom. Unhappy with things at home."

"So he jerks off to relieve stress?!"

Brinks shrugged.

"Take a valium or whack off in the bathroom. But no, I think I'll whack off at my desk," Brenner said with aggravation. "We got Wi-Fi in the john."

"I erased his web browsing history and deleted the porn site he was on. I put Wolfe's penis back in his pants before the EMTs arrived."

"Quick thinking, Marvin," Brenner commended. "Your girl said the police came. Went through his office. Saw a vial of nitro pills. EMTs said it was a heart attack."

"And his girl?" Brenner continued anxiously.

"Brandy."

"We need to worry about her?"

"She's as loyal as they come. I told her that she needs to forget about whatever she thinks she saw on his laptop."

"You think she will keep it quiet?"

"I mentioned that our group would need her more than ever now that our boss had passed on. More responsibility could mean bigger things for her. And we needed to honor the man's character. She got the drift."

Brenner thought for a second. "Let's give her a new title. Like senior admin. And a nice salary bump."

"Good idea," Brinks said, seeing that Brenner piggybacked his idea.

"What about the Chinese?"

"I have most of the accounting information they'll want," he lied with the innocence of a cherub.

Brenner nodded approvingly. A moment passed, the man thinking about his new investors and any potential hiccups that could interfere with their financial backing.

"I'm sure the accounting end will be easy for them to evaluate. But you should also go over our acquisitions history as well. Stock transfers. Arrangements made with any of our acquired entities. Our Hong Kong friends will want to see that too."

Brinks took a moment to sort out what Brenner had said. "Stock transfers and agreements?" he said uncertainly.

Brenner nodded. "Go up to Legal. They work with our transfer agents for companies we've bought. Sometimes these acquired companies have contractual baggage. Don't want any fine print surprises."

"What do I look for?"

"Paper ghosts."

"Excuse me?"

"Most of these old contracts we might have inherited were just 'Let's make a deal' deals. Straightforward exchange of money. We'll pay you this for your shit. Usually physical inventories. Maybe transferring intellectual properties like some guy invented a new sound technology. As long as I've run this place I haven't seen any gotchas surface. I wouldn't worry, but let's cover our asses just to make sure."

Brinks hadn't thought about past arrangements because he had been so focused on the present and covering his own ass.

"Better safe than sorry, right?" Brenner said, giving Brinks a can-do smile.

"Right."

"Legal can help with recent contracts, but the really old ones are on paper. Before everyone went digital. See where we store them. Give them a look-see just to cover our butts."

"Then I'll start with Legal," Brinks concluded, putting on a can-do face.

Brenner stood and extended his hand. Brinks got up as well. "I don't need to tell you this, but our Asian amigos are pretty tight-assed for facts and figures. Between you and me, we need their cash for this project. We need to convince them we run a tight ship."

"I'm sure Wolfe had everything in order." He said this, deliberately making his now-dead boss a patsy for anything that might blow up.

"Can you handle it?" Brenner asked.

"You mean the investors?"

"That but more. Taking over Wolfe's job," he elaborated.

Brinks froze for a split second. These were the words he had wanted to hear ever since he began working at Glowball.

He processed the proposition and measured his words as modestly as he could. "Pretty sure I can. Wolfe was a good teacher."

"Let's see how you do for the next two months. An interim appointment. You get the Chinese squared away, and I don't see any reason why we can't make you our new CFO."

Brinks suppressed his desire to smile. He settled for a second handshake. "Don't worry, Mr. Brenner. The Chinese will be fine. I'll hit the ground running."

Actually, things may not be fine, he thought. People who were tight-assed about getting accurate facts and figures were people he didn't need right now.

As he left Brenner's office, he wondered what old deals had been made that could be an issue for him. He drew a blank. Brenner said Glowball didn't have any problems pop up from the past. Just as Brenner ordered, he would sift through them. He let out a hard breath. His visitors would pose a much bigger problem depending on how deep they dived compared to digging through musty deals made decades before.

CHAPTER 29

ABOUT LAST NIGHT

I felt her eyes even though I was still half-asleep. Maybe it was the force of her gaze that made me stir. I started to come out of my slumber. My eyes slowly blinked open. She was watching me from her pillow, and her eyes were intense.

"What?" I said, returning her stare.

"You were kind of smiling for a time, and then you weren't. I hope the last bit of your dream wasn't about me," she said.

Zena slipped out of bed, and I followed her naked body as she headed to the bathroom. "I am not, repeat, not your porno Kewpie doll," she warned as she watched me gawk at her.

My grogginess evaporated while putting together the sequence of events of the previous night. It had been different. Very different. Maybe strange…if I thought about it too long. Something I never dreamed of doing before. Not just having sex with her but having sex with someone like her. It was not what I was used to, but it was unexpectedly pretty hot. That was the strange part.

Zena came out of the bathroom, showered with a towel over her wet hair wearing a kimono bathrobe that fit quite nicely.

"I have a question," she started.

"Shoot."

"It's about what you want to write."

I could see she was puzzling over something.

"It has to do about what the difference is between fiction and non-fiction."

I sat up, leaning on my elbow. "Go on."

"You wanted to write about me and Holey John, right?"

I nodded.

"Are you writing fiction or non-fiction?"

"I am not sure I follow."

She closed her eyes, tapped her bottom lip with a forefinger, and then looked right at me. "You write based on what I tell you. But then you interpret what I say. I'm not writing it. You are. You make it into a story. You present it as fact. You drop in real places like where we ate or things like my alluring belly dancing."

"Alluring it was," I confirmed.

"You trick the reader to think that that is the way whatever you write really is or was. But it's not. Non-fiction becomes fiction. You create a story of what you heard and saw filtered through your eyes."

"Poetic license," I offered.

"That's all you got?"

I had to think for a moment. Zena pretty much nailed how a writer hears or sees something and then makes it into a story. "Everyone filters their experiences."

"Deep," she said mockingly.

She was calling me out. Her pronouncement was sharp and insightful. Her comments addressed the age-old issue of factual relativity in journalism.

"Isn't all art made by people like making a meal?" I finally answered.

"What's that mean?"

"A painter looks at her subject. Another painter looks at the same subject. Will the paintings be the same? Probably not. It will be their unique interpretation. The world fuels our imagination. It's our food. We digest what we see and experience, and then we—"

"Shit it out." She completed my digestive metaphor but not in the way I would have used. "So I am your meal or, should I say, meal ticket."

"That's harsh," I replied.

"The way I see it is you're going to explain my world to your readers. You're going to explain my world to me."

She said this with a toughness I hadn't heard before. I wondered if she was mad at me because she had opened herself up about her life, and then we had slept together, and her vulnerability had been exposed in a too-intimate way. *Have the boozy feelings that eroded her defenses last night changed as she sobered up this morning?* I wondered.

"Is this about last night?" I decided to ask.

She didn't answer and looked away.

"Look, Zena. I can write what I write, and if you hate it, you can rip it up. I will erase it from my laptop, and that will be that."

She then looked at me, trying to see if I was just saying that or if I meant it. Trust was not a commodity she had in great supply.

"I'd rather talk about you and me," she said, taking a hard left turn away from what we were talking about.

It made me nervous when a woman wanted to talk in terms of *you and me*. "What's this about?"

"It's about last night for starters."

"You mean the sex or the talking and getting-to-know-you stuff?"

"I mean the sex." Her tone changed, the roughness tamped down.

"You said you hadn't had good sex for a while. You said it felt great," I said, confused.

"Well, I hadn't had *any* sex for a long while would've been more accurate. I thought my vag was dead."

"It was just in a coma. Just needed a little resuscitation, is all," I reassured.

"So it was okay?"

"Hot," I answered. I wasn't lying.

"Not weird?" she asked, feeling slightly insecure.

I didn't answer right away.

"Come on, Fenn. You had sex with a little person. It was your first time."

"And so it was."

"And you were thinking, 'Oh, cool, I'm screwing a cute dwarf.'"

"The words *screwing* and *dwarf* never entered my mind."

"Never?" she asked, not buying it.

"At first...but..."

"But then what? Like later, this was all pretty much normal for you," she said accusingly.

"Look, Zena, all this shit ran through my mind at first. Was it weird? Maybe when I first started thinking about it before we actually had sex. I mean my reference point for normal is what you already think."

"So it wasn't normal," she said, scrutinizing my face.

"Sex never seems normal to me. Exciting, boring, anxiety-producing, maybe silly once in a while. But if you're wondering about me thinking about having an erotic encounter with a petite beauty as yourself, then yes, I was aware of it for the first few minutes once we got into it."

"And after that?" she probed.

"I was in the moment."

"In the moment," Zena repeated. "Kinda like Zen sex."

"Look," I said. "You have a great body. *Different* but great. All the working parts are where they should be as you pointed out. And they seemed to have registered the right responses as far as I remember."

"That they did," Zena said with a suppressed smile.

There was something that wasn't exactly hot the previous night, but I didn't bring it up with Zena. When I first tried to kiss her, she had pushed me away from her lips. And I remembered what she said. That she didn't have relationship issues, right? Wrong.

"So everything was pretty much normal once we got started?"

"My penis didn't tell me it had any issues," I answered clearly.

"What about you and me?" she asked again.

The free pass, no-strings-attached agreement seemed to have been revoked now. "I like you, Zena. You're smart, good in the sack, and so very mysterious." I knew I was dodging her real question.

"Mysterious, huh? At least for the forty-eight hours since you've known me."

"Short but sweet," I said.

She smiled and then asked, "You said you have a girlfriend in New York City. That didn't seem to stop you."

"You reminded me she was not there. Love the one you're with as the song says."

She gave a look that demanded more details.

I hesitated as a picture of Lilly reentered my mind.

"You sleep with her?" Zena asked.

"What does that have to do with anything?"

"Is it good?"

"Yes, it is," I answered without hesitation.

"Does she think she's your forever and forever girlfriend?"

I wondered why Zena was giving me the third-degree.

"She thinks we could have a forever relationship."

"But...?"

"She says I disappear. Not physically but emotionally. That's her complaint."

"Is that true?"

I thought for a moment. "Yes. I get busy with my life and work. I don't put as much focus on her or on us as she would like."

"Or that's what you tell her and maybe yourself."

I felt like Zena was trying to crawl inside my head playing therapist. Not the kind of wakeup pillow talk I had expected.

"How would she feel about you and me and last night?"

And this was really not the conversation I wanted. "What do you think?"

"Not great, I bet."

"You feel guilty?"

She was doing her best to mind-fuck me for reasons unknown.

"I think this part of playing truth or consequences is over," I said, exhausted.

"You can keep our torrid night together in your back pocket and use it if you want to break up with her."

"Did I say I wanted to break up with her?"

That was an unexpected insinuation. *Was this a wish on Zena's part?* I wondered again.

"Thanks for the advice and your permission," I said sarcastically.

"So what about us?" she asked once again.

"I didn't realize there was an *us*."

She frowned. "You and I together last night." She held back a moment. "There was something more going on than us just getting it on."

She was reading a lot into our night together.

"And you think last night makes us an *us*?"

"Just asking what you think."

"I said I liked it. It was hot."

"That's all? No *us* vibe?"

"You mean as boyfriend girlfriend? Or *us* as in 'Let's get married'? Or do you mean it was a great one-nighter with no strings attached that will be eternally etched into our memories? Just to be clear," I said, trying to gain some control of what was and would be, "I think option three was where you agreed this would be."

Zena stared at me like someone caught in a tangle of their own design. I saw that she was going down some kind of mental check-off list trying to consign what had happened between us the previous night into her world. Her history of abandonment, society's pigeonholing, and not being like everyone else in the world of tallness had made its way into this discussion.

"Yeah, option three might work."

"In what way?"

"No strings attached so we can further etch new memories."

"Probably a bad idea now," I said, seeing her previous *What about us?* questions had more strings than a hundred violins.

She was back on attack mode. "Yeah, but maybe fun for your research. Unless you need to ask your girlfriend for permission to walk on the wild side."

"Fuck you." I got out of bed, found my clothes, and went into her bathroom.

"Pussy," she yelled as I slammed the bathroom door. "You're as wild as a turd in a punchbowl."

I splashed water on my face to wake up and figured I'd better sort out my arrangement with her. Zena had gone into eerie land with that "What about you and me?" shit. I saw her choice the previous night to bed me as a safe but consequential choice. Maybe her

141

brief interlude with someone approaching decent, which according to her wasn't that often, was actually a seismic event.

I got dressed and left her trailer without saying goodbye. She was one of the most complicated women I had known. This morning, she had thrown me one mixed message after another like a wind storm that didn't know what direction to blow. Finishing a story about the midway, her, and Holey John was about as likely as a fish learning to tap dance. I thought about Lilly and an uncomplicated life, which would be as exciting as the people who Instagram their food.

My brief time with Zena and the midway was exciting, but where I was going with her, my story, and my life was murky at best.

CHAPTER 30

EVERYONE WANTS SOMETHING

Brinks got to work the next morning, feeling jittery as if he had main-lined a gallon of Red Bull. He saw Brandy, who looked up from her desk with a desolated expression and gave him a sympathetic batting of her eyes, thinking he was similarly devastated by the untimely passing of his boss. He returned a weak smile like a family member at a relative's funeral standing on the mourners' line.

"I was thinking," Brandy said, "about Mr. Wolfe."

Brinks clenched his teeth, not knowing if she had recognized the woman in the video and made the connection to him. But instead she said, "The circle of life ends in death."

He relaxed, and she continued. "The past is past. The present is present."

"So true," Brinks said at her insight, which sounded more like a line from a self-help book for the grieving.

He entered his office just as his phone rang. It was Freddy.

"Called to offer condolences with Wolfe making a grand entrance to the greenroom in the sky."

"Very poetic."

Freddy reminded Brinks that he was available if any other problematic situations needed his help.

The second call came in right after Freddy said goodbye. It was from Dianne Silva. She owned WaddaFX, a special effects studio. Silva was one of the people who had a very special arrangement with him. She and two other people were part of his subterfuge to hide the money he'd skimmed from Glowball. He had approached them to cook their books so he could cook his. The invoices they billed Glowball were more than what they actually received. The difference went to Brinks minus a 10 percent commission for their efforts.

"Pity about Wolfie."

"Pity, yeah." He waited for her to say more. She didn't. "You have something on your mind."

"Depends."

"On what?"

"A promotion. Yours. Someone has to carry on. Means a bigger piece for me if you continue our arrangement. I'm thinking twenty percent now."

She was pulling out the blackmail gun, thinking she could drop a dime on him.

"Just saying." Silva ended her call

He stared at his dead phone. In Los Angeles, everyone was out for themselves. Everyone wanted something. Just like him.

After his chat with Brenner, he saw he had to think things over—different things—more clearly. So much was on the line. Brinks pushed himself away from his desk and went to his picture window, staring into the distant Santa Ana Mountains. The LA haze had lifted, and he could clearly see their ragged shapes.

What wasn't clear was what Brenner said about the forgotten contracts. What if there was wording that could jam him up? Wording which could lead to more scrutiny. Wording that led people to expose his sleight of hand antics. Scrutiny was not what he needed.

If getting Wolfe out of the picture was Phase 1, then Phase 2 had just begun. The Chinese accountants added a new threat on top of the nameless contracts Brenner had mentioned. *Paper ghosts* he called them. The accountants would inspect Glowball's books. He had to make sure that the six million dollars he had siphoned off over the past several years was buried deeper that the remains of the *Titanic*.

CHAPTER 31

PINK, 1939

Pink loved his backyard garden. The summer had been good to his vegetables. His tomato crop would be plentiful; the cucumbers were getting ready to pick along with yellow squash and zucchinis. The gophers had had a field day with the carrots and onions, but his handyman found the entrances to their tunneled homes and flooded them out with a water hose.

"Hey, Unc," a woman called from the back door of his house, "some guy on the telephone."

Pink turned from his garden. "Say who he is?"

"Nope."

Pink dropped the small garden hoe he was using to rake the weeds around his string bean plants. "Be right in."

He liked having his half-sister around. She came by every week from Freeville, where she lived with his second wife's parents. Susan liked coming by and hearing his back-in-the-day stories about making movies to take a break from caring for them. She was twenty now, had a job at Hathaway's General Store and was seeing this young man, David Burke. He didn't care for Burke. He sold Nash automobiles in Binghamton, and in Pink's opinion, the guy seemed pushy and slick. He knew guys like that when he ran DimaDozen and didn't like them then and didn't like them now.

Pink picked up the telephone. He was wary of having a telephone in his home, afraid that the switchboard operators could listen in to his private conversations. He wasn't the celebrity of the 1920s, but he had intimate conversations with a few women he saw from time to time. Marriage and the woman of his dreams hadn't arrived at his house on College Avenue, but he was just fine with his life.

"This is Maxwell," Pink said.

"How formal," the voice on the other end of the line responded. "Mazer?"

"The one and only. I'm honored you remembered."

Pink was at a loss. He hadn't spoken to Theo Mazer in close to a decade.

"How's the cows and chickens?" Mazer poked.

"Making milk and laying eggs in that order."

"At least some things don't change."

"So to what do I owe the pleasure?" Pink asked, a bit of suspicion laced into his words.

"Just catching up with an old friend."

Pink's gut feeling about Mazer's real reason for calling was confirmed. Old friends they were not.

"You make millions yet," Pink asked. "I would love to have me and my boys cash out. By the way, how are the boys?"

"Needles is shacked up with Roy Baker."

"The Singing Cowboy Baker?"

"Ain't that a pisser? The heartthrob of millions of women is a *faygala*."

"And Crank?"

Mazer hesitated. "Went with Selznick. You seen that *Gone with the Wind* thing? He was part of that. Came up with some new contraption for overhead shots. Used a crane, I heard."

"Good for him."

"Yeah, but that movie wasn't good for the *shvatsas*. Makes like slavery was a good thing. Not a movie that a kike like me likes to see. I ain't big on the coloreds, but my people know slavery and worse. The South is still fighting that *fakakta* war."

"So about those millions?" Pink repeated.

"You can use those contracts for wallpaper. My last three pictures were as popular as a quiff with leprosy."

"So…"

"Outta business. At least for now."

"Someone bought you out?"

"Dublin Pictures. 1939 has not been a good year...yet."

Mazer stressed the word *yet*.

"Dublin Pictures," Pink said.

"Jameson brothers bought it. Like the Mick whiskey."

"Never heard of them."

"No one had. But they liked the idea of getting into the glitter business. Probably needed to hide their whore and dope money when prohibition ended. What a couple of schmucks, but they paid, so what can I say?"

"And they know about our agreement?"

"Sure. But then some other outfit took 'em over during those gangland wars."

Pink said *oh* and shrugged. He never had much faith in the agreement, so this news didn't bother him. His boys were doing fine. And so was he.

"So I have an idea," Mazer started after giving Pink his update.

"I figured."

"This new thing that's coming." He paused for emphasis. "Television. See, you have this tube contraption in a box in your home. What tube I don't know just yet. You get some kinda transmission, which is sent out like radio—only moving pictures show up on the tube. There's a station that broadcasts this from the General Electric company in Schenectady. They call it WGY Television. That's the station name."

"Interesting."

"I bet my last dollar that every house in America will have one. Movies and newsreels. Maybe other stuff. Who knows? The movie theater business will get crushed."

"Hmm."

"It's a ground-floor opportunity. We could put together our own station."

"Sounds interesting," Pink said again but not able to wrap his head around this television thing beaming moving pictures into a tube.

"I'd do everything. You would be a silent investor. Sit back and rake in the dough."

Pink raised his eyebrows. It sounded like another harebrained scheme from the king of schemers.

"Let me think about it."

"Not too long," Mazer urged.

"I'll let you know." Pink took in a breath. "Thanks for calling. Say hello to the boys if you see them."

"You bet, kiddo. Remember, I was the first one who told you about it."

Pink hung up the phone and shook his head. He would not think about it. Television. Moving pictures in a box. One in everyone's living room. Crazy talk.

Instead of going back to the garden, he went up to the attic. He wandered over to where he had kept the Mazer contracts. He had them all for safekeeping. Maybe he would send them to his boys as souvenirs. They could wallpaper them if they wanted.

CHAPTER 32

SWINDLE

Brinks mulled over how Brandy had put Wolfe's death into a context she could understand. Her simple words echoed in his head: "*The circle of life ends in death.*" It was like a clichéd line from a Tony Robbins seminar. He sat at his desk when an inspired scheme began to form. Brandy had unintentionally planted its seeds. What was Brandy's second insight? "*The past is present.*" It sparked an idea.

"God bless you, Brandy," he said under his breath. She had kick-started a new plan, more like a crafty ploy. It was a different ruse to show how Glowball had lost money, money that had mysteriously found its way into his pocket without digital or paper breadcrumbs exposing him. He could kiss her. Out of the mouths of babes. *The past is present.*

Sarah's Shadow Light. It was a movie that Glowball made two years ago. It was supposed to be an art house flick, one of Brenner's attempts to show how deep he was. It was meant to be thought pro-voking. Lots of clever, moody dialogue. Set in Paris. Shot in black and white. The director was Czech and was acclaimed in Europe. He might have been the indie Prince of Prague when it came to making films, but the movie he made for Brenner was the laughingstock of every major critic in the States. Bergman and Truffaut on nitrous oxide was the way one reviewer described it. Ticket sales were as brisk as a three-legged tortoise running a 10K.

Then there was *RoachMan.* A not so subtle rip-off of *The Fly* meets Franz Kafka's *The Metamorphosis.* A pissed-off grad student living in a slumlord shit hole gets zapped in the physics lab by some mysterious beam as a cockroach crosses through it. Viola, *RoachMan*. When he turns into this eight foot tall, creepy-crawly thing, he has all the disgusting attributes of a roach. The *RoachMan* storyline was about killing off all of New York's slum lords. It wasn't silly enough to be campy or thrilling enough to bite your nails. It stink-bombed at the box office like rancid road kill.

He could easily pad both movies' losses and accompanying expenses to hide his siphoning, making them appear like they were as out of control as a bipolar yeti. If the Chinese were going to look at the bottom line, then why not have *Sarah's Shadow Light* and *RoachMan* be the patsy along with Wolfe, who had, in theory, overseen the finances of these flops?

The accountants would see that Glowball was being forthright with them. No one in the movie biz made box office hits with every release. These would simply be Glowball's two major clunkers. But at the end of the day, it was the almighty bottom line that investors cared about and Glowball would still look like solid company for backers.

Brinks tried to poke holes in his new swindle. He settled back in his chair and worked some numbers through his spreadsheet. An hour later, he felt smug. This could work. Fix the past, and the past becomes the present.

His momentary self-satisfaction ended as his thoughts returned to Brenner's remark about old agreements. Paper ghosts. What he couldn't control was what had happened before he arrived at Glowball. What went on before. The past could be present but in a bad way.

Brenner said nothing had surfaced in all the years he had been at Glowball. That was good news. But it would haunt him if he pretended that there was nothing to be concerned about and did nothing. He decided to go ghost hunting to make sure.

He picked up the phone, and Brandy answered. "Yes, Mr. Brinks."

"I'll be staying late tonight, Brandy."

"Is there anything I can do?"

"Actually, you can. Call Pitkin in legal tomorrow. Tell him I need our stock transfer records."

"Sure."

The stock transfer records would have the names of every company and deal Glowball held. "I need one more favor."

"Yes."

"I have to check out old files that Glowball might have kept. Probably stored away somewhere, not on anyone's computer."

"Oh yeah. Paper days. Can you believe that?"

"Yes, when dinosaurs roamed," he said, trying to be lighthearted.

Brandy sniffled. "You know dinosaurs died off. Like poor Mr. Wolfe."

Jesus, Brinks thought. He hoped that would just be a passing phase for her.

"Yes, the cycle of life again even touched those old creatures," he said, sounding like a philosophy teacher.

"So true." Brandy sniffled.

He waited as she blew her nose then asked, "Where do we keep old files?"

"They would be in storage over in the old Clagett building. That's the one next to Studio B in the back lot where they store damaged props."

"Oh right, that building," Brinks said as if he knew that all along. "Remind me how I would get in there."

"I'll call Mac over in Security, and he'll golf-cart you over," Brandy answered brightly like a student giving the right answer to her professor.

"Thanks."

"Sounds like it'll be a fun night for you."

"Fun like acid reflux."

"My grandmother has that."

"Which is not fun," he said.

"I guess."

"You have a good night. Try not to think about what happened with Mr. Wolfe...if you can."

Brandy said she would try and said "Thank you" before hanging up the phone. The next challenge would be where the hell to start looking. He would burrow into the archived files and wondered how far back he needed to go. An uncomfortable thought skimmed across his mind. What in the off chance he found something in an agreement that might cause trouble for him? He shook the thought away and waited for Mac to show up.

CHAPTER 33

FINDING A FOUR-BREASTED WOMAN

I was steps away from my car when I heard Zena's trailer door open.

"Hey, fuck face," she yelled.

I turned.

"At least you know your name."

"Go to hell."

My bedroom encounter with Zena wasn't part of writing a great story for Stan's plan, but as the bumper sticker says, "Shit happens." Life is full of lefts when you should go right. I did that a lot. I had a wandering dick, Lilly would say if she ever knew about my sexploits.

"I want to tell you something." She jerked her thumb toward the open trailer door.

I returned, and we sat on the edge of her sofa. I tried to gauge her mood and what kind of new IEDs were circulating inside her head.

"Sorry," she said.

I looked at her, and she took my hand and kissed my fingertips.

"Forget my relationship bullshit questions. I had no right to bring your friend into the picture. I guess I'm just not good with certain people situations."

"Booze and instant intimacy are not best for next day assurances of devotion."

"How about some makeup sex to test your devotion?" she suggested.

"Maybe not a great idea."

"Not a bad one, though."

"Sorry if I screwed that up for you. Sleeping over. What you thought it meant."

She winked at me in an effort to diminish the single-mindedness of her previous discussions about *us*.

"This was the kind of screwup I like. Look, if John is off the table, let's have you meet some of the other folks that work here who you haven't talked to. My way of apologizing."

"Okay."

"See if they are willing to let you into their heads. We can start with Louie and Big Eddy."

That could be a possibility. Two sides of a story. The people of the midway. Focus on Zena. Flavor it with Dolly the sword swallower, Duffy who paints with his feet. Mention the lady with the fading tats who was trying to figure out a different career angle since body inking was in vogue. Then tip to the flip side. Their bosses. What they saw as the future of the small time-traveling circus. Whom they hired and why. How they survived against the bigger circuses and cable TV that kept people at home glued to unreality shows.

We stepped out of her trailer and squinted into a bright midday sun. The circus and midway were already coming alive for the day.

"Let's go to the cook shack," Zena said. "That's where the roustabouts hang. The G brothers are usually there, ensuring they don't lose their body-to-fat ratio."

I could smell coffee and deep fry grease linger in the breeze as we approached the tent. The tables were plywood on sawhorses, and the benches looked like castaway church pews. There were a few people sitting at the long tables inside the tent, swatting away summer flies as they drank coffee from heavy mugs. People who stood outside smoking cigarettes watched as Zena and I got closer. I noticed two men quickly walk away as I approached.

"You're not a known quantity," Zena explained.

She led me up to the kitchen tent. I followed her in, and all eyes were on me. If she and Holey John were the oddities at Maxie's Supper Club, the roles were now reversed, me standing out like a two-headed baboon.

Zena spotted the Brothers sitting with a man in a white shirt and skinny black tie shifting through a stack of receipts, punching buttons on an oversized calculator and scribbling numbers into a ledger. The man with the tie had bug eyes and chewed gum like a cow chewing cud, his looks not giving a convincing portrait of an accountant.

"Hi, Louie," Zena said. "Eddy."

The two men were in their sixties and wore more pounds than were healthy for them. They both had pork pie hats on, the kind that men wore in the 1940s. The hats were tipped back, so whatever breeze was blowing through the tent could cool off their foreheads, which were dappled with sweat. Louie had sagging jowls that framed a mouth with a cigar stuck in it. Eddy had a baby face with pink skin from too much sun or high blood pressure. The weird thing was that both brothers were walleyed.

"Make sure your joint ain't empty cause you're here, not there," Louie said, looking annoyed. "Same with Holey John. You guys don't work, we don't get our cut. No cut, no money. This place don't run on love, you know."

"God forbid," Zena said, trying to tamper the sarcasm. Louie pointed at me, a pinky ring glistening on his hand, one that Tony Soprano would have loved, catching the morning light. "And what's with this scribbler coming over here? We already made with the introductions to you and Mr. Sparkles."

"He wanted to chat with you," she explained. "I told him a story without mentioning you guys would be flat."

This time, the sarcasm dripped from her voice like oil from a leaky engine.

"Really?" Louie said, oblivious to her tone. His voice like his face belonged to a younger person, the pitch too high, as if puberty had passed him by.

I jumped in, seeing an opening. "Mr. Blanker, my editor, must've spoken to you about how publicity is worth thousands."

"He said that?" Louie made his face crease like a prune.

"Sure. I write a great story, and you get good press. More people come to your circus. More money is spent. You win. I win."

155

"Depends on the story, don't it?" Eddy said. "Maybe we should take a peek."

Everyone wants to be an editor. I didn't say anything and just smiled.

"Maybe we can find some time, and you fellas can tell me how you got started here."

"Sure," they both said with sloppy grins.

"So where is Holey Moley today?" Louie asked. "He's been disappearing a lot more than usual. He wasn't on last night. That's two days. He skip town? If not, he's in a shit load of trouble."

"You know he gets his spells," Zena said, making up an excuse to hide her concern.

"Yeah, but we don't have a health plan to cover that," Louie explained.

"You don't have a health plan at all," Zena shot back.

"You and pin man can always find a job somewhere else," Eddy said, his threat coming out squeaky so that any menace was lost.

Zena didn't respond.

The man with the skinny tie cleared his throat. "Mr. John is in the hole."

"That right?" Louie asked.

"Owes us about six hundred bucks in back rent aside from the vig."

Louie's face got even redder, this time from anger and not the summer heat. He opened his left hand then punched it hard with his right hand, a fist the size of a small cannonball. "He better not be playing me for a chump. Make sure he knows he's going to be in a world of hurt if he don't fork up."

"Of course," Zena said and pulled me by the sleeve, walking out of the tent.

"Louie means what he says. I've seen a few of our folks after he had a talk with them. Faces looked like hamburger meat."

"Lovely people," I said. "So what's the deal here with you and Holey John?"

She walked me toward the midway. "We rent space and give the brothers a cut. The vig."

The arrangement sounded like Mafia rules.

"I'll introduce you to a few people and tell them what you're doing. Some may talk to you, but don't get your hopes up. Then you're on your own."

"What are you going to do?"

"I need to find John," she said. "The brothers said he missed his act last night. Not a good thing for him. I'll check his trailer."

"You worried?"

"Always."

Zena introduced me to a few of the midway denizens and then left looking for Holey John. I was able to interview a few people I hadn't spoken with before. I hoped that Zena would be able to track down Holey John and hoped even more that I could break through his armor so we could talk again and give me a second chance.

I introduced myself to a woman who was tagged as Dolly Daggers: The Beautiful Blade Eater. Dolly Steele was the name she gave me. She was a sword swallower. Steele offered to demonstrate her art when I told her that I was writing about fascinating people on the midway. She liked that I said *fascinating*.

"A picture is worth more than a thousand words," Dolly said with a flourish. With that, she demonstrated her talents with a small crowd watching behind me. She bent her head back so that her mouth and throat were like a straight pipe. Slowly, she dropped a sword into her mouth and down her throat until all but the handle could be seen.

I watched her and was dazzled and scared shitless at the same time. The idea of eviscerated innards would do that to me every time.

The crowd clapped then melted away after her demonstration, with a few people depositing money in a box at the edge of her stage that read "Money for Blood Transfusions" with a smiley face next to it.

"That's quite a skill," I complimented her. "Unique."

"If everyone could do what I do, then I wouldn't have this gig," she said proudly.

I smiled a confirming smile.

"You must learn to overpower the gag reflex to swallow," she explained after removing the sword from her throat when we were alone. "So what did you think?" She referred to her performance. "Think you might put me in it?"

"Very good chance," I said, thinking about B-roll people to fill out my story.

She smiled hopefully.

"How about telling me how you decided to become a sword swallower?"

Dolly considered the question. "I like danger." She motioned me closer to talk. "And I have this oral thing," she said, bringing her voice down to a near whisper. "I love giving head."

This was a twist that piqued my interest, professionally speaking of course. A cock is not a sword, and a sword is not a cock...at least in my experience.

"Hmm," was all I could say.

"Peculiar, maybe? Or kinda strange?"

Crazy images flew around my head as to how her sideshow and bedroom skills merged. "There is good strange and interesting strange."

"What about *weird* strange?"

"There's that too. But I think you fit into the good and interesting."

"I can also swallow umbrellas, canes, and garden hoses. What people like the most is when I swallow neon lit tubes at night, making my neck glow in the dark."

"Maybe I can add that to my story."

Dolly looked at me with a sudden admiration in her eyes. "Maybe works. And maybe I can show what else I can swallow... later."

Smiling, I wondered if an unfulfilled outlet to alleviate horniness was the price you paid being in the always-on-the-road midway life.

Leaving, I said I'd be in touch and went past other performers. There was Roscoe the Fire Eater, who could stick a flaming stick into his mouth. I thought of Dolly and wondered if he had an oral thing going too. He also did this fire-breathing act, sipping flammable liquid and spewing it across his stage, producing great fireballs. I bet he was a big hit at the campfire when s'mores time came around.

I talked to a snake charmer who would wrap snakes of all sizes around her neck. Basically boring unless you are a reptile enthusiast. Then there was Harry the Contortionist, who could turn himself into a human pretzel. Maybe thrilling for people who loved yoga classes.

Tillie the Tattooed Lady whistled at me as I walked by her space. No one seemed interested in looking at her, and her tip jar was just about empty. She was at least sixty, overweight, and covered with tattoos that had seen better days. Most of them were faded and lacked color, an inky water-downed blue the predominant shade.

"So you the guy that Zena has been chatting up."

"That's me," I answered. *Ah, Zena, my midway promotional pimp.*

"An article you're writing about us, right?"

"Yup."

"Look at that young guy by the ring toss game with his girlie," she directed.

I turned and saw the man wearing a wife beater T-shirt.

"You see his tats?"

I studied his arms and neck, where colorful designs of snakes, foliage, and images of Jesus next to half-naked women were inked into his skin like a Kandinsky meets a Dali collage.

"Twenty years ago, I was unique. The only people that had tats were service men that got drunk and were tatted on a dare. Now half the youngsters get them. Guys. Chicks. Grandmas even." She sighed. "I need to find some other gig."

"Any ideas?"

"I could light my farts while I eat worms. Or how about sucking a condom up my nose then cough it out through my mouth?"

"Honestly?"

"Yeah."

"Disgusting comes to mind."

She smiled. "Disgusting works real good here."

"Try it out for a couple of days. Your audience will let you know if they like it."

"Like a focus group."

"Exactly," I said. "Good luck."

I went past Zena's booth to see if she had tracked down Holey John. She had a customer who had tears running down his cheeks. She mouthed "No, John" and then gave me a "Do not disturb" look, so I walked by, even more worried about her worrying about her friend

My cell phone vibrated in my pocket, and I took it out. It was a text message from Stan.

"You fine the flour-breasted woman nyet?" the message poked.

"Still looking," I texted back, seeing his texting skills lacking.

"Call miff," Stan texted back. "Time for an upflate."

CHAPTER 34

DWARF STANDARDS

I called Stan back.

"There was a time if you were called all thumbs meant you were clumsy," Stan started. "Now you see all this people texting their asses off with their thumbs jumping over their keypads like coked out grasshoppers." He took a breath. "How's it going?"

I gave him a rundown on the people I had talked to so far.

"This Holey John guy. Hundreds of pins, plugs and piercings," said Stan. "Gotta be a heck of a story right there."

"Didn't like my probing questions."

"So he's a no? That sucks."

"My hope is that if Zena nudges him to talk…"

"And Zena is what to him?"

"A very good friend." I told Stan about her fortune-telling shtick that was spooky because she seemed to see right through people. The fact that she was a dwarf but looked like a knockout hottie just miniaturized and intrigued him. I ended with Zena being baby-dumped like in my New Yorker story. That really caught his attention.

"Some fucked-up people out there." He paused a second. "Look, the Zena angle is cool. But the story needs a Yang to her Yin. The Holey John guy is the Yang. You need to get him back on board. Deep-dive into his mind. You're close to actually writing something good."

This was the closest thing to a Stan compliment, although his firm instruction to get Holey John back in play made the compliment seem irrelevant. Holey John, as far as I was concerned, had his own mental zip code that didn't include me, and if silence was golden, the dude was Fort Knox.

"I might have some leverage," I said, not knowing what it was.

"Great." And Stan clicked off.

Ten seconds later, my cell buzzed.

"So?" Thelma said when I pressed Answer. "Your phone is dead or maybe your fingers are broken?"

"It's not Monday," I answered.

"So there's a rule about me not calling on other days?" Selma pronounced her accusation today, sounding like Fran Drescher with a country-and-western twang.

I guessed midweek guilt from my mother was now on the table.

"Of course not," I answered, making my reply sound as honest as possible. My relationship with Selma was complicated. I assumed most children could say that about their folks; it's just a matter of degree.

"How's it going?" she asked. This could be a very open-ended question for Selma. I chose a simple answer.

"Good. I'm talking to some very interesting people."

"Sideshow people not like us, right?"

I wasn't about to argue her 'not like us' comment. "Right."

"Well, it's a living, if that's what you want to call it."

"They do."

"I bet they have a fortune-teller?"

This question freaked me out, wondering if Selma had telephonic ESP.

"Zena," I said. "She is what you'd call a fortune-teller."

"Interesting name. Maybe she can tell you when you will get a real job and find a nice lady even though you already have one."

I groaned.

"What?" Selma said as though she said nothing wrong.

"She's not that kind of fortune-teller. She reads people. Like you, sort of."

"Really? Like me? I'm flattered."

"Sort of like you," I added.

"She went to college to study this?"

"Yes," I said to confuse her.

She had no comeback.

"You can compare therapy modalities." I said this and heard a snort and continued, "Zena can tell a lot using applied psychology, deciphering facial micro expressions, and also a person's body language."

Selma remained silent. I threw all of this at her, repeating what I had found on my trusted source of information… *Wikipedia* along with my Zena notes for the article.

"You like her?" This was another Selma hand grenade that I needed to dodge.

"She's a very interesting story subject." This was a noncommittal response that avoided a yes-or-no answer.

"I have a surprise for you," Selma said, changing the topic. I heard her talk to someone nearby and thought it must be my dad. It wasn't.

"Who is this interesting Zena person?" Lilly asked. Selma must've had the speaker on. There was a bite to her question.

"Lilly," I replied, surprised, "what are you doing at my parents'?"

"Brunch and who the hell is Zena?" she grilled me again.

"Someone I'm interviewing for my story."

"Interviewing, huh," she repeated mockingly as if that was journalist code for screwing someone.

"She's a dwarf who tells fortunes," I quickly said. I felt ashamed using the dwarf card, thinking that would immediately dissuade her from thinking Zena would be an object of my desire.

"A pretty dwarf?"

I guessed that saying Zena was a dwarf didn't quash her reservations.

"She's okay if we are using dwarf standards." I avoided any adjective that fell into the *pretty* neighborhood.

"She's okay, huh?" Lilly adopted my mother's snort. Distance was supposed to make the heart grow fonder. In my case, it was making her distrustful.

"Something's going on, Fenn," she confronted. "I can sense it in your voice."

When I paused too long, she said, "Fenn?"

"What?"

"I bet even dwarves have vaginas. Especially okay ones by dwarf standards."

"They have to pee like the rest of us," I said, hoping humor would douse the flames of concern.

"Vaginas can function in other ways."

I figured she must've been taking Selma's conspiracy lessons.

"Come on, Lilly," I said as unbelievably as possible, hoping it would make her contention seem baseless.

"You better not be eating off the menu," she ordered.

"Come on," I protested again, pretty sure what menu she had in mind. I heard a rustling noise and the muffled sounds of discontent in the background.

"A dwarf you are liking now." Selma was back on the phone.

"Yes. For my story. And a man that pierces his flesh with hundreds of pins. And sword swallowers, a tattooed lady, snake charmers. I can't believe you guys," I said, trying to sound indignant.

No response.

"I need to go," I said, giving up.

"Of course you do," Selma said, and with that, the phone went dead.

I could see that the home front had become as frosty as a Nordic ice floe. Heading back to my motel, I decided to escape from a demanding world filled with relational expectations. Perhaps *Lethe* and a few hits on my vape would help. I also realized my double-teamed call with my city ladies meant I had to end my flesh-on-flesh encounters with Zena. All these ladies, including Zena, were slamming me with expectations I could not meet. It was becoming too thorny. *Keep it purely professional*, I reasoned. I started the engine, heading back to my motel, thinking that Stan's assignment to renovate my career felt like having a blind date with a gorilla.

CHAPTER 35

THE HOUSE

The first beams of sunrise trickled over his face. It felt warm, and Holey John slowly opened his eyes. He was confused at first not seeing the name written on the ceiling of his trailer. The name he'd seen just before he fell asleep, and the first thing he saw when he woke. Instead, he saw the orange morning sky breaking through the branches of the pine trees above him.

He sat up. The leering face of the devil rock greeted him in silence. He stared back unafraid. He believed that there was a devil. It inhabited people feeding their darkest sides. There was certainly a place called hell. It was right here on earth, some versions more hellish than others, some occupants even worse.

Holey John got up and stretched. He heard the sound of water falling and birds chirping as the new day started. His recent memory kicked in, and he remembered coming here, that douche bag Wally trying to run him over, finding that tree with the hollow, and the rounded rocks deposited inside like a hallowed hiding place that, for some reason, seemed all too familiar. He had missed yesterday's performance at the Brothers and they would give him shit. Maybe hurt him. He didn't care about the pain or his job. Now more than ever before, he felt there was something that could replace the hole in his soul.

"Fuck 'em," he said to himself. He would skip the midway again. It was the house pulling at him. He decided to go back there and talk to the old man.

It took him less than an hour. He stood across the street staring at it. The *For Sale* sign on the lawn gave him the same disquieting reaction he had felt the day before.

As he studied the house from the other side of the street, a feeling of sadness settled over him. Why did the sale of this house matter to him? He slowly walked to the front steps. He had to think. He sat down and spread his fingers over the painted wooden steps.

He heard a door open behind him. "You look out of sorts," said the same man he had talked to the day before. He came down the steps.

Holey John took a moment before answering. "I'll be...fine."

The man was thin as if youth had evaporated from his flesh. He wore suspenders to hold up a pair of trousers too big and loose for his spindly legs. The short-sleeved white shirt he wore had a few spots where food had landed. His socks didn't match, and one shoelace was untied.

He stiffly sat next to Holey John, putting a bony hand on his shoulder for support, his joints creaking in the effort.

"You got quite a sparkle there," the old man said as he surveyed Holey John's face.

"People say...that."

"Bet a lot do," he chuckled.

"You're gonna sell...this house, right?"

"Yup."

Holey John looked at the lawn, which needed some weeding.

"Bought this place not long after the owner died. Been here a while."

"You know the guy who...died?"

The old man rubbed the side of his face. "Pink was his name. Like the color. His nickname. Percy Maxwell was his real name."

"Maxwell," Holey John said, taken aback by the name for a reason he didn't understand.

"Yup. I met him a few times. He'd stay here most of the summer then leave for the winter after the leaves finished. He was a friend of my older brother. They worked together a long time ago. But my brother left Ithaca back in the twenties for the West Coast where I was born and raised. This guy Pink decided to stay. My brother and a few other guys—must've been friends and all—used to come back here for reunions. Talk about the good ole days and such. When I was old enough, my brother brought me here summers."

"Your brother alive?" Holey John asked.

"He's long gone. Died in a terrible fire with his friend. Santa Monica it was."

"Sorry."

The old man waved the unpleasant thought away.

Holey John wondered about his own family again, something he did for so many years. He tried to squeeze out any scrap of recall and always came up blank. No recollection ever surfaced about his mother and father or any siblings.

The old man went on. "When I would come here, there was something about this part of the country I really enjoyed. The fact you had actual seasons, not like out West."

"So you moved," Holey John concluded.

The old man nodded. "I got a nephew who lives in California. Got wife. His kids all grown up out and launched. Going to move in with them, them having extra room now. He's been insisting on that for a while now. Winters get harder to deal with here. They have a nice room for me. I finally gave in." The old man studied Holey John for a moment. "What's your name, anyway?"

"They call me Holey John."

The old man chuckled. "Kind of a play on words, huh?"

"Gets peoples' attention…which helps if you are…a carny."

"Carny, huh. In that circus outside of town?"

He nodded slightly. "And your name is…?"

"Ralph Gilmore." Ralph extended his hand, and they shook. Holey John felt the old man's bony fingers wrapping around his.

"My older brother Delmar, the one who died, had a nickname like you got. Not the same one, course. They called him Crank."

"Crank?"

"He was a cameraman for that man, Pink. Made movies in Ithaca before the talkies came along. They used to shoot them around here before the studios moved out to California. Better weather. Can't make too many movies when your nuts turn blue from the cold."

Holey John stared straight ahead as a distant memory surfaced for a moment and then sank below the surface of his mind.

"Lots of the old stars came here. Crank told me the stories. The town went a bit crazy with them for a while, not being used to these actors' lifestyles. Women smoking and drinking like men. Fast cars. A lot of people shacking up. But I think the townies actually liked them despite the hullabaloo. Gave a jolt to a sleepy rural town. And a lot of the locals got bit parts in the movies or had jobs helping out."

"So you're really thinking…about moving?" Holey John asked to reaffirm the old man's intentions.

"Back to where I started."

"Like…bookends."

"Funny about that, the way life works sometimes. You finish where you start."

"You remember what happened to…the man…who owned this place?"

Ralph scratched his head. "He just dropped dead one day. Out walking his dog. Had a place in Key West he'd go to in the winter. If you have to go, that would be a good way. No cancer dragging things on. Just boom—drop dead, lights out, no suffering."

"When was that? When he…passed away?"

The old man scratched his head again, trying to remember. "Must have been around 1980 because I bought the house in '82. Me and the wife had been saving up to buy something out this way. I remember picking up Alma—that would be my wife—and carrying her into the foyer, like it was our wedding night. She passed on last year."

"Sorry…to hear that."

Holey John waited as he put a question together. "How'd you know this place…was up for…sale?"

"Funny thing the way things work. I read Pink passed. Some California paper mentioned it cause he was in the movies. I called some real estate folks back here. Said the town was putting it up for sale 'cause of back taxes not paid for a while. I wasn't sure I'd have the chance. I knew Pink had a younger sister who had a husband and a kid. A nice boy."

Holey John frowned. "He had some…family?"

"He did. That came up when I called about the house. The lawyers had to file some sort of papers to make sure the deed was free and clear. I guess that after some time it was obvious that none of Pink's relatives were ever going to come round to claim the property, and the city wanted to collect back taxes. Seems Pink had no will neither."

"You have any idea what happened…to his family?"

"Nope. I did meet Pink's nephew, his sister's boy, when I visited. But her husband. Not a nice man, if you ask me. Tough on the kid. Yelling at him all the time. His mom trying to protect him. Pink tried to shield the boy. He'd take him out and do things when the parents were at each other's throats. Then the kid stopped coming."

The old man studied Holey John's face through his rheumy eyes and pointed a shaky finger at him. He saw him finger his scar. He opened his mouth with a question but then pulled the thought back.

"You remember the…parents' names?"

Ralph stroked his stubbly chin. "Well, Pink was a nickname. The sister married so she wouldn't be a Maxwell, assuming she used her married name and I don't know what that was." Ralph shrugged a sorry shrug. "This old brain ain't what it used to be."

Holey John's stomach fluttered as he talked to Ralph about the man called Pink, this house, and the street he kept returning to. It had to be for some reason.

"Me and Alma moved in and the place was like he left it. Like he thought he'd be coming back. Furniture, kitchen stuff. Left behind other things. Mostly stuff they must've used when they made them movies. Props. Costumes. Stored those things up in the attic."

"That'd be fun…to see."

"I found something in the attic when I repaired some old loose flooring when me and Alma first moved in. There was one loose board that looked like a kind of a hidey hole. I felt around and I found a box. Just some old papers stuffed in it. Alma said I should just leave it be."

"Under…a floorboard."

"Yup. And someone painted a giant chess board on those planks to boot."

"Chessboard," Holey John said hollowly, seeing a washed out image emerge from some recess in his head. He was silent for a moment. "You think I could take a look…around…see that attic some time?"

"Be happy to."

Holey John's mood changed as a new thought came to him. He stared straight ahead. All the jewelry on his face couldn't hide a sad expression. "They have a funeral…for this Pink guy?"

"Oh, sure. Nice turnout from what I heard. He was well-liked and kinda famous."

"He buried around…here?"

The old man shook his head and just about giggled. "Nah. Had himself cremated. They sent his ashes back here from Florida. The funeral director down there said Pink had made prior arrangements. Maybe he had an idea that he wasn't long for this life. Had them all paid for and all. Said that his friends, what may have been still alive, take some of his ashes, pack 'em inside a fireworks. Shoot them over Seward Park. He had his movie studio there I believe. What was left he wanted sprinkled over Devil Falls, at least that was what he used to call that spot. I guess that place had some sentimental meaning for him."

"Devil Falls," Holey John said, catching his breath.

"You know the place?"

A chill had passed over him, and he nodded.

The more he talked to the old man, the more perplexed he felt. He had just spent the night in the state park staked out in front of a water fall with an outcrop of rocks that looked like a devil. Then there was the tree hollow with the stones. And now this house with a chessboard in an attic that seemed strangely familiar.

Holey John changed the subject. "How long has your house been up…for sale?"

"Not long. Maybe a few weeks. A couple of nibbles but no real offers." The old man waited a beat then asked, "You interested in buying this place?"

The idea excited him, but he wasn't sure why. "I think I might." He considered it for a moment. "Kinda crazy...me living here...the pin cushion man."

Ralph raised his eyebrows. "Betcha them pins come out."

"They can."

"Timing is everything they say."

"Could you give me a...tour?"

"Past my nap time today, but I can give you one tomorrow."

"Okay."

"I got me a nice real estate agent. You wanna talk to her?"

"Sure."

"She can bring over papers to look over if want to make an offer after you see the place of course."

"That agent lady of yours...can find me on the midway...for the next few days."

"I'll tell her to come by. Tell her to look for Mr. Sparkles."

Holey John grinned and got up from the step, looking at the house. The old man started to get up and then reached for Holey John's hand to help him stand. Ralph went over to the *For Sale* sign. There was a plastic rack that held sheets of flyers. He took one and handed it Holey John. The latter looked the sheet of paper over.

"It's got the particulars about this place."

The old man shuffled up the stairs. When he reached the front door, he gave Holey John a salute. Holey John nodded then turned and looked down the street. The runt who had been tucked into the shadows the day before was nowhere in sight.

CHAPTER 36

BREADCRUMBS

Marvin Brinks heard his footsteps echo against the cement walls of the old building. The guy from security had driven him over to the old Clagett building and let him in.

"Kinda late to be working," Mac said, his false teeth clattering as he spoke.

"Hollywood never sleeps." Brinks offered.

"I'll turn the lights on for ya," Mac said, using his flashlight to find a bank of switches. "Brandy said you'd be lookin' through some old files. The oldest ones we got are on the shelves, way down there. Got 'em organized by year. Dates written on the side."

"You seem to know your way around here."

"Yup," he agreed, giving Brinks a wide grin. "One of my jobs. Puttin' boxes away here. Not many these days since everything is on them computers. I guess the trees don't mind."

"Gotta point there."

"There's a big desk and chair down the aisle if you wanna sort through them boxes," Mac added.

"Thanks."

"I'll leave you my flashlight. Use it to smack the rats if they come out to see who's nosin' around."

"Rats?" Brinks asked uneasily.

"They come out at night. They like to eat the paper. Real literary vermin they are," he explained and chuckled.

"Then I guess I'm all set," Brinks said, anxious to start.

"Just call me and I'll bring you back to your office when you're done," Mac offered, and with that, he headed out the door, and Brinks heard the golf cart put-put away from the building.

He walked to the desk and looked around. He wasn't sure what the best way to find what he wanted was, but then again, he wasn't exactly sure what it was that he needed to find. Paper ghosts were all he could think of. He needed his mind to be sharp, and it could be a long night. He knew one thing for certain as he focused on the job at hand; just as Brenner had said, every studio in Hollywood since the 1920s and maybe even earlier had a history of buying other studios. There were mergers and acquisitions, buyouts, bankruptcies, and more name changes than immigrants going through Ellis Island.

He knew Glowball Productions wasn't always Glowball. When he first started his boss told him that Glowball acquired Arlington Road Productions. Before that, Arlington had been Cranes Neck Studios. So he got up and walked down the aisle, searching for Arlington Road cartons. An occasional squeak made him freeze, fearing a rat would see him as a better meal choice than a sheet of moldy paper.

He then found a carton labeled Arlington Road. He brought it back to the desk and removed bundles of letters, agreements from suppliers, and a few contracts with B-movie actors who had their fifteen minutes of fame then disappeared from the footlight parade. He found a publicity photo in a file marked PR. A man with dark rings around his eyes dressed in a white suit and collarless shirt stood with a man and woman on each side of him. On the back of the photo was a date—1971.

Someone had written, "Mr. Venzenta, Stephen Perry and Sabrina Lansing at the Monarch Hotel." Venzenta had meaty hands wrapped around Perry and Lansing's shoulders. He smiled crookedly. Perry's lips were straight as a razor blade. Lansing looked stoned. A news clipping attached to the photo stated that Venzenta, the new head of Cranes Neck, had acquired their studio.

Another clipping caught his attention. It was a news story about Perry and Lansing. The pair had made one movie that was a hit. Perry, a trust fund kid, brought his camera to Woodstock. He and

Lansing, who liked to imbibe in mind-altering drugs, put together a documentary with great footage of the bands that played there, the hippies stoned on an alphabet of drugs and nude bodies sliding down muddy hills. The story also said that they were both arrested for dealing the drugs they liked to take. What struck Brinks as wildly weird was that Venzenta was the one who bailed them out and paid their legal fees. In exchange, he acquired Arlington. Brinks found one document he put aside. It was the P&S for the sale of Arlington to Venzenta along with revoking the existing power of attorney to create a new one.

Brinks closed up the carton and returned it to the shelf. He walked down the aisle and found the Cranes Neck box. Inside were a few files listing assets, most of them acquired from Arlington. One thing jumped out. An affidavit issued by a Los Angeles judge indicting Venzenta for money laundering, prostitution, and mail fraud. The judgment stated that Venzenta used Cranes Neck to launder the money gained from his illegal operations. Maybe why Cranes Neck never produced a single movie.

Brinks was working backward like a man inside a time machine. He went back to the power of attorney paperwork and discovered a letter that referenced a corporate filing for Lansing Perry Productions. The letterhead showed that the law firm of Lightman Capital had handled the acquisition paperwork. The firm's letterhead had a Los Angeles address. He'd pay them a visit and see what other paperwork they might have just to make sure if Lightman's firm had other agreements. It seemed this exercise was a wild goose chase, but CYA was in order.

A squeaking noise behind his head startled Brinks. He turned and saw a pair of tiny red eyes staring down at him from a top shelf. The rats were up and hungry.

It was a sign for him to go. He had one lead to follow. He did a quick search on his computer and looked up Lightman Capital. He then took all the files that contained references to Arlington and Cranes Neck, specifically the one that had Lightman handling Cranes Neck and Arlington Road business. Just in case his Hong Kong visitors were steered to these cartons to practice their own due diligence.

Brinks then called Mac and asked him to pick him up.

He heard the golf cart rumble a few minutes later and stop by the desk.

"You find what you needed?" Mac asked.

"Not really."

"Grab a seat and I'll give you a ride back."

CHAPTER 37

JUST EYES

Back in my motel, I watched dusk settle over the hills of Ithaca, casting a shroud of crimson over their peaks. I could tell that housekeeping had recently been in the room. The bed was made with starched, clean sheets, a new set of shampoo and conditioner bottles on the sink next to the tiny bars of soap that I could hardly hold in my hand.

I lay down and took a hit from my vape. Feeling the buzz, I opened my laptop thinking about how much had happened in the last two days. Hooking up with Zena, the pressure from Stan wondering about my interviews, trying to get through to Holey John, Lilly pretty much guessing I wasn't leading the chaste life out on the road, and of course, Selma adding new weekday guilt calls as if her previous weekend assessments of my life weren't enough.

After firing up my computer, I connected the USB cord from my phone into my laptop and downloaded my notes and interviews. The software magically created Word files from my uploads. I read over what I had written and closed my eyes. I could vividly recall everything at the G Brothers, including the smells, the colors, the crowds—the atmosphere of the midway's otherworldly world. When you write a story, it has to be like a good dish. The meat is the people. The background is the spices and flavorings. As I thought about my culinary analogy, I heard Zena's accusing words that she was my meal ticket and I shit out stories.

My mind was so absorbed in what I was doing—no doubt the weed helping—that I didn't hear the knocking at first. The knocking grew louder, and I went to the door.

"Who's there?" I peered through the peephole, only seeing the wall across the hall.

"Me, jackass!"

I opened the door, and Zena barged through. I saw she was agitated since being called a jackass was not an endearing form of a greeting even though I'd been called worse by her.

"John is missing," she said. "He didn't show up all day. Last night either."

"How did you get here?"

"Dolly drove me after the midway closed. She said you like her swallowing act and you bonded. You are quite the charmer," she snorted.

"It's what I do," was the only thing I could say.

"I went to his trailer. Nothing."

"You don't have a key."

"Duh." She headed for the door. "I need you to come back with me. See if we can get in. He may be dead or something."

I turned off my laptop, found my car keys and wallet.

She took notice of the bed. Her agitated mood disappeared for a second. "We should try that sometime. Like fucking on a football field with sheets."

When I parked my car, Zena and I walked over to Holey John's trailer. It was attached to an old Ford Ranger pickup truck. The trailer, a beat-up Sunline Sunray, looked like it had been on the road a while. From the outside, it was nothing special. No tourist stickers of places he had visited. No bumper stickers about whom he wanted elected or whether there was a baby on board. There was one sticker I did spot. An innocuous peace sign on the driver's side door.

I knocked on the trailer door and waited. No one answered. I knocked again, this time much harder. Nothing. I put my ear to the door as Zena looked at me with anticipation. I shook my head.

"Not here," I said.

"Damn it. It kills me when he goes off like this."

I turned the knob, and it didn't budge.

"I tried that, numb nuts."

"You try the credit card thing?"

You could slip a credit card into the crack between the door and door frame next to the lock and push the deadbolt back. It worked in the movies.

"Yeah."

I took a card out of my wallet and tried. "American Express. It has more advantages."

Zena punched my thigh. My card didn't work either. She punched me again.

"Now what, Einstein?"

I took out my cell phone.

"What are you doing?" she asked. "John is a troglodyte when it comes to anything that involves electronics. You can't call him. He doesn't have a cell phone."

"YouTube," I said. I tapped on my Internet browser icon and got onto YouTube. I keyed in *lock picking* and found what I was looking for.

"Look at this video." We watched the clip. It was a Memphis news station feature on home invasion.

The clip ended. "Lock bumping," Zena said. "Fucking A."

"Do you have any keys?" I asked. "House keys. Any kind."

"In my trailer. Old keys I kept for god knows what reason."

We drove to her trailer, and she came out a few minutes later, holding a baggie full of keys. She dropped them in my lap, and we headed back to Holey John's trailer.

I tried a few keys until one fit. I looked on the ground and spotted a rock the shape of a hardball. I picked it up and tapped the key several times. I heard something click and moved the key, turned it. The door opened.

"After you," I said.

She stepped into the trailer. I followed and found a switch by the door and flipped it up. An overhead light came on. We both stared at the walls and what few furnishings Holey John had inside his trailer.

"Jesus, Mary, and Joseph," Zena exclaimed, totally blindsided by what she saw.

I looked around, taking in what was beyond strange. "You mean you never—"

"He never invited me inside," she said, completing my question. "I can see why."

Zena saw what I was seeing. "This is some crazy shit. No wonder no invites."

I looked at the walls and moved close to them, running my hand over them. "He glued these. You can feel the edges."

What Zena and I gawked at were the cutout eyes from magazines that covered all the walls. Just eyes. Hundreds of them.

"Look at this," Zena said, pointing to a few brown paper shopping bags.

I came over and peered inside. They were filled with cutout eyes, just like what were pasted on the walls.

"Interesting interior design motif," I said. "Any idea what this is all about, you being a therapist?"

"Retired therapist." And she shook her head.

We wandered through his space, which took less than a minute since a trailer is, by its nature, fairly space challenged. I poked my head into the bathroom. No Holey John hiding there. The rest of his place was an open shell. A kitchenette, a few built-in cabinets, a small card table, a lawn chair.

I looked at his stove and refrigerator. "Zena."

"What?"

"His appliances have locks." I pointed at the stove. There was a bike lock wrapped around the oven door.

"Trust is in short supply around here," she explained. "Some people steal food, and whatever isn't nailed down. Mostly it's the transients that show up just while we're in a town."

His bed held my interest now. It was an army cot. Olive-green blanket. A pillow. The bed was made with hospital corners tucked tight. There was no clutter.

"The eyes thing must have a story."

"Not a good one, I imagine," she said.

Zena was silent, turning her head from one wall to another. She looked up, and her eyebrows furrowed. "What's that?"

I looked up at the ceiling. No eyes glued there, but a design had been painted. Precise strokes of black paint. It reminded me of something. Zena saw it in my face.

"Want to share your thoughts?"

"Calligraphy, maybe."

"Like letters?" she asked.

"I've seen this design before. When he grabbed Wally. On the top of his right hand."

She moved through the trailer, eyeing Holey John's place more closely. "No backpack. The one he always carries."

She walked to his bed and sat down. A moment later, she put her legs up on the bed and lay down, staring at the ceiling.

"So this is what he sees every night before he goes to sleep," she said reflectively.

"This man becomes more interesting the more I know about him, which isn't much. He's a riddle, wrapped in a mystery, inside an enigma."

She gave me a look. "Profound," she sniggered.

"I stole that one from Winston Churchill."

"I figured."

I took another look around. "So where would he go?"

"My guess is he was doing his walkabout thing and lost track of time. I just hope he didn't find trouble."

"Or trouble found him."

Zena swung her legs off the bed and dropped to the floor. As she smoothed the blanket on the bed and fluffed up the pillow, she spotted something sticking out from underneath the pillow and pulled it out.

"It's a photograph." She stared at it for a full minute and frowned before handing it to me.

I could tell it was old. The black-and-white image was a bit faded. A young Asian woman stood erect facing the camera. She wore a light, white sleeveless shirt. Behind her was a stand of bamboo. She had captivating eyes, and her straight, black hair was pulled back. The woman held a little child by the hand. She was smiling at the person who had taken the photo. I flipped the photo over.

"Okay now," I said.

"What?" Zena asked.

I handed her the photo, and she examined the back. Her eyes stayed on the back of the photo then moved to the ceiling and then back again to the photo.

"It's the same. The letters or whatever this is."

"A riddle, wrapped in a mystery, inside an enigma."

"Stop with the Churchill shit!" Zena snapped. She paced back and forth, her arms wrapped across her chest, as if she needed to keep herself together.

"You want to call the cops?"

She shook her head.

"So what do you want to do?"

"We wait and see and hope he comes back in one piece."

Zena took one more look around Holey John's trailer. She went back to his bed and slipped the photograph back under the pillow. As she picked up the pillow, she spotted something else and picked it up. She turned to me and held it on her palm.

I came over. There were two medals. A heart-shaped design with the bust of George Washington attached to a ribbon and a bronze star hanging from a ribbon.

"This one is a Purple Heart medal," I said. "You get one if you were wounded in combat. I think the other is a bronze star. I believe it's for bravery in combat."

She was silent as she took the medals from my hand and slipped them back under the pillow with the photograph.

"It's late," I said. "We can come back in the morning."

Zena bit her bottom lip, worry pressing hard on her face.

I saw her distress. "You can spend the night with me and take advantage of my gimongous Motel 8 bed."

She shook her head. "I don't think I'd be much company."

"I understand."

I looked around one last time and took out my cell phone. I selected the camera app and took shots of the writing on the ceiling, the wall of eyes, and went back to the photograph that Zena had slipped back under the pillow. I took a photo of the photo and then replaced it under the pillow.

We left the trailer just as we found it, in and out as stealthy as a cat burglar. If my editor fired me, I could try my hand as a second story B&E man. Of course, Selma would not see this as a brilliant career move. Naturally, it would be a deal killer for Lilly as well, which might be one way of getting out of having dinner with her folks.

CHAPTER 38

A MAZE OF CONTRACTUAL CACA

The secretary looked like a spitting image of Loretta Young. Brinks thought that the woman's hairstyle was straight out of the 1940s film *A Night to Remember*; an assortment of complicated bobs and pin curls. She sat at her desk, inhaling a lungful of cigarette smoke then blowing it out through a wide set of nostrils. Loretta Young meets Puff the Magic Dragon.

The office was small and located in a building that had seen better days. The secretary sat in the middle of the reception room. The chairs were a slightly worn, the magazines a bit dated, and the carpet needed cleaning. This was not an investment company that had made good investments.

He stood in front of the secretary and introduced himself.

"Hi. I called yesterday," he said. "Marvin Brinks from Glowball. A two o'clock appointment with Mr. Lightman."

The secretary picked up her phone and dialed an extension number and said his name. She then pointed to a door with a head shrug.

Brinks entered an office, and it looked as if a Kansas tornado had organized the room and its contents. Alfred Lightman stood in front of a file cabinet that had all of its drawers open. Files were scattered on the floor at the man's feet as he shuffled through one file after another.

"My apologies," Lightman said, lifting a manila folder off the floor. He gestured to a chair that had a stack of books on it, inviting Brinks to sit.

Lightman, like his office, looked wind tossed, his thinning hair pointing up in all directions, his bow tie shifted at an odd angle and his wrinkled shirt looked like it was afraid of ironing boards. He was in his fifties, a bit overweight with a beer belly pressing against the buttons of his dress shirt. Clearly, standing in front of a mirror in the morning to assess his looks was not a priority.

"Just put those anywhere," Lightman instructed.

Brinks sat and watched as Lightman found another chair with a briefcase on it, which he placed on the floor.

"Clearly I am organizationally challenged," Lightman said with an ironic smirk.

"I assume your secretary doesn't help."

"She's not allowed in here. The only filing she does is on her nails. She is not displeased since her only duties are answering the phone, sending e-mails, printing copies when I need them, keeping my appointment book up to date, and experimenting with hairstyles. Last week, she was all in with Elsa Lanchester. You know, the Bride of Frankenstein."

"In LA, having a likeness to some celebrity even dead ones seems to be a thing."

"So your call yesterday referenced a company in which a client of ours may have used our services."

"That's correct. I'm trying to locate former agreements that my company might have inherited. Mergers and acquisitions of other studios are common in the movie business."

"I see."

"I found a document that shows your firm handled a company called Cranes Neck Studios."

"A movie production company, I gather."

"Correct," Brinks confirmed.

"If we did, it's not one of my more recent clients. Could be one of my father's old customers. He had a lot of investors that thought studios were a good place to place a bet."

"Your father?"

"My dad was a hot ticket in his better years. I took over once he started to have conversations with the autographed photos on that wall, convinced they talked back."

Lightman then pointed to a wall that had over three dozen framed photographs hanging on it. Each was of a well-known actor or actress from the 1930s until the mid '70s.

"Alzheimer's," Lightman explained. "Dad was a real good schmoozer. He did well for his clients."

"And Cranes Neck could have been one of them?" Brinks asked.

"Perhaps. Is Cranes Neck still in business?"

"Actually they were bought by the company I work for. I know that Cranes Neck bought another company. Arlington Road."

"A lot of buying and selling, eh?"

"Big fish eat the little ones."

"Tell me what you've found so far," Lightman said, wanting to know more.

"We know that Cranes Neck was taken over by a Mr. Venzenta, and your firm was mentioned as handling a transfer of ownership from Arlington Road."

Lightman shook his head and offered a small smile. "My father got rid of a lot of paperwork when legal requirements of archiving them were over seven years."

Brinks wondered if this was the end of his wild goose chasing, which wouldn't be a bad thing since nothing problematic had surfaced.

"But some of his clients' records may still be filed away. When his Alzheimer progressed and his mind hit a fog bank, he stopped shredding old records."

"So you might have some."

Lightman nodded. "I'll check. How about you come back in an hour while I dig around? There's a deli that makes a great corned beef sandwich around the corner."

*****

Brinks found the deli and seated himself next to a wall that was covered with celebrity photographs. Unlike Lightman's father's collection, these people were still alive and kicking. He ordered the corned beef. It was tasty, and he washed it down with a Dr Peppers. An hour passed quickly. He paid the bill, left a nice tip, and headed back to Lightman's office.

When he entered, Lightman was sitting on the floor with a few files in between his legs. He looked up at Brinks with the right corner of his mouth twisted upward in an expression of confusion.

"I'm not sure how much help I can be," Lightman started.

"You find something?" Brinks asked.

"A maze of contractual *caca*."

"Meaning what?"

"You find one thing that leads to another that leads to something or someone else. It's worse than figuring out a genealogical tree of dead ancestors who were all in witness protection programs."

"But you found something."

"I did, but be patient. It's a bit confusing. First, I'm glad you gave me the big fish eating the little fish analogy."

"Why's that?"

Lightman had a file folder on his lap. He held it up to Brinks. FUBAR was written in large black capital letter on the cover.

"FUBAR?"

"It's an old army term my dad used to say. Fucked Up Beyond Any Recognition."

"That doesn't sound good."

Lightman opened the folder. "Let me guide you through this chronologically."

"Okay."

"We'll start with what you already found and work backwards."

Brinks sat down on the chair that he had occupied before.

"Okay, so Mr. Venzenta bought Lansing Perry productions to get his own production company started."

"Right. I found that paperwork last night," Brinks confirmed.

Lightman continued taking out a page and looking it over. "This is a purchase and sale agreement. By doing so, Cranes Neck also acquired all of Arlington Road baggage."

"Baggage?" Brinks asked.

"It's an agreement," Lightman said, pointing to another sheet of paper. "Remember what I said about finding one thing that leads to another."

Brinks kept quiet, waiting for him to continue.

"I went through the entire file and all the paperwork my father kept. What I found was more buying and selling."

"Beyond Cranes Neck and Arlington?" Brinks asked.

"Correct. It seems like each time any of these film companies acquired another company, they shared a common problem."

"Which is what?"

"Each new owner was obligated to honor the contractual provisions of the acquired company. This included any agreements made in the past."

"And Lansing Perry wound up with one of these provisions?"

Lightman nodded. "It's tricky. Most of these previous deals that were inherited didn't mean *bubkis* for the new owners."

"But you found something," Brinks said, sensing there was a deal that actually meant something.

"So as we go backwards, we can see handoffs. It turns out that my father arranged funding for a company called Dublin Pictures." Lightman then held up a new sheet of paper. "Not sure what happened, but they auctioned their assets. And guess what bidder won and acquired whatever equipment and property they owned?"

Brinks shook his head.

"Lansing Perry, aka Arlington Road."

"Who was acquired by Cranes Neck," Brinks added.

"And this is where your analogy of the big fish eating the little fish comes in." Lightman held up a new sheet of paper. "It seems Dublin Pictures had acquired an outfit called HocusFocus Productions in the late thirties," he went on. "A guy named Mazer ran it."

"Okay..."

"Here is where we get into the contractual caca. When Mazer started HocusFocus, he bought equipment and other tangible assets from yet another movie outfit called DimaDozen to set himself up. Again all this buying and selling."

Lightman picked up another sheet of paper, this one yellowed by age. "From what I can tell, Mazer bought them out with money and stock. The stock was issued to four men. I assume this was part of his agreement when he acquired DimaDozen's assets."

He then gave the yellowed paper to Brinks. "This is the contract Mazer made with Percy Maxwell, the guy who owned DimaDozen. It gives each man a percentage of Mazer's company. All totaled, it adds up to a ten percent share of the value of the company's profits when they sell their shares."

"It's dated 1926 when they all signed it. I doubt any of these men are still above ground," Brinks pointed out, scanning the document.

"Sure, but here's where you may need a strong stomach and a very big bankroll."

Brinks didn't like where this was heading. "Why should I be worried?"

Lightman pointed to a section of the old agreement. "You will notice an *in perpetuity* clause."

"What's that?"

"It means 'of endless duration, not subject to termination.' The stock the four men received and any associated value carries forward for each acquiring company. From Maxwell to Mazer to Dublin Pictures all the way up to Cranes Neck and beyond."

Lightman pointed at Brinks since beyond was Glowball. Brinks looked at the contract and saw a large HocusFocus logo at the top. He saw the *in perpetuity* wording and signatures at the bottom of the agreement. Mazer and Maxwell and three other men. A sudden tightness formed around his chest.

"But this HocusFocus company doesn't exist anymore, right?" Brinks asked. "The stock and the agreement would be meaningless since dead men can't cash in their shares."

Lightman palms pointed up to heaven with an *I know* gesture. "I'm sure they're all dead. But read the agreement. The part about descendants."

Brinks took a closer look.

"If any of the signatories' descendants are alive, this agreement is still binding. I bet it was Maxwell who added that clause to protect his investment, probably assuming that putting his money into another movie outfit was like a blind man playing poker."

The tight feeling grew into a steel band wrapping around Brinks's chest. "So in effect, my company would have to honor this clause."

"From a legal perspective, yes. Assume all the signatories are dead, but who knows if any of them have living heirs? I have no record of that. That's your next step. Looking into that. Because you'd be liable for whatever the present value of their shares are if cashed in. If no heirs are alive, you have no legal responsibility."

Brinks closed his eyes, charting the flow of turnovers that got him to this point. There had been no one to hit up for whatever the stocks were worth—until now.

Clearly, the four men were deceased. No descendants had come forward to claim their shares from Glowball. Wolfe would have known that. So would Brenner.

He looked at Lightman, who went back to studying the Mazer contract. Brinks would have to steal this copy of the contract. Stealing this copy wouldn't take care of the remaining ones floating around. But no sense having one of the Chinese accountants stumble upon this if they started digging too deep. Glowball would take a major financial hit if any of the heirs came forward. And that would trigger an all-out, full court press on determining Glowball's financial wealth which he knew was about two billion dollars. Ten percent would be $200 million.

Brinks imagined a domino effect if a really good forensic number cruncher was hired to check every penny of Glowball's expenditures. Brinks's accounting sleight of hand was good enough to trick the average bean counter but maybe not for a determined auditor.

His *Sarah's Shadow Light* and *RoachMan* ruse may not hold up to that kind of deep dive scrutiny.

Lightman struggled to get up. "One more thing."

Brinks waited for the next bombshell.

"My dad represented Venzenta in a criminal case. Embezzlement."

"How did that turn out?"

"Venzenta went to jail. That's all I found."

Brinks didn't see this information hurting him. "You reap what you sow I guess," he said, hoping his own reaping didn't come back to haunt him.

"Can your secretary make a copy of this contract for me?" Brinks asked. This was the only evidence he needed to bury. The other paperwork Lightman showed him was of no value in terms of exposing his activities.

Lightman gave Brinks the contract, which he let fall to the floor. He picked it up along with another sheet of paper, a letter to one of Lightman's clients.

"You can leave it with her after she copies it," "I'll file it later."

"Thanks for your help," Brinks said. He walked to the door, opened it, and waved a goodbye to Lightman. As he shut the door, he slipped the Mazer contract into his jacket pocket.

Brinks went to the secretary and gave the letter to her. "Can you make a copy of this for me? You can file it later."

"Fat chance."

The secretary got up from her chair and made a copy for Brinks, handed it to him, and then put the letter into a file tray spilling over with papers. A drop of water hit Brinks on his forehead, and he looked up.

The secretary saw what he was staring at. "Shitty building, shitty office. Sprinkler system likes to spit once in a while."

"I'd call and have your building maintenance guy take a look," Brinks suggested.

"Fat chance," the secretary said again.

Brinks shrugged and left the office.

When he got to his car, he took out the old contract and read it more closely. Mazer had signed the contract along with Maxwell and three other men: *Delmar Gilmore, Ollie Gustafson, and Marcus Ellwell.* Their names were typed out with their signatures inked in above each name along with the date, January 1, 1926. He wondered why it was signed on the first day of that New Year. And why had DimaDozen studios closed shop.

Brinks then started his car and began driving home. He found the from the past just as Brenner warned. But he had four names. If they had been in the movie business, even decades before, he could hunt them down and find out what happened to those men and their contracts. If they had families, a good private detective could find them. If any of them were found, he would figure out a way to con them into giving him their copy.

There might be some difficult people to convince or con. But he decided, if necessary, extreme measures might be needed. It was a matter of survival. He would distance himself going forward. Nothing done traced back to him. No breadcrumbs.

Brinks knew that, in his world and for the right price, he could get someone to track down those agreements. Use a hired goon with not a lot of smarts. Someone who did the job and didn't ask any questions about it. Brinks knew just the right person to call.

CHAPTER 39

A SPECIAL DEAL JUST FOR YOU

The call came on his personal cell phone. It was Freddy returning his call.

"I got a guy for you."

"Tell me."

"Remember the killer video?" Freddy asked.

Brinks did not appreciate the *killer* adjective.

"Sure."

"Same guy. Name's Leon."

"The nose buster."

"Him."

"What did you say?"

"Not much. Nothing about Wolfe's sad ending. No connection to you. Said I had a man in Los Angeles who needed to find a few people."

"Vague," Brinks said in an agreeable voice. "I like that. You talk money?"

"You can do that when you meet the guy."

Marvin Brinks hesitated. "Is that necessary? Can't you just tell him what I want over the phone? I can give you what I need him to find. Some names to start with."

"Not the way he works. If he gets screwed, he wants to see who screwed him. He's not the kind of guy you screw. Just saying."

"I have no intention of doing that," Brinks said defensively. "So where do I meet this charming fellow?"

"At the bar we met at," Freddy replied. "I make the introductions and then split. My finder's fee will be five Franklins."

"When do we meet?"

"You said you're in a rush, so it's set for tomorrow. Be there at seven."

*****

Brinks parked his car near the bar. He had an envelope for Freddy with $500 in it. He wore dark sunglasses and a beat-up leather jacket he had picked out from Glowball's costume and props room. He nixed a wig, thinking Freddy would start laughing like a hyena on crack.

He saw Freddy at a booth sitting next to a big man, built like a guy who spends time lifting heavy things. The man had a good-looking face that complimented his build. Brinks headed to the booth.

"Leon, this is Marvin," Freddy said, introducing the two men. "I'll leave you two."

He slipped out of the booth and put out his hand. Brinks knew this wasn't a goodbye handshake so he removed the envelope and handed it to Freddy.

"See ya when I see ya," Freddy said as he left.

Brinks sat down and faced Leon. "So, what did Freddy tell you?"

"Not a lot. Said you want me to track down some dead people. Not clear why."

Brinks noticed that Leon made a slight whistling sound when he said certain words. He wore a white silk shirt, tucked into fitted black trousers and a light gray sports jacket. He had a full mane of black hair combed straight back with some kind of gel and a face that had its muscles tightly laid over a rugged but handsome bone structure. Brinks thought of a young Victor Mature. Everyone wants to look like a celebrity, he thought once more.

"That's about it. Find some people and what happened to them."

"You got names, addresses?" Leon asked. His eyes were slate gray and penetrating.

"Names. Maybe lived around here once upon a time. Need to know any living relatives if they have any."

"Just names, huh? That's pretty slim information."

"Well, that's why I wanted to hire someone like you. Do the legwork that's needed."

Brinks took out a copy he made of the agreement he'd swiped from Lightman's office. He handed it to Leon. "The people I want to know about signed this. Their names are at the bottom. If you find any relatives, I need to know that too."

Leon took the copy.

"These men probably worked in and around Los Angeles. Back in the 20s and 30s. Movies. Silent ones at first and then probably talkies."

Leon scanned the agreement. His eyes stopped as he studied the HocusFocus logo, then the names of the people who signed the paper.

"These fellows actors?" he asked, seeing that they were names he didn't recognize.

"My guess is that they were behind the scenes guys. The only name that sticks out is Maxwell. I know for a fact that he directed silent movies."

Leon put a finger to his lip and tapped it, thinking a moment. "I see a lot of movies. New ones…old ones."

Brinks wondered why Leon had segued into this topic.

"You can learn a lot from them. The actors. I did some acting, you know. Nothing special. TV commercials mostly. You like Lon Chaney?"

Brinks blinked at the man's non sequitur. "Sure. The Man of a Thousand Faces."

"Yeah. Amazing how he could change his looks. I watch a lot of TV too," Leon said. "Improves my diction."

Another non sequitur, thought Brinks.

"I like to imitate accents too. Famous actors mostly."

"Sounds fun," Brinks said, not knowing where this guy was going.

"I did snacks and auto parts commercials. Maybe you heard the Sparky Sparkplugs one."

"No, but that's quite a range you have," Brinks said, clearly unimpressed but acutely aware of his hissing *s*'s. He imagined that was not one of the accents he learned to imitate.

Leon paused and studied Brinks's face.

"You mind taking off those sunglasses, buddy? Not much sunshine coming into this room of gloom."

Brinks removed his sunglasses and gave Leon a threadlike smile.

The man looked Brinks's face over as if he were memorizing it. His eyes returned to the sheet of paper Brinks had handed him.

Brinks was about to take back the paper. Before he could, Leon grabbed his wrist and squeezed it.

"You mind if I look this over some more?"

Brinks wanted to say he did mind, but the bones in his wrist felt as if they would snap. He let go of the paper.

Leon took a few minutes reading it over.

"So this Maxwell guy sells all his movie equipment to Mazer for some chump change and a piece of the action for himself and his boys."

"That's right."

"So let me get this straight. I go hunting for these men who we assume are six feet under. And also track down any relatives who are above ground."

"That's the idea."

"My question is why," Leon said, still looking at the agreement.

Brinks said nothing.

Leon fingered the copy of the agreement. "I'm no Einstein, but I have a hunch you want this as well."

Brinks realized this guy was not a brainless muscle head.

"Kinda go together. The people and the paper."

Brinks squirmed in his seat.

"Leon waved the sheet of paper. And you want these back for some reason."

Brinks said nothing, uncomfortable that Leon already presumed the agreement had some importance. Clearly, this guy was not the goon he'd hoped for.

"And it looks like there are five of these little puppies may be floating around somewhere."

"Actually four," Brinks replied. "I have Mazer's. The one you're holding is a copy."

"So what's the deal, brother?"

"I work for a business that needs to keep track of agreements that have been made in the past. It's a bookkeeping issue. Outstanding shares need to be accounted for. Loose ends need to get straightened out."

"What's the name of your business?"

Brinks tried to think of what to say. "My clients like to remain anonymous."

"You know, buddy, I really hate a liar."

"What do you mean?"

"In my *business,* I need to spot a lie. If I don't, it's bad for my reputation. A guy says he paid a loan but never did. Or he doesn't know where a certain somebody is but maybe he does. So I listen and separate the BS from the truth. And everyone's got a tell."

"A tell," Brinks repeated.

"Yeah. Like in poker. A guy does something if he has a good hand. Something else when he has a bad hand. Maybe he pulls on his ear or takes a deep breath. It's subtle but detectable." Leon leaned forward across the table. "You have a tell when you lie."

"Is that so?"

"Yeah. Your cheek gave you away. The twitch."

Brinks unconsciously rubbed his right cheek.

"It's your left cheek. Let me see your wallet," Leon said.

"What?"

"You fucking heard me. Your wallet or I leave and you can find someone else." The man was all business now, his demand sounding more like a threat than a request.

Brinks reluctantly pulled out his wallet. Leon opened it, started laying out its contents and shuffled through the owner's credit cards. Leon scanned Brinks's driver's license and business cards.

"Marvin Brinks," Leon said. "Glad to meet you."

Brinks said nothing, waiting for Leon's next move. Leon took out his iPhone, pressed a symbol, and an Internet browser filled the screen. He quickly fingered a small keypad like a concert pianist and brought up Google. His fingers tapped in a name. Marvin Brinks. He then pressed the search icon. The next screen displayed a series of news bits about Brinks.

"Nice," Leon said. "*Variety* says you just became the interim CFO at Glowball Productions. Some guy Wolfe stroked out or something, huh?"

Brinks offered a hesitant nod.

"Lucky break for you but not Mr. Wolfe." Leon looked at a news clip photo next. "Wolfe's wife was some looker."

"I guess," Brinks said blankly.

Leon narrowed his eyes on the photo of Wolfe and his wife. "I know her from somewhere." He then said nothing for a long minute and then looked up at Brinks. He pointed his finger at him and chuckled. "You're the guy."

"What guy?"

"The guy who wanted to have this babe captured in what they call a compromising position. Or in her case *positions*."

"I have no idea what—"

"Cut the crap rap." Leon tapped his head in a *I know your shit shit*. "Wolfe. Wife. Copulating video. Wolfe underground now. Maybe the vids I took sent him over to the next world. Then your well-timed promotion. And here we are. The two of us sitting across from each other playing bullshit patty cake."

Brinks said nothing.

"Okay, the Web is a wonderful tool. My life is an open book. I plead guilty."

"Not so open, I'm guessing. We okay now, Marv?"

"You tell me."

"Since we straightened out this little communication issue, we can move on with our business arrangement. You want me to find out what happened to these dead guys. See if these agreements went with them into the grave or maybe their offspring have them. Clearly, it's important to you. I don't know or care why, but I'm getting the vibe you need this done sooner than later, right? I'd be guessing something about them would be bad for you, huh?"

Leon was getting too close to what Brinks was trying to keep hidden. Brinks inhaled a deep lungful of air and held it, letting it out slowly as if his anxiety might flow out with his breath.

"So here's the deal. I work on a daily rate with all expenses paid. If I find what you're looking for, I get a bonus to be determined."

"And your daily rate is what?"

"Fifteen hundred a day plus expenses."

"That's steep."

"My Hollywood mogul rate."

Brinks didn't quibble. He could dip into Glowball cash as needed.

"And this bonus thing? What's the to-be-determined part? How much are we talking?"

Leon gave Brinks his best smile that would make an orthodontist proud. "Not money."

Brinks frowned. "No money. What's the catch?"

Leon tapped his finger on his head again. He was thinking about how to explain what he wanted. "It would've been money with someone else but the world works in mysterious ways."

"You mean God works…"

"Nah. He, she whatever doesn't give a flying fuck. But the *you meeting me and me meeting you.*"

"So no cash. What then?"

"A special deal just for you. Did I mention I did a bit of acting?"

Brinks nodded.

"I auditions," Leon said. "I got untapped talent. I need to get on the radar. Too many people are crowding the audition room for me to get noticed. I need a leg up on them. You can give me that."

Brinks thought this over and nodded. What harm could that do? If he had talent, maybe a few bit parts would come his way. If he bombed, so be it.

"I can do that."

"Good answer."

"Find these agreements and leave no trails."

"Got it."

"Good."

"But I do this and not for bullshit walk-ons or a character that has five lines. I want something bigger. I'm not talking leading man or supporting but a role where you see my name on the credits five down from the top. Somewhere after Clooney, Pitt, Wahlberg, or Giamatti. Whoever is this month's hot property."

"I can't just hand you a role. That's what directors decide, and the people who cast a film."

"You must have some juice being the temp CFO."

"You still need screen tests. I don't even know if you can act."

"You get me the screen tests. And a special coach."

"What kind of special?"

"I am sure you noticed that I have a distinct quality to my speech."

"I noticed," Brinks said.

"I need you to find someone who can help me get rid of it. My little impairment is a career killer."

"I can find you a speech coach. We have them at Glowball when actors need to use a particular accent."

"And if I suck at screen tests, you get me acting coaches. And if there is a role that I have the slightest chance of auditioning for, then you use your pull, your position at Glowball. That's the deal. And don't even think I'll be the fall guy if things go into the crapper. If I fall, you fall."

Brinks mulled Leon's terms over. He decided time was not on his side, and this guy seemed to have smarts and muscle as needed.

"You want me to do this job, have Freddy call me. And you saying yes means all the things I mentioned. Don't need you to dry hump me. Zippers up and we are all in."

Brinks bit his lower lip, thinking again.

Leon kept his eyes hard on him. "Nod your head if you understand."

Brinks absorbed Leon's rules and gave him a nod.

"If you want to get started right away, we'll use burner phones. That's how we talk. Leave no trails, right? Do this under the radar."

Brinks blinked that he understood.

"Good boy." Leon slid out of the booth and headed for the door.

Brinks watched him leave. A waitress came over, and he ordered a double bourbon, straight up. He hated bourbon, but he needed to swallow something that would kill the bad taste in his mouth after agreeing to Leon's terms.

The bourbon came, and he knocked it back. He took out his cell phone. He punched in a number. Two short rings later, Freddy answered. "It's me," Brinks said in a disheartened tone. "Tell Leon we have a deal."

CHAPTER 40

AN UNDERSTANDING

He knew Brinks would hire him. His vibe was desperate. Desperate men don't have the luxury to take their time and go window shopping. He agreed to meet Brinks back at the same bar the next day. When Leon walked in, he saw Brinks in the same booth nursing a drink.

Leon sat down and gave him a tooth-whitened grin. Leon was quite familiar with the showbiz necessity for perfect teeth in this business. Just as important as your complexion. A close-up on your face could be your worst enemy, revealing acne scars, pimples, and blackheads. He had a cabinet full of moisturizers, anti-aging and wrinkle creams, acne treatments, even concoctions for dark circles around eyes. Casting insurance.

He was no slouch for keeping teeth and skin perfect. But then there was his cobra-like hiss. The fucking hiss that Brinks would remedy or else.

"So we have an understanding," Leon said as he sat down.

"We do." Brinks gave him an envelope with five grand in it. "Some start-up money for expenses."

Leon opened the envelope and a copy of the HocusFocus agreement along with his business card. He eyed the card, which had handwritten notes on it.

"Make several for yourself. Reinvent your identity. People look at a business card and never question what it says, within reason." He paused. "Whatever you do, we don't want anything traced back to me or you. I suggest you get several different business cards."

Leon thought about all the actors and actresses he admired. How from one movie to the next they had assumed different characters. Changes to their looks, the way they talked, the personalities they adopted. Good guy to bad guy.

"Reinvent myself. Should be fun."

He read over the names. "You have any ideas to share beyond what you already told me?" He pointed at the Mazer contract.

"Nothing important," he lied.

Leon thought for a few moments. "Like our little chat yesterday, we both can assume the guys that signed this are long gone. I'll search for their obits and death certificates, find out if they had relatives. Ones that are alive. If they are, I'll track them down. See if they have the agreement you want back."

He then stood, pocketing the envelope with cash and copy of the agreement. "I got that you're in a hurry. I'll check in with you every day."

Leon took three cell phones out of his pocket and handed them to Brinks.

"What this?" Brinks asked.

"The burner phones I said we'd use. You'll only get calls from me. And use that one speed-dial number for me."

Brinks nodded.

"One more thing. It's what you need to do from now on."

"Which is what?"

"Don't use the Internet to search for information about these people the way you probably already did. You're leaving digital footprints. People can track where you go, what you download. Like you said, no traces, in case you're worried about people looking into whatever hanky-panky you're up to."

Brinks didn't like Leon referring to what he imagined he had been doing as hanky-panky but knew that Leon was smart enough to he know he had pressing reasons concerning the contract.

"Won't you be using the Internet to help track down these people?"

Leon smiled. "I use Tor."

He explained that Tor was used for the Deep Web, which kept your searches impossible to trace since your activity was bounced around hundreds of IP addresses.

"Web anonymity." Brinks thought of his routine searches for escorts. That Tor thing would be handy to keep his personal life secret.

Leon looked at the business card. "Goodbye, old me. Hello, new me."

Brinks pressed his lips tightly together.

"What?" Leon said.

"I'd hate to have you take off with my money and never see you again."

Leon jabbed a finger at him. "I don't roll that way, my friend. Bad for business. Besides you're going to make me famous. Right?"

"Right," Brinks replied, stretching the word out.

He then watched the big man leave and sighed. All he could do now was wait.

CHAPTER 41

CHASING GHOSTS

Leon sat at his desk in his office located on Vermont Avenue. His office bordered Koreatown. He liked it there. The place had history. During the Roaring Twenties, the head of United Artists bought his wife, Norma Talmadge, an apartment building, which he named the Talmadge. Charlie Chaplin and Gloria Swanson followed soon after moving into apartments near the Ambassador Hotel where the Academy Awards ceremony had taken place for several years. The Brown Derby and Cocoanut Club opened nearby and saw the likes of Crosby, Sinatra, Judy Garland, and Louie Armstrong. The history of the area, however, had a stain when Robert F. Kennedy was assassinated at the Ambassador Hotel in 1968.

Leon got up from his chair and went over to a waste-high filing cabinet. He made a mug of green tea with water he boiled on a hot plate that sat on top of the cabinet. He preferred tea since coffee was known to stain teeth. He set the mug down on the cabinet and opened up the top drawer and pulled out the file he'd labeled *HocusFocus*. He then returned to his desk and opened up the folder and read the single sheet of paper he had filed, the contract with the names of the people who originally signed it over ninety years before.

Leon ran his index finger over the four names: *Ollie Gustafson, Delmar Gilmore, Marcus Ellwell, and Percy Maxwell.* He turned on his laptop, opened the Tor browser, and started with the main player in Brinks' drama. He Googled "Percy Maxwell." He knew from Brinks that Maxwell was in the movie business when silent movies were being made.

The search came up with a Dr. Maxwell in Des Moines and a minister of the Crossroads Church of Christ in New Hampshire. There were five more Maxwell hits but none in California and none in the right time frame. Leon went to the last page of hits and found an obituary from the *Key West Citizen* dated from 1980.

> Key West, Florida—Percy Maxwell, 86, died unexpectedly on September 23 at his home in Key West.
>
> Known as "Pink" to his friends, he lived an understated life in Key West. He had been a Key West resident since 1926 and previously resided in New York. He is survived by his half-sister, husband, and son. Maxwell was a celebrated silent movie producer and director. A memorial service will be held at the Sea Side Chapel.

"Call me fuckin' Colombo." Leon's body vibrated with excitement. He printed out Maxwell's obit, took it from the printer, and placed inside his *HocusFocus* folder. Back at his laptop, he searched for more information about Maxwell. The man was mentioned in a few articles about the silent movie era. Some notable names of stars appeared in his films, names that Leon was familiar with.

He ran through some numbers. Maxwell died at eighty-six, so he must have been born in 1894. Now Leon knew he died in Key West and resided in New York. Maybe New York City.

He searched more sites for news about Percy Maxwell. There were a few more items in newspapers. He was honored at the Thirty-Ninth Academy Awards, honoring him in 1967, at the Santa Monica Civic Auditorium in Santa Monica, California. It was hosted by Bob Hope, with Maxwell given an award as a national treasure in cinema. A Maxwell retrospective of the few films that had survived was shown at the San Francisco Silent Film Festival. The others had been lost because most of the old films had been combustible, containing nitrite, a substance used in explosives.

The next thing he did was search Census Bureau data. Census records could help but had a caveat. The Feds did a nationwide census every ten years. But public access was limited to records that were no more than seventy-two years old. The most recent publicly available census records were from the 1940 census and released in 2012. Anything after 1940 was not yet available. He entered Percy Maxwell, New York, and California and waited.

The screen displayed *No Matches Found.*

Leon frowned and reentered the same name and Key West. *No matches found* was displayed again. He was puzzled. There was no doubt Percy Maxwell lived in both places. He tried variations of Percy: Percival, Perseus, Perry. Nothing.

He tapped his temple, wondering why no census data popped up for this guy. He searched census records from 1870 to 1940. *So how could a celebrated person not appear on any of the records?* He wondered. Something odd had gone on with Maxwell, but he didn't know what. But he still had good news to share with Brinks.

"I got a lead on Maxwell," he started when he heard Brinks pick up the burner phone.

"I'm listening."

"I found your guy's obit. Maxwell's."

"And?"

"He punched his ticket in Key West in 1980. Seems he had a place down there for years."

"That's almost over forty years ago." Brinks waited a moment and then asked, "You thinking of going there?"

"Maybe but first I got an old buddy who lives down there. Let's see what he can dig up first. I assume something happened to his Key West place. Sold it or was inherited. Maybe some of his belongings were left there. Stored maybe. You die, you leave shit behind."

Brinks understood that concept well. Like his collections. He never really owned them in the long run. Nobody did. He just rented them until his third act ended and then someone else got them. That was the business of antiques.

"You find out anything else?"

"Good bet he didn't wind up in LA. He sold his studio to that Mazer guy, and I can't find anything about him coming to Sleazywood." Sleazywood came out in a hiss. "Obit implied he made flicks in New York but not where."

"Silent movies were in a lot of places not here," Brinks explained.

"Good to know if I need to track him there. After he sold out to Mazer, maybe he stayed in the business somewhere else." Leon waited a moment then said, "This news you won't like."

Brinks moaned *a what*.

"He had a half-sister."

"Shit. Fucking shit!"

"Obit mentioned a half-sister who married and had a kid."

"Is that a lead?"

"Not really. There was no other information."

"So we have to worry about living relatives."

"You mean *I* do."

"Right," Brinks said, irritated by this guy whom he depended on. For now at least. "Anything else?"

"I checked the census records, but they only go up to 1940."

"And?"

"It was weird. No mention of Maxwell at all. Feels like I'm chasing a ghost."

Ghosts again. "What about a will? Some estate information. A deed?"

"Finding stuff drawn up over fifty years ago may be harder than picking snot out of a broken nose. Besides, if he had a will, why hasn't anyone shown up to collect on the agreement that's twisting your jock strap?"

"Collect what?" said Brinks, playing dumb.

"You being cute again, Marv? I read the contract. You know what *Wikipedia* is?"

"I do."

"Great online encyclopedia and reference tool."

Brinks said nothing.

"I found this term: *In perpetuity.*"

"Where is this going?" Brinks asked.

"Your outfit has to honor whatever Mazer's shares are worth in Glowball bucks. I can smell your sweat over the phone. Not sure what it means to you. Maybe your boss would shit gold bricks so you're saving his ass if this piece of paper landed on his desk. Maybe you'd get a fat bonus and you'd be promoted as their permanent CFO if you found them and conveniently made them disappear."

"You don't know shit," Brinks replied as indignantly as possible.

"Maybe." Leon tried to sound unsure, not wanting to piss off his career meal ticket. "Look, you gotta chill. We got Key West. Be happy I got this far. I'll catch up with you in a while, crocodile." With that, Leon cut the connection.

CHAPTER 42

THE STRANGER YOU SIT NEXT TO

The morning after Zena and I broke into Holey John's trailer, I drove back to the fairgrounds. A warm breeze blew across the field, mixing the weirdly intoxicating aromas of fried dough, grilled Italian sausage, and cotton candy—not an aroma that wafted in the neighborhoods I had traveled before arriving here.

Zena was already at her booth. When she saw me, she shook her head. I nodded back and started searching for Holey John on my own. As I roamed the grounds, I studied the crowds and took notes using my phone's recorder app. I still had a story to write, and Stan said any story needed background fodder, so I thought that I might as well make the most of my search for Holey John even though he had told me to fuck off.

I walked through the crowds and studied the people like an anthropologist coming across a newly discovered tribe. Hyperactive kids shouted as they ran from one ride to another as if they had just popped too much Adderall. Grown men of all builds and sizes grunted as they tried their hand trying to win stuffed animals for their wives and girlfriends by throwing hard balls at lead-bottomed wooden milk bottles or shooting basketballs into impossibly small hoops.

After a while, I headed back to Zena's spot, hoping for a cheery nod. An elderly man sat across from her. I saw the man take a five-dollar bill out of his wallet and hand it to her. He had a single tear run down his weathered cheek. As he got up, he gave Zena a slight bow then left, disappearing into a throng of people.

I saw that she had no other customers waiting for her after he'd left, so I stepped into her booth.

"No Holey John yet?" I asked.

"I'm going to kill that man even if he's already dead."

"That guy okay?" I asked about her last customer.

"He wondered about his dog. What he had done."

"Oh."

"He had to put him down yesterday. The dog was old and sick. It was his best friend for over fifteen years."

"Did he feel guilty?"

"A bit, but he knew it was the right thing."

"Did he want absolution?"

"I don't pretend to be a priest. I simply listen. People telling me something that was hard for them is an absolution they give to themselves. It confirms in their own mind that as hard as something can be to do, in most cases, they do the best thing. Most people are basically good."

"Thelma would say it's therapy," I said.

"A one-time session. I'm the stranger on a train you sit next to. Someone you may never see again. I am a safe person to listen to whatever it is you want to talk about. No judgments made. It helps people to move on."

"You are a really amazing person."

"We already slept together, so this can't be a pickup line."

I smiled for an instant, and then my expression turned.

Zena noticed. "What?"

I pointed. Holey John was heading to his empty booth. He was cut off by Louie, who put his meaty hand over Holey John's shoulder and began to squeeze. We both saw Holey John wince. Through the din of the midway crowd, we could hear Louie screaming at him.

"This can't be good," I said.

Zena stuffed the cash from her money jar into her purse, and we both sprinted over to the two men.

Louie had Holey John's knees buckling as the big man squeezed even harder. "Nobody screws with me, pal," Louie shouted. "You think you can just show up and come and go as you please? I ain't a charity talent show for weird fucks like you."

Zena and I stepped in close to Louie, while a small crowd gathered to see what was going on.

"What's this all about?" Zena asked as she pushed her way forward.

"You know what this is about. He's like a magician with a disappearing act. Only he ain't no magician, and magicians usually pop back on stage after they wow the crowds. This guy just disappears."

"Is this about money?" she asked.

"You bet it is. He's in the hole for over six hundred smackers. I'd give this creep a beatin', but my knuckles would be torn to shreds with all that shit he has all over his face." He continued to squeeze Holey John's deltoid muscles like a vice. "Maybe I should rip some of his gold studs outta of his face and hock 'em for the scratch he owes me. Gold is up, and he's like a two-legged walkin' jewelry store."

"I'll give you what you think he owes you," Zena offered. "Let him go."

"That's on you if you wanna bail his sorry ass out. But him taking a hike ain't good for my business. He and you, my little psychic midget, are what brings people into the midway. It ain't the tattoo lady with her faded ink or the sword-swallowing bimbo that brings horny goes in. Shit, my old lady can swallow my dick, and it's a lot bigger than Dolly's daggers."

"Great to hear we're so valuable and that you're so well-endowed," Zena replied with a smirk. "So you actually need us so these nice people can lose hard-earned dough, trying to pop balloons with dull darts or try to knock down weighted bowling pins to win cheap stuffed animals." She made sure the crowd heard what she was saying.

Louie gave her a deadly look, seeing the reaction of the crowd.

"You keep talking like that, you'll be dumped faster than a hooker with cooties. You think we can't find other freaks just dying for a steady gig?"

"Yeah, I'm sure there are plenty of us advertising on Craigslist." Zena reached into her purse and took out a roll of bills. She pulled off seven one-hundred-dollar bills and pushed them into Louie's groin.

"What da fuck!" His hand went down to his crotch.

"Keep the change and let him go," she demanded.

Louie removed his right hand from Holey John and took the bills from Zena. He fingered the money and looked down at Zena's bank roll.

"Business must be good," Louie said. "You sure I'm getting my vig from you?"

"You count my money jar every hour I'm on," she said, sounding like a cobra ready to strike. "John is square with you. Don't touch him like that again."

Louie laughed. "Or what?"

"Sometimes I have this dream about sneaking into your trailer one night and cut you and your brother's nuts off. It's just a dream, Eddy, for now."

Louie laughed a nervous chuckle. "You're the one with balls."

He waved the money at Zena and patted Holey John on the top of his head. "Don't be late again or you might wind up as supper for Hilda the lion." He gave Holey John another shot to the top of his head, his diamond pinky ring leaving a red mark.

The people who had gathered stood around for a few moments, hoping for more drama. When none came, they took off in all directions.

"Thanks," Holey John said, rubbing his shoulder. "I'll pay you back. I got…money."

"You okay?" Zena asked, sounding genuinely worried.

"No pain…no gain."

She gave him a quizzical look. "That makes absolutely no sense."

"I'm trying to be…" He paused, searching for the word.

"Stoic," I offered.

"Yeah, that."

"Where were you yesterday? I was scared to death."

"I made a friend…in town," he said sheepishly. "I met this old guy…after we had lunch. I went back and saw him…again."

"And last night?"

"Took a long walk…after I left Ralph."

"Ralph?" she repeated.

"The old guy I met."

"And you went where? Alabama and back?"

"You're funny."

Zena waited for a better answer.

"Into some woods…outta town. I hiked into some…park. There are waterfalls. I think I remember being…there 'cause they're special."

"Special?"

"Yeah and I needed to clear…my head. It gets full of spiders… sometimes."

Zena gave Holey John a concerned look and then looked at me. She patted his hand, but she didn't press him about his mental state. She studied a sheet of paper he was holding tight against his side. "What's that?"

"Something the old man gave me. He's selling…his house."

"This man Ralph?"

"Yeah."

"And what? You're thinking about buying it?" She said this with blindsided incredulity.

He shrugged guiltily, his eyes cast down at the ground like a boy scolded by his mother. "It's a special house," he stuttered.

"How?"

"Hard to…explain."

"I see that."

"Maybe you could see…it."

"Sure," she said in a flat tone. "Anything else happen you want to tell me?"

I could tell Zena was not thrilled with Holey John's idea of buying a house, and I could see a dozen reasons why this would upset her.

"I saw that…punk."

Zena took a guess. "Wally. He stalking you?"

Holey John gave an imperceptible nod. "Tried to run me over."

Zena exchanged an apprehensive look with me then went back to questioning Holey John. "So what about this Ralph person? And what's so special about this house?"

"Dunno. Just a feeling I…get."

He said nothing more but offered a fleeting expression that she couldn't discern. He then clutched the sheet of paper and said, "I better get…changed."

I watched him head toward his trailer. "Never a dull moment around here."

"I wouldn't mind a bit of dull," Zena said and then considered what her friend had told her. "It feels like John is acting stranger than his usual kind of strange."

"How so?"

"Disappearing like that. That house and the old guy. Him thinking about buying it is like wanting to get a ticket on the *Lusitania*. He leaves here, and he would sink without…"

She didn't finish her sentence, and I said, "He'd be sunk without you. And maybe you would too. You guys are a team."

We started walking back to her booth. A few people were waiting nearby. "Customers," I said.

"Gotta pay the rent."

"Looks like you have enough to pay a lot of people's rent," I said, pointing at her purse. "Mine included. Maybe I'm in the wrong biz. I could write haikus for five bucks a pop."

"I don't think we attract the ionic pentameter crowd here."

As Zena was about to step into her booth, I pointed at her purse again, curious about her stash of cash, which I knew wasn't the result of her fortune-telling gig.

"We can talk about that later. I have more Scotch to loosen your inhibitions and any girlfriend guilt you're suppressing. You never told me her name, by the way."

I hesitated and then said, "Lilly."

"And there she be and here we be. Love the one you're with as the song says. I'm your secret love muffin. Until you leave."

"Love muffin. Sounds tasty."

"From the man who gets his lovin' on the run."

"Ouch."

"Come by after I am done today."

I recalled having resolved not to continue my dalliance with Zena. Keep it professional. This was the moment to bring this up.

"Oh, he hesitates," she said, seeing me hesitate.

"It's just that—"

She cut my excuse off. "Tonight, you can bring the appetizers and leave the guilt trip outside my trailer. I'm thinking caviar and pate. And good crackers, not Ritz."

I sighed, seeing my resolve melt faster than climate change at the North Pole. My trip back to the city and meeting Lilly would be like me doing summersaults across quicksand.

"Oh, and find some good chocolates." She gave me another one of her devilish looks. "I like a nice piece of chocolate after I have an orgasm."

CHAPTER 43

CAN'T PAINT WITH MY SOCKS ON

Zena went back to her booth. I castigated myself for not standing my ground—my "no more cha-cha" ground. As I belittled my weakness, I roamed the midway once more, hoping to find a Holey John replacement. When I approached whom I thought might be a possible replacement, they quickly declined, wondering if I was a cop or with ICE.

One person who didn't was a man who painted portraits with his feet. His name was Duffy and had been an art student once, felt like his career was going nowhere and joined the army, hoping to get assigned to a drafting unit. Instead, he wound up in Afghanistan. A roadside bomb in Kandahar blew off his arms and left half of his face badly scarred.

"Funny way to get me back into art," he told me.

"Not exactly funny, but life has its ironies."

"My biggest challenge is when it starts to get cold outside. Can't paint with my socks on," he said and laughed.

He had his artwork pinned to the wall behind him. This man was brave. Able to move on with his life and retain a sense of humor.

I moved past Holey John's booth. He was back in action, having people lance his skin with jewelry. Egged on by a young man, a squeamish woman took a gold safety pin, pinched the skin above his left pectoral muscle, and inserted the metal needle. She smiled apologetically at him then stepped off his stage, looking like she was about to faint.

I thought I spotted Wally tucked away in the crowd, eyeballing Holey John. I didn't see his main squeeze, the young woman who was carrying the little man's child. I felt sorry for her. What makes a person stick it out with a loser? Of course, who was I to pass judgment? I was sure that Lilly would take a red-hot branding iron with the letter *L* to my forehead if she knew what kind of intimate munchkin shenanigans I gave myself permission to indulge in.

I walked back to Zena's booth and stopped about fifteen feet away from her booth, hidden among the passing crowds, keeping a watchful eye on her, making sure that Wally wasn't making any rounds for revenge against her or Holey John.

A sensation of protectiveness came over me as I watched her. I wondered why I felt this way. Was it what a friend felt toward another friend? Was it that we had shared bed time? Or was it the fact she was diminutive, and therefore, I assumed she was vulnerable, me feeling some wacky sense of fraternal protection?

I stood in the background, being vigilant, and after a good half hour, I felt it was safe enough to leave her. Taking one more look at Holey John's booth, I noticed a woman dressed in a pants suit step to the stage and hand him a large envelope. To my surprise, he hugged her. That was weird, was all I could think.

A list of shopping chores awaited me, and I walked across to the parking area and found my car. I turned the engine on and started to drive, steering my car away from the Giambolvo Brothers. I was in Ithaca twenty minutes later and parked in front of Wegmans supermarket. I had a shopping short list from my friend: caviar, pate, and good crackers. And of course, after-orgasm chocolate.

CHAPTER 44

NICKEL TOUR

While Holey John waited for the next customer, he rubbed his shoulder, which still ached from Louie's bruising grip. He made the pain dissolve this time by thinking about the waterfalls and what he found there and the house that the old man was selling.

A woman who wore a pants suit with a blue blazer that had a RE/MAX logo embroidered on her breast pocket approached him.

She extended her hand. "Mr. Gilmore sent me. My name is Tish Mansfield. I'm with the real estate agency helping Mr. Gilmore sell his house."

Holey John took her hand, then she handed him a large envelope. "This is a purchase and sales agreement. You can look it over just to see what's required if you're interested in acquiring the property. If you apply for a loan, we'd do a credit check. Then you probably want someone to inspect the property." The woman tried to look at him as if there was nothing unusual about a man who looked like a chandelier.

"I still need to see...the place," Holey John said, taking the envelope. From across the grounds, he saw that Fenn was watching over Zena and then Fenn glanced over at him. He figured that Fenn saw the woman had given him something. Holey John quickly looked away.

"Other people are interested. The early bird gets the worm, so you may want to act fast," she urged.

This bullshit pressure angle, Holey John assumed, was what real estate people do. He didn't mind. People had to make a living.

"About the house tour. Mr. Gilmore said you could come over today after seven o'clock. Does that work for you?"

Holey John thought for several moments. He could steal away, pretending to go on a break around supper time. Louie and Tony might get a little steamed, but he would be back before they went totally psycho.

"Seven is…okay."

"I'll come back tomorrow after you see the house, and you can let me know what you think."

The RE/MAX lady was about to leave when Holey John gave her a hug. She was caught off guard by the strange man she was embracing—a man that felt like a studded porcupine.

When it was time for Holey John's break, he stepped off his stage and headed to his trailer. He put on clothes and drove his truck to College Avenue. Traffic was light, and he got there in less than twenty minutes. He parked and went up the steps and knocked on the door. He heard the slow shuffle of shoes. The old man, Ralph Gilmore, opened the door and greeted him.

"The real estate lady came…around. Said I could come over… and see the place today."

"Yup. Come in and I'll give you the nickel tour." Ralph Gilmore swept his hand, beckoning Holey John in.

It was the smell of the first room Holey John entered that struck him right away. He, Holey John, wondered whether a person's brain had an olfactory memory. He tried to place it, the scent. He closed his eyes, filtering out the furnishings of the room, the light coming in from the windows, the paintings on the wall. He just concentrated on the scent of the house. He swore he could smell the air in his lungs. Oiled wood, like mahogany or teak.

Ralph tugged on Holey John's arm. "Straight ahead is the parlor and dining room. Kitchen to the right of the dining room. And a library to the left. At least it was a library when Pink had this place."

Holey John was guided into the parlor. He looked around and noticed a sofa and a loveseat a bit worn. A small table was on one side of the sofa with a lamp on it. The shade was amazing. It was made out of stained glass.

"That's a real Tiffany," Ralph described as they moved along. "It belonged to Pink. Like I said, he left things behind just as if he thought he'd be coming back. That's what snow birds do. Leave when winter hits and then come back in the spring."

Holey John noticed old movie posters hanging on the walls.

"Pink made those back in the day," Ralph explained.

Holey John took a closer look and something stirred, a memory maybe, but he wasn't sure why.

The landlord shuffled out of the parlor and moved down the hall that led to kitchen. He stopped before they got to the kitchen and turned into the dining room. A large oak table surrounded by ten chairs dominated the room.

"Didn't use this much myself. But Pink must've had some fine dinners here. All those actors and sweetie pies and all."

Holey John moved to the table and let his fingers glide over the wood. On impulse, he stooped down and moved a chair aside. He craned his neck and looked under the table. He found a faint set of scratches. His eyes settled on the markings. They were initials. *JB*.

"You see something?" Ralph asked.

"Initials."

"That right?"

"Crazy but…I think they're…mine."

"Now ain't that something."

In the kitchen, Holey John found a fire hydrant sitting in a corner that caught his eye. A dog stood next to it with its right leg lifted.

Ralph smiled and patted Holey John on the shoulder. "A prop," the old man said. "Dog's been taxidermized. Pink had these old props scattered around the house in places you wouldn't expect. Had him a sense of humor, all right."

He then led Holey John out of the kitchen. "Let's see what we got upstairs."

Holey John held the man's elbow. Shifting his backpack, they ascended the stairs. "Three bedrooms on this floor. Bathroom with a tub and shower. Toilet of course. Also got a half bath. Just a commode and a sink."

Holey John went into each bedroom. Ralph's master bedroom was quite spacious. The old man kept it neat, the bed made, no clothes on the floor. Like his own trailer. The other rooms were smaller and sparse. Twin beds, simple dressers, throw rugs on the floor. Holey John went to each window and looked at the views. From one window, he could see Cayuga Lake. He stared intently at the shimmering water, sunlight bouncing off the small white caps like silver crowns topping the crests. He thought he remembered a playground edging the lake. An older man holding his hand taking him there.

"Quite a view," Ralph admired. "And it could all be yours." The old man cackled. "That's what the real estate lady says when she shows off the house."

"You mentioned a checkerboard...painted on the floor," Holey John reminded.

"Yup. In the attic."

"Can we go...there?"

"Don't see why not." Ralph showed him the way to a narrow door. He twisted the doorknob and it creaked open. Ralph gripped the wood banister and hefted himself up the flight of steps. Holey John followed behind. He felt a stitch of anticipation of what he might find.

CHAPTER 45

A FAVOR

Leon put in a call to his old army buddy Jabo Jabowaski. Jabo had moved to Key West after his stint in the service. He was Leon's sensor operator when Leon was launching Hellfire missiles at the bad guys in Afghanistan. They kept in touch with occasional catch-up calls, usually when they heard about one of their drone crews getting divorced, went into rehab, or took themselves of the board.

"Is Jabo there?" Leon asked when a woman answered, her voice having scratchy sound of a heavy smoker.

"Who's askin'?"

"Tell him Leon from Creech."

He heard the phone clatter down on the bar and the woman shouting *Jabo*. A few moments later, a man came on the phone.

"Someone die?" Jabo asked.

"Someone always dies somewhere."

"Asshole. You know what I meant."

"Nah. Least I hadn't heard."

"You remember that dago Corica from Syracuse?"

"Yeah. Had beady eyes like a squirrel."

"He ate a bullet a couple of weeks ago. His wife told me. Said it was cause of what he did. Couldn't get the images of Hellfires slamming into civilians out of his head."

Leon grunted. That was not a thing he'd ever consider.

"How are you doing otherwise?"

"Pretty good."

"You liking the Keys?"

"Sure. Still a bartender at a place that looks like a biker bar but without the Hell's Angels. The tourists don't know the difference between a Ducati and a Harley. And who doesn't love wet T-shirt contests."

"Depends on who's wearing the T-shirt."

Jabo chuckled. "You should come down. Catch up. We got a pond out back. Got a fence around it. Tourists throw chicken gizzards we normally throw away. Sell 'em for five bucks a bag. Throw it into the water and see the gators move faster than greased lightning. Chaw that shit down like starved junk yard dogs."

"Maybe I'll buy a few bags and see for myself."

"Be on the house, man."

"On the house," Leon repeated. He thought about his Hellfire Predator days with Jabo. He knew what happened when his missiles hit a targeted house like a painter interpreting his color pallet. If the missile blew up a cloud of gray, he had hit an empty building. If the color was the shade of coffee grinds, he had hit dirt and earth. And if it was a combination of gray and pink, then he had vaporized a building with people inside.

Dispensing death anonymously hadn't been gratifying. What would have been would be looking directly in his victims' eyes as he put their lights out, seeing the last glint of life leave their eyes. Like the difference from watching porn to actual face-to-face fucking,

"Listen, I need a favor. There's three Franklins in it for you."

"As long as I don't have to knock someone off."

"Nah. More like finding a house."

Leon told him about Percy Maxwell, his background making movies and that he bought a place down in there.

"He kicked in 1980," Leon said. "I need to know where he lived. See if anyone lives there now."

"Can do buddy. So what's your line of business? I saw a commercial you was in 'bout a year ago. Some dessert you was hawking. You a private dick now?"

"More like a fixer for people with too much money who get into trouble."

"You still thinking about being a big star?" Jabo asked.

"Could happen faster than I thought. Got a connection now."

"Cool." He waited a second. "You mind me asking about that hiss, Snake? That gonna work for you in Hollywood?"

Snake was the nickname he was called back at Creech.

"I gotta guy that's gonna deal with that. Speech coach. Hollywood big shot."

"Cool."

"So we good with what info I need?" Leon asked.

"I'm on it like white on rice."

"You find anything, call me." Leon gave Jabo his cell number.

"Keep it tight and right, Snake."

"I always do."

CHAPTER 46

OPEN SESAME

Dust motes floated through the shafts of light that filtered through the attic windows. Cardboard boxes, old trunks, and broken household items were scattered around. A heavy tripod that once held a camera lay on its side, one of its legs a broken stump like an amputated soldier. An old movie poster, not like the ones downstairs, was tacked to the wall with its corners curling from age. Holey John could read some of its faded letters: Lionel Barrymore and Pearl White in some film he could not decipher.

He went over to an old steamer trunk and lifted its lid. A musty smell wafted up. Holey John bent over and lifted out costumes that were stitched beautifully, though moths had made their way in and left a few holes.

He opened other boxes and found papers yellowed with age. There were actor notes, a list that appeared to be locations for scenes, daybooks with appointments penciled in. He saw a few names repeated: Needles, Loci, Crank, Gustafson and women's names with exclamation marks next to them.

"You want to see the hiding place I mentioned?" Ralph offered.

"Okay."

"It's under the chessboard." He pointed and said, "The one on the right side. The board that has a slight warp. Pink's hidey hole."

Holey John went to the bowed board. He removed his knapsack laying it on the floor. He pulled on the board. It resisted, the summer heat having swelled the wood. He gave it a few gentle tugs and the board loosened and came up.

"Feel around down there," Ralph said as he pulled up a crate to sit on.

Holey John circled the dark space with his hand. His fingertips hit something hard. It was a large metal box with a handle. He pulled it up.

"Like I told you, I came up here to store some things. One of the boards had lifted. That's when I discovered Pink's hidey place like it was a safe deposit box."

"You look inside…this?" Holey John gestured to the box.

"Nope. Didn't think it was mine to open. Like a grave with a coffin inside. So I let it be."

Holey John squatted on the floor, resting the box between his legs. There was a rusty latch. He yanked, and the latch creaked like an old rocking chair. Inside were photos on top. He shuffled through them. There were portrait shots with names scribbled on the back. Some had the names in the daybooks he had found in the trunk. A group photograph had four men with their arms linked around each other. Holey John flipped the photo over and saw names written in neat cursive letters:

Delmar "Crank" Gilmore, Ollie "Needles" Gustafson, Marcus "Loci" Ellwell, Theo Mazer, and Percy "Pink" Maxwell. New Years, 1926

He put that photograph aside with one of the men in the group catching his eye.

Another photo was a head shot taken by a professional photographer. A name had been printed at the bottom of the photo: Percy Maxwell. The same man who caught his eye. He added that one on top of the group picture.

There were receipts for supplies, pay stubs for employees, and cancelled checks. One thing that all the paperwork had in common was the name of a company: DimaDozen Productions. And the one person that seemed to own the company and paid the bills was Percy Maxwell.

Holey John picked up the photograph of Maxwell again and studied it for several minutes. The man was maybe in his thirties, dark complexion, open face. It was the eyes that got to Holey John. They were familiar eyes. He put the photo of the man aside once more.

He took out the entire contents of the box and sifted through them. A woman's handkerchief with a faint color of lipstick in the shape of a kiss. Then a sequence of folded drawings, a storyboard that showed a woman pursued by a man. In the last panel, the woman was on the edge of a waterfall, the man right behind her, her face revealing total fear. The sketch of the waterfall had a rocky background. Holey John squinted. He saw the blurred shape of the devil rock.

He held another photo. A couple dressed to the nines as bride and groom. The woman was pretty, smiling at the man. He looked stern, his hair high off his head. Holey John flipped the photograph over. *David and Susan, July 14, 1946.* Holey John studied their faces. There was something eerily recognizable about them. He put the photograph on top of the others with a growing sense that this house held secrets from his past.

His fingers glided over an envelope which he opened. Inside were two pages. The top of each page had an old fashioned cameraman with his cap turned backward shooting his camera, his hand on a wind-up crank. Holey John read the page.

"You ever heard of…HocusFocus Films?" He held it out to Ralph.

"Not a name I know."

"What's this look…like?"

Ralph took a few moments as his eyes scanned the document.

"It is some kinda agreement. This one is signed by Percy Maxwell and someone named Theo Mazer. Percy. That'd be Pink. The second is same as the first. This one is signed by a man named Gustafson and that same guy, Mazer. They signed it New Year's Day, 1926."

Holey John saw Ralph's forehead crinkle.

"Interesting."

"What?" Holey John asked.

"Mazer bought DimaDozen. Some language here about shares for both men."

227

He gave Ralph a blank look. "So what's that…mean?"

"Looks like the men from DimaDozen got shares from this guy Mazer's company." Ralph thought for a moment then said, "My guess it doesn't mean much being written so long ago."

Holey John saw him purse his lips.

"Something else?"

"I wonder why Pink kept his copy and Gustafson's. Not the others."

Ralph handed it back to Holey John. He kept the Maxwell agreement and put the Gustafson one aside.

He kept sorting through the tin box. Inside was another legal-looking set of papers. It was the deed to a house. On the last page, he saw names. The people who signed the deed. The address of the house. The former owner, the new owner, an attorney with a notary public stamp next to his name with a date. March 31, 1927.

"This is a deed for…your place." He studied it a bit more. "Ralph, you ever hear of a guy named…Pinkus Moskowitz?"

Ralph scratched his chin thinking for a moment. "Not that I can recall."

"His name is on the deed…for your house."

"Not Percy Maxwell?"

"No."

"I'll be doggoned," Ralph cackled.

"What?

"Pink. Pinkus. Of course," he giggled. "Pinkus Moskowitz had to be Percy Maxwell. You know, lots of guys came over from the old country and changed their names to fit in. My kin came from Ireland. MacGilmartin. Changed it to Gilmore. Must've been like that for Pink."

Holey John was still puzzled as to why Pink or this man Percy had used a different name on the deed. He handed the deed to Ralph.

There was one last group of papers at the bottom of the tin box. Two newspaper clippings. The first was a back page from the *Chicago Sun Times* listing local news. There was a photograph of the couple he had found before. The wedding photo. Holey John studied the two faces. A shiver ran down his spine, when he read the article dated *April 3, 1985.*

> A man and woman were pronounced dead at the scene of an automobile accident last night. Police say that the driver, David Burke, age 65, veered off the road hitting a tree. There had been a light rain and heavy fog that night. His wife, Susan Burke, who was a passenger in the car, died a short time later at Mercy Hospital. They are survived by a son.

The woman, the article said, was the half-sister of Percy Maxwell, a well-known producer and director of silent movies in Ithaca, New York.

Holey John repeated the names of David and Susan Burke under his breath and put the clipping to the side, his face drained of blood.

Ralph picked up the clipping. He rubbed the back of his head and read the obit. He looked at Holey John in a funny way. "That's the couple. The ones that fought like cats and dogs when they were visiting here."

"My name is…Burke. My last name. Those initials…under the table. JB. John Burke. It's mine."

"That couple killed in that car crash. They'd be your parents?"

Holey John didn't respond, his body stiffened. His memory as always was like a broken mirror where fragments reflected distorted pieces of what might have been. He said the two names again. "I think…" He didn't complete the sentence. He exhaled heavily and then slowly lifted the second newspaper clipping.

He read the date. *August 22, 1973.* An Ithaca newspaper. His eyes traveled over the front page. On the bottom right there was a photo of an older man and younger man.

The older man had his hand on the younger man's shoulder. His head was turned to the younger man, and he was smiling at him. The young man was dressed in army fatigues. There was a jagged scar along his temple, still pink from a recent injury. The soldier stared straight into the camera. His eyes were vacant and hollow, his lips tight. Holey John recognized the soldier and it took his breath away as if punched hard in the stomach. *The soldier in the photo was him.*

Holey John lifted his hand from the old clipping and felt the ridges of the scar on his temple. He showed it to Ralph. The old man read the clipping, his eyes shifting between the photo in the paper and Holey John.

Ralph's eyes now stayed on Holey John. "Son, are you okay?"

"Dunno."

Ralph read the photo caption out loud. "Percy Maxwell greeted his nephew John Burke, who recently returned from Vietnam. He was awarded a Bronze Star and Purple Heart."

"Well, I'll be damned. Pink's your uncle."

Holey John closed his eyes tight. Another one of the broken fragments of his life came into view. It was the man with his hand on his shoulder. He was the person who took him to Devil Falls, the man who looked after him when the yelling between the two people from the wedding photo was out of control.

"Bronze and Silver," Ralph started. "You must've done something very brave."

Holey John had no memory about anything he had done over in Nam that would warrant those medals.

"I have to go," he said to Ralph, his voice tight. His chest was crushing him, his head bursting, his thoughts a ball of confusion.

"You know any of this before?" Ralph asked.

Holey John shook his head.

"That's a lot to digest, son," Ralph said sympathetically.

Without a goodbye, Holey John grabbed the photos, the newspaper clipping of him with his uncle and the police report about his parent's death. He shoved them all into the tin box, and then he pushed it into his knapsack. He stood quickly, feeling lightheaded and moved quickly across the attic room and disappeared down the stairs.

Ralph sighed as Holey John left. He gathered the remaining photos, Gustafson's contract, the deed, and the scattered papers he'd left behind. He put them with the other DimaDozen papers and memorabilia, placing the stack of papers back into the hidey hole.

Ralph struggled as he got up from the crate. He hoped Holey John would buy this house. Keep it in the family now that he knew why this strange man was drawn to his place. In any case, everything up there in the attic would still be safe just as they had been for so many years.

CHAPTER 47

SHARDS

Holey John unlocked the door to his trailer. His evening act was done in a trance-like daze. He couldn't remember or care how many people had pierced him, his mind totally adrift, trying to make sense of everything he had learned just hours before.

The midway was closed now as were the rest of rides, midway performances, and circus acts. He was exhausted. He put his knapsack on the floor by his cot and lay down, staring at the ceiling. His eyes hardly blinked, but his eyes were misty like morning dew on a windowpane. Holey John wiped the tears away with the back of his hand. As he lay there, he felt different. Something had dramatically shifted for him. He could feel it inside his body and brain. The unknown he'd endured for so many years didn't seem as nameless. The shards of his broken past began to piece themselves together— the busted mirror showing a clearer reflection of who he had been, although still fractured but more graspable than ever before.

He reached for his knapsack, opened it, and took out the tin box. He opened it and sat back down on his cot. He took out all the photos, the news clippings, the bits and pieces that his long forgotten uncle, the man called Percy Maxwell, had squirreled away. More important, he had found who and what happened to his parents. And the gossamer memory of a kind man who had been his guardian angel was no longer a figment of his imagination.

The contents inside the tin box had revealed pieces from his past that had been secreted away for over forty years. Had his guardian angel steered him to this house? Had Pink with unseen hands pushed him so that, at the right time, he would find these things and find part of himself, the lost soul he saw in the newspaper photograph?

Holey John rubbed the scar on his head. A battle scar. The newspaper made it clear he had been in Vietnam. The medals he received were given for something he had done. He stared at the ceiling and the letters he had painted so long before, still not knowing what they meant. He ached to know what went on before August of 1973. The medals and scar. Were those nightmarish dreams that faded when he awoke connected to them? He shuddered, wondering what had actually happened over there.

That asshole Fenn suggested something painful occurred in his past, his midway act something he did as atonement. The reason he chose to be a human pin cushion. That he thought he deserved his self-inflected punishment.

Holey John pulled the photograph from under his pillow and stared at it for a long time. Was she the specter that appeared in his dreams? The woman whose eyes understood his pain. The woman who forgave him.

He sat up and spotted the large envelope that the real estate lady gave him. It was lying there on his small card table. Holey John put the photo down and went to the table, bringing the envelope back to the cot. Opening it, he let the sheaf of papers fall to the blanket. Most of the papers were forms. A purchase and sales agreement. Credit history forms. Employment history. Request for banking information and income taxes.

His mind swirled like a dust devil. No fucking way could he handle all this paperwork. Worse, most of the shit it was asking for was information he couldn't provide. What he could provide was something that might avoid all this form-filling bullshit.

Cash. Hard, cold cash.

He went to his stove, turned the combination lock, and heard it tick as he found the right numbers. At the last tick, he stopped and opened the stove's door. There was a banged-up cash box with a handle on top. He took it to his bed and opened it, lifting out several stacks of money. All were rubber banded around hundred-dollar bills.

Holey John had been getting checks for over forty years. Government checks. Disability checks. He knew why now. Over $3,000 a month. They were sent to a bank that had offices all over the United States. Once a month, he would withdraw most of what was in his account in cash using his given name.

He touched the stacks of bills he had saved. He didn't make much money with the G brothers. Most of his food he got for free at the cook tent. Maybe he'd spend a little on a few snacks and drinks he kept inside his frig. His wardrobe was meager, seasonal clothes he'd pick up at thrift shops; the pins people stuck him were bought at Dollar Stores.

He scanned the broker's papers. His eyes rested on the asking price for the house. He smiled. He had more than enough cash to buy Ralph's house and then some. He would call the lady who gave him her business card.

A new idea took hold as he thought about buying this house. He held the faded photograph of the woman and child and closed his eyes. A thought came to him, imagining the three of them sitting on rocking chairs on the porch of the house. As always when he looked at the photo, he wondered who they were and if he would ever find out.

CHAPTER 48

CRAZY TALK

Twenty candles were placed on two nightstands by her bed, casting a warm glow inside the trailer. *Miles for Lovers* was playing soft jazz in the background.

"Another one, please," Zena said.

"Your wish is my command," I said, placing a small spoonful of black Beluga caviar on a Capeachio water cracker.

Zena closed her eyes and opened her mouth as I placed the cracker on her tongue. She closed her mouth, making orgasmic sounds as she chewed. "Caviar on a Communion wafer. Thank you, Jesus."

I smiled as I sat on her bed. We both had a glass of Scotch sitting on the night tables that flanked each side of the bed.

"Peel me a grape," Zena said, mimicking Mae West.

"I forgot the grapes."

"Then peel my clothes off. Caviar makes me horny."

"I thought that was oysters."

"Any seafood makes me horny."

Her eager expression faded when I didn't make any moves.

"Something wrong?"

I shook my head. "This is our second time."

"Are you the kind of guy that remembers things like the first time we met and shared a special moment? Or the guy who thinks a second time means we are no longer one-night standees and are shifting into something a bit more serious?"

235

I started to say something but held back. Zena was a bundle of contradictions. When we had first met, I was as important to her as a piece of gum stuck to the bottom of her shoe. Then something changed, and she spilled her guts to me about her life. After that, I was promoted to boy toy and into the sack we went. If I really thought about her, she was a human Rubik's Cube, a puzzling challenge to understand what went through her head. I finally brought up one of the things that did bother me.

"About kissing," I ventured, "or the lack thereof."

"Skip that track," she insisted.

I thought of the ladies of the night with their "no kissing" rules. Was it the same for her, kissing meant crossing into the too-intimate zone?

"What's on your mind besides that?"

There were many things on my mind.

"Is guilt keeping you from pouncing on me besides your smooching issue? Or did my previous rant about the significance of our comingling bubble up?"

"I have put any guilt inside a box to be opened at a later date. The rant I will dismiss as a momentary aberration of a sex-starved woman who was amazingly serviced."

"A man who can compartmentalize."

She totally nailed that one.

She gave me an *uh-huh* and crossed her arms, waiting for me to say more. Another thing troubled me even more. "Actually, there is something we should talk about other than what we're talking about."

"Oh?"

"What happened today. At the fairgrounds. That shit that went down."

"What shit?"

"I think Wally is stalking Holey John."

Zena frowned. "You saw him do that?"

I nodded. "He might give the little tough guy more than a black eye the next time they rumble. Holey John in lockup might unscrew the few screws he has left."

"You actually seem worried about him. The guy who basically told you to fuck yourself."

"He's your friend who you care about."

"And since you care about me, you care about him."

I shrugged, but maybe her suggestion had some legs. Her implication felt strange, making me wonder about my feelings toward her again. Fraternal protection or something else. She had played relationship ping-pong as to where I fit into her life. But as for her in mine? I'd be gone soon enough, and in any case, I'd be back home where I could think about what Zena had really meant to me, how I may have changed my views on what was normal, what intimacy actually meant.

"You have more thoughts about him?" she asked.

"You ever question why he does what he does? The piercing-his-flesh shtick?"

She thought for a moment then said, "I do."

"And...?"

"I feel something happened to him before he joined the midway. It's connected."

Zena confirmed what I had thought when I told him there was a term for people who liked to inflict pain on themselves and immediately he told me to go fuck myself.

"Have you asked him?"

"What I let him know is that I would like to talk to him about anything. Past, present, and future."

"And he said what to that?"

"Thanks."

"But no heart to hearts?"

She shook her head. "When people want to talk, they will. Just like me telling you about my past."

"Would it help if I tried to find out what happened?"

I could tell she wasn't sure about me probing into his past.

"What if I found some things out that would help him? I mean, being a human pin cushion can't be a pleasurable way to live for the rest of his life."

"What if you found things that would send him over the edge? He's always just a few steps away at any given time."

"What if whatever I find I share with you and you can decide if you want to share it with him?"

Zena considered the suggestion for a long minute. "Okay. He can't get wind that you're doing this or that I said you should try."

"Deal."

"There's another thing," she said with a worried expression. "The house thing."

"A big-time change if he buys it. For both of you."

She was quiet. I guessed she was processing the possibility.

"Why now? Why here?"

"Maybe he's growing out of his crazy stage."

"And that's as likely as when Saudi women can go topless. Let's put all of this shit on hold. My head feels like it's going to explode."

"Good idea."

She patted her bed. "I believe we had been heading down a different path before."

"We digressed," I agreed.

She shed her clothes and took my hand, putting it on her breast. "The naked lady beside you is waiting."

I looked down at her lying on top of her silk sheets, her hair falling around her neck, framing a striking face, Zena giving me her best *come hither* look. Her fingertips slid lightly over her nipples, down to her stomach, and then over her *conejo*, now giving me the look of an innocent virgin. I was getting a very interesting performance that night and wondered if that was an act.

And so we made love. I was less cautious that time, having been there before. The awkwardness and uncertainty of a new lover lessened. The acute awareness of making love to a woman who was not the body type of women I had been used to was now replaced by a man who wanted to please. I let my mouth explore every inch of her body, my fingers pressing into her back and buttocks like a sculptor molding clay.

Zena moaned as I touched her, the quality of her sighs indicating where my touch responded best, sending shivers across her body, her fingernails digging into me. Her hands wandered over my body, feeling my muscles, stopping for a second when she felt a scar, continuing to places where, when stroked, I would accompany her sounds of pleasure with my own. I, for one, was not acting.

CHAPTER 49

GETTING CLOSER

"I found some things out about your guy," Jabo said right after Leon answered his phone.

"That was fast."

"Yeah, so the day after you called, I went to the address you gave me. I put on my only white shirt to cover my tats, shined my black dress shoes, trimmed my beard, and slicked back what's left of my hair."

"A regular makeover."

"Didn't want to spook nobody. A man lives there. Older guy. Probably retired. Anyways, I said I was selling a pest protection plan."

"Which is what?"

"We got roaches down here you could put saddles on. Termites that will eat through steel doors, and these ants, crazy ants they're called 'cause they run around like they're on meth."

"Not a good promo for living down there."

"Anyways, got a regular who drinks here. Works for Ornix Pest Control. Asked if I could borrow his van for a few hours. Said he could drink for free till I came back."

"Nice move."

"So I show up and the guy opens the door and point to the truck and sez the first visit is free. Everyone likes free. I'm chatting him up, which I do good being a bartender, so we chat, right?"

"You find out anything?"

"He's been in the house for twenty years. Bought it in the late eighties. Real estate agent told him it was vacant for some time. Said the previous owner was down here in the winter then split when it got so hot that you could cook eggs on the sidewalk."

"Another not so great Key West selling point."

"And that's why God invented AC. Anyways, the guys sez the owner would go north somewhere then come back again in the winter. Seems the owner passed away. Property taxes built up so the town auctioned it. I guessed nobody in his family claimed it."

"He let you poke around?"

"Yeah. I told them I could do a free inspection. See if he had an infestation that needed attention."

"He let you in?"

"Sure. Like I said, everyone likes free."

"Excellent."

"He had an attic. Bunch of old books, records from the vinyl days, clothes in hanging bags. Had time to rummage through boxes he had up there. Found one box with tax returns, some photo albums, and things that you can't figure out what to do with."

"Anything connected to Percy Maxwell?"

"Some old framed movie posters were lying against a wall with his name on it. Directed them, I think."

"Anything else?"

"That was the funny part."

"What?" Leon asked, becoming more interested.

"There was a trunk. I was alone up there, so I opened it. It had photos but not this guy's family. Real old pix. And letters. Found one dated from 1930 from some guy named Needles. Funny name, right? Another one signed Crank. There was also one envelope wedged inside a book. It was mailed to someone. But it had *Return to Sender* stamped on it. I opened it. Some kinda paper folded up inside."

"You get a chance to read it?"

"Not the whole thing. But it had a bunch of names on it. Looked like they all signed it. Legal like."

"You see any names you could make out?"

Jabo took a minute to think and said, "I think some I saw one name. Like Marco or something?"

"Marcus?" Leon asked, pushing Jabo to think.

"Could've been. Had a funny kinda of picture of a guy on the top. Like a letterhead or something. Like he was shooting an old-fashioned movie camera."

A shot of adrenaline suddenly spiked through Leon's body. "You take it?"

Jabo hesitated. "Nah. The guy came into the attic and got all weird on me for looking inside the trunk. He saw me holding the letter, took it from me, and put it back in the envelope. Asked me if I was looking for termites in there like he knew I wasn't. So I sez they build nests inside dark places, and he sez I maybe should finish up. So I pretend to look around some more and tell him there are some trouble spots and I could come back later. He sez he'd let me know, and I could tell he thought I was doing something hinky."

"That it?"

Leon's mind drifted as he pulled Jabo's details together. He looked at the mirror on his desk and put his index finger on his cheek. He touched a spot. A pimple breaking out was like having carcinoma.

"Leon," Jabo said. "You still there?"

Leon put a dab of ointment on the potential zit. "Yeah. Good work, buddy."

"You ever need me to do this kinda thing again, lemme know."

"You bet."

"And think about a visit. Got a special bottle of Jack we can break into."

"For old times."

"That piece of paper I found. Important?"

"Could be."

"You thinking of visiting this guy? Take another crack getting it?"

Leon made a sucking sound. "Maybe sooner than you think."

CHAPTER 50

DUSTING FOR FINGERPRINTS ON THE INVISIBLE MAN

Afterward, she lay across my chest, my arm around her waist, our breathing returning to normal. Our bodies were covered in a sweet sweat made of the energetic lovemaking that had us both smiling and wondering at the same time.

"Don't ask," Zena warned almost breathlessly.

"Ask what?"

"Yes, it was good for me. Actually pretty great."

"Yeah."

"Yeah, it was great for me or great for you?"

"Both," I answered, filling my lungs with air like a runner catching his breath.

"I think I'll have a chocolate now."

"Ah, the orgasm has generated the desire for a bit of chocolate."

"Yup."

We lay there in silence for a while. Having sex with Zena was good that time. Different to be honest but nonetheless good. Making love to her and completely ignoring she was a dwarf would be a lie. Maybe it was the increasing familiarity of knowing her body by sight and touch and knowing her as a person. I thought of a roller-coaster ride. When you go on it the second time, you know what to expect.

"How is your story going aside from John bailing on you?" she asked, giving my thoughts about her a breather. She propped her elbow on the pillow to hold her head as she faced me.

243

"Mostly notes so far. A few descriptive paragraphs. Like what the midway and circus look like, the smells. The sounds. The people that come here or work here. I'm trying to get the feeling of this place."

I could see that she went to another place inside her head, her expression going from a pleasured state to one of concern.

"What's bothering you?"

"About you helping find out about his past," she said simply.

"You're having second thoughts now?"

"Are you helping John or helping yourself if you find anything…" She paused a beat and then added, "Juicy."

I sat up now, our eyes meeting. "I am only trying to be the good guy here."

I could feel Zena suiting up her old protective armor.

"Come on, Fenn. I don't have to be a psychic. You came here with a mission. Get a good story. John is part of that. He won't spill his guts to you, but you could find out things about him on your own."

"I told you what I would do with anything I find. If you don't trust me, then just forget what I said I'd do."

"I'm sure you get that trusting people has always been an issue for me." There was an edge to her comment.

"I do, and I have no idea what I'd find. Your friend's past might be like dusting for fingerprints on the invisible man."

"I hope you're a man of your word. And I hope I won't regret it later."

"You won't."

"What's your plan now? About your story assuming John is out of the picture."

"Well, I need to find another person as fascinating as you."

"You already got inside my pants, so you don't need the smooth talk lines."

"You are fascinating. I mean it."

Zena puzzled over what I had just said. I immediately wondered if that was too much of an affectionate disclosure on my part.

"So you want to be a Zena groupie."

I gave her a sideward glance. "I don't want to be your groupie."

"What do you want to be?"

"How about a friend?" I suggested.

She thought about this for a moment. "We'll see where that goes. Let's be real, Fenn. Once you're done here, we will be distant but pleasant memories. Maybe be friends until then. When we first slept together, I was driven by…"

"My incredible looks."

"No, numb nuts. By my neediness."

I tilted my head, taking in that admission. I wanted to ask her what kind of neediness, but I let it go. I kissed her cheek. "Can I ask you a question and not get a bullshit answer?"

"Maybe."

"You gave Holey John a wad of money. Just like that. Peeled it off a roll that would have given Bernie Madoff a boner."

She lay back down with her head on her pillow, and then she stared at the ceiling, silent for a while. "I have a trust fund," she eventually admitted, "from those lovely people who dumped me. More of a shame fund."

"You ever wanted to find them?"

"No. I can't see any therapeutic value in doing that. But I'm cool taking their guilt gelt. Not an even trade for what they did, but life doesn't deal out fair trades."

I waited a moment, thinking, then asked, "So if you have this nice bit of income coming in, why are you doing this, working here? You could do anything."

"I guess we just entered a judging-my-life-choices moment."

"Not intended."

Zena was quick with her answer. "I like the life. I like the people here for the most part. The Giambolvo buffoons I could do without, but it is what it is. Nobody likes their landlords or their bosses, right?"

I could see why she chose to work here. She had said enough in our previous conversations about not feeling comfortable in the world outside the midway. I had no idea if she thought about anything other than staying with the Giambolvo Brothers for the rest of her life.

An odd thought crossed my mind about how similar we were. Did fear keep her here, living in a protective bubble just as I had about leaving the Big Apple? I knew about bubbles and feeling safe in that comfort zone. Was her life safe and predictable? Maybe like mine.

"You're thinking," she observed.

"I am."

"About me?'

"Yes," I admitted.

"More deep thoughts and questions."

"Of course."

"Maybe I won't be able to answer them. Or want to."

"Maybe not. Too penetrating."

"Ah."

"Ah, what?" I asked.

"Penetrating. Let's continue the penetrating things that I have no problem with."

I smiled, and she slid her body over mine. Round two. *Ding-ding.*

CHAPTER 51

REPRESSED BEAN COUNTERS

When Brinks picked up the phone, he heard Brandy's sing-song voice. "Mr. Brenner for you."

"Pass him through."

"Marvin," Brenner started.

"Yes, Mr. Brenner."

"Our friends from Hong Kong have arrived."

"Good," Brinks said, not thinking it was anywhere near *good*.

"They're in the executive conference room. Brandy sent coffee and cakes up from the commissary. Had her order tea too. That's what they drink, right? Just in case."

"Either way we're covered."

"I want them to be happy while they're here," Brenner stressed. "You need to make sure of that. Anything they want, you get it for them. Anything."

"I can do that." Brinks knew what Brenner meant by *anything*. It was Hollywood code for delivering anything and anyone to satisfy the unspoken indulgences that help people make decisions in your favor.

"Big bucks at stake," Brenner reminded unnecessarily.

"Got it."

"The books look okay?"

His stomach tightened but gave Brenner a smooth. "They're good to go."

"Head up there and introduce yourself. I'll meet you in five."

Brinks put down the phone. The accountants had arrived, making him feel like a reminder call for colonoscopy. In the last few weeks, he moved most of his bogus costs around so that Glowball's movie house flops, *RoachMan* and *Sarah's Shadow Light* looked like major fiscal disasters. If those guys didn't dig too deep, his sleight-of-hand ledger maneuvers would be enough to avoid closer inspection. Glowball's other movies had done fairly well, so the company was legitimately in the black. Production costs, salaries, and overhead were all being paid. Bonuses were given. People were happy. The big skim shouldn't be noticed.

His real worry was making sure no trail to the Maxwell and Mazer contracts would surface. If an heir popped up, a serious effort to determine Glowball's cash value would follow unearthing things that had to remain buried. His reliance that that wouldn't happen was all on Leon. One fucking piece of paper and Brinks would lose his entire world. Worse yet, depending on a person like Leon was like having faith in a juggler juggling bottles of nitro.

Brinks got up from his desk, reciting Brenner's instructions in his head. Keep them happy. That was one thing he knew how to do and do it well, having done those favors before. He slipped on his suit jacket, smoothed the wrinkles out, ran his fingers through his hair, and exhaled a sigh like a man blowing out candles.

When he opened the door to the conference room, he saw Brenner and Brandy next to three men. All three wore Armani suits, not Hong Kong knock-offs, which he could spot twenty feet away. They were in their forties, seemingly fit, fairly good looking. He put on his best smile and stepped towards them.

"This is Marvin Brinks, our numbers guy here," Brenner said, introducing Brinks to the three men.

The first man shook Brinks's hand. "Edgar Foo Young," he said. "These guys call me Eggy."

The second man did the same, shaking his hand. "Charles Chan. You can call me Charlie."

Brinks noticed both men spoke very good English.

"Welton Hung," the third man said. "My friends call me Welt."

The three men stood around Brinks stone-faced for a few moments them burst out laughing.

Brinks frowned, not catching what was going on.

Brenner was laughing too. "Come on, Marvin. You're slower than a three-legged turtle."

"Christ. Got me going for a minute. Charlie Chan, Eggy Foo Young. Well Hung."

"I'd say for more than a minute," Charlie said. "My last name is really Zheng. Welton is William. William Qian. And Edgar's surname is Wang."

"My college roommate at Harvard Business School was Alvin Weiner. Wang and Weiner. They called us the two dickheads. Didn't help us get laid."

Brandy looked at the carpet and giggled.

"Harvard, huh?" Brinks said.

"Wharton boys," Charlie added, pointing to William and Edgar.

"Nice creds," Brinks said.

"We all have Chinese Tiger moms. Get high marks or die a hundred little deaths through humiliation."

"One way to motivate,"

"No carrot, lots of stick," Edgar said. "Little time for dick."

Brandy blushed this time.

"Okay, Marvin, I'll let you men get started," Brenner said, changing the subject. "You need anything from me, let me know. Otherwise, Marvin will get you any information you need about our financials. We look forward to working with your group."

Brinks nodded.

"Can I do anything more?" Brandy offered. "If not, I'll leave you gentlemen to your work."

Brenner walked by Brinks and, in a soft voice, said, "Anything they want," he repeated.

Brinks nodded.

When Brenner and Brandy left the room, Brinks said, "Shall we sit and talk business for a few minutes. See how you want to do this. I can give you access to a secure area of our accounting information. Accounts payables and receivables. Liabilities, fixed costs, projections. You name it."

"Blondes," Edgar said eagerly.

"For each of us," Charlie added.

"Excuse me?" Brinks replied, his eyebrows raised.

"Screw the books today," William said. "We need to kick back. The plane ride was a bitch, even in first class."

Edgar added, "My ass needs a massage."

"By a blonde," William emphasized and chuckled. "And not just his butt."

"And we want a kick-ass meal tonight," Charlie added. "A great steak place. Not Kam Hong Garden or Mr. Chow's. We get plenty of that shit back home."

"And the blondes," Edgar reminded. "Barbie Doll or Midwestern farmer daughter types that like to party. Do very nasty things."

"The nastier, the better," William said and laughed.

"And some coke," Charlie said under his breath and tapped his nose.

Brinks's head felt as if it had whiplashed, his visitors firing off their requests.

"Can you get us the ladies tonight?" Edgar asked.

Brinks chuckled. "You guys cut right to the case."

"We are repressed bean counters," Charlie joked.

"I'll need permission from your Dragon Mothers first." Brinks kept a straight face. "And your wives if you have them."

The three men looked at each other, baffled by Brinks's prerequisite.

"You're fucking with us, right?" Edgar said apprehensively.

"Absolutely," Brinks said and smiled. "Gotcha, Eggy."

"You're a slick dick," William chuckled.

"I'll set you horn dogs up," Brinks said with a conspiratorial grin. He had done that before. Horny businessmen that needed to be bribed with call girls, party enhancements, or things more exotic. He called it the Triple P: the Pussy Party Package. He'd call his escort agency. Freddy would supply the blow.

"You are a glorious person," Charlie commended.

Brinks wasn't sure that was the right word but said, "Thank you." This was good. Those guys would have a glorious time. The girls would wear them out along with the blow and whatever they drank. Mixed with jet lag, their attention to his cooked books might be as focused as a hyperopic astronomer. He could keep a daily girl train going for them that was as dependable as a sunrise.

"I'll have our limo take you back to the Marmont where you'll be staying." Brinks glanced at his watch. "I'll make a reservation at the Cut on Wilshire. Greatest steak place in Beverly Hills. After dinner, the young ladies will show up at your suite with presents." He tapped his right nostril.

After dinner, when he parted ways with his new pals, the ladies would rock their worlds. Add some coke and they'd rock till they dropped. Their level of bean-counting fastidiousness would be more slipshod than he'd ever dreamed.

CHAPTER 52

MUGGA BOOMBA MUMBO BUBBA

I was back at my hotel, concerned about tomorrow's call with Stan. When we had talked last, he wanted me to deep-dive into Holey John's head, which was like sending me out to talk to a tombstone. Zena might try to turn him around, but I didn't have much hope my taciturn subject would suddenly open up to me like an oyster offering its pearl. Moreover, in the afterglow of sex with promises made, I agreed to channel my Sam Spade detective skills to help unearth Holey John's secreted history, which might explain his recent change of behavior. There were murky clues. His midway act, the trailer décor, the hidden photo, the scar on his scalp, the medals. And the house in Ithaca that seemed to have cast a spell over him. And as promised to Zena, whatever I discovered was not to be used.

Without Holey John, I needed a new and captivating subject. Someone as intriguing as Holey John. Someone that I could sell to Stan. I drove back to the G Brothers and wandered past the rides and the midway. The big tent was empty now, the matinee show having ended. A few roustabouts were cleaning up animal poop and empty popcorn boxes in the big tent, while others were tightening the ropes that secured the tent poles.

I could hear the animals behind the big tent and headed that way. The lion let out a hoarse roar. One of the horses neighed; a dog yipped. The horses were tied up in the shade of their trailer. I saw a long chain attached to the stake stretched out along the ground with its end wrapped around a camel's front leg. I looked around and saw a woman who had ridden horses in one of the big tent performances.

She had changed into jeans and a T-shirt, shedding her sequenced outfit and glittering makeup. Now she looked like a forty-year-old tomboy with a clear face and a healthy-looking, strong body. The kind of woman you'd want to marry if you had farmland in Iowa in 1885. She was brushing down one of the horses and saying soothing words to him. A horse whisperer. Might be a good story here. I went over.

"Hi," I said.

She stopped brushing the horse and asked, "Can I help you?"

"I'm doing a story on the people who work here."

She ignored me.

"I didn't catch your name."

"Because I didn't give it. Good luck with your story."

"Come on," I persisted. "I'm sure you have great stories to tell. How you got into what you do. The circus life. Stuff like that."

"I'm in witness protection."

I knitted my brow, not falling for that. "Come on. I need interesting people to make this story come alive."

"You talk to Babur. He'd have a good story."

"Okay. Is he around?"

"See those bales of hay over there. He'd be behind them."

"Thanks."

I headed to the stacks of hay. A man was humming, but it wasn't a song I knew, more like a windshield wiper thwacking in the rain. I went around, and there was a man whom I assumed was Babur. He was lying against one of the bales with his purple turban on the ground. Babur had a buzz cut, his hair as short as a Marine, a skull that looked unusually lumpy. Maybe six feet tall and thin as a rail, his overalls baggy and loose as a Mumu. He was doing something with his hands as I stepped closer.

"You Babur?"

The man quickly covered himself, putting his hands over his crotch. I guessed what he had been doing. I pretended to look behind me, giving the man a chance to put his junk away. I let a minute go by and turned back to face him.

I stated my question again. "Are you Babur?"

The man nodded and gave me a gummy smile.

"The horse lady said I should talk to you. I'm a writer doing a piece for my magazine," I said, introducing myself.

He nodded again.

"So you work here?"

He smiled again.

"What do you do?"

Babur got up, smoothed his overalls, and pointed to the camel standing by the horses.

"You ride him?"

He shook his head.

"Take care of him?"

He grunted with what sounded like a yes. He pointed to a long-handled broom. *Great.* The man cleaned up camel poop. Maybe there was a cool story about how he'd got the camel. Maybe he was a camel whisperer like the equestrian lady. Maybe he knew Lawrence of Arabia. I had a lot of maybes that could pan into something. Or so I hoped.

"The camel yours?"

He gave me another gummy smile again, and then he got up and did a little dance. I thought he was trying to imitate a camel hopping over hot coals. I had no idea what he was trying to convey.

So far, my line of questioning wasn't priming Babur's storytelling pump, and his little dance wasn't doing much for me either. I needed words from Babur, not Irish step dancing. What the fuck was the horse lady thinking?

"What the camel's name?" I asked.

"Mugga boomba mumbo bubba."

His words came out thick and slow as if rags drenched in molasses were stuffed inside his mouth.

I tried a different question. "So where did you get your camel?"

"Mugga boomba mumbo bubba," he repeated with spittle following his words, and I moved a step back out of range.

A flash of suspicion hit me, so I asked, "What color was George Washington's white horse?"

"Mugga boomba mumbo bubba."

"Let me tell you about Ahab the Arab, the sheik of the burning sand," I sang, doing an injustice to the lyrics of Ray Stevens, my coprolalia kicking in.

He did a jig to my rap and said, "Mugga boomba mumbo bubba."

I smiled at Babur and would've shaken his hand as I left but knew where that hand had been ten minutes before. "Thanks for your time," I said and waved goodbye.

"Mugga boomba mumbo bubba."

I went around to the other side of the hay bales and saw that the woman who had been brushing the horse was still there.

"You get that story you wanted?" she asked, giving me a teasing smile.

"More than I could've hoped for." I waited a beat. "You knew."

She laughed.

"I've been through the desert on a horse with no name," I sang.

She gave me a *WTF* look.

"Something I do," I explained.

"Cute," she said.

"What's up with Babur?"

"Tongue cut out in Afghanistan before the stoning."

This could be an interesting story.

"The story goes that he was stoned for having sex with another man's wife. They were both stoned. The woman died. Her husband's honor redeemed."

"I guess Sharia law doesn't include couple's counseling."

"He was left for dead. One of our army units found him. He had been an interpreter for them, and I guessed they felt they owed him. The sent him to the States. How he wound up at a zoo that went out of business is unclear. The G brothers bought Bertha at auction, and Babur came along with the deal."

She pointed a finger up to the sky like when Big Papi would hit a home run. "Kismet."

"Moves in mysterious ways," I agreed.

"I see you with Zena a lot. Remarkable lady."

"So you know her?"

"Share a coffee now and then."

"She has quite a story," I said as obliquely as possible. The horse lady gave me a twitchy look. "Been having interviews with her and other folks here."

"Interviews? Is that what you call it? Be nice to her, okay?" The equestrian was clearly protective, guessing what I might have going with Zena.

"I am." I paused. "Can you suggest any other interesting people I should talk to?"

"Holey John comes to mind."

"I got crossed off from his Christmas card list."

"I'm thinking you have a knack for pissing people off."

"Goes with the job. Anyone else come to mind?" I asked her.

"Fodder for your story." She thought for a moment. "Well, there's two people."

I waited.

"The G brothers. You got colorful, and if poundage counts for substance, you got that."

"Zena had the same idea. Could be something there if I feel hopeless."

"Desperate times calls for desperate measures." She went back to grooming her horse, and I waved goodbye.

I left thinking about Holey John. With another series of dead ends and time on my hands, I promised Zena I would try to uncover what I could about him. I had a few ideas about how to do that. I'd call my father. He had been a first-rate detective for over thirty years. He still had connections that might help me track down his background.

As for my story, maybe the Muses would visit me with some fresh ideas. The thought of getting shit-canned by Stan was making me depressed. Maybe it was time to head back to my motel room and hit the vape for inspiration.

CHAPTER 53

PUZZLE PIECES

Holey John sat on the edge of his cot and looked at the open cash. He would sign the purchase and sales agreement and buy Ralph's house, the house that had belonged to Percy Maxwell—the uncle who had been his guardian angel.

Holey John's mind whipped around like tumble weed being blown down a prairie road. His visit to the house led to the discovery of the box that held pieces of his forgotten life which had been MIA for most of his life. He knew what the connection was to this town, a fuller understanding of the man he had been. His discovery might be the start of lifting the fog of a life lived like a madman.

His visits to Ithaca over the past years and what this city's sway on him made sense now. This town, unlike the dozens of others, had always been different. A primordial feeling buried deep in his DNA was unearthed as he sifted through the treasure trove from his uncle's hidden cache. He was overwhelmed by what he found, yet a feeling of peacefulness also spread through him.

Holey John realized he didn't have the entire set of pieces to complete the puzzle that was his life. Some key things were apparent now, but there were other things that weren't clear at all. He leaned back on his bed and stared at the writing on the ceiling. He wished he knew what the design meant, vaguely remembering drawing it after waking from one of his nightmares. And the old photo. The woman and the child must have been important to him. But how and why?

He glanced around his trailer. His walls were covered with eyes staring at him every day. Were they watching over him? Or condemning him for the things he had done in his past? And why was he driven to paste them there at all?

There were the piercings. What the fuck had been up with that? The piercings hurt, but he went to some place where he didn't feel it. That guy, that writer, had implied something. Fenn suggested some fucked up form of self-punishment. Maybe that asshole was right. But for what? Maybe it was time to scrap off the eyes, remove every piece of jewelry.

He picked up the large envelope the real estate agent had handed him. He worried about Zena, his best friend. She didn't know exactly what attracted him to that house. He was afraid to tell her. Afraid to lose her. She was the anchor than kept him from going totally over the edge. At some point, he would have to tell her, but he didn't know how she would react. He decided to tell her that day. Take her there. Show her around. Maybe she would like the place. She might even leave the midway and live with him and begin a new life as well.

He brought the cash box over to the table and looked down at the bundled stacks of cash. He studied it for a moment. A shadow moved across the table. He looked up. It was Wally. That fucking asshole was standing on a wooden crate.

Holey John slammed the top of the box lid down and pushed himself away from the table. He bolted to the door, opened it, and saw Wally scampering away across the field of parked trailers.

He went back inside his trailer. "Goddamn shit!" He picked up the box and looked at his makeshift oven safe. The asshole could have seen the oven door was open. Wally was trouble. He was crazier than a methed-out rat. The money wasn't safe now along with everything else he'd taken from his uncle's hiding place. Holey John closed the box and locked it. He had to hide everything now along with the key.

Suddenly, an idea entered his head. He thought of an ideal place to conceal the key. He rummaged through the glass bowl filled with his flesh-piercing jewelry. He found a sturdy brass safety pin. He unclipped the pin and ran the needle through the small loop at the top of the lock box key. Getting up, he went to the small bathroom and stood over the sink and looked into the mirror. His eyes roamed over his chest and found a small open spot on his left pectoral muscle. Clenching his teeth, he pushed the needle under his skin. When the needle poked through, he clipped it closed, the key blending in with all the other jewelry that decorated his chest.

He needed to hide the box and money. It couldn't be inside his trailer, that was for sure. He had to hide it someplace else. He grinned. He knew the perfect location. A place his uncle Pink would have seen fit. He headed to his pickup truck, got in, started the engine, and drove off and out of the grounds.

CHAPTER 54

ABOUT THIS MAN

The phone rang three times before Selma picked up.

"Hi, Mom," I said.

There was a long silence before she answered. "Oh my god," she said in a voice that sounded like a cable tightened around her vocal cords.

"It's me, Fenn," I said, thinking she didn't know who called.

"You need money," she said without missing a beat. "It's fine if you do."

"No, Mom. I'm swimming in cash," I replied, making use of my skills in hyperbole.

There was a stark silence.

"Your coprolalia acting up? You've been arrested? You got in trouble and need a lawyer."

"Mom," I said, exasperated. "I'm just fine."

I felt her panicked mind rolling around like a roulette ball trying to explain my call.

"Oy, you've got cancer," she said in a more constricted voice. She was thinking in extremes to rationalize my phone call. Why else would I call? If I wasn't asking for money or wasn't on death's door, then something even more terrible must have happened if I called home.

"No, Ma, I'm fit as a fiddle." I wondered what a fit fiddle actually was. Another opportunity to consult my other brains: Google and *Wikipedia*.

Selma was down to her last catastrophic reason for my call. "You get in trouble with the midget?"

She meant, did I knock her up?

"Dwarf," I corrected and then said no.

More silence followed by the sound of her lungs expelling a mixture of relieved breaths coupled with annoyance. Not many people can make that sound.

"I'm okay. I need to talk to Dad."

"Just like that."

"What?"

"No 'How are you doing'? No, what are you doing these days? It's called a conversation with your mother, Mister Big-time Reporter. Isn't that what you do for a living? Ask people questions? A call from you is like buying a winning lottery ticket. Rare and far-fetched."

I should have known that this kind of exchange would go down when I called. Selma was right. I rarely called. I had parental telephonic avoidance syndrome, although I expected this was not a real DSM diagnosis.

"Sorry," I apologized, trying to sound repentant. "So how are you?"

"Fine," she answered flatly.

"And how have you been feeling?"

"Fine."

I was getting the monosyllabic treatment. "Anything interesting happening with your work? Interesting cases? New techniques to explore your clients' inner demons?"

"Sarcasm won't get you anywhere."

Selma was in her "hurt mommy feelings" mode. "You wanted a conversation," I said.

"I'm still in shock."

"So while you're recovering, let me talk to Dad. We can talk later."

"He's busy."

"Doing what?"

"Yelling at the TV."

Selma took the phone away from her ear and pointed it into the room where my dad watched television. I heard faint but clearly decipherable accusations from him.

Dad was on a roll. "You think your lies become facts!" I heard him shout. "Entertainment for fascists!"

"Fox?" I asked.

"What else? He can't scream at me about the world going to shit because I agree."

"He can't skip a news cycle, you know."

"It's good therapy for him. He needs to let it out."

Mom, the eternal therapist.

I heard her call my dad's name. "Marco," she yelled, "take one of your heart pills. It's your son."

I half-smiled as I heard footsteps approaching.

"You okay?" my father asked.

"I'm fine. You?"

"These frauds. They took lessons from the Goebbels propaganda playbook. That bastard said, "If you repeat a lie often enough, people will believe it, and you will even come to believe it yourself." The fanatics have figured that out." He took a needed breath. "So what's up?"

"I need your help."

"Money."

Here we go again. "No, Dad. Professional. I need to track down a person. Not actually find him. More like find out about their history. Their past."

"Why?"

"It's this story I'm working on."

"Those midway people."

"Yeah. There's this one guy. He goes by Holey John." I explained what Holey John did on the midway, how old I thought he was, and how, according to my new midway acquaintance, Zena thought he was acting even more strangely than usual.

"A man making a living having pins stuck in him, and he's acting stranger than usual," Marco contemplated.

"That's what Zena thinks," I said.

"Zena. She's that dwarf that your girlfriend and mother detest."

"Detest?"

"You think you'd get a free nooky pass?"

"Nooky pass? Selma said that?"

"Hmm."

"Not in her usual vocabulary."

"Hard to predict what comes out of your mother's mouth. Like you. Just different."

"I never said I was intimate with this woman."

"Women have this sixth sense about men. If she's attractive and willing, they assume we go after it. In your case, they don't think size matters."

I grinned at his short people jibe. "Probably true."

My father had a good idea about my boudoir mattress hopping and thankfully passed on judging me, at least out loud.

"So about this man," he asked.

"When you were a cop, did you ever have to track down someone's past?"

"Sometimes. You know what his real name is?"

"I don't, and he won't say."

"Your little friend know?"

"She may but won't tell me. Seems that's the way these people roll on the midway."

"Hmm."

"You have anything you can give me?"

I thought for a moment. "He lives in a trailer. His wall is covered with eyes he's cut out of magazines. Hundreds of them glued to the walls."

"Peculiar but not something I can use."

"He has something drawn on the ceiling."

"What is it?" he asked curiously.

"Dunno. I took a picture. I can send it to you."

"Okay."

"He drive a car?"

"A truck."

My father was quiet again and then said, "Get his license plate number and the state it was issued in."

"Okay."

"Any chance you can get his fingerprints? One of my buddies from the FBI can run it through IAFIS."

"IAFIS? I think I heard something about that at the academy."

"Let's not talk about that."

It was still a sore subject for my father, although he had warned me that a career as a cop would not fit in with the way I was wired. Smart man, but who listens to a parent when you are twenty-two?

"It's their Automated Fingerprint Identification System. If we get a match, we can see if Mr. John has a criminal history. Also gives us mug shots, any scars or tattoos, characteristics like height, weight, hair, and eye color. Even aliases. If he served in the military or was employed by the government, we may get a hit."

"Thanks, Dad."

"Sure thing. Hope I can help."

"Selma want to talk to me now?"

"Selma," he shouted. A moment passed. "She's shaking her head."

"Still in shock."

"Call more often. That'll help."

I ended the call and thought about getting fingerprints and his license plate numbers. The plates would be easy. Not so for finger-prints unless I could swipe something of his. That would be a real challenge since we weren't on buddy-buddy terms.

CHAPTER 55

OOPS

The four men sat around the mahogany conference room table. Three of the men made snorting sounds. Brinks was not joining in the snort fest. Their snorts seemed to come as they studied the various online spreadsheets that he had given them. After delivering a week of Dionysian distractions to his new Hong Kong buds, they decided it was time to get down to business. They too had bosses who could not be put off forever.

He anxiously watched the men, whose eyes were glued to their laptops. The eyebrows on each of them were downturned like arrows pointing to the ground. Concentrated. Probing. Looking for red flags. Serious about understanding the financial health of Glowball Productions.

A week of supplying these men with drugs, booze, and babes was having the effect he'd planned. Their brains were mushy. Their ability to dissect the masses of financial information numbing. They were coming to the end of examining the expenditures for a five-year window of all Glowball properties.

They all had been in the conference room for five hours straight. Charlie Zheng looked up. "What you are doing is bad."

Brinks smiled stiffly; the hairs on his bristled, thinking some slip-up caught Zheng's attention. "Bad?"

"Our dinners every night with you. Too rich. My fucking stomach," he said, rubbing his belly. "Sounds like temple gongs on Chinese New Year."

A false alarm, Brinks thought with relief. "I know a good salad place," he suggested.

"Fuck salad. My appetite for that other stuff is still good," Qian said. He lowered his voice and pointed to his crotch.

"You sure ate a lot of bushy wushy salad," Wang joked. The men howled at that, and Brinks joined in. Their laughter settled down, and silence fell over the room for the next half hour until Qian broke the silence, pointing at his laptop.

"Are you kidding me?"

"What?" Brinks asked, his voice suddenly tight.

"RoachMan?"

Brinks waited for more.

"No wonder it lost money."

Zheng and Wang got up from their chairs and came to Qian's side. They all started to snigger. Brinks heard screams, but they were coming from Qian's computer. He got up to check out what the three men were seeing.

"The freakin' Japs did this shit forty-five years ago with *Mothra*." Wang was in a huff. "No wonder this bombed."

Brinks breathed a soft sigh of relief. "In this business, you don't get them all right. But the ones that hit made us lots of money."

The men went on for another hour in silence without citing any issues.

Brinks figured it was time to call it a day. "You guys ready for my favorite salad place?"

Wang gave him the finger, but then Qian frowned. "Just a moment."

"What?" Brinks asked.

"Where did you shoot RoachMan?"

Brinks closed his eyes for a moment, remembering. "Morocco."

"Morocco," Qian repeated.

"And this Sarah movie?"

"Toronto," Brinks replied. "Canadian government gives us nice tax breaks when we shoot there."

"Funny though."

"No, it was a drama."

"Not funny that way."

"What then?"

"Casting company in Morocco."

"They did a good job."

"You hired the same one for both movies. Mahal Films," Qian said, pointing at an entry in the spreadsheet. "Puzzling."

Brinks had an *Oh, shit* moment.

"How does a Moroccan casting company have connections in Toronto?" Qian asked, looking directly into Brinks's eyes. Wang and Zheng were also looking at Brinks, their usually cheery dispositions not cheery now.

Brinks hesitated. He quickly saw how he had fucked up. He had rushed his cover up and just cut and pasted certain cells into his revised *RoachMan* and *Sarah's Shadow Light* spreadsheet.

"Probably a data entry error," he said a moment later. "Summer interns. Temp workers. It happens once in a while. The oops factor."

Qian nodded. "Maybe there are other oops errors."

"It's possible. I can run a data duplication search program." Brinks suggestion was a shot from his hip, a quick answer that might satisfy his suspicious investors for now. "It will duplicate file names and cell values that are the same. Numbers, names, meta tags."

"Good idea. Data oops are not good for us…or you."

Brinks felt a sense of reprieve thinking he had a reasonable explanation, although duplication search was a stretch and may even catch more errors he'd made.

"Paper." This came from Wang.

Brinks turned to Wang with a question mark expression.

"We want to see a paper trail. Best way to cover our asses. Invoices, contracts, purchase orders, shit like that. Wang pointed at the laptop and said, "Need to compare what's here to paper. Not digitized, real paper."

"Not a problem," Brinks replied, knowing it was a major ass fuck to his scheme. A lot of the numbers were entries he simply made up. For that, there was no paper.

"One more thing," Wang said, looking at the other accountants. They knew what he was about to say and sang out one word like choirboys. "Tank!"

Brinks's frown was deeper than an Arizona dry gulch. *What was a fucking tank?*

CHAPTER 56

CAN'T MAKE SILK OUT OF A SOW'S EAR

After returning from the G Brothers fairgrounds, I went over my notes. I was still looking for captivating story subjects where my chances of success were getting slimmer than getting a date with Emilia Clarke.

I was about to hit the vape when my phone rang. I hoped it wasn't Lilly telling me she had killed my cat and plants. My dad's 411 on the free nooky pass that Selma and Lilly had a hunch about might make my girlfriend, if that was what she still was, have lethal ideas.

It was too soon to hear from my father since I had only texted him Holey John's license plate an hour before. Ruling that out, I figured this call would come sooner than later, and sure enough, it did. I looked at the caller ID and groaned.

"Hi, Stan," I said, my voice flat as Kansas.

"I am not sensing mirth and joy."

"You sense correctly."

"Ah, the dreaded publisher's call where the freelancer has hit a wall."

"Once again, you sense appropriately."

"Are we talking Great Wall of China size, Berlin Wall, or a farmer's field stone boundary marker."

"How about half a Berlin wall."

"As in Zena's in your pocket but her bejeweled friend is AWOL."

"How did you guess?"

"A man who sports himself as a human pin cushion must have some cruel demons he wants locked away. Kumbaya sharing with the

269

likes of you or any journalist is too much to hope for. And the odds of having his dark side published is not a race horse I'd bet on."

"Stan the Man can see through the spam," I rapped in honest praise.

"And so do you have just as interesting backup characters?"

I left his question hanging in the air.

"Your silence is not golden," Stan said with dagger pointedness.

"Let me be honest," I started.

"I would expect nothing less."

"My backups are basically people that you would call freak show folks, although Zena would whack my nuts if she heard me say that. So who are my choices? Biological oddities and risk taking acts like sword swallowers, fire eaters, a tattooed lady, and a dude that does nasal flossing with bungee cords."

"Bungee cords?"

"I made that one up, but you get the picture. Take away the theater and biological bad luck, and they are pretty normal for this setting, and *normal* isn't very interesting."

"You have to dig deeper, my friend. That is what a great journalist does."

"I can't make silk out of a sow's ear."

"I will ignore your dusty proverb. Getting your story to sing, that's the challenge. Find another character amongst the gaggle of characters that do the fascinating things that they do there."

"Right," I said, trying to keep Stan's hopes up as well as mine.

"A piece of journalistic advice."

"Sure," I said, wondering if he was going to lay some trite guidance on me.

"It's not what they do." He paused for effect. "It's why they do what they do. They all made choices, right? What drove them? You don't stick pins into your flesh because you think it's a cool idea. Or decide to swallow swords for a living because it's more exhilarating than working in an office cubicle. You need to get the psych behind the why."

Stan took a moment and then continued, "And you know the upshot if—"

"Yes, Stan," I interrupted, not wanting to hear his threat again. "Well, I might have a substitute for Holey John." I remembered the horse lady's suggestion.

"That's my boy."

"Not a sideshow character but characters they are."

"Plural?"

"The Giambolvo brothers. Think Boardwalk Empire meets the Fatty Arbuckle twins."

"Your metaphor is lost on me."

"These two brothers own the traveling circus with its midway acts you banished me to, to create a sink-or-swim story. They are obese cartoon character versions of old mob movie sleaze bags. They roughhouse people who don't fall in line. But Zena, one more than half their size, never takes their shit. She scares them."

"So where's the story? These brothers are just overweight bosses manhandling the help. That's what bad bosses do."

Stan was right. Maybe I was grasping at straws.

"It has legs," I insisted, although weakly. "I'll find the angle."

"I'll give you another week. You want to put the brothers into the mix, fine. Go back to the peeps you mentioned. Get the 'why they are here' point of view. And make Zena the headliner. If not midway people, then the guy who shovels up the elephant shit."

"Camel shit," I corrected, thinking of Babur the camel custodian, who was as articulate as a babbling brook.

"Whatever. Our audience may not choose these folks' lives, but we'd like to make our readers understand what choices they've made and why."

"Curiosity sells," I agreed.

"One week," Stan repeated and ended the call.

CHAPTER 57

EVEN CLOSER

Brinks heard his burner phone vibrate in his desk drawer. "Leon?"

"Who else would it be?"

"Right."

"Got some Key West Maxwell news."

"And?"

"There's a retired man living in the house Maxwell owned. Had my friend case the place."

"And?"

"He found a contract. It was Marcus Ellwell's. Might be others there."

"Excellent."

"Actually not. He wasn't able to take it." Leon heard a deflated sigh.

"Then we better run it down."

"You actually mean *I* should."

"Right. That's why we have a deal."

"Of course," Leon said, holding back a go-fuck-yourself given that Brinks held the keys to the make-me-a star kingdom.

After he ended his call with Brinks, Leon went back to sleuthing for the former's lost boys. Firing up his laptop, he clicked on the Tor browser. He typed in a name, Ollie Gustafson, and accessed an online database—the California Death Index, assuming Gustafson exhaled his last breath there. Leon typed 1940 through 1997, assuming good old Ollie was born around 1900 give or take a few years. The index displayed thirty-six names. That was workable. Next, he searched obituaries for each Gustafson that had gone on to greener pastures. The obits listed next of kin, surviving relatives, children and grandchildren. Leon printed out the names.

The white pages were next, and Leon cross-referenced the dead Gustafsons with an online list of phone numbers and addresses for the deceased's extended families.

Leon felt good. He was getting closer and would need a call script. What to say when he vetted what he called the *liklies*. How he would introduce himself. Find out if Ollie was any relation to these people and if they knew if he ever worked in the movies.

Of course he would use one of the new business cards he had printed. He selected his Lex Barrymore. A variation of Lionel Barrymore, one of his fav actors of the past.

Leon spent the next few hours trying to reach the people on the list. He programmed his disposable phone so his new name would appear on the caller ID. When voice mails greeted him, he didn't leave a message. When someone answered, it only took a minute to confirm if they were in his Ollie sweet spot. On his twenty-third call, he lucked out.

"Is this Nancy Kelley?" he asked when a woman answered. Nancy Kelley was listed as a niece in one of the Gustafson obits.

"Yes. And I ain't buying or donating."

"Not asking for money or selling anything. My name is Lex Barrymore, and I work for Brigham and Cross. Our firm audits companies and their stock trades, any lapsed contracts, and closed book payouts."

Nancy Kelley was silent for a few seconds. "I have no idea what the hell you're talking about. If you're trying to sell something, I'm not buying."

"No, ma'am," Leon assured, pouring on a syrupy response. "Just trying to see if you have an old agreement that entitles you to some money."

"I'm busy. Get to the point."

"You ever have a relative named Ollie Gustafson?" Leon spouted out before she hung up. "In the movie making business a long time ago?"

A few seconds passed, and she said, "Might've been." She played it vague, seeing what that guy was up to.

"Like I said, we help audit companies' stock records." Leon found a site called *Investopedia* and slapped together a mumbo-jumbo pitch for people without an MBA could understand.

"Go on."

"I'll keep it simple."

"Simple is good," she said.

"Companies have a period of time to handle monetary adjustments concerning shares of stock that might have been owned. It's called a book closure date."

"You said *simple*," she snapped.

"It's the cut-off date stock owners would have. If Mr. Gustafson was your uncle, he would've been entitled to a dividend payment. However, Mr. Gustafson's agreement was void since he never sold his shares or contacted my client. But our firm likes to close out the books for unresolved agreements. So what we do is offer compensation to the holder of the lapsed agreement even though they are not entitled to anything."

"How much compensation are we talking about?"

Leon waited before answering so he could goose her interest. "Typically, two thousand dollars for this kind of thing. We get the old agreement, you get the money."

He could hear a small gasp from Nancy Kelley.

"So I need to ask you again. Was Ollie Gustafson a relative of yours?"

Her answer was as swift as a lightning bolt. "Yes. He was my uncle. I was a teenager when he died. But I remember him saying he worked at the studios around Burbank. Sewed costumes for the actors and actresses."

"Movies, huh? He must've had quite a life."

"You'd think, right?"

"Your uncle had any other kin?"

"No one left. Just me. Mom and Pa passed a while back."

"Sorry," Leon said then asked his next question with caution, not wanting to sound too eager. "Did he leave you anything after he passed away?"

"Nothing for me to retire on," she harrumphed her disappointment. "I got rid of his household stuff and old sewing crap," Nancy explained. "Goodwill got his clothes and furniture. I kept some personal souvenirs from his picture days. Still need to sort that out."

"That could be fun."

"Hmmm."

Leon went on. "So there might be his papers. Letters. Photos. Those types of things."

"Most likely," she noted.

"You have any idea where they are?"

"I have a box or two in my basement."

Leon could feel her frown over the phone when she asked, "What exactly am I looking for? You said something about an old agreement."

"It would be a sheet of paper. Kind of an unusual design on the letterhead."

"What kinda unusual?"

"A guy filming with an old style movie camera. Guy with a cap on backward."

"That'd be Crank," Nancy Kelley chuckled. "He was a cameraman."

"A cameraman," Leon repeated.

"Yeah. My uncle told me they used to hand-crank the film when they shot movies."

"Sounds cool," Leon said. He caught himself hissing on the word *sounds* but hurried on with his conversation with the woman.

"Yeah. Delmar Gilmore—that'd be Crank—lived somewhere around here. Uncle and him used to visit, talk about the good old days, like old people do."

Leon smiled to himself; Nancy Kelley was giving him a possible new lead to another name on Brinks's list. He came back to the conversation. "You come across anything with that letterhead?"

"Like I said, I haven't gone through his papers real thorough like. But that designy thing rings a bell. I gotta feeling I seen it on something. Not sure what it was though."

Leon felt a glow grow like the feeling he'd had when he had a good facial at Purity, the West Hollywood spa he visited once a month.

"I have some business in your area next week," Leon said. "How about I come over and we can see what you have?"

"Just gimme a call."

"I'll bring a checkbook just in case we find it."

"Sure," she said then gave him her address. "Next week then," she said brightly and hung up her phone.

CHAPTER 58

ONE THING AT A TIME

Zena said she had something for me when I came by her booth. She reached into a box under her chair and carefully pulled out a bag. I opened it and was about to reach in when she said, "Careful, cowboy."

I saw something wrapped with tissue paper. She handed me a handkerchief. I unwrapped the tissue paper and saw it covered a Betty Boop coffee mug.

"A gift?" I asked, confused about the 'Do not touch' order.

"It's got John's fingerprints on it, like you wanted." She smiled and asked, "You talk to your dad again?"

"Gave him Holey John's license plate number. His truck is registered in Chicago. But the address he gave to their DMV was a feline rescue shelter."

"Really? Never thought he was a pussy guy like you."

"Cute."

"He get a name?"

"John Burke. My dad is tracking that name down." I raised the mug. "This will help a lot."

She offered a sad smile.

"What?" I asked.

"I'm violating his privacy."

"You're worried about him, and we're helping him."

"I think it's more than that."

I looked at her, waiting for her to complete her thought.

"That house. If he buys it, then—"

"Then what?"

"Then what will I do?"

"Without him?"

She nodded, a look of loss and apprehension crossing her face.

A customer came up to her booth and waited for me to leave.

"One thing at a time," I offered. I put the mug back into the bag and said goodbye.

CHAPTER 59

FREAKIN' YOUR SHIT

When Leon showed up at Jabo's bar, Jabo screamed out, "Holy fuckin' shit man."

Leon smiled. "In the flesh."

The man came from around the bar and gave Leon a bear hug. He guided him to a booth where the wall was decorated with 1960's Kitsch: calendars with women in skimpy bathing suits, old movie posters of Easy Rider, Mad Max, and the Wild Angels. He broke out the Jack Daniels, and they began catching up on life after delivering death.

"You know what sticks a broom handle up my ass," Jabo started.

"Not a good image, Jabo, but go on."

"If you was boots on the ground with all the rag heads you sent to Allah, you would've got medals. But this PlayStation drone shit we did got us zilch."

Leon nodded. "Covert works that way."

"Fucked up." Jabo thought for a moment then said, "But that one thing you did."

Leon knew what was coming next.

"It was a bit fucked up, you know." Jabo shook his head back and forth. "Maybe more than a bit."

Leon nodded again.

Jabo was referring to Leon's unauthorized Hellfire missile he sent into a building that killed a family who were just civilians.

"You were freakin' your shit. What the fuck made you do that?"

Leon didn't think too long about his answer and said, "'Cause I could."

"You one crazy motherfucker, you know."

Leon shrugged. "People say that."

They drank some more and went through a half bottle of JD.

They chatted some more about Iraq, how fucked up that place was, how the politicians who started the war should suck sand.

After some time had elapsed, Leon changed the subject. "You think I can borrow your friend's van for a couple of hours? The pest control guy."

"You gonna try and get back into the house?"

"Yeah."

"My pest guy is regular," Jabo explained, looking at the old Jax beer clock on the wall. "Should be here in half an hour or so."

Leon laid five one-hundred-dollar bills on the bar. "Here's what I owe plus whatever you need to give the man."

Jabo took the bills and put them in his pocket.

"One more thing."

"Sure."

"I need a dead rat. Maybe a couple."

Jabo smiled. "Always up to something, you crazy son of a bitch."

Leon smiled back. "Props."

"Just tossed a few in the bins outside. Unwelcome after-hours visitors chompin' D-Con will do that."

Leon pulled up to the house that Maxwell had owned. He wore an Ornix shirt which was a little tight around his chest, the one that the pest control guy had lent him for an extra twenty bucks.

Leon knocked on the door and heard someone shuffle, stop, then put an eye to the peephole.

"I don't need your service," a man said, with the door still shut.

"You may want to rethink that, sir," Leon said. Wearing a pair of blue latex gloves, he held up one of the dead rats in front of the peephole.

"What's that?" The man's voice sounded puzzled.

"Rats. I found them belly up behind your house in your swimming pool. Looks like it ate some of the pellets that the last guy from my company had left behind. I'm just following up."

"He didn't say nothing about rat poison."

"Part of the inspection he did. I can take a look inside. Free of charge of course."

The man hesitated and then opened up the door. Leon gave him a warm smile.

"What's that you got there, son?" He was pointing at the canister of insecticide Leon was holding.

"For termite, roaches, ants. Spray it around the edges of the foundation and floorboards."

"That free too?"

"Why not?" Leon said, offering him his best smile.

The man led him into the house as Leon made a convincing show of looking for rat holes and insect nests.

"You have anything upstairs?" Leon asked.

"Just an attic. The other guy was up there."

"I know. He made a report and suggested we spray the baseboards. Check the boxes he missed. Critters love hiding in them. Build nests."

The man rubbed his chin thinking and then said, "Okay, I guess."

He led Leon to the attic. Leon circled the perimeter of the room, going through the motions of spraying along the baseboards.

"Let's take a look at your boxes," Leon said, stopping at one of the cardboard boxes that came from a moving company. "Can you open it?"

He let the man take the lead. The man nodded and Leon said, "Feel the bottom of the box. Does it feel damp at all?"

The felt the bottom and said, "I don't think so."

"Good. Now smell the contents. Put your nose inside a couple of inches." Leon instructed, watching the man. "Any mildew or moldy odor?"

The man sniffed. "Might be."

Leon had a good hunch that any paper stored for over twenty years would smell funky.

"Everything in there should be moved to a plastic bin. Put some activated charcoal or briquettes in the bin. Charcoal will absorb the odors."

They went through the same routine with a few other boxes, and Leon shared his recently Googled pest control advice. As he went from one cardboard box to another, he spotted the trunk that Jabo had mentioned.

"You should check that one too," Leon said, touching his nose with his forefinger to remind the old man about the sniffer technique.

"Right."

He opened the trunk and put his head in a few inches. A moment later, he surfaced smiling. "I think we're good here."

Leon came over and knelled. "Need to be sure. Take some of those things out and see if there's a slight layer of what looks like dust. If there is, you have a problem. That's not dust. It's roach eggs."

The man began removing the contents of the trunk. Leon kept a vigilant eye on what he was taking out. That was when he spotted the envelope. "Don't see no dusty stuff," the man said as he got up from his knees and stood in front of Leon, pointing down to where he had piled up the contents inside the trunk.

"That's a relief," Leon said. He bent down and pulled out the envelope that Jabo had described.

"Whatchu doing with that?" the man asked, suspicion clear in his question. "That other guy had his eyes on that. What's in it?"

"Dunno," Leon said. "Looks old. Has an old stamp on it. I collect stamps. My hobby."

"Maybe I want to collect old stamps. Put it back." He snatched it from Leon's fingers.

Leon stared at the man for a few hard seconds. He smelled the man's fear. Then it came to him. He saw what he waited for, for so long. Handed to him at last. It was like the angel of death had blown its hot, acrid breath into him, giving him permission. Leon stepped away from the man, studying him. His lips twisted into razor-sharp lines as he lifted the pressurized spray nozzle, aiming it at the man's face. It took a second before the man could process what Leon was about to do. Before any words of protest left his open mouth, Leon gave the man a full blast of the insect spray hitting his eyes, keeping it going into his gaping mouth.

The man lurched backward and dropped the envelope, his hands thrusting outward, trying to stop the spray. Then his hands went to his eyes, trying to rub away the spray which only made his sudden blindness even worse. Words didn't leave his throat, poison constricting his vocal chords. He stumbled past the trunk, resembling a character from a zombie movie.

Leon put down the canister of inspect spray and grabbed the man by his arm, pulling him close. With his other hand, he wrapped his fingers around his throat and squeezed it. The man tried to remove the claw-like grip from his neck, but his strength left him like a leaking balloon.

"Open your eyes," Leon ordered.

The man shook his head, his eyes burning hot coals.

"Open them!"

The man lifted his eyelids, halfway seeing through a blur of tears Leon smiling. This was what Leon had wanted for so long. Not the anonymous death he had delivered but death close up and personal. Death that came slowly as the light went out of his victim's eyes.

"That's right, my friend," Leon whispered. "If there's a heaven, you'll be there in no time at all."

The old man gurgled, and then he sank to the floor. Leon followed him down, his hand still wrapped around his throat until he took a final breath, his eyes open, seeing what would be the last thing his brain processed, and then he sagged like a wet washcloth.

Leon finally witnessed what he had hoped for and smiled. Death made intimate. An invigorating sensation flushed warm across his entire body. Better than sex although sex was never that satisfying. He picked up the envelope. Inside was a contract like the one Brinks had given him. He read the signatures—Marcus Ellwell and Theo Mazer—and then he smiled again.

Brinks's "Leave no trails" mantra came into his head. He went downstairs, went into the dead man's bedroom and came back with a blanket.

He parked the van in the back of Jabo's bar, which was then closed. He saw some people hanging around outside, tourists no doubt; the few that were, were drunk and oblivious to Leon's presence. After a while, they staggered back to wherever they were staying. When it was clear, he opened the back of the van and removed the blanket that was wrapped around the man he had killed hours before. Instead of throwing bags of Jabo's chicken gizzards into the alligator swamp behind the bar, Leon hoisted the old man over the fence. The body made a splash, and several gators beelined over to inspect what hit the water. In the moonlight, Leon made out an explosion of surface water churning madly. He saw pink slime surface within a whirlpool of water. It only took a few minutes and the water was calm again, the pink no longer visible.

He leaned against the side of the van and called Brinks. A sleep-heavy voice answered the burner phone.

"It's in the fucking middle of the night," Brinks grouched.

"Your beauty sleep can wait, although no amount will make you better-looking."

"So you also want a career as a comedian?"

"I got Ellwell's paper."

Leon heard Brinks's breath quicken. "You sure?"

"As sure as fish don't blink."

"What about the guy in the house? Is he going to be a problem?"

"Not now. He made a bunch of gators very happy."

Brinks saw an image he didn't want to see emerge.

"Also we have another lead. The envelope that Ellwell's contract was in was postmarked Ithaca, New York. Had *Return to Sender* on it."

"Ithaca. You thinking that's where Maxwell lived. Any return address?"

"No." Leon wondered about that. Why there? Hollywood was the center of the film industry.

"You thinking of going there?"

"After I see a lady about another lead."

"FedEx the Ellwell agreement to me," Brinks said and gave him his home address.

"What's going on at Glowball?"

"I got bean counters crawling up my ass. The faster you get the others, the better."

Leon grunted his acknowledgment and killed the line. Brinks's ongoing urgency about getting the contracts bothered him like an itchy mosquito bite he couldn't scratch. These accountants were making Brinks sweat bullets. But what was the connection to the contracts he was hunting down? He knew one thing. If he could figure that out, it would give him more leverage once he was done. And having leverage was always good.

CHAPTER 60

NEW KINDA LIFE

The three of us sat in Zena's trailer, not saying much. I sat next to Zena. Holey John sat across from us on a trunk that held Zena's assortment of costumes.

"Why is he here?" he asked, jabbing his finger toward my chest.

"I asked," Zena replied.

"Why?"

"To do something for me," she said, looking guilty.

"What...thing?"

Zena squirmed in her seat and then said, "I asked Fenn to find out what happened to you before you came here...your *past*."

"Why?" Holey John asked uneasily.

"You were acting funny." She said *funny*, but I knew she meant *weird*.

He let out what came close to a laugh. "More than...usual."

"What's up with that house?" she asked accusingly, not being part of his decision.

"It's...special."

Holey John turned to me, and I sensed something in him had changed.

"What did you...find?"

I looked directly at him. "To tell you the truth, not much. Your name."

"John Burke," he said, beating me to the punch.

I blinked. "Right. And that you were in the service but no more than that."

Holey John thought over what I had said over for a long minute and then turned to Zena.

"I got some things to tell…you. Personal stuff. Things I'm… doing now. Like the house. And things I might've…done," he said then turned to me and added, "I can save you the effort…of digging into my…past."

I exchanged looks with Zena.

"But I'm not sure I wanna share that…with you." He said this to me, his eyes steely.

"I can leave." I started to get up, but Zena pulled me back down from my chair.

"It's okay," she said. "Whatever you say won't be in anything he writes."

It was clear that Holey John was uncomfortable with me there. He gave me an unbelieving look.

"Scout's honor," I said.

"You were a…scout?" he asked, still unbelieving.

"No, but I mean it. I swore to Zena that I wouldn't write anything about you. She's worried about you. Thinks something went on before you came to the midway."

He took that in. Zena nodded.

"Okay," he said as if my pledge to Zena was enough.

Holey John shifted in his seat and ran his tongue over dry lips. He brought a knapsack which lay at his feet and pulled out two envelopes. There was a large brown business envelope that had seen better times and a clean, crisp white one with a logo on the top left corner. He laid both down on his lap.

He took the brown envelope and opened the flap, pulling out a yellowed newspaper clipping. He handed it to Zena. Her fingers gently pinched the sides of the clipping, respecting the age of the paper.

"Read it."

Zena looked down at the paper and read it, then tilted it in my direction to do the same. We both read it, letting a minute pass before saying anything. I looked at Zena, who looked at Holey John. I knew she was processing the information uncovered by her friend.

"Vietnam," she finally said. "That scar? You were wounded and—"

"And my brain got...scrambled. That's why..."

"It's okay, baby. It's okay."

Zena handed me the clipping and went over to Holey John. She placed her fingers over the old scar and then bent over and kissed it.

"I think that's why I have...nightmares," he said, softly putting his hand over hers as she touched his scar.

"About what?"

He shrugged. "I don't know. About something I did over there. I just wake up feeling...really bad."

"You received medals," she said, reading the paper. "For bravery."

"Yeah. But...for what?"

She looked at him, hoping for more.

"I dunno. My brain hurts if I try to...remember."

I didn't say anything. Bravery in war usually meant killing. His scar was most likely a testament to an encounter of some sort. This man who tried to come across as impenetrable on the midway was as fragile as Murano glass.

"You never talked about this to me," she said, sounding hurt.

"Talking makes it...worse. Besides...nothing is clear, just jumbled shit."

She came back and sat next to me. "That man was your uncle," Zena said, reading the newspaper again.

"Percy Maxwell," he said. "He's dead. So are my...folks."

"How do you know that?"

"I found another clipping in...Ralph's house. That old guy I met...owns the house I'm buying."

He showed us the obit about his parents.

"That's quite a lot to handle," I said after a respectful minute, seeing Holey John's armor shedding as he revealed what he had found.

"There were all these papers and photos...in the attic." He paused for a long moment. "That house was my uncle's...why it's special to me."

He held up a sheet of paper from the other things he had retrieved from the old man's house.

"Ralph says it was some kind of…business arrangement. Not sure if it's worth…anything. There was another one. A agreement I found…for a guy named Gustafson. I left it there."

I looked at his uncle's agreement. He had owned a movie company and sold it to a man. Mazer. His uncle and three other men who worked for him got one as well. Shares were part of this agreement.

"I'm no lawyer but see this," I said, pointing to the contract. "This language." I read a sentence to Holey John. "There's two words here."

"And you being a writer can explain them," Zena teased.

"You love to combine zingers with a compliment," I said.

"How I roll with you, sweetie. Get to the point. The words."

"There's a *in perpetuity* clause. It means there's no end to the agreement and has to be honored. Whoever this agreement affects has to honor it."

"I still don't…get it," Holey John said. "What it means…to me."

"The shares your uncle got would go to you as his heir. Maybe worthless but more digging may be a good idea."

One of Stan's lawyers could help, but on second thought, that probably wasn't a good idea since I'd promised Zena I wouldn't reveal anything I uncovered about Holey John, and Stan was a like a shark smelling the blood of a good story.

After I said what was in the contract, he looked at Zena.

"I'm going to buy…his place. My uncle's. Remember that flyer I showed…you before."

"You sure about buying it?"

He nodded, offering up a nervous smile. "Special…like I said."

"So that lady the other day. Fenn saw her."

He nodded and led up the white envelope. "Papers for me to sign…if I want to buy the place. Look at that clipping…again. That photograph. Me and my uncle…in front of his house."

We both studied the clipping. It made sense now, his mysterious meanderings in Ithaca.

We sat in silence for a time, the minutes hanging heavy in the air. I looked at Zena. I could tell she was sorting out this information.

These two people were joined at the hip. He was her protector. The tough guy always on hand as her personal bodyguard. And she was his protector. A soulful guardian to fend off the jerks that would beat him down emotionally or take advantage of his mental vulnerability.

I looked at Holey John and saw that delivering this news to Zena was probably one of the hardest things he had to do. Maybe ever. Leaving the G Brothers was an act of courage. Leaving Zena was even bigger like taking off his inner tube, thinking he could swim in the deep end of the pool.

"You can live…with me," he said. It wasn't offered in desperation but as a good idea. "The carny life sucks…right? The Giambolvos… are goons. What are we giving…up? We can start…fresh. A new kinda life."

Zena gave him an uncertain smile. "That'll be good for you."

"So what do…you think?" he asked. "About staying…here? Be my…roomie." He let out a coarse chuckle. "I close on the house…in a couple of…days. Please think…about it."

Her chest expanded, taking in a deep breath, then it slowly deflated. "Okay."

I thought that was the end of our conversation. But Holey John sat there, and I saw tears welling up in his eyes.

"What's going on?" Zena asked, concerned. She got up once more and moved close to him, holding his hand.

I assumed it was his anxiety about the life change he was making, the possibility of losing his best friend and going into a new world alone.

Holey John removed her hand and slipped his fingers into the brown envelope again. This time, he removed a photograph, the one we had discovered hidden under his pillow. He held it up to Zena. She pretended to see it as if for the first time.

"Pretty lady."

A teardrop streaked down his cheek, dodging around his jewelry. "She comes into my…dreams. At the end. After the bad…stuff."

"Who is she?"

"I've had this photo…forever. I'm thinking now she's from my time…over there." He paused and banged his knuckles against his skull, this time with an unnerving viciousness as if he were trying to dislodge a memory stuck hard like a barnacle fastened onto the side of a freighter.

He flipped the photo over and held it up to Zena and me, showing the scribbled text. "See that?"

It was the same writing we had seen on the ceiling of his trailer.

"What does it mean?" she asked.

He shook his head as another tear fell from his eye.

"I need to find out...who she is, and the little girl," he pleaded, his words anguished.

"I may be able to help," I offered.

He looked directly at me for the first time without resentment.

"I have experience digging up information. And my dad can help too. He was a detective. He may have access to records or people who can help find out things."

"What kind?" Holey John asked.

"Military for one. Do you know what branch you served in?"

"Army, I think. Don't remember a...unit." He paused. "But I think I was a point man."

"May sound weird." He paused again, thinking. "Quirks of... mine."

"Like?" Zena asked.

"Bridges. Hate going over...them. Highways too. Break out into...a sweat. Feel trapped."

If he was the point man, it made sense. An after-the-war consequence of trying to survive. Jungle paths with no escape.

"And smells. Can't stand the smell of a burnt match, cigarettes... aftershave."

That made sense as well. Scents wafting through the forest could tip off the enemy.

"Can I see the newspaper story?" I asked.

He handed me the clipping. I studied the picture of him, a young man maybe twenty or so, dressed in what looked like Army fatigues. I squinted at his uniform.

"See that," I said, pointing at his uniform, "on your shoulder. It's a patch. Probably indicates your unit. That can help find where you served. I bet there is a military archive we can check. They'd have your service records. It'd be things like that which might turn up clues to find out who that woman and girl are."

"And what I…did?"

"That too."

I nodded, and for the first time, I saw an expression of thankfulness coming from him.

"You'd help me?" he asked in a soft voice.

Zena looked at me, and I didn't hesitate. "Of course."

"I can take a picture of the new clippings stories and the photograph. The agreement your uncle signed. Send it to my dad. Have a lawyer look into that agreement."

I could see him waver, still not trusting me.

Zena patted his hand. "It's fine."

He nodded an okay.

I placed the photos on her bed along with the newspaper clippings and agreement. I took several pictures.

"We'll see what my dad can find."

"I could show you…my house." He looked directly at Zena with soulful eyes, hopeful now. "Then we can talk…about me and you…there."

"I can do that."

His face lit up.

"I'd like to tag along," I suggested.

He nodded, wiping his cheek with the palm of his hand. "Thanks, Fenn," he said then got up, turned to us, gave Zena and me a crooked smile, and left.

Zena let out a big breath. "Wow. This was a big day for John." She looked intensely into my eyes. "And me."

"Big," I agreed.

She took my hand, squeezing it. "Thanks."

"For what?"

"Helping him find out about that woman and any other stuff that can help."

I could see that Zena was overwhelmed with everything that he revealed, the way he was breaking out of his mental prison.

We sat for a few minutes in silence. I watched her and assumed she was digesting all the information that Holey John had given her.

After a while, she said, "I have a mystery you can solve." I gave her a puzzled look, and in return, a look that was sultry and sad came over her. It was a strange combination.

"You liking to investigate things."

"True." I had learned in my brief time with her that when things became too uncomfortable, she favored distraction.

I was spot on as she got up, took my hand, and led me to her bedroom.

CHAPTER 61

THE TANK

Brinks parked his car in the Glowball parking lot. As he opened the car door, his burner phone rang.

"I'm back from the Sunshine State," Leon said.

Brinks didn't pursue what had happened to the occupant of Percy Maxwell's old home after Leon mentioned a bunch of gators being his big fans.

"You have Mazer's original, and I now have Ellwell's. Two down and three to go. That should make you happy," Leon summed up.

"Except the Hong Kong crew isn't done. It's like they want to find something bad." He understood if Brinks was in trouble, his own LaLa land dreams would go sideways.

"I'm making progress, buddy. Got good news to cheer you up."

"Okay, cheer me up."

"Gustafson. I may know where his copy is. I'm going to meet someone today. I'll let you know how it pans out." With that, he powered off his phone before he could hear any more of his client's anxiety.

*****

Brinks walked past Brandy, and they exchanged smiles. As he entered the conference room, the three men who had been scouring his worksheets moved their heads close together. They were speaking Chinese. Brinks knew this couldn't be good, seeing their conversation was agitated.

"The Tank," Qian said to the other men in English and then turned to Brinks. "We've been thinking that the oops thing is not so good. Why we want Tankowitz."

Brinks closed his eyes as his brain ricocheted an *Oh, fuck* pin ball inside his skull. That Tank. He realized they were talking about Sherman Tankowitz. His visit was never a good thing. He had the reputation of a numbers bloodhound and could smell bad ink a mile away.

"He can help sort through your books and papers. If all's kosher, you get a green light and our funding. He's faster than us when it comes to ledger dumpster diving."

Everyone in the movie biz knew who and what Tankowitz was all about. He made his bones in forensic accounting for movie studios. Men and women went to prison. Tankowitz specialized in analyzing fiscal data to reconstruct and detect financial fraud. His forensic analytics skill could drill deep, find wherever and whenever money exchanged hands, and uncover any transactional diversions for unexplained reasons. He could find shit even when people thought there wasn't any.

Brinks had an ominous thought. What if Tankowitz started looking outside the box, the inside box being Glowball? The outside was finding the Maxwell. All of his other sleight-of-hand tactics might be safe. Cracking his accounts in the Cayman Islands would be nearly impossible since he had leapfrogged his money using Bitcoins into more shell companies than a Nigerian email scam. But the Mazer agreements were a weak link if it ever surfaced along with any heirs. That would trigger a full-scale audit where the Tank would surely uncover his tricks, sending him a one-way ticket to Lompoc federal prison.

Zheng took out his cell phone and made a call.

"Sherman. This is Zheng." Pause. "Family is good thank you." Pause. "Yours? Good. Listen, I have a job if you can take it." Zheng explained his presence at Glowball and what he and his two colleagues were doing. "Maybe it's nothing more than some data entry glitches, but we need to be sure before we invest anything."

There was another pause. "Due diligence, right?" Then Zheng said, "You can help?" Pause. "Great. Tomorrow? That'll work. I'll give you Marvin Brinks's number." He then smiled at Brinks, who smiled back with a pathetic nod. "He just took over from Mr. Wolfe after his untimely death." Pause. "You heard, huh? Tragic, right." Pause. "Okay, see you later."

"We'll be back tomorrow with our guy," Wang said. "Might as well call it a day until the Tank gets here."

"You guys want company again," Brinks offered, referring to the ladies he'd set them up with. Better to have them on his good side, the ever dependable provider of pleasure.

"Maybe skip that tonight," Wang dismissed. "Gotta be fresh when the Tank arrives."

As they all walked out the conference room, Brinks saw that his fate was then in two men's hands. Leon doing his search-and-destroy mission. And now Tankowitz, who could uncover his peculiar book-keeping if his track record was as good as the people he destroyed had said.

CHAPTER 62

STICKY STICKS

Leon passed a strip mall before he reached a small white stucco house in Boyle Heights, a neighborhood on the east side of Los Angeles. Her place needed a new coat of paint, the harsh southern California sunlight baking the paint into flakes. The lawn was brown and burnt. A few scraggly bush berry shrubs lined the front of the house. Several lawn ornaments of cement bunny rabbits that had seen better days were scattered around the wilted sod in an attempt to add some cheerfulness to the surroundings. The effect was lost on Leon. He drove past and parked his car a couple of blocks away behind a van that advertised a pool cleaning service, his car out of sight of Nancy Kelley's next-door neighbors.

Leon looked around. The street was empty of people, most of them at work, he guessed. Satisfied he wouldn't be noticed, he opened an attaché case that lay on the passenger seat. When it clicked open, Leon fingered through its contents. This held his disguise parapher-nalia. Leon enrolled in an actor's workshop three years before so he'd be ready for any casting call. Along with acting lessons, they taught how to use makeup, apply beard and facial hair, use prosthetic aides to alter ears, nose, and bone structures. His job for Brinks was per-fect. If ever anyone he encountered were questioned, their descrip-tions of him would never come close to the real Leon. *Leave no tracks.*

He decided to use a wig and thick-framed eyeglasses. A pen-cil-thin moustache would be the final touch. Leon removed a hand mirror from his case and studied his transformation. He gave his reflection a perfect smile. Show time.

Leon spotted Nancy Kelley peeking through the curtains, watching him approach. She opened the front door before he had a chance to knock.

He gave her a wide smile as he mounted the two steps to her door. "Lex Barrymore," he introduced himself. He took out the business card with telephone and fax number for a law office in Kansas.

"Come in, come in," Nancy Kelley beckoned. The idea of ending up with two grand for some useless agreement made her scalp tingle.

The living room was small and decorated with paint-by-number paintings. He spotted a framed poster with Pearl White seated in a biplane cutting across a bank of clouds, goggles lifted up on her forehead as she smiled out of the frame.

"Crank shot that one," Nancy Kelley boasted. "My uncle did the wardrobes. Must've been a hoot to be working then."

Leon stood close to the poster and read the names of the actors. His eyes squinted at the name of the director. Percy Maxwell.

"Very cool," he said, feeling an inch closer to the Hollywood honey pot.

Leon then stepped away from the poster. "You said you might have old papers that your uncle kept."

"Yup. Found them in the basement. And that letter. It's in the kitchen."

Nancy Kelley led Leon into the kitchen. The walls were painted a hideous yellow that would make a banana ashamed. "Coffee?" she offered.

"No, I'm good."

She pointed to the kitchen table. An envelope lay there next to a jar of Dr. Perricone's Cold Plasma Sub-D. Leon knew it was a neck rejuvenation treatment to tighten sagging skin along the neck. Of course, it wasn't the high-end products he used.

Kelley handed Leon the envelope. He eyed it closely. Gustafson's name and address were handwritten in a distinctive style but with no return address or name. Leon studied the postmark and stamp. The postmark was smudged, but he could make out the date, 1973, and three letters, *ITH*. Had to be Ithaca again. He slipped a page out of the envelope.

"I need to check something out." Leon moved to the living room out of ear shot of Kelley. He called Brinks, who answered after four rings.

"I have Gustafson's."

Brinks let out a relieved breath that blew over the receiver. "That's good."

"Actually not."

"Why's that?"

"No contract. Just a letter with that logo on it."

Leon felt Nancy Kelley's eyes drilling into his back as he kept his voice low into the cell phone.

"What's it say?"

"Give me a sec…it says…

> I still have the one you wanted me to save.
> Heard you did well in Tinsel town…not like our
> palsy Mazer. You want it, let me know. You could
> frame it but the frame would be worth more
> than his deal with us. Life's a crap shoot, right?
> Ha-cha-cha.

"It's signed with a single letter. *P. P* as in Percy," Leon continued.

"What are you thinking?" Brinks muttered in a not-so-happy reply.

"Seems that some roads lead to Ithaca. And Gustafson's agreement."

Nancy Kelley stepped into the living room and gave Leon a "What's up" look. He smiled and pointed at the cell phone as if he was confirming something. He raised his index finger, making a "Just a minute" gesture. She nodded and went back into the kitchen.

Leon then ran through what he thought he knew and what he knew he didn't know. "I have to ask myself about why he kept the original."

"Good question."

"So for whatever reason, he held on to Gustafson's and maybe held onto the others."

"Why would he do that?"

"The letter says, 'I still have the one you wanted me to save.'"

"Time is running out. This bloodsucker Tankowitz is arriving tomorrow."

"So if I gather from your pee in your pants frame of mind, hurry the fuck up and go to Ithaca is what you're telling me."

"Right."

"But I got a closer lead to check out first. The Kelley lady mentioned that Gilmore used to visit her uncle."

"What about your Ms. Kelley?" Brinks asked, clearly nervous.

"Relax. I'll give her the two grand and she'll be happier than a pig in shit."

"Two grand for a letter?" Brinks complained.

"No trails. Your mantra, right? Be bad news if someone other than me finds her and asks questions."

Brinks sighed and said, "Okay, give her the cash."

"I'll be in touch," Leon said quickly and ended the call.

Nancy Kelley came back into the living room, watching Leon as he turned around. He led her back to the kitchen table and slipped the letter into the envelope, putting it into his jacket pocket.

"This what you wanted?" she asked.

"Yes." He pulled out another envelope, his fingerprints wiped clean from it with twenty-one hundred-dollar bills inside.

"This is your lucky day," he said, handing her the cash.

Her anticipation of something gone bad left her, replaced by the bouncy excitement of a high school cheerleader. She stepped away and looked into his face.

Leon smiled at her. But something changed as she gazed into his eyes, a puzzling look tilting her head to the side. The lids over her eyes came down halfway as some unclear recognition entered her consciousness.

"I seen you," she said suspiciously, wagging her index finger while squinting at him. "The snacks guy."

Leon took a step back, not understanding at first what Nancy Kelley was referring to. He had never seen her before in his life. So what the hell was she talking about?

"Sticky Sticks," she finally blurted in a sing-song voice. "I loved them. Cinnamon and sugar over that soft doughy stuff."

Leon's gut twisted, but he forced a smile. "Sticky Sticks," he repeated.

This was not good. This broad could place him. She could gossip with her girlfriends about meeting the Sticky Sticks man. He wasn't going to let his dream die because this woman had blown his cover.

"You look different now and all. But I'd never forget that voice. Your cute, toothy whistle when you said 'Sticky Sticks' on the TV. You still got that when you speak normal, you know. The way you said *this* before."

He nodded. "Not many people remember me."

"I have a funny memory thing going about silly things like that." She paused for a minute then asked, "So you gave up being a star, huh?"

"On hold for now," Leon replied without thinking.

"How about an autograph?"

"Sure. And how about giving me a big hug from an old fan?"

She smiled brightly as they embraced.

"A career change, you being here," she said into his ear. "Funny about how things work out."

"Man plans and God laughs." He began to squeeze her tighter.

"You're hurting me," she said as her breath was being squeezed out of her. "Come on now."

Leon squeezed harder.

"I mean it. Let go. I'm serious. I can't breathe," she wheezed.

She swatted at him, hitting his back, and then sunk her teeth into his hand drawing blood.

"Bitch," he said in a tight voice.

He didn't let go and squeezed even tighter. She beat her fists against his back in a pitiful attempt to get away, her body trembling. Leon heard a dull, cracking sound as her spine snapped. Her head fell back enough so that her face was inches from his own. She looked him in the eyes.

He smiled, seeing her life drain. This was better than the old guy in Key West.

"Why?" she said in a confused, guttural plea as his grip squeezed the remaining air from her lungs.

"Don't like having fans."

He stared into her eyes until her breathing stopped.

A minute later, her body went completely limp, and he let her go. She dropped to the floor, her eyes wide and mouth contorted into a frantic plea that never had a chance to leave her lips.

Leon thought of the man from the Keys and how he had savored seeing his life leave his body through terrified eyes. And now Kelley. The pleasure of stealing her was replaced by troubling thoughts. He had planned every detail of his visit except this was not in the script. He knew he couldn't just leave and have someone find her. Cutting her up into pieces and stuffing the parts in a trash bag was not an option. Too messy. There was only one option. Remove the body and quickly. Leon wiped down everything he touched, except the anti-wrinkle cream which he pocketed. Nancy didn't need it anymore.

Carrying her to his car parked a few streets away was not an option either. People might recall his car even though his was a rental using an alias. That's when he remembered the van.

Leon left the house using the back door. He took a quick peek and didn't see any neighbors in their yards. No dogs barked. People still at work. He hopped a fence and detoured to a side street. The pool service van was still parked in front of his car. He walked by the van three times. He heard a heavy-duty vacuum behind a house filling the air with noise. The pool guys were still doing their thing.

He stepped around the van, pulled the driver's side door handle and slipped into the seat. Looking around the vehicle, he spotted a large flat head screwdriver. He jammed the screwdriver into the ignition, turned it, and the van started.

A few minutes later, he backed into Kelley's driveway. He drove the van to the back of the house and opened the vehicle's back door, leaving the motor running. Nancy Kelley lay where she had fallen.

Leon looked around. Her pocketbook was hanging on a kitchen chair. He took the money and credit cards from her purse, leaving her driver's license. He also retrieved the envelope of cash that had excited the woman who thought she had died and gone to heaven. Maybe she did if there was one.

Leon grabbed a kitchen towel and wiped his fingerprints off of everything again for safe measure. He looked for any blood that might have come from the bite he had received. Her teeth didn't puncture the skin but left a nasty bruise. Satisfied, he scooped Kelley's body up from the floor and carried her into the back of the van along with her pocketbook. He closed the van's door, hopped into the driver's seat, and left the white stucco house in Boyle Heights behind.

Leon drove a few blocks to the corner of Saint Louis and Fourth Street and stopped the van. He saw a deserted parking lot next to a picnic area. He pulled the van under a tree and called Brinks as he began walking back to his car.

"It's me again. Our friend recognized me."

"How in sweet Jesus's name was that possible?" Brinks screeched.

"I told you I did some acting. Must've been good enough to leave an impression." Leon hoped this self-promotion would make Brinks see him in a better light.

"So now we have another problem to solve," Brinks countered, exasperation tightening his words.

"Chill, brother," Leon reassured. "Already solved. She won't say a thing to no one, no how."

Brinks had a bad feeling about how Leon had handled this new problem. "I don't want any details."

Nancy Kelley would turn up later that day near the picnic area in Hollenbeck Park. He knew how this would play out. Police would say it was a mugging gone badly. He parked the van at the strip mall and walked back to his rental. Another case of a stolen vehicle that no one would care about except the pool guys. He would probably hear about the dead woman on the six o'clock news. People who had a funny memory thing about anything about him would always be a problem.

CHAPTER 63

POKING AROUND

I ate a quick motel buffet breakfast. I wasn't enthusiastic about pans filled with lukewarm scrambled eggs, undercooked bacon, or boxed cereals. This wasn't the New York City fare served at my usual hang— Brooklyn Bagel and Coffee Company, which isn't in Brooklyn but in Manhattan. But the buffet had enough carbs and coffee to clear my morning cobwebs. I went back to my room, brushed my teeth, and put on a fresh shirt.

I started investigating Percy Maxwell as I had promised Holey John. I thought about the old newspaper with Holey John and his uncle. I fired up my laptop, searching for more info. According to Holey John, he was a silent movie producer and director right there in Ithaca. Using DuckDuckGo, I found a small scattering of info. Several awards. A place in Key West. Not much more except an obit saying that Maxwell died in Key West. Nothing about what he may have done in this Ithaca after he quit the biz and sold Mazer his inventory of moviemaking equipment. I looked at the time and realized I would be late if I didn't leave soon to pick up Holey John and Zena. We were going to get a tour of the house that Holey John was in the process of buying. My cell phone rang as I was leaving. It was my father.

"Hi, Dad."

"The miracles of caller ID," he said. "Nobody's anonymous."

"Screens out old girlfriends who may still have an attitude."

"And that would be a good feature for you."

"Extremely."

"I have some information about your friend," my dad said, changing gears.

I went to the bed and sat down.

"That image you sent me. I had one of my buddies who works in my old precinct's forensic lab blow up the photograph of the two men. The old guy and the soldier."

"Any luck?"

"Yeah. My buddy was able to zoom in on the patch on his uniform. It's got an eagle's head and the word *Airborne* on top. It's the insignia of the 101st Airborne Division. They were active as an airmobile unit from 1967 to 1972."

"Airborne?"

"Airmobile units could move rapidly. Get to their objective despite any terrain complications or enemy concentrations. These guys saw a lot of action."

"So he had to parachute—"

"No. 'Copter into a hot zone and land. Land in a paddy or field and head into the jungle," my father corrected.

I had a hard time taking the Holey John I knew then and spinning him back forty years with a weapon heading into a firefight.

"They were known for speed, surprise, and aggressiveness," he recited as he read off the notes he must have taken.

"What about military records?"

"I got enlistment information, but medical was off limits."

"What's up with that?"

"The guy that's helping me found a record of an incident, but it was redacted."

"Meaning...?"

"That someone didn't want to make public whatever happened, so it was heavily sanitized."

"And if the incident became public—"

"Certain people might not have liked it back then. I saw that cover-up crap when I was a cop. Like a bad shooting of an unarmed civie."

"You think government people did this?"

"Your guess is as good as mine. He won some medals, so I assume some shit went down. Maybe the kind certain people don't want revealed. If your friend ever cracks through his memory wall and remembers whatever it might have been, then who knows?"

"Maybe it should be kept hidden," I concluded, wondering if Holey John's nightmares were ghosts of things he did that were best forgotten.

"Maybe," my father agreed. "Remember Mai Lai? They tried to cover that massacre up."

"What about the photo? The woman and little girl?"

"Now that's another interesting bit of information I found."

I waited for my father to tell me what it was. He didn't say anything right off. He liked to do that just like a reporter would, wait until the end of a story to land the punch line.

"First of all, there's that scribble on the back of the photograph. And the same one on the ceiling. Only it's not a scribble. It's Vietnamese. A name. Of a woman. *Linh.*"

"Linh," I repeated.

"Records I got from a man I know down in DC say she was his wife. Linh Burke. Showed that he married an in-country girl."

"He's got a wife?" That news hit me for a loop. Holey John had never mentioned a wife. "And the little girl in the photo."

"Maybe his daughter, I'm guessing."

"Married and a kid. You sure?"

"Good hunch. Seems like over eight thousand soldiers married Vietnamese women."

"So where are they now?"

"The sixty-four thousand dollar question. Some came back with the men. Some got left behind when their tour was up and didn't take the marriage thing seriously."

"A marriage of convenience."

"Could be or if a grunt got his ticket punched over there and they stayed, maybe went back to their family."

"There was no mention in the article from that newspaper," I clarified.

"Who knows what his mental state was when he came back? If he was airlifted to a US-based hospital like Walter Reed and his head was scrambled by a head trauma, he might not even know or remember he was married."

"So no record of them coming over here?"

"None that I could find. Saigon fell in April of 1975 to the North Vietnamese. American civilian and military personnel in Saigon were evacuated with thousands of South Vietnamese folks who were allied with us. You ever hear of Operation Frequent Wind?"

"No."

"It was the largest helicopter evacuation in history. Anyway, there was no record of his wife being evacuated. Records had been destroyed before the military left. Who knows what could've happened? Maybe the ones that were left behind had to go off the grid when the VC won the war. Maybe killed for marrying a US soldier or sent to some up-country rehab work farm. Reeducation, they called it."

I let out a troubled breath. "Not sure how Holey John will take all this." I waited a moment. "Any idea if she may be alive?"

"Well, there's no record of being dead. I had one of my old contacts in the Fifth Precinct help me out. They cover Chinatown. Phuc is from Vietnam. Parents came over before the North won. He covers the gangs down here. Chinese and Vietnamese mix it up. Territorial turf shit. Long story short, he contacted his uncle over there and asked him to search for a Linh Burke. The uncle came up blank. No death certificate. No address. She could've changed her name. Or kept her family one. The police over there are useless when it comes to helping about things that happened over forty years ago, but you can hire a PI over there if you want to do a more thorough search. Said he'd give me some names."

"So she could be alive over there."

"Could be. If your friend can handle it, maybe he should go over there and see what he can dig up. Maybe some memories would be worked loose."

"Thanks, Dad. I'll see what he has to say."

I had a hard time imagining Holey John making a trip like over there with the possibilities of bad war juju unearthed, but you could never underestimate the power of will and love.

"That's all I have for now." My dad paused then said, "There's something else."

"What?"

"Not sure yet but maybe related to your friend. I checked the National Personnel Records Center. I got some of what I found about your friend because a buddy of mine pulled some strings. Normally, you can't get information unless you're next of kin."

"Okay," I said, knowing there was more info coming.

"You have to fill out forms and prove you're related. But someone with some authority has been poking around. And not next of kin."

"What kind of poking?"

"Like your friend is a person of interest. Can't say who or why so that's all I know right now."

I heard a voice in the background on my father's end, growing louder.

"Here's your mother," my dad said.

"So?" Selma started.

"So?" I said back.

"You have your father playing detective."

"I do. He's good at it."

"He's happy to help. Gives him something to do instead of managing what I do and yelling at the news. Retired men are a pain in the ass. So how's the story going?"

"I've hit some bumps in the road."

"Oh. With the midget?"

"Little person," I corrected. "No, my other subject."

"He a midget too?"

I let that one go. "No. He's the friend of the little person."

"What's he do there?"

I hesitated but decided to tell her what Holey John's shtick was and served in Nam.

"Oy," she twanged. "The man must have demons."

I didn't disagree. "He doesn't want to be in my story. He's very private."

"Maybe bad memories if he'd talk. I have patients that fall apart when their shit bubbles up."

Mom saying *shit* threw me off for a second, *shit* not part of her usual list of medically approved terms.

"Maybe I can recommend someone who treats vets," she offered.

"We'll see." I knew I was getting into treacherous water with my next question. "How's Lilly?"

"Your cat and plants are still alive. You may not be when you come back."

"Right."

"I have to scoot. Marco and I are having brunch with the Cicala's, your father's cousins. I hope we don't get spaghetti and eggs again."

Selma hung up with a quick "So long." I thought about all the things my father had found out. What could I tell Holey John? His unit in Nam. Sure. What they were known for. Maybe. What he did. That wasn't anything my dad had found. If there was a cover-up there, I had nothing to tell. But I could say that the woman and child in the photo were his wife and child. I'd talk to Zena first, about what she thought about telling him what my dad had found. I grabbed my keys and headed out to the parking lot.

CHAPTER 64

LOOSE ENDS

The day after he read the news and the cops trying to solve Kelley's murder were going south of nowhere, Leon went back to his hunt. Finding Gilmore. Finding Gustafson. And of course, Maxwell.

He thought it sounded like a movie. It wasn't. He picked Gilmore as his next attempt to track down one of the three remaining signatories on the Maxwell Mazer agreement. The Kelley woman mentioned that he had been around to chat with her uncle, so he may have remained local.

Leon repeated the same cyber hunt routine he had used to track Gustafson and tapped a few keys. While the computer blinked out an initial result of over twenty-four thousand results, he let out a deep "Here we go" breath.

He decided then to use an advanced search engine with more filters only displaying hits within California and a range of birth dates. It only took two blinks of an eye and his search was narrowed down to less than one hundred hits.

It took him about two hours to read through the results. He found four that were of interest to him. The third was an obituary. This Gilmore was buried in Forest Lawn cemetery in Glendale. Date of his death: 1944. The obit mentioned his career in the film industry, that he was an early innovator of technology for sound, lighting, and camera tracking. Leon's heartbeat thumped faster as he read that this dead guy had worked with Percy Maxwell during the silent movie era. He mouthed *bingo* and slapped his desk, palm down. His last studio association was with RKO. He retired to Santa Monica.

Leon read on and was taken aback. Gilmore had died in a fire with a roommate. His building was totally destroyed along with all the occupants. The fire company's captain had said in one of the newspaper articles that the fire was caused by old movie reels that had been stored in Gilmore's apartment. The captain went on to explain that those older films were coated with nitrate, which was highly combustible.

There was a photo of people with their names mentioned in the obit who attended his memorial service. A few were Hollywood celebs he recognized, others he did not, but Maxwell was mentioned.

Leon printed out the obit and slipped it into his Glowball folder. He called Brinks and told him what he had found.

"What about family?"

"None mentioned, but it seems Gilmore had a roommate. I found an old photo of him from a gala with his special friend. They were standing together. His friend was gazing into Gilmore's eyes. I know that look. A tell."

"You mean Gilmore was—"

"Could be. But nothing and nobody survived the fire."

"Bad way to die." He took a moment then continued, "So we can assume the agreement went up in smoke."

"I would." Leon didn't ask Brinks what a good way to die was. He paused a moment. "Has the guy showed up? The one that makes you want to take a dump?"

Brinks intestines tightened just thinking about Tankowitz's arrival.

"Tomorrow. Gotta go," he said to Leon, cutting the call, and quickly headed to the men's room.

CHAPTER 65

THE BIG GUN

No one needed to remind Sherman Tankowitz that he was a big man. He clocked in at over 300 pounds at 6 feet 4 and thought he looked just fine. Big men made smaller men feel smaller. In his case, size mattered, especially in his business where he had to make people squirm. Most would have thought that a forensic accountant shouldn't look like him, more like Woody Allen, but Tankowitz gave the impression of being a Sumo wrestler strangled inside his Armani suit. The seams were close to bursting even when he stood statue still. His neck had a layer of flab that hung over the starched collar of his off-pink dress shirt. The tie he wore had a pattern of handcuffs, a joke gift from a happy client who had his million dollars of embezzled funds returned.

When he showed up at Glowball, he was directed by Brandy to the conference room, where the three Chinese accountants were sitting. The room had glass walls that faced out into the hallway. Tankowitz saw each man had their respective noses inches away from their laptops. Then he saw the white guy watching the Chinese men. That would be Marvin Brinks, the newly appointed and temporary CFO of Glowball Productions.

Brinks was the first to notice Tankowitz when he came through the door. Standing up quickly, he extended his hand to the big man. Tankowitz's hand wrapped around Brinks's like a boa constrictor wrapping around his rodent dinner. Brinks smiled through the pain of his hand being crushed. The alpha numbers dog had come to Tinsel town and was claiming the neighborhood.

Tankowitz let go, and Brinks was able to talk then, his breath having been held to stifle a handshake from hell moan.

"The troops have arrived," said Brinks as close to a joking introduction he could muster to the accountants.

"Troop, singular," said Tankowitz with a broad smile that showed off gapped teeth that resembled pickets on a fence.

"Right. The big gun is here."

Tankowitz gave Brinks a sidelong glance.

The three accountants stood, pushing their chairs away to greet Tankowitz. It was like a line at a wedding reception with introductions given and hands shaken; this time, Tankowitz not using his crushing grip. He had saved that for Brinks to show him who was in charge now.

For the next two hours, Tankowitz circled the conference room table like a vulture looking for carrion. He stopped at each man's laptop, where a discussion ensued. Qian, Wang, and Zheng reviewed what each had done, what accounts they scrutinized, where one ledger intersected information on another man's ledger.

It was common that each movie had hundreds of people connected to its production. On top of that, there were scores of outside companies and vendors who were also involved. Materials needed, services rendered, inventories warehoused, props bought or made and stored, freight charges, electrical costs, rentals of every kind, catering, and salaries.

In the conference room were dozens of boxes from the warehouse with five years of paper that the accountants had requested. Stacks of receipts, invoices, and assorted documents were arranged in neat piles by year on the floor. Wang had mentioned a few bookkeeping inaccuracies so they double checked the entries, but nothing irregular popped out. The list of what and who had to be tracked and accounted for was endless. In Brinks's mind, endless was good. He wanted Tankowitz to fall down the Glowball rabbit hole with blinders on.

"Where's the head?" Tankowitz asked. "My prostate is talking back to me."

Brinks gave him directions and saw the big man disappear for ten minutes. When he came back, Brinks spotted Tankowitz by

Brandy's desk chatting with her. He worried about what he was asking her. Questions about Wolfe's death. Maybe the warehouse that Brinks visited. His mind drifted, thinking of all the worst things that could be told, but then Brandy was laughing as if Tankowitz had just told her a joke.

"Nice gal," Tankowitz said when he came back into the room.

"The best," Brinks agreed.

"I asked her to send up more coffee. I hope you don't mind."

"Of course not."

"She said Mr. Brenner wanted to have lunch with me this week. Have a chat about how I'm doing. Pretty sure he wants a clean bill of health so he can get funding from Hong Kong Capital."

"He's a good guy," was all that Brinks could say. He suppressed any sign of uneasiness, worrying what Brenner might say.

By the sixth hour, Brinks could feel the energy within the room drain. Since Tankowitz had arrived, he never stopped by to check in with Brinks, ask him about Glowball's business, what was in the pipeline, or the latest juicy Hollywood gossip. The man was as conversational as a dead clam. Except for two requests to refill the coffee carafes and pastry baskets, the man kept Brinks at arm's length like a nudist with a boner.

Zheng startled everyone with a guttural yawn. He blinked his eyes open and shut as if he had been staring too long at a sun lamp. His colleagues followed with their own yawns since yawns are known to be contagious. Even Brinks let one out. Tankowitz, however, did not.

Brinks felt a sense of relief. Tankowitz had arrived ready to rumble, looking for blood, and after a good part of a long day, nothing popped up on the radar. The mighty Tank was going to be his bitch, sent back to his cave with his tail between his legs.

"Wimps," the big man said, clearly disappointed at the accountants lack of staying power. "The lion never sleeps."

"We are not lions," Wang stated. "Just pussycats since we do like pussy."

The other two accountants guffawed, but Tankowitz only offered up a thin smile.

"My mind is *mushi*," Zheng admitted. His friends chuckled at the food gag.

"It's been hard to keep up with our good pal Marvin, our honored host," Qian explained. "My brain has been fried over the last few days."

Tankowitz's eyebrows came together in intersecting lines. Brinks saw the look and didn't like it.

"You never partied with Marvin?" Wang asked. "Man, you don't know what you're missing."

This was not the kind of advertisement that Brinks wanted voiced right then. It was a reputation that was good when you needed a resistant star signed who you knew liked to have a good time or an investor that wanted more that some profit for his or her money.

But Tankowitz was on a singular mission. Brinks was guilty until proven innocent.

"Really? Sounds fun," Tankowitz said, encouraging an explanation wanting to hear a bit more.

"I don't wanna talk outta school," Zheng said in a loud whisper, "but there is nothing like a good steak, excellent wine, and ladies with the nicest ta-tas you could imagine, to rest your face on them for eternity." Zheng pretended to close his eyes and produced a contented smile.

"More than rest." Wang made a suckling sound. The other men joined in a chorus of suckling sounds.

Brinks let out a small congenial laugh as if indicating that in this business he was the host and that's what a good host provides.

"And for dessert…" Qian finished his thought by tapping his right nostril.

"I guess I should've come a lot earlier," Tankowitz said to Brinks. The big man filled the room with a belly laugh, making the accountants join in but the look he gave Brinks could melt a glacier.

Brinks shrugged. "That's me. Party central for our out-of-town guests. It's the Hollywood way as Brenner would say." Brinks shifted some of the blame to his boss as if that was just routine protocol when you hung out with the *Jollywood* crowd. He gave Tankowitz a boyish smile, holding both palms up, guilty as charged.

"Well, the partying is over, boys. We all need to be clear-eyed in the morning," Tankowitz directed, his delivery far from being convivial. "No more distractions. You can rest your heads on hotel pillows and dream of ta-tas and get a good night's sleep." The way he said that made everyone in room feel like they were errant frat boys being lectured by the dean of students.

"Tomorrow we come here laser-focused." Tankowitz locked his eyes on Brinks, who thought he would die right then and there. Or maybe he just hoped he would.

Tankowitz was no dummy. He saw through what Brinks had done with the accountants for the last few days.

The five men left the conference room after packing their laptops away.

"I have reservations at the Savoy for dinner," Brinks announced. "Best Kobe steak this side of the Mississippi."

"We'll all pass," Tankowitz said. "You guys can order room service."

When they all left the conference room, Brinks stood calmly next to Tankowitz at the elevator as if that day was the most normal day ever.

"For a mid-budget kung-fu movie, I never expected we'd get the famous Tank to look over our books."

"It's a brave new world," Tankowitz replied. "The days of wine and roses and careless cash are over. It's all about ROI. The bottom line. Shareholders. *Capeesh?*"

Brinks nodded, feeling instantly threatened by what the big man meant. "Well, tomorrow is another day," he replied, making it sound like he couldn't wait for the sun to rise with nothing to hide.

"Have a good night's sleep," Tankowitz said, putting his meaty fingers on Brinks's shoulder. He squeezed just as he had when they first shook hands.

At home several hours later, Brinks submerged his body into his hot tub and couldn't help thinking. In the dark, he gazed up at the stars and went over all the possible scenarios. He was squarely in Tankowitz's gun sight. He wondered if there was anything else he could do to throw off his scent to sidetrack this oversized bloodhound. If Tankowitz did find a bread crumb, would the trail lead to a blind alley? Hopefully. He covered his ass with that Lightman lawyer by stealing Mazer's contract. He had taken two incriminating chess pieces off the board with Leon, who took care of the Kelley woman and the man who met a swampy end. His offshore accounts and anonymous LLC holdings made it almost impossible for the fat man to track down Brinks's activities unless he had FBI connections.

Brinks did not feel like he could see light at the end of the tunnel, his troubles magically disappearing while Tankowitz was still spilling over the books. There were two other contracts lost in the wind. Gustafson and Maxwell's with Leon still chasing them down. Only one had to surface while Tankowitz was hunting for bear. If one did, Tankowitz would go into full press gotcha mode.

He slipped his body under the warm, bubbling water with only his head above the water. What happened tomorrow made close auditing a bigger threat. *RoachMan* and *Sarah's Shadow Light* were good diversions like throwing raw steak to a rabid dog to escape being bitten. His anxiety remained, his fate not entirely in Tankowitz's hands. It was also in Leon's. He let the hot water jets in the hot tub pummel his bruised shoulder where Tankowitz had clamped his fingers.

Counting on Leon's success wasn't a comforting thought, but if he succeeded, two major exposures would be reduced to one. He dried his hand and reached for his cell phone and dialed a number.

"The Romanian tonight," he requested.

The agency woman said, "I'd like you to consider another woman."

"Oh?"

"Yes. Someone special for you tonight."

"How special?"

"Great experience in the art of pleasure giving. But more. She is smart. She is sensitive. She appreciates beautiful things as you do."

Brinks was intrigued. "Her name?"

"Mona. As in the Mona Lisa. She is as precious as that one is. Treat her well. It will be worth it."

CHAPTER 66

ARRIVAL

Leon woke up early. In customary order, he shat, showered, and shaved. Drying off, he stared into the bathroom mirror and spotted a potential pimple rebelling against his almost perfect skin.

"You are so dead," he threatened the blemish and swabbed an acne drying ointment over the dermatological intruder. He put the ointment on a shelf that had over thirty tubes and jars of skin-care related products—all acquired as his ammunition to fight the body's drift toward decay. If his body was supposed to be treated as a temple, he took care of it more like a majestic cathedral.

Satisfied, he got dressed and went to his laptop. He checked the weather where he was headed. It would be hot and humid. He packed light, making sure his shaving kit had all the facial creams he would normally use. He packed a second piece of luggage, a small cosmetic case. This one contained his Man of Many Faces props. It contained wigs, fake moustaches, prosthetic moldable latex to change his face, and an assortment of cosmetics to alter his skin tones. As he traveled in his efforts to locate what Brinks wanted so badly, he'd never look the same. If another Nancy Kelley occasion occurred, any witnesses would describe a man that never was.

The last thing he packed was driver's licenses and corresponding credits cards in various names courtesy of Freddy who used Bratva, his Russian mafia connections, to supply him with any number of fake documents for a price.

Leon ordered a taxi to LAX and had the driver drop him off at the Delta Airways terminal. Brinks was paying for his expenses so he got a seat in first class on the Delta flight to Binghamton, New York. The flight attendant offered him a drink, and he ordered a Scotch on the rocks. He would be landing in the Greater Binghamton Airport. He could have flown directly into Ithaca, but he learned over the years that if you got into a nasty situation and people wanted to track you down, it was best to make your comings and goings harder to figure out.

Once the jet leveled off at eleven thousand feet, he took out his iPad and got connected to the Internet using Delta's inflight Wi-Fi service. He found a Holiday Inn located in the Commons which was some kind of outdoor promenade in downtown Ithaca, a few blocks from Cornell University. He booked a room for several nights. He found an Avis car rental place in the terminal next and reserved a Chevy Impala.

He searched for Ithaca's public library next. The Tompkins County Public Library would be open in the morning. This would be his first stop in trying to locate records pointing him to the illusive Percy Maxwell.

He landed five hours later. Leon headed to the men's room after he picked up his baggage. He found an empty stall and changed his appearance. A wig and goatee gave him a professorial look. In a college town, this was a get-up that made him look like he belonged there. Leaving the stall, he stroked his goatee as he appraised himself in the bathroom's mirror.

Leon picked up his rental car. The gal at the Avis counter smiled at him and asked if he was here on business or pleasure.

"Educational." Leon gave her his driver's license and credit card.

"Ah. Going to Binghamton University?"

Leon nodded. "Nicholas Ray once taught there." He threw out this piece of cinema history as a red herring since BU was not where he was headed.

She gave him a blank look.

He gave her three clues. "*Rebel Without a Cause*. The movie. James Dean."

All he got back were more blank looks, obviously a millennial that preferred insipid sequels of *Pitch Perfect*.

"Love your accent," she said, not knowing what else to say. "I like men who speak special." The Avis lady took the card and swiped it. She looked up at him with a twinkle in her eye. Leon waited for the card to go through. It did.

He found the Chevy Impala in the numbered space, put his luggage in the trunk, and got inside the car. The radio came on to a station that filled the car with country music. He had a strong dislike for that kind of music. Drunk men kicking dogs, kids, and women. Like his father had.

He changed the station and found a Broadway show tunes station. He hummed along with Ethel Merman as she sang "You Can't Get a Man with a Gun."

He headed north on Route 81. About twenty minutes later, he got off the interstate highway and went through the village of Whitney Point, which you could miss if you sneezed too hard. He passed Aiello's Restaurant, an Ace hardware store, and then saw an old Sherman Army tank that adorned an athletic field.

Leon turned onto Route 79, past makeshift farm stands, run-down mobile homes, and pasture lands that could use a brush-up. He came into Slaterville Springs, and gradually, the houses looked like they were evolving into more expensive living quarters and better groomed front yards. Barns were painted, some with signs advertising not hay for sale but Earthworks pottery, Finger Lakes yoga, and Intouch holistic massage.

He was on the outskirts of Ithaca when a line of cars ahead slowed him down to a crawl. He strained his eyes to see what was up, thinking it could be an accident

It turned out that there were police, but they were directing cars into an open farmer's field where people were parking. Right behind the field was a circus of some sort. He saw the lights of a Ferris wheel and caught the greasy smell of fried sausages and the noise of the midway. A memory surfaced. That summer he spent steering unhappy losers away at the fixed games of chance, offering them a beer that the carnival owners suggested as a first option or throwing their asses out if they refused his offer of hospitality.

He decided to check it out for old times' sake, entered the field and parked his car. He had time to kill. Leon paid the price for admission and walked around the grounds. Immediately, the midway caught his attention. He saw the same games of chance: Ring toss with impossible odds of landing over a bottle. Balloon rarely popping with the help of dull darts.

He left the games and wandered by the sideshow acts. Not as many mutants as there were back in the day. The regular freak show cast of characters were on their stages: A bored-looking tattooed lady. A sword-swallowing cute girl, a magician with tired tricks, the fire eater, the fat lady, and some amputee drawing pictures with his feet.

One guy caught his eye, a freak that got paid by people to stick pins through his flesh. The man didn't wince; just stood there like a wooden cigar store Indian. He watched this act for a while who billed himself as *Holey John—The Human Pin Cushion*. People stuffed bills into his jar, picked out a jeweled pin, and pushed it through his flesh. They looked at him for a reaction and got none. The women seemed more squeamish but did it anyway. The men tried to find spots where they thought it would hurt the most. But the guy would swat away their intended location when they aimed for his face, groin, or knees. Leon decided he liked this guy. He had mental armor like himself but decided he had to be fucked up.

Before he walked away, he spotted a short, tough guy giving the pin-pricked freak the evil eye as if his furious stare would make the pin cushion guy keel over dead from fear and dread. It didn't work. The tough guy stepped onto the stage and moved right up to him. They exchanged unfriendly looks. The punk took a twenty-dollar bill out of his pocket, dropping it into his jar, and said something to the pin cushion man that Leon couldn't hear. The freak didn't react. The punk sorted through the pins and labrets, pulled out four, and studied Holey John's torso for a place to lance him. He picked a spot over his collarbone. Instead of piercing his flesh, the tough guy jabbed the pin into Holey John's cheek just below his right eye. Blood immediately spilled out and ran down his face. The crowd gave out a collective gasp. Holey John held back any sign of pain and grabbed the man's arm with one hand and wrapped his fingers around his attacker's throat with the other.

A woman rushed forward from the crowd and screamed, "Wally! What the hell are you doing?"

The man called Wally dropped the three other pins and tried to remove Holey John's fingers from his throat.

"I can't—" Wally choked out.

"Now you cut…me and tried to run me down…before!"

"Breathe," Wally gagged as his face turned gray.

Holey John loosened his grip and gave his attacker a solid punch right into his ribs. Wally howled and clutched his ribs, his breathing coming even harder now. Holey John kneed Wally in his groin then threw him off the stage, where he landed on his back, dazed and struggling to catch his breath, grabbing his balls. Holey John pulled the pin from his cheek. He dug the twenty out of his tip jar, balled it up, and threw it at Wally. As Wally struggled to get up, a small Glassine packet fell out of his pocket.

"Don't come round here…again," Holey John spitted the threat.

Wally brushed himself off and eyeballed Holey John. "You're a dead man, pin sticker."

A woman stepped from the crowd and grabbed him by the arm.

"What the hell is the matter with you?" she yelled, shoving him along away from the midway area.

Leon witnessed this display by the pin cushion man. He also saw the packet that dropped to the ground. He looked at his wristwatch and decided he had enough along with the stink of fried dough and sausage grease that felt glommed onto his face. When the crowd dispersed, he saw that the packet had been trampled on but still lay there. He picked it up. Brushing off some dirt, he opened it up, wet his index finger and tapped into the powdery contents. When he tasted the powder with the tip of his tongue, he nodded.

"Bad boy." He watched the punk and his lady walk away and put the packet into his shirt pocket.

Walking back to his car, he passed a very small woman telling fortunes. They exchanged looks. He stared a long moment and she returned his gaze, lines in her forehead furrowing as if she sensed something about him. He ignored her look and strolled away. He remembered fucking a midget just to say he did. It was okay except her voice sounded like she had sucked helium out of a balloon. Her talking dirty like one of *The Wizard of Oz* extras was an erection killer.

Leon found his car and noticed Wally and his lady friend heading toward a rusted Chevy pickup truck. He watched them as she yelled at the beaten punk.

"What is wrong with you?" the woman screamed. "You want to violate your parole?"

"Go screw!" he shouted back.

"You are a shit bag, you know."

"Keep your voice down," he said, noticing a man watching them.

Leon turned away as the couple got into the truck. As he got into his car, he saw the truck tires spit up dust, heading out of the parking area. Leon read the hand-lettered writing on the truck: *Anything Goes Junk Removal.*

Figures, Leon thought to himself. The guy removed junk but also used it. Life's moments of absurdity come to all of God's children. Leon smirked. This place had more characters than a bad Hollywood movie.

CHAPTER 67

LEAVE ME BREATHLESS

He couldn't get over the woman in the hot tub. She was more than he had ever expected. It was the third time she had been with him. She was in her late twenties with a firm and flexible body. Her face was pretty in a natural way. No makeup. Girl-next-door look. Innocent but eager to please. No surgery to enhance her breasts or any other part of her. No ink or piercings. Her hands were skilled, touching him in all the right places, never rushed, attentive to his reaction. She knew he wanted to climax later, in the bedroom, and not out there in the tub, under the stars.

Brinks closed his eyes while Mona rubbed his chest. He liked the fact that she had a normal name. Not Crystal, Jade, or Amber. Why did these girls pick names based on gemstones? This thought passed, and he was reminded of his incredibly good fortune for the last week. Tankowitz, the ace forensic accountant, hit one dead end after another as he tried to find a chink in Brink's accounting armor.

He looked at his fingers, which were wrinkled from being in the tub, and decided it was time to adjourn to his living room for a nice bottle of champagne, which he had chilled to celebrate his escape from the crow bar hotel.

"Shall we?" Brinks said to Mona, tilting his head toward the door that opened into his living room. She smiled and rose from the tub fully naked and faced him. She lingered in front of him, letting him admire her body, which he did and sighed. He was a lucky man indeed.

They put on the bathrobes he had laid over a chair and, holding hands, walked into his house.

"You like jazz?" he asked her.

"Yes, I do."

"Anyone in particular?"

"Something romantic. Do you have this album *Coltrane Plays for Lovers*? Very sensual."

Brinks was impressed. She was not a bimbo with a great body for rent but a woman with much more sophistication than any other woman he had requested.

"I like 'You Leave Me Breathless,'" she added.

He smiled at her. He wondered if he spent more time with her that his arrangement might become more than a business transaction.

He went over to his turntable and scanned his shelf of LPs. He liked the vinyl records, thinking that the sound was better than the digital music. He found the album and slipped the record out of the sleeve and placed the record on his turntable.

He heard his cell phone vibrate. The one Leon gave him. He had laid it down on the coffee table next to the champagne, which was chilling. Mona noticed it too and smiled at him.

"You can answer it, you know."

He didn't want the mood to be broken. "Whatever it is, it can wait." If Leon had the good news he promised, he'd call back.

"Champagne?" he offered in a gentle voice that he didn't know he possessed.

She nodded, and he took the bottle of Armand de Brignac out of the ice bucket. He popped the cork, and Mona giggled as it bounced off a wall next to one of prized Henry Moore watercolors.

"Your house and everything in it is like an affirmation to expensive taste," she said as she sipped the glass of champagne.

He frowned, not sure if this was said as an admiring comment. "You think these things ostentatious?"

She thought about his question. "Perhaps. But I think you like to acquire these things not only for their beauty but for the thrill. I think you get a rush like a man snorting cocaine. The feeling lasts for a while, and then it goes away and then you need another rush.

Another beautiful thing to acquire. Like me for this evening and the previous ones."

"Food for thought," he said in a flat voice. Of course she was right, but he had never been with anyone who actually understood his obsession that was very close to an addiction. He wasn't offended by her frankness for some reason. He actually liked that about her. No bullshit like most of the movie people who slung it every day.

"We all have desires," she said plainly. "This is yours. I am not judging. I am merely observing." Mona then pursed her lips as if she had more to say.

Brinks saw that and asked, "Something else?"

"Not just a thrill for you." She tightened her lips as if she didn't want to let her words come out.

"I'm a big boy. Tell me."

"I think these things fill a hole inside you. Like a man who is hungry but can't find a meal that fills him up."

Brinks raised his eyebrows. "Wow."

"I'm out of line."

He thought for a moment then said, "No, no. Just an interesting way of looking at what I do."

"No offense, I hope."

"None taken. I might drop my therapist and go to you."

"Good," she said and kissed him deeply, her tongue warm and soft in his mouth.

When she stopped, he asked, "What are yours? Indulgences."

"I have them but I am not here to talk about myself."

"Why not?"

"That would change the nature of our arrangement, don't you think? I must remain mysterious."

He believed it probably would best. But maybe that wouldn't be a bad thing for once in his less than fulfilling string of paid for relationships, if relationships were even the right term to use.

Mona saw he was thinking too much. "I enjoy the fruits of your passion. Better than collecting stamps or baseball cards."

He laughed. "You underestimate the beauty of stamps. They are like miniature paintings. Do you want to see what I mean?"

"If you like."

Brinks took her to another room, a study, which held collections of stamps, coins, and Netsuke ivories from the seventeenth century used in Japan to secure pouches. He opened a safe and returned with an album of stamps, placing it on his desk. He opened it and pointed to one of the stamps.

"The plane is upside down," Mona pointed out.

"It's rare. It's known as the inverted Jenny stamp. The design has a Curtiss JN-4 airplane that was accidentally printed upside-down."

"It's valuable?"

"Very. The most expensive one I have."

He showed her other stamps. He stopped for moment and asked, "You must have things you value. Maybe not objects. Maybe experiences."

She caressed the side of his face. "Again, you probe. Maybe I'll tell you some day when I feel comfortable about revealing myself."

Brinks held her hand against his face. He kissed her fingertips. Something stirred inside him, and it wasn't what was underneath his robe. He wanted to know her not as a woman hired for the evening; he wanted something deeper. He hadn't felt this way for a long time. Maybe ever.

"Can we forget what you call our arrangement for a minute?"

She smiled curiously at him. "Okay, for a minute."

"Do you have a number that I can call you? Invite you out on a real date. Dinner. Maybe dancing."

She was silent for a minute, thinking it over. "I still may charge you for my time." She laughed, not trusting his proposal. She had been with too many men who after the glow of sex offered her the world or made promises that they would never honor once she left their side.

"I can live with that." He looked at her for a long moment, and she could tell something was different with this man.

"Let's see, shall we?" she said.

"Of course."

She kissed his cheek and wrote her private number on a pad that lay on his desk. "No expectations, okay?"

"Okay."

He smiled at her, his heart beating a little faster, a thrill filling his gut, like a high school crush a boy might have. He held her hand and led her to his bedroom. They both sat on his bed and she moved close and pressed her lips against his. They kissed a long kiss, and when she pulled away, she whispered into his ear, "But tonight, I am your fantasy woman."

He leaned back and looked directly into her eyes. "Can I ask you one question? Be straight with me when you answer, okay?"

"If I can."

"You ever think about getting out?"

"You mean out of my work?"

"Yes."

"Sometimes. When I am too old and my looks don't work for me anymore. Gravity and wrinkles are not a friend for a woman like me."

"What if one day before wrinkles and gravity betray you, you could have a new life? Have all the money you could ever need. Live anywhere you choose. Would you consider leaving?"

"Perhaps. Are you my white knight riding on a white stallion who will whisk me away?"

"I can be."

"Then I will keep my ear out for the sound of approaching hooves."

He smiled, but he saw she was deep in thought again. "You have a question for me?"

"You are offering me quite a lot without really knowing me and yet—"

"I know. It's a feeling I've had ever since the first time I was with you. Not the after-sex kind that makes men say crazy things they regret later."

She smiled, having had the same thought a moment before.

"Let me ask you this," she said.

"Shoot."

"Imagine I am in a room. And in this room, there is your most precious and beloved painting."

"Okay."

"Just me and your priceless possession."

"Go on."

"Suddenly, a fire breaks out, and you can only save me or your painting. What do you run into the room to save?"

Brinks did not hesitate at all. "Why, you of course."

Mona smiled as he moved close to her and, they kissed another long kiss. He slipped his hand inside her robe and felt her breast, and gently pinched her nipple between his thumb and forefinger. She broke the kiss and exhaled a warm breath into his ear. Her hand moved inside of his robe and found his penis, making him hard right away. He looked into her eyes and his heart skipped a beat, an exquisite feeling pulsing through him.

She removed her robe. Brinks stared in wonderment as before. She was more beautiful than the statue he had longed for at the Hammerstein estate sale. Her hands were gentle, and she began to stroke him, his chest, his face, his penis. He responded and guided his hands over her warm body. They lay back, and Mona took his penis and placed him inside her. Their bodies intertwined. Their movements matched each other, slow and rhythmic, then building up in a delightful frenzy as she moved on top of him, moving him inside her. They both made breathy sounds of pleasure, and he climaxed. He felt the inside muscles of her vagina spasm, a throbbing spasm, and she moaned; a throaty gasp fluttered into his ear.

His eyes were closed, and a contented smile crossed his lips. "I think I am falling in love with you."

She removed his penis and lay besides him, rubbing his chest.

"I'm sure this isn't the first time a man said this to you after making love."

"No. But I like the way you said it to me." With that, she turned his head and gave him a long and deep kiss.

CHAPTER 68

SO DONE

I found Zena alone in her trailer. She had finished her afternoon shift and was taking a break. "I need to change," she said.

As she changed, I avoided gawking at her so I could concentrate and told her what my dad had found.

"A wife and a kid," Zena said. Her face showed total shock. "Like in the photograph? That's so crazy. And he had no idea, right?""

I nodded. "Any thoughts you want to share?"

"About the house and Holey John and what to tell him?"

"Yes."

"Honestly?" I mentioned the other thing my dad had told me: that someone seemed to have an interest in Holey John and there were redacted records in his files.

"A cover-up?"

"Could be."

"This thing about someone tracking Holey John is weird. Why and who would be interested in him?"

I shrugged.

She paused. "This change." She gestured toward the fairgrounds. "This has been my life for over ten years."

"Change is hard," I said, trying to comfort her, my words sounding trite like a platitude a life coach might offer. "Can you imagine living in Ithaca?"

She shook her head. "What would I do here? Open up a fortune-telling storefront on the Commons?"

"Sure. I see students coming to see you. Find out if they should major in accounting or become professional beer pong players."

"Funny is not helping me."

"How about going back to school? Try another run at psychology."

"I don't know. I have a few more days here before the G Brothers move on to Syracuse. I'll decide then."

"Holey John is going to seal the deal tomorrow."

"I know."

"He seems happy. Right?"

"He does," she said with a thin smile.

"We should be supportive." I waited a few moments.

"We should tell him what my dad found. About his wife and kid."

"But not the cover-up shit. That'll rattle his head."

"The nightmares."

"Yeah."

"Maybe have him come here later, see what he thinks about all this."

Kissing her forehead, I left her and walked back to watch Holey John's performance. A fresh crop of gawkers were gathered. I sensed something different about him as people came up on the stage, dropped their five-dollar bills into his jar, and looked for a place to run a pin through his flesh. I was reminded of a painting I had once seen of a saint. It was *The Martyrdom of Saint Agatha* by Sebastiano del Piombo. It was almost pornographic, a Renaissance scene where a topless Agatha had her torturers clamping down on her nipples with what looked like pliers. She looked to her right, seemingly at peace with no trace of anguish on her lovely face. Holey John, like Agatha, seemed at peace for once despite the pins lancing into him.

People came and went. A man stepped up to the stage. I could see he was drunk.

"Hey, freak. Love them pins and all that shit you get decorated with."

"You do, huh?"

I watched Holey John do something totally surprising. He reached into his jar of pins and studs and threw handfuls into the gathered throng. People scrambled to pick them up. I wondered what that was all about. Then it struck me. A symbolic gesture. Out with the old, in with the new.

One of the Giambolvo brothers broke through the crowd, hearing a commotion as people were on their hands and knees, picking up Holey John's discarded pins.

"Hey!" shouted Louie, the brother with jowls that hung low like uncooked pork chops. "Whatta fuck are you'se doing?"

"I am...so done," Holey John shot back. "This is my last... show, fatso."

"Oh yeah? Whatchu gonna do? Be a hobo like you was before?"

"Nah. I'm buying a...house. Right here. In town."

"Kiddin' me, right?"

"Straight up, Louie."

By now, carnie workers had gathered as Louie grabbed Holey John's wrist, trying to pull him off the stage. "I could make an example of you," he said loud enough for me and the workers to hear. "Cops wouldn't care about finding some dead hobo under a bridge."

"Sound like a threat...and I got...witnesses," Holey John said, breaking away from his grip and smiling at his midway comrades.

"You won' last a month."

"Come around...next year. I'll have you over...for dinner. Double portions."

Louie looked around, seeing midway performers and roustabouts taking in the scene. He turned to lecture them like a street corner prophet. "You think this guy is brave. Well, he's nuts. Always has been. Stickin' pins and shit into himself like a voodoo doll."

Louie's face was red as a beet, clearly enraged that Holy Holey John made his exit so publicly. He glared at him with eyes as deadly as a sniper, his jowls jiggling like Jell-O as he stormed off.

I came up to him. "Quite an exit. You worried about the fat man?"

"Nah."

I smiled. "What's next?"

"Trish, the real estate agent, said to…meet her back at Ralph's…tomorrow. Sign papers…and stuff."

"Don't forget about giving us a tour."

"Happy to. Zena may actually like…my idea. Right now…I need to start packing." With that, he gave me a salute and turned to head off to his trailer.

"Wait a sec." I tapped him on the shoulder, and he turned around. "I have some news for you. My dad dug some things up."

He gave me an expectant look.

"What did he…find?"

"I'll walk with you."

"Okay."

As we walked, I talked. "Info about your tour in Nam." I told him about what unit he was in. I could see he was struggling with something. I had already told Zena that info and knew it was okay to lay it onto him.

"They do anything…messed up?"

"What do you mean?"

"My nightmares."

"Nothing we found so far."

"We did find something about the woman in the photograph."

Holey John gave me an expectant look.

"The writing on the ceiling matches the writing on the back of the photo."

"So?"

"It's a name."

"What kinda…name?"

"A woman." I paused and took in a deep breath before I continued. "Her name is Linh."

His eyes became slits as if recalling something. I put my hand on his shoulder again. "Linh is your wife."

I watched his reaction. He stopped walking, as if he was suddenly spiked into the ground. It took a few seconds for him to get that notion processed, making it past whatever cobwebs were getting in the way.

"I have a…wife," he said in disbelief. "That woman…is my wife?"

"Yes."

"Where is she?" he asked excitedly.

"Don't know yet."

"Is that my daughter in the…photo?"

I shrugged a *Could be* shrug. "That's all I know for now."

"Oh my…god."

I saw his expression morph from a look of surprise then disbelief then a smile.

"I have a…goddamned wife." He held that thought for a moment. "I need to find…her. The kid too." More gears turning inside his head. "Fenn, they can live…in my house." He was excited like a kid opening presents at Christmas.

"Sounds like a fine idea."

He mulled some ideas over and then looked me straight into my eyes. "Can you help find them for…me?"

I didn't answer right away.

"Come on," he pleaded.

"I can try, but it won't be easy."

His face folded into concern.

"Might have to go back," I said. "See what we can find."

"Nam?"

I nodded. I could see Holey John getting fidgety. He was on information overload.

"Zena. She would want to…help."

"Of course."

We started to walk again. "Gotta start packing my…shit."

"You should come by Zena's place later."

He gave me a thumbs-up.

I gave him a wave, and he headed off. I wondered how I could track down a woman and young girl who had disappeared from a man's life over forty years before. I had just been asked to help the man I had told Stan was as stable as a bottle of nitro on a rollercoaster ride. Of course, Stan would see a good story there even if things blew up.

CHAPTER 69

TRACKING DOWN A DEAD GUY

Leon left the creatures on the midway, thinking what losers they all were. He would never be a loser like them. Maybe they thought they were entertainers, but unlike himself, they were at the bottom of the barrel of entertainment scum.

He drove off the dusty field and headed to the hotel he had booked. It became hillier as he approached the city of Ithaca. Houses were closer together, and the two-lane road began a descent into the town's center. Route 79 became East State Street, and he took a left onto South Cayuga. Leon spotted the ten-story Holiday Inn and pulled in front. He popped the trunk, got out of his car, and waited for a bellhop but gave up after a few minutes. He guessed that bellhops were outlawed in a liberal college town and people were meant to schlep their own luggage.

He then entered the lobby and saw a few leather sofas and chairs arranged around a round marble-topped coffee table with a bouquet of plastic flowers placed dead center. A sweeping staircase was on his right, and the front desk was to his left. Leon carried his luggage to a bored man doing a crossword puzzle at the reception area.

"Can I help you, sir?" the receptionist asked.

"I have a room under Fairbanks."

The receptionist tapped on a keyboard looking up reservations, humming a tune Leon could not figure out. "Ah yes. Fairbanks. I have you booked for a week."

"Correct," Leon confirmed.

"Business trip, huh?"

"Something like that," he answered, still wearing his disguise and used his recently adopted O'Toole accent, wanting to add "monkey business" to his reply, but held back. Wisecracks made people remember you.

The receptionist gave Leon a key card to his room. "Elevators are to the right of the staircase."

Leon got to his room and went inside. It was typical Holiday Inn décor. Queen-sized bed, small closet, dresser, flat-screen TV on the dresser. At least the TV was updated. He unpacked his clothes then went to the bathroom and removed his disguise. He needed a hot shower after a long day of traveling, sitting on a plane for five hours, then driving almost another two. And the carnival grease had to be scrubbed off.

He stripped down to his underwear and socks. Sitting on the bed, he picked his briefcase up and opened it. Leon pulled out the large envelope that had all the information he had collected so far. He read over the contract for the umpteenth time that had Brinks's knickers in a twist. He thought the odds were in his favor to find why Brinks so desperately needed them. It was only logical that the remaining contracts had to be there since Maxwell dropped dead in the Keys and there was nothing of value he had left behind. His letter to Ellwell was posted in Ithaca, so it only made sense that he lived there, and that meant he had a house.

Based on his deal with Mazer and getting rid of all his movie-making gear, it was a good guess that the man had enough of the silver screen biz. But what happened after that was what he'd hope to find out.

In the shower, he washed off the road grime and the greasy food vapors from the carnival. He turned the shower up as hot as he could take it, letting the water beat on his back. Then he turned it all the way to cold, to shock his body awake.

Drying himself off, he went to the mirror and wiped off the shower's steamy mist to look at his face. He dried it with delicate pats and searched for any facial imperfections. As a precaution, he opened a tube of skin rejuvenator and, satisfied, walked back to the bed. He put the papers in the room safe and stored the briefcase in the closet.

When he was dressed, he called down to the concierge, who turned out to be the receptionist guy.

"I need a place to eat."

"We got Pete's right down the street. It's a bar, but they have food."

"Thanks." He paused, looking out his hotel room's window. "I saw a building across the street when I pulled in here."

"It's the Tompkins County Public Library," the receptionist explained. "Pretty good collection, being a college town and all."

Leon thanked the man and hung up the phone. It was a short walk from his hotel, and tomorrow, he planned to make it his first stop. Good place to start when you're tracking down a dead guy. He put on a wig that made him look like an old hippie, covered it with a baseball cap, went out the back stairway, and headed for the bar.

CHAPTER 70

JACK-IN-THE-BOX

After Tankowitz had arrived, the three Hong Kong accountants morphed into different people after they outted Brinks's giving them their "anything they want" requests.

Gone was the convivial atmosphere. No more jokes about getting laid or talk about party drugs. They were either glued to their laptop screens or shuffling through paper files. Tankowitz circled around each man, stopping to double-check what they were doing. When any of the accountants grunted or raised their hand, he would examine whatever caught their attention.

Brinks sat on one of the conference room chairs with his laptop open. He had several financial programs running, each containing specific data that the men asked about.

On the second day after Tankowitz had arrived, Qian tapped his laptop screen, pointing to an SAP program for financial planning and analysis.

Tankowitz stepped over and looked at what Qian was puzzling over. He turned to Brinks. "Can you explain what we're seeing here?"

Brinks got up and studied the screen. "Can you scroll down the page?"

Qian paged down, and Brinks nodded.

"That's our software that gives us a very granular dive into our profitability with cost analysis."

Tankowitz squinted at the numbers. "What are we specifically looking at?"

Brinks looked again and said, "That's what we invested in one of movies." He then shook his head, giving Tankowitz and Qian a look that bordered on shame.

"RoachMan," Brinks said. "One of Mr. Brenner's ideas. Not a good one, but please don't repeat that I said that." With that, he feigned a pleading look. "Mr. Brenner and Wolfe had a shared desire to make a horror movie. Childhood fantasies, maybe. I don't know. They never defended why they did it. My boyhood fantasies were about *Playgirl's* tits and wanting to be as cool as James Bond. The Sean Connery one."

Tankowitz shook his head, hearing Brinks talk about tits and how he supplied the accountants with a supply of women.

He wasn't surprised that *RoachMan* would catch Tankowitz and the other accountants' attention. Tankowitz most likely would give a pass on *Sarah's Secret*, which was Brenner wanting to get creds as a serious maker of movies in the league of Bergman, Altman, and Cassavetes. Anyone in the business knew that making a movie was a gamble. Hollywood had a long list of box office bombs. But like any gambler, you wanted to reduce your risk. *RoachMan* had been a clear and unchecked risk as far as Tankowitz was concerned.

"Some of these costs are crazy," Tankowitz continued.

"I told Wolfe his budget was running way over," Brinks agreed, "but it's hard to tell your boss they're nuts."

Tankowitz pulled a chair next to Qian and studied all the expenses that were attributed to RoachMan. Brinks stayed nearby, holding his breath then letting it out then holding it again. This tortured breathing pattern lasted almost an hour, his fear that one of his many ruses would turn up.

"Some expenses look out of line," Tankowitz pointed out.

"Which ones?" Brinks asked, trying to sound doubtful.

"From some company called WaddaFX."

Brinks pretended to rack his brain about this particular outfit. This was the company owned by Dianne Silva, with whom he had a special arrangement to overbill Glowball where he and Silva put money in their respective pockets. Brinks felt the hairs on his neck stand up. Was this the red flag that Tankowitz found that would shatter his world?

After a long minute, he pointed his finger up acting as if he finally recognized the name. "Right. WaddaFX. It's the special effects studio we employed. A lot of computer-generated imagery was used. Complicated stuff. A lot of retakes for blue screen scenes that were shot at night."

Tankowitz knew all about numbers, but his understanding of the technologies that movies employed was above his pay grade. "Like what they did with *Star Wars*."

"Exactly," Brinks blurted. He saw that the big man seemed satisfied with his explanation, and he relaxed.

The next three days went along with some of the same questions. These were not "gotcha" problems with the ledgers, expenses, or contracts. Most were easily explained especially where the activities were as kosher as a ballroom full of dancing rabbis Brinks had told Wolfe.

On the fourth day, the three accountants and Tankowitz were winding down with no jack-in-the-box surprises. Brinks felt a weight lift from his shoulders. One more day and he hoped no surprises would pop up.

He saw Wang puzzling over something on his laptop.

"What's this?" he asked Brinks.

Brinks went over. Wang wasn't looking at any financials. It was a news story.

"I thought we should see what Glowball acquired...you know, other movie companies. We see that shit with Hong Kong studios."

Brinks stiffened, wondering what Wang had found.

Tankowitz came over and bent to see what Wang had pulled up.

"It's a news article. Seems that an affidavit from a judge indicted this guy named Venzenta for criminal activities. Says he used Cranes Neck to launder the money."

"Interesting," Tankowitz said. "Mr. Brenner said that Glowball had acquired a few companies in the past over lunch when I first got here. Cranes Neck was one he mentioned. I shared that with the fellows here."

"Before my time here," Brinks clarified, keeping a straight face.

"See what else you can find Zheng," Tankowitz suggested.

Brinks watched as Zheng searched for more information. After ten minutes, the latter smiled and said, "I got something. I found the docket number from the judge who issued the avadavat."

"Anything else?" Tankowitz asked.

"It refers to the case. A law firm represented Venzenta. Lightman. Office in LA."

Tankowitz thought about this new development. "Give me the address, and I'll pay a visit tomorrow. Never know if there are other entanglements from the past we need to know about."

"Good idea," Brinks agreed. "Cover your ass."

Tankowitz didn't smile.

Brinks left the office and headed to his car, sweat dripping down his back. "Fuck!" he yelled inside his car and banged on the steering wheel. He was convinced he had removed any incriminating evidence at Lightman's office. He swiped the contract. What else was there that could harm him? But a visit by Tankowitz would have Lightman tell that Brinks had visited him and copied something. That would raise suspicions he didn't need. Leon was out of town, so he couldn't help. Only one person could help him now.

He called Freddy.

"I need your help."

"You sound desperate."

"I am."

"What do you need?"

Brinks explained he visited a law firm and took something important. He told him about Tankowitz. If he visited the firm and talked to Lightman or his secretary, the numbers sleuth would go after Brinks with a vengeance, grilling him about what he had pocketed.

"Tankowitz can't talk to Lightman."

"I'm not into murder," Freddy asserted.

Brinks thought for a while. "I have an idea. Not murder."

He then explained what might work.

Freddy said *hmm* and asked him for the name and address of the law firm.

CHAPTER 71

QUE SERA SERA

The three of us were in Zena's trailer. Holey John rubbed his knees nervously with the palms of his hands. She watched her friend and guessed he had something to say to her.

"You weren't at your booth when I came back to do my evening shift," she started.

"Yup," he said with a smile that came as close to a shit-eating grin for a man with studs pierced around his mouth could offer up.

"Tony didn't come after you?"

Holey John cracked a big smile and said, "He did."

"And?"

"I told him I…quit."

Her eyes rolled up like window shades. "He'd he take that?"

"Not so good. Kinda threatened me…but he's all blubber."

"Bluster," I corrected.

"Both," he said.

"So this house thing is real."

"I'll take you…for a look-see."

"I would like that," Zena said as sincerely as possible.

"Fenn gave me some…news."

She turned to me and nodded, already knowing what I had told her, then turned back to Holey John.

"Found out I have a…wife. That's her name…on my ceiling. Linh. And that photo. It's my wife…and the girl could be my daughter."

"A house and now a wife. Wow. Quite a day for surprises."

"Good ones. Fenn said he'd help me…find Linh." He hesitated for a moment. "You could help…too."

My cell phone went off. I could tell by the ringtone who it was. "I better take this outside." I left the trailer and walked about twenty yards out of earshot.

"Hi, Lilly," I said sheepishly.

"Are you being an asshole on purpose or is this behavior firmly rooted in your DNA?" she scolded.

"You're mad."

"OMG. My boyfriend is a psychic." She huffed a moment then said, "They have cell towers up there?"

"Sorry."

"It's been days since you left and not one call."

"It's this assignment," I said as an excuse. "Stan is breathing down my neck, and one of my key subjects has bailed on me."

"So a five-minute call is too much for you to handle?"

"I'm an asshole. You know how I am when I get involved."

"Involved," she harrumphed. "Involved as with your assignment or a person?"

This conversation was heading down a slippery slope.

"Of course it's the assignment. Look, Stan has me on tender hooks for this piece. If I don't hit this one out of the park, it's pink slip time. He's my meal ticket. No other clients."

I told her about Holey John and how I was helping him, how I needed to find a substitute character for my story. I didn't mention Zena.

She didn't respond right away. Then she said, "Maybe that's a good thing."

"What? Losing my job?"

"Yes. It's an opportunity."

"What? For living under a bridge in a refrigerator box?"

"Come on, Fenn. You're a smart and talented writer. You could do something else."

"Like…"

"Write a book."

"You think?"

"Sure. Find some creepy topic you like. You like doing creepy."

"A book can take months to write. How do I support myself?"

Her answer was quick. "We could live together. I make enough in my job. I can cut out Pilates and yoga classes. Other things."

I was taken aback by her offer. It was generous. And it showed me how much she wanted us to be together.

"Really?" I said, responding to her offer.

"Yes."

A few things held me back from saying okay right away. The first was how much of a cad I was. There was my recent bathroom romp with Fiona, which went well beyond research along with the other ladies I had bedded for my rejected story. And now what I was doing with Zena, whatever that was, made me realize that I was as loyal as an alley cat in heat.

"I think your offer is amazing," I said.

"Amazing is not a yes-or-no answer," she said sternly.

I needed to sidestep this one and buy some time.

"Let me finish this piece. See what Stan says."

"You're doing your 'Fenndango' dance," she said. "It's a binary answer. Yes or no."

If I say yes, will I confess my most recent wanderings to clear my conscience, making myself feel better and wind up making her feel worse? Or keep compartmentalizing my cad-like behavior, which I perfected, keep it in a closet never to be opened, and see where Lilly and I wind up?

I heard exhaustion before I could say anything as she said, "Look, if it doesn't work, then *que sera sera.*"

Her *que sera sera* offer was generous. She realized I was a loose cannon, and living together would give us both a relationship thumbs-up or—down reality check. I gave her a plus on my fuck-it list.

"You are really amazing."

"Yeah, so you said before. I wish you would honestly believe that."

"I know I can be a jerk."

"Can or are?"

"Both. This article should be wrapped up in a few days."

"Just man up and don't be an asshole, Fenn. Don't waste my time or yours."

"I have deep feelings for you, Lilly. I won't."

"Conflicted ones I see."

"Let's talk about your offer when I get back to the city."

"You better," she said and clicked off with my head left spinning.

I came back to the trailer, and both Zena and Holey John looked at me.

"Probably not your editor to see where your story is going," Zena said, her sixth sense on active duty. "Why not just tell her?"

I was about to say "Tell her what?" and then realized that Zena's "Tell her what?" was me telling Lilly whatever Zena and I were doing.

Holey John looked at both of us, confused.

"It was his girlfriend," Zena said.

"You okay with him having a…girlfriend?" Holey John asked.

"He's fun and smart and not half-bad in the rack."

He grinned and said, "Half-bad is better than…bad, bad."

"Wish I was a fly on the wall when he's back in big city. If he comes clean about little ole me, it'd be better than watching a bare-knuckled cage fight."

I gave her a scathing look.

CHAPTER 72

A VERY BUDDHIST ANSWER

The next morning, Leon walked to the library from his hotel, exiting through a side door, having altered his looks again. He chose a Chevron moustache, thick and wide, covering the top of his upper lip, his Tom Selleck look. A pair of eyeglasses in the latest metrosexual style was added to promote a cool journalist impression.

He passed by people who looked like refugees from Woodstock, real ones and student wannabes. He liked the hippie look. What he didn't like was their skin. The au naturel lifestyle wasn't big on taking care of things facial, and anybody with bad skin was not on his "I love the flower children" dance card.

In his briefcase, he carried his laptop, Maxwell notes, and one of his various business cards to be used in the appropriate setting. Today, he was Doug Fairbanks, a freelance writer. Entering the library, he spotted a reference librarian's desk.

"Yes, young man," the librarian asked when she looked up. She was about sixty-five and had an open face. No makeup. Hair in a bun. Unlike the youngsters he passed, she probably was at Woodstock, sliding in the mud without a stitch on her in '69.

"Hello." Leon took out his business card and slipped it across the desk. "I'm researching an article on Ithaca and its silent movie history." He used his Truman Capote enunciation since Capote had a lisp, and he figured a man researching cinema history might be a bit fay with a natural tendency to hiss.

The librarian smiled. "Mr. Doug Fairbanks," she said, reading his card. "An appropriate name for someone looking into silent movie history."

"And your name, if I might ask?" He beamed a spotlight smile at her.

She pointed to the desk, where a nameplate indicated she was Erna Edmonds.

"A pleasure, I am sure." Leon thought his little inside allusion to the star would go unnoticed, but you don't become a reference librarian without having a healthy recollection of things both significant and trivial.

"Not many people know about that time," she said, "or about our place in cinema history. I'm sure you know that. There were other places that made silents. West Orange and Fort Lee, New Jersey, New Rochelle, Staten Island."

This new information disturbed Leon. Did Maxwell pull up stakes here and go to one of these cities?

"Didn't know that." He tried to appear glad getting this news.

"I have a few books you could peruse." She tapped on the keyboard on her desk. Looking at the monitor, she made a few *ummm* sounds. A printer kicked in, and she handed Leon a sheet of paper.

"I can recommend these. But Kaplin's *Take Two: The True Story of Ithaca's Movie Making Era* is my favorite. Really gives you a flavor for how the city had a love/hate relationship with movie people here."

"This will help for sure." He waited a beat and then asked, "You know anything about a director named Maxwell?"

"You mean Percy Maxwell? Just a bit. Seems he was pretty much of a recluse after he shut down his company."

"Another question."

"If I can answer, sure."

"He must've lived around here, right?"

"I imagine so," she agreed. "At least when he was making movies."

"How would I find his residence? I searched the Internet and came up blank."

The librarian thought for a moment. "I'd try the county's department of assessment. They have real estate tax records. You can access that on line." With that, she pointed to a carrel and gave him the web site and the library's Wi-Fi password.

Leon walked to the cubicle, sat down, and opened up his laptop. He logged into the assessment site. He found a search form and typed in Percy Maxwell. A long minute went by, searching through all real estate tax records for Tompkins County. When the search ended, a text box popped up with a message. *No records found.*

Strange, he thought, since the librarian agreed that Maxwell must have lived there while making movies. He tried *P. Maxell, Maxwell* without a first name, *Maxwell* with one *l*. Again, zilch.

He went back to the librarian. "No tax records under Maxwell."

"Strange. The database goes back to the 1930s."

"Is there a post office in town?"

"A few. I assume you are trying to see if Mr. Maxwell had a mailing address."

Leon gave her another bright smile.

"There's an archival database of post office records. You could try that," she suggested, giving him a new web site link.

"You're worth every cent they pay you."

"Which isn't enough, I assure you."

It took him almost an hour to find that there was a Percy Maxwell with a PO Box number. His mood lifted. Maybe he stayed put and didn't go out west or to New Jersey or those other places the librarian had mentioned. But his dark mood returned when he saw that the archive had no associated physical addresses.

"Shit," he said softly to himself. This didn't make any sense. How could a known celebrity be so far off the grid with no official records attached to him?

Leon returned to the librarian and told her what he had found or, more accurately, what he hadn't.

"You can try the Tompkins County country clerk's office. Should have copies of deeds, land sales, court records, and old census records. I wrote down their address for you."

Leon delivered an appreciative smile, headed to his car, and drove to the country clerk's office. His morning mood was still up. No need to call his ulcer-prone pal to hear him complain about the Chinese guys and the big-deal forensic blood hound.

In his car, he Googled the clerk's office on his cell phone. He shed his library look and transformed himself into another character for his visit to the Clerk's office. His challenge was showing up at different places making specific inquiries without being identified if things went sideways.

He went with a film historian look, picked a salt-and-pepper wig, a different goatee, and wire rimmed eye glasses. His pitch would be the same as with Erna.

Leon entered the Tompkins County clerk's office. On their web site, he noted that a Ms. Amber Valentine was the county clerk. There was a photo of her, and it was she who was entering something on a computer as he entered the office.

"Can I help you?" she said, standing now as she came away from her desk. She was an attractive woman, with the dark eyes and raven hair. Unlike the reference librarian, Ms. Valentine was no stranger to lipstick and eyeliner.

Leon gave her a thin smile that sheltered his pearly white teeth. No flashy grin needed for a historian who needed a favor.

"Ms. Valentine, I presume." He used his Cedric Hardwicke accent borrowed from the Stanley and Livingstone movie.

She nodded. "And you are…?"

Leon handed her a different business card. She looked it over then looked up at him.

"Researching the silent movie people who worked and lived here," he explained. "The reference librarian on Greene Street said your office may have some records that could help me. Erna Edmonds."

"Lovely woman. So what are you looking for?"

"One man in particular. Percy Maxwell. Name ring a bell?"

"Can't say it does."

"I'm trying to get background on him. Where he lived. I can't seem to find his residence in Ithaca."

"You try the post office?"

"No physical address. Just a PO box."

"Obituaries?"

"Died in Key West. But no mention of his Ithaca whereabouts."

"So no address." She looked at the ceiling, hoping to have a thought drop on top of her head. "Your Mr. Maxwell is like a man in the witness protection program. Off the grid." She gave him twinkly smile.

"Exactly. I understand you may have records of deeds, mortgages, liens. He could be listed on one of those."

"Could be. We're talking about someone living here around when?"

"Probably 1915 to 1980 when he died."

Ms. Valentine rubbed her index finger against her bottom lip. "We started digitizing records about ten years ago." She picked up a telephone and dialed. "Hi Peter. Can you come to the front for a sec?"

She hung up, and a few moments later, Peter arrived. He was introduced as the office IT guy, young and as hip-looking as a county official can get away with. She explained what Leon was trying to track down.

"Give me twenty minutes. I'll run a sort program on your guy."

Peter disappeared, and Leon schmoozed with Ms. Valentine. She was married, had one kid, two cats, and three goats, lived in Richford down the road, and took tai chi classes. Clearly a New Ager who had no issues using eyeliner and lipstick.

Peter returned with a thumbs-down gesture. "The Maxwell well is dry. No taxes, voter registration, or deeds in his name. You sure you have the right name?"

"I am. But thanks for trying."

"No worries," Peter said and took off again.

"Too bad, huh?" Ms. Valentine said.

"Yes." Leon's mood went dark again. What was left for him to do? This guy was a phantom. A freaking ghost. Like Brinks had said before he left, finding the house just might cough up the ghosts that had been squeezing his balls. Now it felt like his balls were being squeezed. How could this guy just disappear?

"I have a suggestion," Ms. Valentine started.

"Sure."

"Go back to Erna and ask about old telephone directories. They may have kept them."

"Good idea," Leon said, not having thought of this himself.

He thanked her and left. Back again in his car, he removed the disguise and looked in the rearview mirror. He became the journalist again, the thankful visitor that Erna Edmonds had helped.

Erna was still behind the reference desk when he returned. She looked up at him when he approached.

"Any luck?" she asked.

"Yes, maybe, and no."

"A very Buddhist answer."

"Is that good?"

"Around here, it is," Erna said, sweeping her hand outwards implying that the United States of Ithaca welcomed this type of answer.

"Ah," Leon said and then explained. "No in that I don't have Mr. Maxwell's address. Yes that I ruled out local county records."

"And the *maybe*?"

"Ms. Valentine mentioned phone directories. Old ones that you might have shelved. Her idea."

Erna Edmonds shook her head. "Not something we have here but it could have been archived at Cornell. They had a grant to digitize everything in sight. If you farted in 1890 and it was recorded, they might have it."

Leon raised his eyebrows at Erna's earthy remark. Once a hippie, always inappropriate.

"Here's the link to Cornell's archive. See if you can find your friend there." She wrote the link down on a slip of paper and handed it to Leon.

Maxwell was certainly not a friend. More of a pain in the fucking ass. At the carrel, Leon logged onto the Cornell site. The landing page had a catalog where thousands of articles, books, photos, and more could be searched. He tried Maxwell and got a list of entries that he had already known about. He typed in *Ithaca silent movies and directors*. Several citations for Maxwell and DimaDozen, his production studio. A news article mentioned it was torn down and bought by the city for a park. Two hours later, he had exhausted any source for Maxwell's house, including the phone book.

He went back to Erna.

"You look like a man who is about to swallow a razor blade."

"Just about. Cornell was a bust."

"You checked out tax records, census data, obits…?"

"Yup, all that."

"Newspapers the same thing?"

"Unfortunately."

Erna squinted. Her eyebrows knotted, and her crow's feet deepened.

"What?" Leon asked, seeing her puzzling over something.

"The newspapers you found. Where did you look?"

"Went online. Like everything else you try to find now."

Erna half smiled. "Except…"

"Except what?"

"The *Ithaca Journal* was and is the oldest news rag around here. The paper was first published in 1815 as the *Seneca Republican*. It was renamed *The Ithaca Journal* in 1823. Most of the paper was saved starting with its first issues…"

"I appreciate the history, but…"

"But anything before 1999 wasn't put online."

Leon waited for more. "But …"

She smiled again and said, "But we have microfiche. For all those back issues."

Leon's shitty mood began to waft away like a stink blown away by a sea breeze.

"There's a microfiche reader over there."

Leon followed Erna's index finger.

"We'll get you reels from 1980 when Maxwell died back to 1910 when he could have first arrived here. It's cumbersome. No search feature. Just slog through every page. Hundreds of them. You might hit pay dirt."

Leon had run out of options, so this was a gift.

"Patience is a virtue unless you wanna get laid," Erna chuckled.

He showed surprise, but then again, Erna was an old school flower child.

"I'll send up for the reels."

A young woman, who looked like an updated version of Erna, appeared. No makeup, Birkenstock sandals, a dress design that was peppered with Zodiac symbols, and shooting stars tattoos on her forearm that matched the dress.

"*Pour vous*," the young woman said, placing a cart filled with boxes next to Leon.

"*Gracias*," he replied in the only smattering of a foreign language he knew.

She giggled, thinking it was a joke.

Leon studied the boxes. Each had a label with a year written on it. He started with 1980, the year Percy Maxwell passed away. The library was open till 5:00 p.m. He had a little over two hours. He would scan through the pages until closing and see how far he could get. If he didn't find anything before he had to leave, there was always tomorrow.

At 4:55 p.m., he was scanning through the 1973 reel. It was the August reel that made his heart skip. The news about the Vietnam War was covered in almost every edition he had read for that year since Ithaca, with its Ho Chi Minh loving college students protesting against it. It was the photo that gave him a jolt: a weary-looking soldier standing next to an old man. The soldier had the zombie stare of someone returning from war. The old man wearing a sad smile had his arm over the kid's shoulder. Leon studied the photo more closely and read the accompanying story.

The page was from August 22. The older man had his head turned up, looking at the younger man. The soldier, dressed in army fatigues, had a noticeable scar along his temple. The caption read "Percy Maxwell welcomes home his nephew John Burke." The story focused on Burke's return, how he had been wounded in a firefight and was home recovering from his injuries.

Leon's pulse pounded like a bass drum. *Maxwell and his nephew!* The next thing he noticed was the house in the photo. They both were standing in front of a house. Leon would bet his last nickel that that was the house that Percy Maxwell lived in. It had to be. He wanted to enlarge the page, but there was no zoom feature. There was a print function though. So he pressed Print, got up from the scanner, and walked over to Erna's desk.

She was holding the printout from the newspaper that he had printed.

"So you found him?" she asked.

"Sort of. It's probably the house but no mention of where."

The woman took a close look at the printout and the photo. "It's a style of an older house we see around town." She then bent down and opened a drawer. She took out a magnifying glass and studied the photo carefully. "There's a street sign. Well, at least the first two letters."

Erna handed the magnifying glass to Leon.

"It's a *C* with maybe an *O* or an *A*. You know any streets that start with those two letters?" he asked.

She typed on her keyboard, and a moment later, a map came out from her printer. She studied it for a minute, running her finger around the streets. "Cayuga, Court, Corn, College, Carpenter, Cobb, Cascadilla are a few."

She then handed the map to Leon. "You could drive around, see if there's a house that matches the one in the photo."

Leon extended his hand for a thank-you handshake. "You were an amazing help."

"Just doing my job." Erna held his hand longer than needed. She looked at the faint bite marks on his hand.

"Dog bit me when I was walking by a frat house in town," Leon explained. It was the Kelley woman trying to ward him off as he crushed her larynx. "Maybe I look like a postman."

"Dog could've been stoned," Erna said. "Might've found the frat boys' stash. Who knows what goes on in a stoned doggie's head. Maybe they see God."

"God is dog spelled backwards," Leon joked.

Erna smiled. "And if God is Shih Tzu, we would be up Shitz Creek."

CHAPTER 73

ALIEN CREATURES

"Well, this ends the nickel tour," Ralph said. "I'll get us some iced tea." He exited the attic, carefully going down the stairs.

"That's where I found…myself," Holey John said, pointing to the chessboard that was painted on the attic floor. "There's a loose board underneath. My uncle's hiding place."

Zena and I agreed to meet Holey John and see the house for ourselves. We met Trish Mansfield, the real estate agent who stood by silently, letting Holey John do all the selling.

We remembered Holey John's description of finding Percy Maxwell's trove of memorabilia, including the two clippings, one about his folks and the other about returning from Nam. Holey John turned, and we followed him to the first floor and entered the living room, where Ralph greeted us with lemonade.

"What do you…think?" he asked Zena.

"Some fresh paint and new furniture that doesn't look like the set design from the Bates Motel would do wonders."

He smiled broadly, which was as rare as seeing Haley's Comet. "Easy enough to…do." He paused then said, "So like it?"

Zena came up to him and reached for his hand. He looked down at her. She squeezed it and said, "I'm happy for you. It's a great place. Lots of room. Quiet street. No far from the center of town."

"That's not…what I meant. You here. Can you…imagine it?"

Zena didn't answer right away. I knew she was playing a movie in her head, the "What would it be like for me here?" movie.

"Maybe. But I need to think about it. It'd be a pretty big change for me."

"Well, that's better than a... *no.*"

He then turned to the real estate agent and asked, "Can I put Zena on my...deed?"

"John," Zena said, taken aback. "I'm not there yet. Here, I mean. On board with your sweet proposal. I said I need to think it over, sweetie."

Trish turned to Zena. "I can do that. Put you on the deed. Has nothing to do with whatever you decide. No financial obligation either way."

"We'll see."

Ralph returned with a tray of paper cups filled with iced tea. We all took a cup and drank it, washing down the attic dust.

Zena asked me for the time.

"Close to five."

"I better head back to the G Brothers. My evening appearance is in an hour. I still need to make a living."

This was an excuse to get of Dodge and any more entreaties from Holey John. I knew that she had enough dough from her trust, so saying she needed to make a living by pulling down a couple hundred bucks a day was on the left side of bullshit. I also understood her hesitation. She'd be leaving her midway community and the friends she made. We all said our goodbyes to Ralph.

Trish walked with us to our car. She turned to Holey John. "We can close tomorrow. Sign the papers. Paying in cash speeds things up. Of course, I had to tell the bank you weren't a member of a Columbian cartel," Trish blurted, laughing at her joke.

"I'll come to your trailer later after I get off. Chat some more," Zena said, holding Holey John's hand as we stood on the porch.

"That'd be...good."

We left, and I still had no clue about how Zena felt about leaving her life. If she agreed, those two would disembark into an alien and unfamiliar world. Fortunately, Ithaca was full of alien creatures, and they would probably fit right in.

CHAPTER 74

GOOD NEWS, BAD NEWS

Leon left the library, full of anticipation. He got into his car and lay the map and copy of the newspaper article on the passenger seat. As he made his way into town, he began looking for streets that started with the letters *Ca* or *Co*.

Cayuga Street was on the same street as his hotel. He made a left. South Cayuga turned into North Cayuga after a few miles. When he reached Remington Road he knew that he had traveled the entire length of his first *Ca* street. He motored slowly, scanning every house, comparing each one to the photo until he didn't need to look at the photo anymore, the image etched into his mind. He backtracked and found Cascarilla Street. It ran less than a couple of miles and ended at the Cayuga Lake front.

At times when he drove very slowly, the people who were out and about took notice. He didn't want to raise suspicion having people think that he might be tagged as someone casing their houses to rob. Occasionally, he would wave as if he was just a rubbernecker looking around town.

Leon checked off Concord and Cambridge Place, Christopher Court, Court and Cornell Streets. He skirted by the Cornell campus when Court Street ended at the Ithaca City Cemetery. He picked up Campus Road, and just before he reached the Pew Engineering Quad within the university grounds, he made a right onto Central Avenue. At the rotary, he entered College Avenue.

Leon slowed to a crawl and inspected the houses. A car in front of him and moving in the same direction slowed. He saw the brake lights and the car pulled to the curb. He couldn't get a clear view of three houses blocked by the parked car. So he made a U-turn to check out the houses he had missed. As he passed the three houses, he saw five people standing on a porch. Two of them looked odd. Odd but familiar. So odd that it made him swerve, his car almost hitting an oncoming car. He looked back in his side view mirror. He had seen them before. Then it clicked. The weird couple were from the midway. He pulled into an empty spot on the sidewalk.

"What the fuck," Leon said, watching them. The pin cushion guy and the midget fortune teller were holding hands. Figures, he thought. Freaks humping freaks. He didn't recognize a third person, a man who looked like a regular human being. A woman wearing a pants suit outfit, like a dyke with a career, stood with them. Then this geezer bent down to shake the midget's hand and then patted pin cushion man on the back.

He watched the people leave the house. Sunlight hit the pin cushion guy. He was saying something to the midget. The midget was nodding. She wasn't in her fortune-telling outfit but wore a tight tank top and jeans. Nice rack and ass. Not bad for a tiny tot.

The pant-suited broad shook the old man's hand and spoke to him. She waved and went down the porch steps then got into a car. Leon noticed a real estate logo on the door as she drove off. The trio climbed into another car and headed down College Avenue. He looked at the car as they passed by, and the midget spotted him. He quickly turned his face away.

Leon took his time and studied the house. He looked at the photo, and it struck him. It was the windows. They were the same. He got out of his car for a closer look. As he did, his breathing came quicker, seeing a growing resemblance. He double checked the photo from the newspaper.

He walked to the spot where the photographer must have taken the picture. He lined up the two letters of the street sign and squinted at the house. Sure enough, it was the house in the photo. He shook his head. "Fuck me sideways till Sunday." He let out a breath like a kid blowing out birthday candles. He found the house. Great. But what in hell were the midway weirdoes doing there?

Leon edged nearer to the house. A signpost was wedged into the front lawn. The house was for sale. A plastic holder was attached to the post. There were sheets from a real estate office with information about the house. He took one and noticed a banner glued across it with *Under Agreement*.

"Shit," he said, wondering about the people who had just left. Did they know the old guy and came to visit? Or maybe the normal guy was family? Or a buyer? Or could it be that the two freaks and the normo wanted to buy this house? A kinky threesome idea, but it was Ithaca after all.

He took out his burner phone and dialed his ticket to the stars.

"Good news, bad news," Leon said when Brinks answered.

"Somehow this is not very reassuring."

"You want assurance, buy insurance."

"That's what I'm paying you for. My insurance. Insurance that Tankowitz who's giving me the googly eye while the bean counters grind through my numbers come up short. Tankowitz knows I gave our overseas friends the Hollywood shuffle. Makes looks at me like I was throwing sand into their eyes."

"They find anything?"

"No, but I feel like I am wearing a suicide vest, and Tankowitz has the remote."

"Just act like nothing's wrong," Leon advised.

"Sure. No problem," Brinks answered, sarcasm dripping from his words like engine oil. "So brighten my day."

"Like I said, I found what probably is his house, thanks to my new best friend Erna."

"Erna?"

"Librarian in town."

Leon gave Brinks the rundown on his pinball deflections from one office after another, trying to locate Maxwell's house when he finally hit the jackpot.

"I spot this article about Maxwell and his nephew who came back from Nam. The newspaper had a photo taken in front of this house. The house I'm currently looking at."

Leon waited for an *attaboy* and didn't get one.

"You mentioned a nephew," Brinks said.

"Yeah. John Burke. He was with Maxwell in the paper."

"That must be the bad news."

"Could be," Leon said.

"Not could. He's an heir."

"He may be dead for all we know. That photo made him look like he was knocking on heaven's gate. Take a breath, dude."

"Sure. Let me deep-breathe this fucking situation away."

"Look. I will get into the house," Leon said confidently. "There's an old guy in there. Old people like to talk to me. They like to talk about their lives. I turn on the charm and they yak. If there is any paper inside, I will find it for you."

"Perfect," Brinks said, again his inference that that was not perfect.

"I'll let you know what I find after my schmooze."

"Schmooze?"

"Yeah. I do that real good. Be surprised what people wind up telling me."

CHAPTER 75

A DEAD BODY IN SUMMER

Leon waited a good ten minutes before heading to the front door. He thought about what he was going to say and hoped the old man would go along with his previously winning pitch. He still wore the same getup he had used with Erna, the journalist in search of Ithaca's silent movie history.

He knocked on the door and waited. He heard footsteps shuffle then stop, and then the door cracked open.

"Yes?" the old man asked.

"The house," Leon said. "I saw the sign."

Ralph grinned. "You're a dollar short and a day late. House is sold."

Leon grinned back. "Oh, I'm not here about buying it."

"Then what can I do for you, son?"

Leon took his business card out from his shirt pocket and handed it to Ralph. "I've been researching the silent movie people who worked around here. Got some leads from a librarian in town."

"Erna?"

"Yes, sir. That's how I found your house. I'm doing a story on Percy Maxwell. Seems he might've lived here."

"He did."

"That's great!"

"An article you say?"

"That's right. You mind if I look inside. Get a feeling for his place, ask some questions. Anything you might know to give me background. Maybe take a few photos."

"No harm, I suppose." Ralph let him in and showed him to the living room. Leon immediately spotted the posters on the wall, walked over, and studied them. He lingered there, making gratifying sounds, his mind relishing a bygone age when actors really acted, not the pretentious shit he had seen that day. When he finished, he turned his attention back to the old man.

"You know my name," Leon said, pointing at the business card that Ralph was still holding. "I didn't catch yours."

"Ralph Gilmore. So what do you want to know?"

"Whatever you may remember."

Leon took out his cell phone and asked, "You mind if I record what you tell me?"

He didn't turn the recorder app on but went through the motions, putting it on a coffee table facing Gilmore.

"Record away." Ralph smiled a full set of dentures and sat down on a sagging armchair.

He told Leon how he had met Percy Maxwell, his own family's connection to the silent movie industry in Ithaca. He recalled some of the times he actually met him when his gang would come back from California for their reunions.

"They spent hours jawing about the good old days. Percy used to take them to a special spot in the state park near these waterfalls."

"Special?" Leon repeated.

"Yeah. Where they shot some of their cliffhanger movies. He had a nephew. Took him there as well. It was nice, the two of them together, away from the kid's parents who were as agreeable as a rattlesnakes inside a paper bag."

Leon heard the word *nephew*, and a sliver of panic made him stop his questioning.

Ralph continued. "A couple of the men stayed in the business. Headed West soon after sound came in."

"Talkies," Leon added.

"Yup. Percy dropped out of the business, but my brother worked till the fifties. Not sure about the other men."

Ralph's recollections lasted almost an hour, Leon hoping the man might give him leads he could follow.

"That's about it," Ralph finally said. "If I remember anything else, I'll contact you." He waved the business card at Leon.

"That would be great. One more thing though."

"Okay."

"I see the posters from movies he shot," Leon said, gesturing to the walls. "You have any other things? I can use my phone's camera and take some photos if you don't mind."

"I have some props scattered around."

Ralph got up from the armchair and pointed toward the dining room. Leon chuckled at the peeing dog and took a shot. "That thing take good pictures?"

"Just like a regular camera. Anything else to see?"

"Nah. Moth-eaten costumes and some broken props that are junk."

"Photos, letters, papers?"

Ralph shook his head, but Leon saw the old man's eyes quickly look up toward the ceiling and then cast down at the floor. Leon knew a tell when he saw one.

"Those costumes and props? Take it they're upstairs in the attic?"

When Leon asked this last question, Ralph noticed a different tone. The question wasn't as innocuous as his previous line of questions. He sensed this man was after something.

Ralph gave a dismissive gesture. "Yup. Just gathering dust. Not worth the effort to make the climb."

"Be great to take a look anyway."

Ralph heard that tone again. He turned his back on Leon and headed down the hall toward the front door, expecting the man to follow. He didn't hear Leon taking his lead and spoke over his shoulder.

"I am awfully tired, Mr. Fairbanks. What's with my visitors and you popping up? Believe me there isn't anything more I can show or tell you."

With the old man's back facing him, Leon came up behind him and squeezed the man's neck, with his claw-like fingers. He turned Ralph around and marched him back down the hall.

Ralph's knees buckled, but Leon kept the old man upright with his grip.

"What are you doing?" Ralph howled. "You're hurting me."

Leon stopped and loosened his grip. "You got an attic, and you're going to show me what's up there."

"It's moth-eaten costumes and broke-down props," Ralph insisted.

"I like old, moth-eaten shit. How do we get up there?"

When Ralph hesitated, Leon increased the pressure around the back of his neck. He felt a tingling sensation, knowing the old man's protests meant there was something he didn't want him to find.

Ralph pointed weakly at the door down the hall. As Leon march-stepped, Ralph, the old man, squirmed, his arms flailing like the broken wings of a seagull. His thrashing hand landed on small table that held the Tiffany lamp. It fell; the shade shattered.

The old man stumbled a few times, banging his bony shins against the edges of the steps as Leon pushed him up the landing. By the time they reached the attic, Ralph's breathing was labored.

Leon let go of his grip, and Ralph crumpled to the floor. He held his chest with his right hand over his heart while he sucked down air.

Leon started opening the old trunks. Like the old man had said, they were piled with old costumes. He dumped everything out of each trunk and rummaged through them, flipping the trunks on their sides. He found one thing that caught his attention. A knife with a bone handle, something a cowboy might have used in one of Maxwell's westerns.

"Just old stuff like I said," Ralph said, his voice trembling. "Take anything you want," he said, pointing to the Bowie knife.

"Nice of you." Leon picked up the knife. More trunks and boxes were kicked open with nothing of interest, not the thing he was after. Desperation fell over him. He chased this fucking piece of paper from Los Angeles to this time-warped college town, and his sure thing hunch about the contracts being there was not so sure at all.

He walked over to Ralph, who had gained some of his strength back.

"I'm looking for some papers."

"There ain't any newspapers up here. We recycle."

Leon smacked him across his face. "Wise guy. I think you know what kind of papers I mean. Papers that Maxwell had."

"He died over forty years ago for God's sake! What in Sam Hill would I know what he did with whatever you're looking for?"

"Just a hunch," Leon said, repeating his belief they were there.

"Play the horses then."

Leon grabbed the old man by his shirt collar, yanked him up, and gave him a backhanded slap across his face. Ralph's dentures went flying out of his mouth.

"You're an asshole," Ralph gummed out his insult. "If I was a younger man, I would've—"

This time, Leon punched him in the stomach, and the old man's breath whooshed out of him. It took a few minutes for his breathing to come back to normal. Leon knew how to inflict pain using pressure points. He hooked two fingers around Ralph's collar bone and squeezed.

Ralph's eyes rolled back inside his head, and he began to squeal, his legs beginning to buckle again. Leon relaxed the fingers. "Are you seeing where this is going? There are papers I need. Signed ones. Ones that Maxwell had."

Ralph spit in Leon's face. The latter smiled and grabbed Ralph's crotch, gripping his scrotum. Ralph began to cry. Leon took Ralph's middle finger next and broke it, hearing the sound of a dry twig breaking. He broke two more fingers leaving the thumb and pinky alone for now.

Ralph's mouth opened wide, and his scream became an inward breath of anguish.

"You got a bunch more fingers to work on," Leon said.

Ralph wanted the pain to stop. He knew what that bastard was looking for. That brute wanted Pink's papers. It could only be one thing. The contract with Mazer. What else had any value? Ralph didn't understand what that meant almost one hundred years later, but there was no doubt that that bastard wanted it bad.

Through tears in his old rheumy eyes, he glanced across the attic, thinking about the hiding place. And that was a mistake.

"You see something over there?" Leon urged, about to break another finger.

Ralph had reached his limit. He nodded toward the chessboard.

Leon took him around the waist and walked him to the painted chessboard.

"Now what do we have here?" Leon asked, looking down at the board.

He dropped Ralph to the floor. He could see scratch marks. The recent ones were around one of the boards. He pried the board loose with the Bowie knife. Leon smiled. He reached in and pulled out the contents of the stash. He tossed aside the photos and receipts from suppliers but pocketed a letter from Irene Castle. That was worth more to him than Brinks's ulcer-producing contracts. He stopped with a breathy hitch when he lifted out one of the missing Mazer contracts. This one was signed by Gustafson. He hit gold. A moment passed, and his enthusiasm washed away like a receding wave. There still was one more he needed. The last one.

"Where is Maxwell's?" Leon shouted, waving the Gustafson contract.

"Dunno," Ralph whispered, holding his broken fingers. "I got nothing more to tell you. What's there is all there is."

"Bullshit." Leon looked back at recent scratch marks. "Someone was here before. The people I saw leave."

Ralph stayed silent.

Leon found another pressure point, and Ralph let out a pathetic whimper. He squeezed harder. Ralph's struggle to keep secret what he knew had evaporated.

"Who the fuck was here?" Leon hissed. He took Ralph's other hand and bent three of his middle fingers back, ready to snap them.

"Holey John and his friends," the old man whimpered.

"Who the fuck is Holey John?"

"Maxwell's nephew," he answered, his voice trembling.

Leon turned cold. The soldier in the old newspaper article. Brinks had flipped out when he told him that Maxwell had a nephew.

"What about him?" Leon demanded, finding a new pressure point.

"Ask him."

A confusion of lines crisscrossed Leon's forehead. "Ask him about the contract?"

Ralph sobbed and nodded.

Leon put pressure on this carotid artery. "How can I do that?"

"When he moves in here."

"What does that mean?"

"He's buying my house," Ralph weakly choked out his reply.

"I can't wait. I need it now."

The old man struggled through the pain to speak and then said, "Then go find him. He took it. Along with other stuff he found."

"When was the nephew here?"

"Just before you showed up."

Leon had seen the people leave that house, but two of them were freaks, no one resembling the soldier in the photograph.

He slapped Ralph. "Make sense, old man. No one came out of your place that was his nephew. I was watching."

Ralph's head dropped to his chest. "You're wrong."

"Fine. Where is he now?"

"Midway most likely," Ralph said weakly, his tortured body weak as a baby.

"Who?"

Ralph sputtered a feeble snort. "If you like sparkles, you'll find him."

In his mind, Leon went through the people who had left the house. "You're kidding. The guy with the midget. The jewel-faced freak."

Leon had a *what-the-fuck* moment. Of course the normal-looking guy was too young to be Maxwell's nephew. That left the other guy. The human pin cushion. He was John Burke.

"Thanks, Ralphy," Leon said with his practiced smile. He put his hand on the old man's shoulder and patted it.

"You got what you wanted. Now leave me be. The real estate lady will be here soon." The old man said that, hoping he would live what little time he had left in California with his family.

That hope was snuffed out when Leon moved his hand from Ralph's shoulder and wrapped both hands tightly around his neck, staring into the old man's eyes as he choked him. Ralph's eyes went wide, but his eyelids didn't close, stayed open, his life dimming like a candle whose wick was spent, his head hanging down and off to one side when he finally stopped breathing, his windpipe crushed. He dropped the old man who crumpled to the floor. He knew the police would show up at some point. He rummaged through Ralph's pants and found his wallet, took out the cash, and threw the wallet on the floor. A robbery that went bad.

Leon then dragged his victim to the corner of the attic and pushed boxes over his body. He pushed the papers he scooped out of the hiding place back into the hole, replaced the board, then laid a trunk on top as added insurance to buy time. He knew the clock was ticking. Leon understood where he had to go next and in a hurry.

He exited out a back door and strode over to his car. As he drove away with a new destination in mind, he imagined the neighbors noticing a retched smell coming from the house in a day or two. Dead bodies in summer would do that.

CHAPTER 76

CLOSING IN

Leon figured it would be pretty easy to find John Burke. He slipped through the crowds, weaving his way to where he remembered the pin cushion man's stage was located when he first visited the midway. He needed to hurry since a frantic call from the real estate broad would send Mr. Sparkles off and running when Ralph didn't answer the door.

Leon hustled to the stretch of midway stages and stopped to think. He couldn't imagine living their kind of life. But it struck him that there was a weird similarity in what they did and what he wanted to do. The audience. People watching you perform. He wanted that badly.

A wave of dread washed over him when he got to Burke's stage. It was empty, everything cleared out.

Leon stopped a man carrying a broom who worked at the midway. "Hey, buddy," he started, "where's the guy that gets pins stuck in him?"

"Gone," the man answered. "Tossed his jewelry and shit into the crowds and packed up."

"You know where his digs are?"

The man scratched his head. "Somewhere on the field with all the other folk. Never been to his squat."

"Thanks." Leon began to search the field, taking quick steps, hoping to spot Burke, zigzagging around empty animal cages. Just as he skirted some stacked bales of hay, a ratty-looking camel tended by a toothless rag head cut him off. He yelled and punched the camel's haunch to get him to move. The poor creature stopped dead and let out an anguished bleat.

The man leading the camel came around and saw Leon draw back his fist for another punch.

"Mugga boomba mumbo bubba," the camel's tender said, waving an admonishing finger at Leon.

"Move this fucking hump!" Leon yelled.

"Mugga boomba mumbo bubba."

"Go mugga mugga yourself."

The man shrugged and walked the camel away.

Leon turned left and right. Burke was nowhere in sight.

"Shit," Leon spitted.

He had to think fast as he scanned the field where over fifty different types of living quarters were scattered. Another *shit* left Leon's mouth. Finding Burke's trailer seemed hopeless. He looked at his watch again.

Things were not going as planned. As he puzzled over what he could do, he had an idea. It was a desperate idea, but time was running out.

Leon walked back to the midway. He saw a kiosk with a young man hawking souvenir programs.

"Let me see one of them," he said to the young man.

The kid handed him a program, and Leon leafed through it. There was a photo of the pincushion man and the midget fortune-teller.

"How much?" Leon asked.

"For you, four Washingtons."

He headed toward the midget's booth, rolling the program up and shoving it into his back pocket. He stopped for a moment and watched her. There was a teenager sitting with her. Zena held the young girl's hands and was saying something. The girl was sobbing. Zena said something more, and the girl nodded. She said a few more things, and the girl stopped crying then smiled. She handed the fortune-teller some money and walked away, giving Zena a princess wave.

Leon took in a breath and headed to the booth.

"Ms. Zena," he said, a noticeable hiss when he said *Ms.*

Zena looked up at him and gave him a guarded smile. His vibe was off, but she didn't know why she felt it that way.

"You tell fortunes?" Leon asked, pointing up at her sign.

"More like I help people with what's going on in their lives," she said. "People make their own fortunes, don't you think?"

"Some do, some don't, right?" Leon thought about how he was making his own fortune. Brinks might hold the keys to his future, but Leon had to give them to him.

Leon sat down and said, "Maybe you help me figure out how I can make my fortune."

"Let's try. Let me have your hands."

He held his hands out in front of him. When her hands wrapped around his, he felt a charge run up his arm, like touching a frayed electrical wire.

"What was that?" he asked.

"Our energies connecting."

Leon faked an agreeing nod but was disturbed by her answer.

She looked directly into his eyes. "You are a complicated man."

He thought you could say that about anybody.

"So they say."

Zena's eyes half-closed for a split second and then opened them into a slight squint. Leon caught that. He was sure it was the way he said *say* picking up on his hiss.

"You want things."

Another softball generalization. "Sure."

"But you are a man with many faces."

Leon tensed at that.

Zena felt his hands tighten, a bit too hard.

"You need to have one face. Too many distract your thinking. Your goals. You must be of one mind. One face to the world. Not many."

Leon relaxed a little. She was spouting philosophical advice you could get from a self-help book. But the "many faces" thing took him by surprise. Did she see through his assembled look?

"Do you understand?"

"Sure. One face."

Zena looked at him more closely. "You must find a way to deal with your anxiety."

"Not sure what you mean."

"Your hands. Your pulse is rapid."

He let go of her hands.

"Many people come to talk about things on their mind. I'm a good listener."

Leon forced a smile. "It's the heat. Makes my heart beat a bit faster."

"I see."

"I have a favor," Leon said, pulling the souvenir program out from his back pocket. "Wonder if you would autograph this for me." He flipped open to the page where her photo was printed.

"Happy to." She had a pen near her money jar. "You want me to address this to you?"

"Lester would be real fine."

"To Lester," she said, signing her name.

"One more favor." Leon opened the page where Burke was shown. "Can you point me to where this guy is. He left the stage. Be nice to get his too before I leave today."

"Can't say I know where he is now."

"A guy that works here said he might be in his trailer," Leon said. "I could go there. Ask him to sign this."

"We don't like having strangers pop in unannounced. Sorry."

"I won't be any trouble being a fan and all."

"Circus rules. Maybe he'll be around later."

"It's really important," he insisted, his tone almost threatening.

She stiffened. "Like I said, circus rules."

Leon gave her an irritated look.

"Fine." With that, he got up then took a five-dollar bill out of his wallet and paid her.

As he walked away, Zena got an uncomfortable feeling about that guy but couldn't put her finger on why.

CHAPTER 77

BLIND LUCK HAPPENS

As he walked away, Leon had a weird feeling about the midget. Her eyes bored into him like she could read his thoughts. The strange sensation when her hands gripped his. The "many faces" thing. She dished out her bullshit as if it was true, but this is what they do to trick you into believing they have paranormal powers. *Relax, she's no fucking mind reader*, he reassured himself.

His cell phone buzzed. It was Brinks.

"What," Leon answered.

"Any news? Things are getting too close for my comfort here."

Leon walked to a spot behind a stand selling corn dogs. "I found the Gustafson's contract. And I know who has Maxwell's."

"The nephew."

"Yup."

"How are you going to get it?"

"Don't worry about that. Keep cool. I'll wrap this up before the sun sets."

"Keep cool. Sure. No problem," Brinks said, sounding uncertain.

"Worry about your gooks and Tankowitz. Anyway, I gotta go," Leon said, not wanting to hear Brinks whine about prison and losing his precious lifestyle. He tamped down his own anxiety, but the clock was ticking louder than the gator in Peter Pan.

He headed back to the field of trailers and campers for another look-see. If he had to, he'd see where tiny tots lived and would make her tell him where Burke lived. It worked with the old man. It would work with her.

It was blind luck, when out of nowhere, he saw Burke at the far end of the field. He saw him stop at a banged-up trailer. No markings on the front to advertise what he did like some of the other ones he had seen. Maxwell's nephew was holding a carton which might've held belongings from his stage. He felt under the stairs that led up to the front door, searching for something. Burke glanced around, found whatever he looked for, then climbed three steps to the door. Leon knew it was a key.

He smiled a self-satisfactory smile. As he patiently waited, he sized up the area. He figured the man had to leave to meet the real estate lady if what Ralph had said was true. Since he knew where the key was stashed, there would be no need to draw attention by jimmying the door. And once inside, it wouldn't be that hard to find the contract that Percy Maxwell had signed. The old man made it clear Burke had it in his possession. The trailer was small. So how many hiding places could there be?

The door opened, and Burke carried the same cardboard box. Leon figured he was probably collecting the rest of his shit from his act. Burke stooped down and hid the key then headed back to the midway, a loopy grin breaking through his pin-studded face. He bet this brain-fucked vet was seeing himself in a new life. Too bad that the deal was going south with the owner decomposing under a pile of boxes. Leon followed him halfway to make sure where he was going.

Showtime, Leon thought to himself, his breathing rapid, his senses on high alert. He walked to Burke's trailer, found the key, opened the door, and moved quickly inside. As he shut the door, he surveyed the space. The freak's curtains were drawn, but enough light made it easy to see the layout. He was immediately spooked by the walls. Hundreds of eyes glued to them.

"Fuck all."

The man lived like a freaking monk. Sparse. Hardly any furniture except for a cot and a table with one hard backed chair. And the eyes. Weird like the freak was weird. There was a fridge and an oven. The oven had a bicycle chain lock wrapped around the appliance. If that was his idea for a safe place for safekeeping, then whatever had mauled his brain had really done a number in the logic area of his gray matter.

Leon knew how to crack the combination of a bike lock. He had done it dozens of times around colleges where kids had expensive bikes that mommy and daddy bought them. There were four numbers on a bike lock cylinder, each with four tumblers. All he needed to do was look for a gap between the tumblers. Find a gap then pull the cable. Find all gaps and bingo, the lock is released. It took him a little half a minute to unlock Burke's.

When he opened the oven, it was empty.

Leon almost slammed the oven door closed but caught himself. Not a good idea to make a loud noise. He looked around. Time was running out. At this point, he didn't need to pretend he was a neat cat burglar. He overturned the mattress and threw it on the floor then stripped off the blanket and sheets. Nothing there except a gook photo of two women. He picked it up and tore it in half. The frig had nothing. The freezer had a few frozen meals and an ice cube tray. He tossed aside all the pots and pans with their lids. Empty. He then went into the tiny bathroom next and took the lid off the toilet. Just a tank full of water. Leon's neck tightened as if a serrated rope had been strung around his neck. Maybe he missed something. He went back to the room with the haunting eyes.

He looked at his watch. Twenty-two minutes had passed. He went to the small table underneath the window and turned it over. Nothing was taped to its underside. Leon became increasingly edgy convinced the Maxwell agreement had to be there, but where? He racked his brain. Maybe he hid it under the trailer. Or what about the midget chick? Would he have given it to her to keep? He sat on the overturned cot, twiddling the Bowie knife in his hand, trying to figure out what to do.

CHAPTER 78

FOUND AND LOST

Holey John returned to finish packing what was left on his stage. A few pins were left in the fishbowl, and he put them in his box as a reminder of his old life. He took one last look at the stage, his public confessional where people became his flagellating adjudicators.

He walked back to his trailer carrying a box with the few things he could use. The ornamental lights could be strung around a Christmas tree; his throw rug for the front hall. Zena would come by later, as would Fenn. Maybe she'd go shopping with him. Help him buy a bed and other furnishings since he didn't know squat about what you needed to outfit a house.

Smiling, he thought that by tomorrow all the papers would be signed and the house would be his. Ralph could stay as long as wanted and move to his family out west whenever convenient. While there, he could show him how the furnace worked along with the fuse box if houses still had them. Things that he needed to know as a home owner.

As he headed to his trailer, he thought about having Zena move in with him again. She, like himself lived insulated lives, shielded from what pretended to be the normal world. He could remove every piece of jewelry. His skin would heal over his perforated flesh in a few months, and like a snake shedding its skin, he would be born again, totally revealed, no distracting reflections making it impossible for people to see what was under the cover. For her, the world would always see her as a dwarf, seeing a deformity in their blinded eyes because they didn't know what was in her soul and how beautiful a person she was.

He put what he had packed outside the trailer. His hand swept under the stairs. The key was gone. He saw that door was ajar. As soon as he opened it, a stranger slammed Burke against the door. Leon held the knife to his throat.

"Make a sound, and I'll slice open your gullet."

Burke blinked that he understood this man's threat. Leon took the knife an inch away from his Adam's apple.

"You John Burke, right? Percy Maxwell's nephew."

"Maybe."

"Don't play cute. You have something I want."

He gave the stranger a blank look.

"That paper. The agreement your uncle made. I need it."

"Why?"

"This isn't twenty questions, freak."

Leon nicked him under his chin, and a droplet of blood waited for gravity to decide when it would fall.

"I'm kinda in a hurry." Leon nicked again.

Burke remembered what Ralph had said about the agreement. Something about having shares in a movie company. He didn't understand what value it could have over a hundred years later.

"Look, pal. We can do this the easy way or the hard way. It's just a fucking piece of paper, right?"

Burke cast a searing glare at the man. He said nothing. This asshole reminded him of some of the guys in Nam. Go jungle crazy at Charlie bed check time. But that guy was a different kind of crazy.

Leon saw that Mr. Sparkles was not going for the threat and that was a problem. He could hurt him. But serious damage and freaky guy couldn't tell him where the fucking paper was.

Burke saw that his trailer had been tossed. He glared at Leon. "You kinda went nuts...here."

Here was a man with hundreds of piercings telling him he was nuts.

Leon decided to tell him a half truth. "I've been hired to find that paper thing of yours. and I was desperate," he said, pointing at

Holey John's scattered belongings. "My job is on the line, buddy. Makes you do crazy things, right?"

Burke remained stone-faced.

"Come on, pal. I don't want to hurt you." Leon waited a few seconds then said, "Or you midget girlfriend."

A streak of rage coursed through him. This psycho had stalked him, maybe saw him at Ralph's house that day. He knew about psychos. Clip a bunch of Chucks in the morning and sleep like a baby at night. And then he saw the photograph of his wife and daughter, been ripped in two. His blood rose, and he clenched his fists into hard balls of bone and muscle.

Leon saw Burke stare at the torn photograph. He gave him a death ray look.

There was no way this asshole was going to get anything from him. "It's not here," he murmured. "It's in a…house."

"Oh?" Leon said. "What house?"

"In town."

Leon saw he was being played. Ralph told him that he had it. This freak knew the contract must have some value, having tossed his place apart and putting a knife to his throat. A barracuda smile crossed his lips. "The one on College Avenue. The man was very cooperative when I pressed him. Said you have it."

At the mention of the house, Leon noticed the change in Burke. "Ralph? You hurt…him?"

"That nice house you're buying won't be so nice if you're dead too."

Burke took a moment to understand what the man had just said. Then he screamed, "You bastard!"

Leon kept the knife against his throat. "Maybe that midget friend of yours can tell me if you don't right now." He kept his eyes locked into Burke's. "Maybe tie you up. Then visit her when she's back in her tiny tot trailer. If I close my eyes tight, I can imagine she has a pretty cute body on her for a midget. Might even do her before I cut her."

A low growl came out of Burke's throat.

"Settle down, tiger. Tell me what I want, and you and your little friend can walk into the sunset holding hands."

"Okay," Burke conceded. He let his body go slack, and Leon lifted the knife away.

That's when Burke kneed the stranger in his groin.

Leon grabbed his crotch, and air left his lungs like a punctured tire. He fell to the ground, gasping. Burke kicked him in the ribs, ran out of the trailer, and sprinted to his truck.

Leon heard an engine start and forced himself up. He staggered out of the trailer as the pin cushion man's truck headed to the highway. He stopped to see where the guy was going, watching the truck bump over the field and make it to the road. He was heading north, not back to town. Not to the house. Leon had to move quickly and follow him to wherever the hell he was going.

"Hey!" a voice called out.

Leon turned and spotted the midget in the distance.

Zena saw her friend flee his trailer and that man come after him. She watched as his truck fishtailed out of the parking lot.

"Fuck," Leon said. This was bad.

She quick-stepped toward him. His mind whirled. He had to catch up to Burke. As she came closer, she continued to yell at him. He saw that the carnie people nearby were staring at her, wondering why she was making a commotion. There was nothing he could do but run.

Leon bolted before she or anyone else could get an even better look at him. He knocked her over as he ran hard and fast, ducking behind empty animal cages, zigzagging to his car.

"Hey asshole," she yelled as she stood up, wiping dirt from her eyes.

He jumped into his car, his car keys already out of his pocket, and started the engine. Clods of dirt kicked up as he sped to the road. He needed to get to Burke, whom he guessed with certainty was heading to wherever he had stashed the contract.

As he drove north, he saw Burke's truck chugging ahead. Two miles out, it slowed down, brakes' lights on, and then turned. Leon followed it down a dirt road that led into some kind of park. A minute later, he saw the truck parked at an odd angle in a parking lot. A couple of cars were there. Leon ran to the truck. No one was inside it. He caught a glimpse of the pin man running through the woods. He listened to the sounds of the woods and heard water falling then twigs breaking. The pin man was running. He followed the sounds of heavy breathing. He would make the man talk just like he had done with the old man. After that, he would figure out what to do with the midget, whom he feared recognized him.

CHAPTER 79

GONE

I walked to my car to head back to my motel. As I strolled, I kicked at the sods in the parking lot. Sure, I was happy for Holey John, but at the same time, I was concerned about Zena. I still had no real idea if she would join him or stay at the G Brothers without her protector. I was also concerned about what lay ahead for me. Whatever engaging story I thought I could write a week before was looking as promising as Sisyphus making it to the top of the hill. My next call with Stan would wind up being a telephonic termination of my employment. I could try interviewing the G Brothers. But there was no gripping thread that connected Zena's remarkable life with the pair of choles-terol-bloated Bobbsey Twins.

I was on better terms with Holey John, but it was clear his story was not an option anymore. He had left the midway. And being a human pin cushion was something he wanted to erase.

When I opened the car door and got in, my cell phone rang. It was Zena.

"You need to come over to John's trailer right now!" she said in a freaked-out plea.

"Something wrong?"

"Just get over here."

I got there with Zena standing outside. The trailer door was open. Her expression was grim, and there was fear.

"Take a look."

I went into his place. It had been ransacked. His little posses-sions were dumped on the floor.

"I came to wish him good luck. Out of nowhere, this man bolts out. Son of a bitch knocked me on my butt."

"And Holey John?"

"Wasn't here."

"Who was the man?"

"No idea." She paused. "Except…"

"Except what?"

Zena hesitated but said, "I don't know. He tore ass out of the trailer and disappeared behind those cages. I heard a car take off." She shuffled through the mess and picked up a torn photograph. "Christ. It's John's wife and kid."

I thought for a minute. Who would do this and why? Holey John wasn't the most amicable man at the G Brothers, but this was pure vandalism. The guy lived like a hermit. Not much to steal unless you needed some cutout eyes for your walls. I looked around and saw the bicycle lock dangling from the oven. The fridge door was also open. If Holey John had anything of value, his oven and fridge safekeeping approach had proven to be pretty lame.

"Think for a moment about this guy," I said. "You see him before? Around here?"

"Maybe. Oh hell, I dunno. I was more concerned about John. I thought he might've been hurt."

I went through possible suspects. "Wally had it in for Holey John. You think it might be him?"

Zena paced back and forth. "The guy fled, knocked me down. It's a blur."

"He told one of the G boys to go screw when he quit," I said. "Could be that they wanted to send everyone else a message who thought they could just up and leave. If it was those lard heads' idea, I wouldn't put it past them to hire some muscle head."

"Maybe," she said.

A few people from the fairgrounds who worked there came to the trailer, peeking in and shaking their heads.

"You see where Holey John went?" I asked the people gathered around.

They all shook their heads. Zena's eyes darted about, hoping that he would suddenly show up.

I went outside and looked for his truck. I went back inside. "His truck is gone. Could be that he left before his place was hit."

Zena chewed her lip. "Didn't he have an appointment with Ralph and the real estate lady?"

"I think so."

Zena held up two halves of the photograph of Linh and the little girl. "I hope we catch the bastard that did this."

We went to my car, and I drove into Ithaca. When we pulled up to the house, I saw Trish standing on the porch. We both got out and walked up to her.

"I've been knocking on the door for the last ten minutes."

I looked up and down the block. Holey John's truck was nowhere to be seen.

"You see Holey John?" I asked with a sinking feeling.

"No."

I went to the door and banged my hand against the door. No one answered.

Trish said, "Ralph takes naps, but you and me banging like this would wake the dead."

"Do you have a key to the house?"

Trish took out a ring of keys from her pocket book. She sorted through them and found a key. The lock turned, and she pushed the door open.

"Mr. Gilmore!" Trish shouted. No answer and she called out again.

We stepped inside. "John!" Zena yelled. "Hey, John!"

No answer.

"Let's check the house," I suggested.

Trish and Zena followed me as we circled through the rooms on the first floor. I stopped when we came to the room with the Tiffany lamp. It lay shattered on the floor. We all looked at each other. I stepped toward the kitchen and saw the attic door was open.

We started up the stairs. When we got to the top, Zena let out a gasp. The attic looked like a tornado had barreled through. The trunks and boxes were overturned. Costumes and props were thrown all over the floor. I held up my hand for the two women to stop. I walked ahead, looking more closely at the floor, and saw something on a floorboard. I stooped down and dabbed my finger in it. It was wet and red. *Blood?* I got up and moved more cautiously. My stomach muscles tightened as if I expected someone to leap out and attack me.

I spotted the hiding place that Holey John and Ralph had shown us, now covered with costumes and boxes. Pushing these aside, I saw the loose board had been removed. The contents had been shuffled through as if someone was looking for something.

The two women came over, and I held up my hand.

"It's like the trailer," Zena said.

"What trailer?" Trish asked.

"John's. It was broken into. Someone tore it apart."

I showed Trish and Zena my finger. "I think it's blood."

Zena let out a soft cry and put her hand on my arm. I surveyed the mess. My belly button pulsed that those two incidents were related somehow, but why, I didn't know.

"Look over there," Trish said, pointing to a mound of cartons and cardboard boxes piled up in the corner of the attic.

I looked. "Don't come over here." I sensed something not quite right.

My tone stopped the two women. I took off my shoes and found a broom handle and turned round.

Zena looked at my feet, seeing I had removed my shoes. "I'm sure there's a reason you did that."

I didn't answer and walked in a straight line to the piled-up cardboard. With my toe and broom handle, I nudged the boxes out of the way. I saw blood on some of the boxes. Then I saw a misshapen hand. I moved the other boxes hurriedly away like a ski patrol digging snow off an avalanche victim.

Ralph lay twisted like a clothing dummy that had been thrown off a building, his arms and legs bent in impossible positions. I bent down and felt his neck for a pulse. His neck was not quite cold, but he had no pulse.

I shook my head. "Dead. Vey recently."

Zena and Trish both let out a muffled sob that hung in the attic air like the sorrowful cries heard at funerals. I quickly reached into my pocket and dialed 911.

CHAPTER 80

FALLING MAN

Burke was running for his life. He was running for his wife. His daughter. He was running for one thing. A chance. Whatever was behind this crazy sicko's desperation to get hold of his uncle's contract could only be about money. Had to if he was willing to kill for it.

He ran faster, and his brain burned bright with ideas. The contract meant he'd inherit shares Fenn said. Not sure how that would turn into any money, but he'd use any of it to find them, Linh, and his kid, have all of them together. A woman from so long before he could not remember what her voice sounded like, just spectral remnants at the end tail of his nightmares.

The adrenaline pumping through him cleared his brain as he ran, making him see things he had not understood before. His revelations in Ralph's attic were so overwhelming that he was not able to process all the things he uncovered. One thing was clear: The guy in his trailer was dead serious. Serious enough to tear his trailer apart. Serious enough to threaten his life. Serious enough to have murdered his friend Ralph. Serious enough to hurt Zena. If this motherfucker was willing to hurt him, even kill him, then this agreement was something that he had to save.

His heart pumped like a locomotive. The most important thing was getting the box with the cash and Pink's contract and getting away. This dickwad was not going to kill his dream. Running, branches of low-handing pine trees tore at his face and arms. Burke zigzagged past boulders and shrubs, dodged trees, and took quick furtive glances over his shoulder, knowing that the man who had attacked him would, no doubt, be after him.

He heard the sound of water falling. He was getting closer and ran faster, the sound of the falls getting louder. He pitched his body to the left on a trail and saw the tree ahead.

When it stopped, he reached into the hollow of the tree. A sound startled him. A branch cracked then another. He knew it was that asshole closing in. His mind raced as his fingers touched the box. A plan formed in his head. He found the handle and pulled the box out of the tree. He turned toward the sounds of running footsteps, a glimpse of a shirt through the trees.

His mind raced. He dropped to the ground behind the tree, the box held in both hands. The sound of a man's heavy breathing cut through the rhythmic splash of the waterfalls. He skimmed across his chest, and his fingers stopped when he touched the key that was attached to the safety pin lanced into his pectoral muscle. He snapped the pin open, and the key dropped into his palm. Opening the box, he fingered through the photos, money, and papers he had saved. The contract lay under a photo of his uncle. He removed it and folded the paper in half then half again.

At his feet, he saw a rock protruding through a bed of pine needles. He moved it aside. Grabbing the rock, he loosened it enough so that he could lift it up a couple of inches. With a gap exposed, he shoved the square of paper into the opening then moved the rock back into place, spreading pine needles around it.

He heard a closer sound, a man breathing. It slowed as he caught his breath. The footsteps stopped every few seconds as the man scouted the woods looking for him, like a hunter stalking his prey. He needed a distraction to buy time. A broken branch about lay near him, and he picked it up. He flung the branch to the right, and it fell about twenty yards away from the spot where he last heard the man breathing. A frenzy of boots crashing in the direction of the fallen branch gave him the time he needed. He replaced the key through the safety pin, lanced it into his pectoral muscle, then sprinted to the tree and dropped the box back into the hollow.

The trampling of twigs stopped. The man halted and resumed scanning the woods. He crawled away from the rock and pine tree. He came across something that looked like a manmade staff lying on the forest floor: an abandoned hiker's stick. The end of the stick had broken into a splintered point. He picked it up, tilting his head in one direction then another. About fifteen yards away, he saw the man's pants, his legs planted firmly as he too looked for movement.

He crawled as silently as he could toward his attacker, using his elbows to edge forward.

"Cute," the man said in a smirking voice, spotting Burke. "You playing capture the flag?"

Burke sprung to his feet and charged the man, the pointed end of the stick thrusting at his assailant like a knight bounding ahead with a jousting lance. Leon was caught off guard and jumped to his right, the limb grazing his left arm.

"Fuck you," Burke bellowed and pointed at Leon's blood on his sleeve, taunting his attacker. He feigned to the left and then to the right for another assault and hurled himself forward, the makeshift spear held tight in both hands. As he charged, he ran over a bed of pine needles with its oily surface. His right foot came down hard on the needles, and the sole of his shoe made him skid for an instant, losing his balance.

Thrown off his footing, he missed Leon by inches. With the reflexes as fast as a cobra striking his prey, Leon smashed his fist into Burke as he stumbled by, his fist landing hard on his back, knocking the air out of him, the stick flying out of his hands. He gasped for a breath, and Leon spun around and punched him again, his fist aimed into his solar plexus. Doubled over, he frantically sucked down air. Leon kicked him on the shin of his right leg then the left, and Burke fell face first onto the ground.

Leon unbuckled his belt and grabbed Burke's arms from behind his back and wrapped the belt around his wrists, pulling the leather belt strap tight. He pulled the belt up, lifting Burke up to a sitting position, and then dragged him to a tree. The knife that he had held against Burke's throat in the trailer appeared again.

"Are we in talking mood now?" Leon hissed.

"Fuck you!"

"You're the one who's fucked."

He spat at Leon.

Leon wiped the spittle from his hand and pulled a piece of jewelry from Burke's face. He did not cry out, emotionless as Spock. He spat at Leon again, who pulled five more pieces of jewelry from Burke's face like he was picking berries off a bush.

Burke remained silent but mouthed a *fuck you*.

"I can stop anytime. You know what I want. This doesn't have to go this way."

"Whatever," was his reply.

Leon ripped off Burke's shirt. He methodically pulled every piercing from Burke's chest and back. He went from left to right and dropped the plucked pieces into a pile. Burke never made a sound. Blood ran over his chest and face as if a bucket of red paint had been thrown across him.

Leon stopped when he yanked the last piece of stud from Burke's stomach above the waistband of his pants. He stared down at the man, impressed with his stoic resistance, not breaking down.

A thought crossed his mind. The midway freak had purposely come to this park, so he must've had a reason.

"You like these woods?" Leon asked.

Burke just stared ahead.

"Special place?"

No reaction.

"Maybe some nice memories with your uncle?"

Leon saw Burke's face tighten. A tell.

"The box," Leon said next. "Ralph said you kept everything you found in his attic in it. My guess is that it's here. Not far." He looked for a reaction from Burke and noticed that the man's breathing had quickened. His bloody prey needed a bit more pain. Leon took the knife and slit Burke's pants then pulled them down past his knees and over his shoes. He yanked off his shoes and socks. He came back to Burke's waist and pulled off his underwear.

"Naked as a newborn babe," Leon chuckled. He considered taking the knife to the man's package, but he might bleed out before he could get the information he needed. He resumed jerking the jewelry off the man's flesh, the ones that covered his legs. Not surprised, his hostage did not cry out, did not beg for him to stop. In less than five minutes, he was done. Over two hundred pieces of jewelry lay in a pile like shining pirate treasure.

"I gave you a chance," Leon said to him, taking a new tack. "I admire your courage, as stupid as it is. But I'm thinking maybe I'll do your lady friend." Leon described in detail what he would do. "Your bad luck becomes your friend's bad luck."

Fear turned Burke's face pale.

The idea of Zena being hurt was unbearable. "You leave my friend…alone."

"Depends on you, pal."

"I'll show you where the thing you want…is stashed."

Leon seemed puzzled for an instant, having put this man through hell and was ready to talk now. Maybe it made some kind of crazy sense. This pin cushion man had spent a lifetime running pins through his body, so maybe pain was never an issue. But maybe he and the midget were more than just friends.

Leon grabbed Burke under his armpit and hoisted him to his feet.

"Where to, pal?"

Burke gestured to a tree. Leon kept him propped up, and he staggered toward a tree, stopped, and then nodded at the hollow.

"Inside…there."

Leon reached inside the hollow. A moment later, he had the old metal box. He tried to open it and saw it was locked.

"Where's the key?"

Burke smiled weakly.

"Take the belt off my hands and…I'll show you. It's in the pile of jewelry."

Leon looked at him suspiciously.

"What? You afraid of a…naked, torn-up…old son of a bitch?"

Leon removed the belt and held the knife against Burke's back. "Lead the way."

Burke retraced their steps to the pile of jewelry that were covered with skin and dried blood. He squatted down and sorted through the pieces. Fingering through them, he found a key fastened to the safety pin.

"Silly me that I missed this," Leon said. "Okay buddy, about-face."

They returned to the tree.

"Stay put," Leon ordered. He kicked Burke's knees out, and he fell to the ground. Leon moved away to a small clearing and slipped the key into the lock.

"Mr. Monopoly," Leon said, riffling through the cash. He continued leafing through the contents. He pulled out the photos and old letters. Receipts that meant nothing to him, the clipping of John Burke with his uncle.

He frowned and went through everything he had removed from the box again. The snap of a twig broke his concentration. Burke was quick-stepping away from the tree.

"Hey," Leon yelled, "where the fuck are you going?"

John Burke started to run, his bare feet crunching on dried leaves and pine needles. He heard Leon chasing after him and ran as fast as he could, his legs and body aching from his ripped flesh and torn-up muscles.

He reached the spot where he had buried the contract. He found the rock and turned it over. The folded paper lay there as if waiting for his return. He pulled it out and got up.

Leon reached him, seeing his captive holding something.

"You fucker!" He tried to grab Burke's hand that held the folded paper.

Burke danced away and ran to the edge of the waterfall. He held the paper up and waved it at Leon, his heels reaching the edge.

"Give me that!" Leon demanded.

"Or what?" Burke shot back.

Leon moved slowly toward him. He held the knife and made cutting gestures slicing the air.

"That won't work," Burke said. "You're not getting…this."

Leon stopped, trying to size up the situation.

Burke watched his attacker. Whatever the power that paper held was not going to be given to this man. He peered around and scanned the rocky walls of the waterfall. It would be a quick death if he just let himself fall backward. He knew the man was going to kill him anyway. He knew that all along. His plan had taken that into account. He had tried to fight but lost that battle. There was only one thing to do: Keep the contract away from this maniac. Fenn had to protect Zena now. He hoped his faith in that guy would be enough.

The attacker took a step forward.

Percy Maxwell's nephew smiled, and his smile cracked the blood that had hardened around his lips. He opened his mouth wide and shoved the folded paper inside. He closed his mouth, his teeth clamped down hard, holding the paper square in place.

He stretched his arms out like a man about to be crucified and made a final step, letting himself fall backward.

He was falling backward and knew he would die. He would be dead in just seconds. In the first split second, he remembered the image of the 9/11 falling man, plummeting in slow motion to his death. In the succeeding split second, he realized he felt no fear. Actually, he felt a peaceful sensation that he had not experienced for most of his life. That was his last conscious thought as his head and neck smashed against a rocky outcrop.

Leon gasped and ran to the edge. He saw the man hit the rocky outcrops, his body smashing into one ledge after another until he splashed into the water. The waterfalls submerged him for a minute, and then he surfaced.

"Motherfucker," he said.

He watched Burke's body pushed to the middle of the pool by the current of the falling water. He stared at him, his broken body floating face down. After a few minutes, there was no doubt he was dead.

Leon moaned as his gut twisted.

"Fuck all."

His brain went into overdrive, taking in the current situation. Should he call Brinks? He nixed the idea. Why deliver bad news now? He thought about the Maxwell contract and with it his ticket to the big screen. The dream of the life he had always yearned for had just died with that man.

Or maybe not.

He couldn't stay here. As he hustled back to the jewelry torn from the Burke's body, a new idea formed, one that still might keep his ticket to stardom intact. He had information he could use to blackmail Brinks. There were people that had been killed. He had snuffed two of them himself, and his slick Hollywood client had turned the lights out on Wolfe.

He ran through what he had to do next: Leave no traces as Brinks had demanded. That meant the midget. She could be real trouble. She had seen his face.

But first things first. He needed to clean up the scene there. He picked up the jewelry and dropped them in the shirt he had ripped off the asshole. He then tied the shirt into a knot. Okay, what now? The box and the papers. He had to do something with that. That's when he heard voices. Two voices. A man and a woman talking. Hikers. They were heading in his direction.

Leon quickly shoved the scattered contents into the box. The voices were getting nearer. He couldn't be seen with Burke's blood-soaked clothes. He looked around. The hollow in the tree. He could stash them inside along with the box. He shoved all the evidence down the hollow and walked away without making a sound, slipping behind trees, skirting the hikers.

He then gripped the shirt that held the jewelry. It was worthless stuff, but he had an idea. It was how the death of the man who would be found floating under the waterfalls would be blamed on the perfect suspect. And it wouldn't be him.

CHAPTER 81

DIVERSIONS

Leon left the woods, strolled into the parking lot, and walked to his car. He made sure his gait was unhurried, not the strides of a guilty man who was an executioner. There were about twenty parked cars, but the lot was empty of people. All in the woods, Leon figured. That was good since it would be hard for anyone questioned by the police to remember a particular car. Especially his.

He slid into the front seat and put the shirt on the passenger's side floor. Leon noticed that the bloodstains were still wet. Collecting his thoughts, he knew he didn't have much time to cover his tracks and get out of town.

His thoughts returned to the fortune-teller. Sure bet that hikers would spot Burke. The police would arrive, and soon enough, she would find out that her pal was dead. Tortured and a floater. She would wonder if there was a connection with the running man who tore the trailer apart and knocked her on her ass. She could finger him, and he couldn't risk that. He was too close to his dream.

Leon drove back to Ithaca. His mind played out the next sequence of events. The real estate woman finding the old man cold, stone dead in the house that Burke was buying. She'd call the cops. The midget would also talk to the cops. Depending on how sharp the cops were, they might see a link between a floating dead guy and the geezer decomposing in the attic.

Leon played the next scenes out in head like a movie's storyboard. If he came up as a person of interest, everyone, anyone he would come into contact with would have a different description.

They would describe a particular man, none the same, all of them his chameleon version.

His burner phone vibrated. It was the tenth time Brinks had called him in the last twenty-four hours. He decided to pick it up.

"Good news. Maxwell's contract and the nephew are taken care of. No tracks back to you or me."

"Taken care of?" Brinks asked, thinking about gators and the Kelley woman. "Want to fill me in?"

"When I'm back in tinsel town. We can talk about you honoring our deal." With that, he ended the call.

As he continued to drive, he thought about how to throw the cops, the midget, and anyone else off his scent. A scheme took shape, a sly grin slowly spreading across his lips. He pulled out his burner phone and dialed 411.

"What city and state, please."

"Ithaca, New York." Leon hesitated, trying to recall the name painted on the truck. "Anything Junk Removal," he finally said.

"Do you mean Anything Goes Junk Removal?"

"Yeah, that's it. Can you connect me?"

"Dialing now."

The phone rang four times before a woman answered. "Hello."

"Hi. Is this Anything Goes Junk Removal?"

"Yes. Can I help you?" It was probably the preggo girlfriend, the woman who had given the runt shit in the parking lot.

"Are you the owner?"

"His assistant," she said, being vague.

"I might have a job."

"Oh," she said tentatively.

"Can we talk about this job?"

The woman didn't reply right away

"Wait a sec."

She cupped the phone's mouth piece and yelled.

"Wally." *Pause.* "Wally." *Louder.* Then "You fucking shit bag, snap out of it. A job!" *No response.* She uncupped her hand from the phone and said, "He's not here."

Of course Leon didn't believe her. What he did believe was that her man was a doper on a nod. He recalled her screaming at him the day before about his little habit. Leon had the little glassine envelope that popped out of his pocket when he was getting the shit beat out of him by the floating dead man.

"I can come by now," Leon said. "Talk to him in person. It's a big job and I'm in a hurry. A house my crew knocked down. I'm thinking a ten grand to haul the sheet rock and lumber away."

Leon imagined the woman seeing that was a job that could take them to a better trailer park.

"Okay," she said, "how about in an hour?"

"What address?" Leon asked.

She stalled a moment again, thinking that coming to their broke-down, double-wide was not a good sign of a reliability.

"He'll probably stop at the Black Crow for a beer. He always does at the end of work." He had no work, but she'd make sure he would be at the Crow so she gave him the address.

Leon said that would work. As he ended the call, he could hear the woman scream, "Wake up, Wally. I gotta job for us."

CHAPTER 82

SIXTY-FOUR-THOUSAND-DOLLAR QUESTION

I stared at the twisted body lying on top of the cardboard boxes. I had written about some pretty dark incidents back in the city but none like what happened to Ralph. And at the academy, I did a few ride-alongs with homicide detectives, watched how they handled ODs, drunks who froze to death in winter, suicides, and the bloody aftermath of bar fights. But Ralph had clearly been tortured.

"What should we do?" Zena asked.

"Call the police," I said and handed her my cell phone. "Give them the address and Ralph's name. Tell them you're at a murder scene. Tell them to come up to the attic."

I walked over to Trish, who was still sobbing, and tried to comfort her. I heard Zena reach the 911 operator.

"A cop said they are sending a patrol car over. Said we should stay put. Don't touch anything."

She then looked at me and my stocking feet and the broomstick I had used to lift the cardboard that covered Ralph's dead body. All three of us looked at Ralph, then Trish turned away as if he might feel uncomfortable about her staring at him.

We heard a siren a few minutes later. Car doors slammed, and footsteps headed up the stairs to where we were.

Two uniformed policemen arrived.

"You the folks that called?" one of the cops asked.

"I did," Zena volunteered.

I pointed to where Ralph lay. "His name is Ralph Gilmore. Our friend was supposed to meet us here. He's buying this house."

Trish stepped forward and introduced herself.

The two cops looked across the attic to where I pointed.

"I went over to see if he was alive. He wasn't, so we called it in."

One of the cops made a call. "Let me speak to Kapinski."

The cop nodded, gave the address, and ended the call. "Stay put," he told the three of us. "Detective Kapinski will talk to you."

It took about twenty minutes before the detective arrived.

"I'm Detective Kapinski. This is Detective Kohl."

Kohl looked young and green. He kept wiping his nose as if the attic dust triggered an allergy.

We all nodded, but their eyes lingered on Zena. Not a surprise.

I pointed with the broomstick to where Ralph had been dumped. Kapinski was about fifty. He had a crew cut that was salt and pepper, a little overweight, a smooth face that showed no expression.

"And you are?" the detective asked the three of us, taking out a notebook.

"I'm a friend of—" I started.

"He's with me," Zena interrupted.

"And you are—?"

"Zena."

"Last name?"

"Zena is fine."

"Actually it's not," the detective said flatly.

Zena walked over to Kapinski, motioned him to bend, and whispered into his ear. He took out a notepad from his jacket pocket and wrote down whatever she had said. *I'd have to become a cop again to find out what her real name was*, I thought to myself.

Kapinski turned to me.

"Fenn Cooper." I knew the drill from being in situations where cops were involved. I reached for my wallet very slowly, held it up, and pulled out my license. He took it, compared the photo with my lovely mug, and gave it back.

He then turned to Trish, who explained who she was and her association with the dead man.

"How long ago did you all get here?" Kapinski grilled Trish.

"An hour ago," Trish answered. "Mr. Gilmore was going to sign a purchase and sales agreement." She tilted her head to where Ralph lay. "I work for RE/MAX." She pointed to her name tag pinned to her jacket. "He didn't answer the door. I waited on the porch outside, and then these people arrived. Friends of the buyer."

Trish then took a tissue out of her pocket book and sniffled her nose into it. She gave one to Kohl, who sniffled with her in two-part harmony.

"The buyer," Kapinski said. He opened the notepad again. "What's the name?"

"Holey John," I answered.

Kapinski and Kohl gave me a contemptuous look like I was being too cute at a murder scene.

"John Burke," Zena corrected me. "Stop with the Holey John shit, Fenn."

"Holy John. Funny nickname," Kohl said. "Like a religious guy?"

"Not *Holy*," I explained. "*Holey.*"

"Wholly? Like completely?"

I didn't answer since we had entered homonym hell and I wasn't going to give the cop a lesson in the grammatical peculiarities of the English language.

"Where is Mr. Burke?" the detective asked.

"Obviously not here," I said.

Kapinski shot me a don't-be-wise-guy glance.

"We thought he would be," Zena said, "for the signing. We were concerned, and we came here."

"Why's that?" Kohl asked suspiciously. Kapinski nodded an approving head bob at his sidekick. Rookie and mentor. Batman and Robin. SpongeBob and Patrick. Beavis and Butthead. Oh, I could go on.

"John's place was ransacked," Zena explained.

She described how she and I came to his trailer and found it torn apart. "There was a guy—"

"A guy?" the detective repeated.

"Who was running."

"Who was running," Kohl and Kapinski sang out together like members of church choir.

"From John's trailer."

"Can you describe what he looked like?"

"I didn't get a good look. He ducked behind some cages."

"Cages?"

This really threw them off.

"We work at the Giambolvo Brothers. The traveling circus outside of town."

"The guy who ran," Kapinski asked, returning to his previous question. "Short tall, black, white, fat, skinny?"

"White and fast."

"Well, that narrows it down," Kohl said sarcastically.

"He knocked me down snot nose, my face slammed into the dirt. That's all I can give you. Didn't see his face."

Kohl's smirk disappeared.

"You'd think your pal would've stuck around if his place had been turned upside down," Kohl said defensively.

"Except he didn't," I said. "We were there, he wasn't. That's why we came here."

Kapinski glowered, not liking my tone.

"Did Burke have an issue with…" Kohl intimated, leaving the sentence hang in the air, pointing to Ralph's body.

Zena pushed me out of the way and jabbed him in the chest. "Look, asshole, if you're implying that my friend had anything to do with this…"

I pulled her away, thinking she might punch the detective in the nuts.

"Calm down, miss," Kapinski urged Zena. "We are just getting information from all of you right now."

Kapinski stepped away and made a call. He gave the address and where whomever he called should find him. He then turned to us and said, "Our crime scene people are on their way. Medical examiner too."

"I should tell you and your people that I touched a few things," I said, remembering my academy training.

Kapinski looked at my shoeless feet and broomstick.

"I disturbed the crime scene. Not on purpose. Just wanted to check on Ralph. Mr. Gilmore. Might wanna mention that to the CSI folks."

I heard footsteps coming up to the attic. A mop of tightly curled blond hair was the first thing I saw, which was attached to a woman in yoga pants and a T-shirt that read "I tried to be good but I got bored" and a forehead that dripped with sweat

Kapinski turned, hearing her arrive, and muttered, "Shit."

"What have we got here?" the woman said, skipping toward him.

"Back off, Angie," the detective ordered.

The woman took in the room. "Woo-hoo, a stiff," she yipped with excitement.

Zena and I gave this creature and then Kapinski a bewildered look.

She introduced herself. "Angie Bowers. I'm a reporter from our local rag. I was coming from the gym when I heard about this little situation over the police band." She pointed to her outfit and said, "Spin class is a bitch."

"And you smelled a good story," Kapinski said. Clearly his regard for Bowers was like having a leper show up at a pool party.

She smiled and said, "That's what I do."

"Smell."

Angie crinkled her eyes, not sure what Kapinski meant.

"So who's the dead guy?" The reporter took out her phone and found the record app.

"Unidentified." Since in reality, he didn't identify Ralph; we did.

"Someone pop him?" she asked. Now she was on her toes, standing in place, doing some sort of toe-heel work out movement to get a better look.

"Back off, Angie."

"You got a suspect for this one, Kappy?"

"You are becoming annoying."

"One of my charming attributes you used to say."

"Used to."

"Come on," she complained. "I heard you guys talking about some Burke guy. Person of interest?"

"Eavesdropping on the stairs?" Kapinski reprimanded.

Angie gave him a sly smile. "Tools of the trade."

"I'll hold a press conference when we have more info."

"Ooh, a press conference. Sounds impressive since we only have two newspapers in town. I thought we had an understanding, Kappy." She winked at him and blew him a kiss.

"Detective Kohl, please escort Ms. Bowels out of the house. This is a crime scene which we don't want contaminated."

"*Bowers*," she corrected and huffed her way back down the stairs with Kohl guiding her out.

Kapinski told the uniforms to go to the front of the house and not anyone in while the investigation was underway.

"I have a suggestion," I said to Kapinski once she was gone. He gave me an "Okay, let's hear it" look. "I would hold off on mentioning Holey John, a.k.a. John Burke, at a press conference for now, fingering him as a person of interest."

"Oh, you would," he said sarcastically.

Without hesitation, my coprolalia kicked in. I riffed a couple of lines from Queen.

> You got mud on your face, you big disgrace
> Kicking your can all over the place.

Kapinski gave me the twitchy look you give someone you think is crazy.

"I work as a journalist. I've jumped the gun on a few stories based on what I was told at the time, and I had to eat my words when it turned out otherwise. I'm guessing Angie seems like she'd love kicking your can all over the place. I sense you have or had a history with her."

"I'll keep that in mind."

"Also, with the perp on the loose, we—or you, I should say—don't want to tip him off that we found his vic."

"The perp?" Kapinski questioned hesitantly.

"The real perpetrator since I am certain John didn't kill Mr. Gilmore."

Kapinski took a deep breath, trying to get back on track with his questions. Kohl reappeared and brushed his hands together like he was wiping off crumbs, indicating that Bowers was out on the street and out of the way.

"If you're so insightful, why didn't your friend stay put and call the police? Report a break-in."

"Maybe he didn't know his place was broken into," I suggested.

"So he was not there when you went into the trailer and he's not here. He just vanished or what?"

"That's the sixty-four-thousand-dollar question," I offered, not recalculating the old quiz show's amount into today's dollars.

"This trailer of his..." Kapinski continued his probe.

"On the fairgrounds," Zena said quickly.

"So Burke works with you at that circus?"

She nodded.

"He does what exactly?"

Zena hesitated then explained his act. Kapinski scribbled more notes, but his face didn't show any judgment about what John did. On the other hand, Kohl's eyebrows rose in surprise. Meeting a little person and hearing about a man who had his flesh pierced were too much for him to deal with.

Kohl looked more closely at Ralph's body, taking a step forward.

"I wouldn't do that," I warned him. "I already contaminated some areas. You don't want to make the investigator's job even more complicated."

Kapinski didn't like that I was instructing his detective-in-training.

"Watching cop shows on TV doesn't mean you know protocols," Kapinski said gruffly.

"Actually I do. I was a cop. Well, almost."

Kapinski gave me a funny look. "Almost?"

"NYPD Police Academy. Wasn't a good fit." I didn't say why I wasn't a good fit, that I flunked out, why my propensity to have the occasional doobie and my coprolalia were a career buster. Some things are best not said.

Kapinski looked confused. A police department he might have given his right nut to be part of. Did he think I was a loser who couldn't cut the mustard? In any case, I really didn't give a shit what he thought.

"Kohl," he said, pointing to his own hands and made a "washing the hands" motion, "latex gloves and booties."

Kohl sighed and went down the stairs again.

Kapinski then looked at my shoeless feet and broomstick. Maybe he appreciated that I had preserved the crime scene as much as possible.

He asked us a few more questions before the crime scene investigators arrived.

Two investigators and a woman approached Kapinski. He gave the three people the information he had gathered from us.

"You guys need to stand back," Kapinski ordered us as the investigators put on their forensic outfits. He pointed to where Ralph had been found.

The ME looked at me since Kapinski said I had checked to see if Ralph was alive.

"I'm Doctor Bernstein," she said, introducing herself.

She was Indian or maybe Pakistani, with her black hair held under a ball cap. The other two investigators, one a black guy with dreadlocks, the other white with a buzz cut, had *Forensics* written on their shirts. Ithaca was in step with diversity.

I wondered how Bernstein got that last name. Not a New Delhi—or Karachi-sounding name. Be interesting to find out. Husband's name? Or maybe she was adopted. Maybe I was undertaking a mental digression to put off what the CSI people would find.

Dreadlocks had a camera and came photographing the attic. Buzz Cut took out swabs and evidence bags and collected the blood on the floor. When he found a new pool of blood, he swabbed it, putting it into a new bag, keeping the samples separate and labeling the bag while Dreadlocks photographed the spot where the blood was taken.

They continued to search the attic and took fingerprints from the overturned trunks and boxes. Collecting fibers and footprints left on the dusty floor would be next.

Bernstein went to Ralph's body and began to examine him. "Multiple contusions on the face. A broken nose. If he had false teeth, they're missing."

More probing.

She held up Gilmore's hand by the wrist. "Some of his fingers are broken. Wedding ring still on."

Trish and Zena both let out a moan.

"And his neck too. Broken."

Trish's fingers flew to her mouth. "Oh, God."

Bernstein pulled a worn brown leather wallet out of Gilmore's pants. She fingered through the folds.

"His money is gone but not his credit cards," she said and put the wallet in an evidence bag.

Kapinski pursed his lips. "Not a typical robbery."

"Or not a robbery at all," I injected. "There's a Tiffany lamp worth thousands downstairs. Was there when we came."

Kapinski gave me an irritated look. I figured we wouldn't be sending holiday cards to each other anytime soon.

"What could Ralph have that anyone would kill him for?" Zena said to no one in particular.

Buzz Cut walked around and bent over something on the floor. "Found his teeth." He put them in another evidence bag and smiled like a puppy who retrieved a ball. "Whoa," he gasped, pushing aside a trunk, "there's a loose board."

"See what's there," Kapinski said.

Buzz Cut got on his knees, pried the board up, and removed a slip of paper. "It's a receipt," he announced. "The Clinton House. To rent their ballroom. Dated December 31, 1925."

Kapinski rubbed his chin. "It was a hotel. Built back in the early 1900s if my memory of Ithaca history serves. Some famous actors stayed there when movies were made here."

"Movies here? No way," Kohl said, not believing movies could be made anywhere except Hollywood.

Zena became impatient, seeing the investigator idly look at the papers and photographs as if he had found booty from a treasure hunt.

Blood drained from Zena's face. She turned to Kapinski. "John may be in danger." Her words were urgent. "You're wasting time."

"Because his trailer was tossed?"

"Someone is looking for something. John showed us some old newspaper clippings and a contract he found in there," she said, pointing to the hiding place. "He said there was another one he left behind."

Buzz Cut rummaged through the opening. "No contract. Just more receipts and pics."

Kapinski turned to Kohl. "Get some cops out to the Burke trailer for a look-see."

He then turned to Zena and asked, "Can you give me a description of your friend? His height, weight, age, distinguishing marks."

"I think a man whose face is covered with more jewels than Liberace's jump suit is pretty easy to spot," I murmured loud enough to be heard.

Kapinski turned his head, his eyes boring into me. I shrugged.

"There is one thing, aside from the studs and piercings," Zena said. "He has a faded tattoo on his right hand. It's a Vietnamese name. Linh."

My cell phone rang. However, it was not me who answered since I gave it to Zena.

"John?" She sounded excited, assuming it would be him. She then frowned and said, "Who? Oh. He's here."

I could hear Lilly's voice even though the phone was not on speaker. *Pissed* would be a kind way to describe it.

"Why do you have his phone?" Lilly asked Zena.

"It's complicated," Zena replied.

I gestured to Zena to give me back my phone. But she hesitated, the conversation not over.

"I'm a what?" Zena said, her voice clearly exasperated. "A miniaturized cunt!"

I squeezed my eyelids shut.

"Honey, that's one part of me that's not only as big as yours, and I also believe mine is actually way finer than yours, so it seems."

Everyone in the attic had their eyes on Zena. I hustled over and grabbed the phone. "You are so out of line," I said, disgusted with her.

"Hello," I said meekly. I held the phone away from my ear as Lilly yelled a stream of obscenities that would make a Flatbush rapper blush. I never said a word after my initial *hello*. My line went dead.

"I couldn't help myself," Zena attempted to apologize, "but what she was calling me—"

I held up my hand.

Zena gave me an unapologetic look. "Did you ever say anything about me? Us? Of course not. I'm just a miniaturized cunt like she said."

Before I could answer, Kapinski's cell went off. "Where exactly are the hikers?" He waited for his question to be answered and said, "The falls, huh?" A pause. "Naked? And what. Torn up. Anything else?"

I saw fear grip Zena's face.

It was clear that Kapinski was listening to a cop reporting something that had happened. "Not an animal attack. You say his body looks more like he was shot? A shotgun, huh." A pause. "Holes?" Pause. "Any ID nearby?" Pause. "What about old scars? Tattoos?" Another pause. "Where is it?" Pause. "On his right hand. What about around the rim where he might've fallen? Any clothes?" Pause. "Nothing yet. Well, keep looking. Get the K9 unit out there and secure the area and detain the hikers for questioning. I'll have CSI and Bernstein go there after they're finished here."

"That call?" Zena asked Kapinski.

Kapinski watched the forensics crew for a few moments, looking before answering. "Two hikers found a man," Kapinski said, "in a pool that this waterfall empties into. State park outside of town."

"A man?" Zena said with the voice of a little girl. "John had lots of jewelry on him. They find have jewelry pinned over his body?"

Kapinski shook his head.

"So it can't be John," Zena said, excited but pleading at the same time.

"Thing is, this man—"

She interrupted Kapinski again. "You said this man was shot. A shotgun."

"A guess right now. He had holes all over his body."

Zena waited for more information.

"Your friend had this pin sticking thing going right? The jewelry," Kapinski said.

"You could call it that," I answered for Zena.

"Best thing is we go down to our medical examiner's office once we recover the body. See if the man that was found is your friend. In any case, we need you down at headquarters for a few more questions."

Zena's face was then pasty with sweat, and I heard her give a hushed *okay*.

CHAPTER 83

RELIEF

Brinks was filled with anxiety. It had been five days since Mitch Tankowitz swept into Glowball's offices like an ill wind. The three accountants and the oversized pain-in-the-ass numbers sleuth had been going at it for most of the day. Since yesterday, they were focusing on *Sarah's Shadow Light.*

"Can I be frank with you?" Tankowitz said, breaking the silence, looking at his laptop.

"Of course," Brinks replied, feeling a stitch in his gut.

"RoachMan was bust. I get the misguided pubescent fantasy about making a horror movie. But that Sarah movie? I watched it on YouTube. Why in hell would Glowball make this movie? Did they do any focus groups, any research, do any audience testing before they committed to making this piece of phony attempt to impress the intelligentsia?"

"None of those," Brinks said

Tankowitz shrugged. "They might've just flushed their cash down the toilet. Would've saved them from the awful reviews."

"I know," Brinks agreed. He waited then asked Zheng, "You find out anything more about that Venzenta guy, the legal thing? We wouldn't want that impacting the funding from your investor."

"Funny thing about that," Tankowitz said.

Brinks held his breath.

"I went there yesterday. The entire floor where the law firm was located was closed off."

"You find out why?" Brinks asked, letting his breath out.

"Flooded. I found the maintenance man. Said the pipes on the floor above busted. Something about a buildup of pressure in their sprinkler system. It's an old building."

"You find the people in the law firm?"

"No one on that floor or the floor above. I'm guessing any files are useless now. Probably nothing we could've used anyhow."

"So what can I do to help you see if Glowball is a good investment?"

Tankowitz looked at the accountants and pointed to Wang.

Wang said, "My management will get our findings." Zheng and Qian gave Brinks a thumbs-up.

"Very confident that you can tell Mr. Brenner *Hong Kong Capital* and its investors will open their check books for your kung-fu flick."

Brinks maintained a neutral expression, trying to conceal a look of relief. It seemed too good to be true. Every rabbit hole Tankowitz and the accountants went down was empty. None of his shell game subterfuges were uncovered. Nothing had been called out. RoachMan and Sarah Secret Light did the trick. No time machine taking these guys backward far enough to find the contact that would have sent him away. He had outmaneuvered the king of uncovering numbers fraud. He took in a long breath and exhaled slowly through a smile.

"I am sure Mr. Brenner will be pleased," Brinks said evenly.

"My friends and I will meet here in the morning and write up our report," Tankowitz said. "How about we sleep in and then come back here around ten tomorrow?"

"Sounds good," Brinks agreed. He didn't suggest a celebratory night out on the town. Better to make this end game all about a business deal successfully concluded.

On the ride home, Brinks thought about Leon returning to discuss their understanding. Once he learned that the accountants found no bookkeeping shams and that the last contract and the nephew were no longer a problem, Leon would want details on how he would get his career moving. First line up a speech coach. Then some acting lessons. Maybe have him tested on a few auditions to see how they went.

He might've dodged the Tankowitz bullet, but screwing Leon would be like dancing the tango with a strapped-on suicide vest. Brinks had no choice but to honor his agreement since double-crossing a man like Leon was asking for an express ride to the bone yard.

Brinks pulled up to his house and entered the foyer. He went straight to his bar and poured himself a single-malt Scotch. Well, if he wasn't going out to celebrate, he would call Mona. He couldn't get her out of his mind. She was more than beautiful. More beautiful than anything in his home. But there was more. Her intelligence. How comfortable he felt when he was with her. The things they had in common. He had seen her a half-a-dozen times. Sometimes they just held each other and listened to music. At times, they didn't make love. Instead, they talked into the early morning hours, lying together in bed, warm bodies wrapped around each other as they drifted into a blissful sleep.

He called her. "I have something to celebrate. Can I see you tonight?"

She did not hesitate. "That would be nice. And what are you celebrating?"

"I'll tell you when you get here."

CHAPTER 84

ROOM THIRTEEN

We followed Detective Kapinski's car to the medical examiner. The ME was located in the Cayuga Medical Center, three miles outside of Ithaca. I pulled up next to his car, and Zena and I got out. Asking her if she was okay would be foolish, so I held her hand instead. Kapinski led us to the elevator, and we got in. The elevator rose, and when it stopped, we followed Kapinski down a hall.

"Room Thirteen," he said as we walked.

It turned out that they had taken the body from the waterfalls to Room Thirteen. That was what morgue workers called it, having a noir sense of humor.

"You sure you want to do this?" I asked Zena as we headed into the room.

She nodded, but her entire body stiffened like a child about to get a flu shot.

When we entered, we were met by Doctor Bernstein, who came to Ralph's house when we first reported his murder.

"Come with me, please," she said.

We went past a sitting room and entered a second room. Room Thirteen was cold and had a smell of formaldehyde and disinfectants. There were two walls with rows of metal doors that had bodies stored behind them. A meat locker for the departed.

It was the middle of summer, but there was a lab assistant standing in front of the lockers wearing a heavy parka.

"We're here to see the man who was brought in today," Dr. Bernstein explained to the lab assistant.

413

"The guy with the holes?"

Bernstein shot him an unkind look.

He looked at his clipboard and walked over to one of the locker doors. "He's in cooler four," he said to the doctor. He opened the stainless-steel door to a locker and pulled out a drawer from a sliding rack. A sheet covered the body that lay on the shelf.

"I'm going to pull back the sheet," Bernstein warned, preparing us for what we would see. "This man is pretty banged up from his fall."

Zena squeezed my hand.

"Are you ready?" she said to Zena, who nodded, gripping my hand even tighter.

Bernstein pulled the sheet back. Zena gasped and closed her eyes for a second and wobbled unsteadily. I held her grip and felt a quivering jolt run up my arm as if her hand was hot-wired to mine.

I stared down at the body. It was John, gray and wrinkled from being in the water. His long hair was straggly, his face crushed. The rest of his body was bruised and cut. We saw that all his pins and jewelry had been torn from his flesh. But the tattoo of Linh was clearly exposed

Zena was crying then. She edged a few steps closer to him. Her eyes filled with tears. "Oh, John," she cried. Her tears came faster along with chest-heaving sobs. "Oh, John." She reached out and touched his forehead, smoothing away a loose strand of hair. She placed her palm on his chest.

I turned to Kapinski. "I heard you say something about some falls when you took a call in Gilmore's house."

"There are waterfalls all around Ithaca. This one is outside of town at a state park. Some folks call it Devil Falls 'cause of a face in the rock. That's where two hikers spotted him. We have the area sealed off. We're treating it as a crime scene. We have crime scene people there. We might have a better idea about what happened after they search the area, interview the hikers."

"We'll examine him more closely to determine what happened to your friend," Bernstein added.

I knew what her job was. As an ME, she had to determine the cause of death, whether it was natural, accidental, or intentional.

"My preliminary examination shows no gun shot or knife wounds. There are unexplained wounds. Torn flesh. There is head trauma, and his neck is broken. That's probably what caused your friend's death."

"He was covered in jewelry," I clarified. "They're all gone."

Zena caught her breath and walked away from the steel table.

Bernstein gave me a puzzled look. Clearly, she did not know what he had done before his death. With Zena stepping away, I explained what he did at the midway.

"What I've done is preliminary," said Bernstein. "We'll see if he had any defensive wounds, check for material under his fingernails. Maybe DNA from an assailant that the detective can match to someone."

"Any idea about time of death?" Kapinski asked

Bernstein looked at John then at Kapinski. "No rigor mortis. His limbs have not stiffened. His death was no more than two hours ago. Maybe earlier."

Zena recovered from seeing her friend's injuries and returned, the emotional armor to defend herself against the world back in place.

"Do you remember what jewelry he had on his body?" Kapinski asked her. "One possibility is that Mr. Burke was robbed, and if any of it shows up at pawn shops or local flea markets, we might get a lead."

"He had over two hundred pieces inserted in his body," she said. "There's a photograph of him in our show guide. You can see what he's wearing."

"What if it wasn't a robbery?" I said, not convinced it was.

Kapinski turned to me and said, "Someone with a grudge?"

"That or something else."

He then turned to Zena and asked, "You have any idea about who might have done this?"

She thought for a moment then said, "There was that man. The guy I saw running from John's trailer after it was ransacked. Like I said, I didn't get a good look at him, but there could be others."

"Others," Kapinski repeated.

She nodded. "John had a run-in with one of the G Brothers."

"And he is…?"

"Louie," Zena said without hesitation. "He and his brother own the circus. He went ape shit when John said he was through with them. He could've hired one of his goons to make him as an example."

"There's that Wally creep," I said.

"What about him?" Kapinski asked.

"He was pissed off at me," Zena explained. "I talked to his girlfriend at my booth. I saw her again at a restaurant where we were eating."

She then repeated what she had said to his girlfriend. "The guy started calling me names, came at me like he was going to punch me out and John blocked him, then roughed him up."

"Typical behavior for a little guy. Someone with a grudge against anyone bigger than them," I added.

Zena gave me an *Oh, really?* look.

She continued, "Wally had a second run-in with John at the midway. He might have a strong motive for payback."

"You might want to check the restaurant," I suggested. "Maxie's. Where we ate. There might be regulars who know Wally and his girlfriend."

"If you think of any others, let me know." Kapinski gave me and Zena his card. "In the meantime, we'll check out your boss. Have my men question people at your circus. I might have you come down to the station again. Look at mug shots."

"Draw a piece of blubber wearing Spandex and smoking a stogie, and you got Louie," I said.

Kapinski rolled his eyes at me, the "You're a wise guy" look again. "I'll be in touch. Same for you if you remember anything."

Zena turned to Bernstein before we left. "I'd like to come back when he's all cleaned up, after you…"

"I can call you." A thought came to the doctor's mind. "He have any relatives?"

Zena looked at me, thinking of Linh. "He had a wife. Maybe a daughter," I said. "But that was a long time ago. In Vietnam. We were trying to find them for him."

"His body," Bernstein said, "if it's unclaimed…"

"I'll take care of my friend," Zena said. "Just let me know when you are done with whatever you still need to do."

Doctor Bernstein nodded and gave her a sad smile.

CHAPTER 85

ALL'S SWELL THAT ENDS SWELL

He wasn't hard to spot in the dim light of the bar. When Leon walked in, Wally's head was hanging loosely and jerked up when he heard the Black Cow's door open. He was nursing a beer, giving every new person who came in a once over to see who the man was that had a big job for him.

Leon gave Wally a wide smile and slid onto a stool next to the man.

"Wally, right?" Leon asked, extending his hand which the man took, his palm moist with junkie sweat.

"That'd be me. Can I buy you a beer?"

"Let me buy."

"Why not?" Wally signaled the bartender to come over.

Leon had hastily changed his looks again, playing the part of a wheeler-dealer. Blond wig styled like a successful businessman and a pencil-thin moustache that David Niven would have adored. He put a ten on the bar and told the bartender to keep the change.

Wally gave Leon a sloppy grin and pointed to a booth in the back. "My office."

After both men sat down, Leon took a swallow of his Coors and held his bottle in one hand with a cocktail napkin wrapped around the bottle. He took out the real estate flyer he had grabbed from the Gilmore house, placing it in front of Wally.

"I've got a purchase and sale for this beauty on College Avenue," Leon said. "Old guy's been living there for years. Needs major renovations. I want a guy to haul sheet rock, old windows, and who knows what. You haul these kinds of things?"

"No problem," Wally said. His eagerness made his pin-holed pupils dance brightly under a neon sign that advertised Genesee Cream Ale.

"I need an estimate. Look at the place to see what I'm talking about."

"I can do that."

"You have time now? We can ride over and take a look."

Wally blinked twice. "Sure."

The two men left the bar. "Your ride here?" Leon asked.

"If you don't mind riding in my shit box of a truck."

"Lead on, Macbeth."

Wally's eyebrows furrowed. "Wally Sullivan," he said, correcting him, "not Macbeth."

"Of course."

Wally pointed to his truck. When they got in, he started it up and pulled out of the parking lot.

They drove two blocks when Leon said, "I need something from my car. It's there on the right."

Wally pulled behind it, and Leon got out. A minute later, he returned to the truck with a small bag. He looked around, saw that the street was empty of people, and pulled out the syringe. Leon had come prepared. The syringe he used for gluing fake moustaches and eyebrows was now filled with all the contents of heroin he had picked up when Wally lost it in a fight with the recently dead pin cushion man.

"Whatchu doing, buddy?" Wally asked, his forehead creased with deep lines, looking at the syringe.

Leon punched him hard in the throat into his Adam's apple. The man gasped, trying to breathe, his left arm flailing around his crushed windpipe, trying desperately to suck in air. Leon grabbed his right arm and plunged the syringe's needle into a vein, pushing down hard on the plunger.

"What the fuck, man!" Wally gasped. He batted Leon with his hands, trying to fend him off, but his arms were losing their strength like a punctured balloon. The heroin acted instantly, his eyes rolling back and forth, a gurgle bubbling from his lips.

Leon kept the needle in and pushed air into his vein, causing an embolism. He kept his free hand on Wally's throat and stared into his eyes. The man that his girlfriend called a loser wouldn't have to hear her invectives ever again. He watched the man's eyes as they rolled under his eyelids, the end coming fast.

White, foamy saliva seeped out of Wally's mouth. He stopped breathing, and his head lolled against the driver's side window. Leon took a pair of latex gloves from the bag and put them on. He pressed a finger against his victim's neck, checking for a pulse. There was none. He left the needle in Wally's arm after wiping off his own prints. He took the guy's fingers and pressed them against the syringe.

Leon got out of the passenger seat and circled around the truck. Opening the driver side door, he shoved Wally over to the passenger seat. His limp torso dropped to the side. Leon got in and pulled the truck into street.

Ithaca was known for its ravines. Leon had picked one not far from the Black Cow. A sagging wooden rail that had seen better days was the only thing keeping passing vehicles from plummeting into a fast-flowing creek. He parked the truck under the shade of a tree that was close to the rail keeping the engine running.

Leon picked up Wally's hand. He reached into the bag and came up with a handful of Burke's pins and studs, which he shoved into the dead man's right hand. He dropped the rest of the jewelry under the truck's seat.

Leon looked in the side view mirror to check for cars. Seeing none coming, he quickly got out of the truck and opened the passenger door. He shoved Wally's dead body back into the driver's seat. Through the driver's side window, he shifted the gear into drive. The truck lurched ahead and pushed against the guard rail.

The rail splintered. A second later, the truck broke through the railing and teetered for a moment. Leon moved to the back of the truck and hefted his foot against the rusty bumper. That was all the encouragement needed to send the truck over the edge, somersaulting as it landed upside down in the middle of the creek. The current quickly flowed into the cab through its broken windows, flooding the compartment. Leon watched the wrecked vehicle for a minute.

Satisfied, he walked back to his car. Driving away, he ran through how Brinks would react when Maxwell's nephew would be found making the news. Brinks would freak, assuming Leon had a hand in his death. Knowing Brinks, he wouldn't probe for any information. The police would be all over the Gilmore house by then. Unless they were as dumb as a bag of rocks, they would see a pattern. Two dead men connected to a house. Somebody would spot the truck and Wally inside. The police would find the jewelry. More connections would be made. His own scheme would pin Burke's murder on the OD'd loser at the bottom of the creek. If fortune was smiling on him, they might wonder if the junkie was also connected to the old man's death.

It was clear he needed to get out of town, get back to the West Coast. He'd drive back Binghamton and leave the rental car in the airport parking lot without turning it in.

Leon reached for his burner phone to call Brinks.

After two rings, Brinks picked.

"I'm heading home. Just one more thing to take care of, and don't ask what."

Brinks remained silent.

"You can celebrate," Leon said, "unless the fat man is still up your ass."

"He came up with nothing."

"All's swell that ends swell, and we have some unfinished business."

Brinks sighed twice. The first was one of relief and the second heavier since he had to manage Leon's acting aspirations.

"Okay. Call when you get back. I need to run. I have company coming over."

Brinks hung up abruptly, which pissed Leon off. He'd deal with his arrogant client when he got back home. In the meantime, he thought about what his next disguise should be as he drove back to the fairgrounds.

CHAPTER 86

PERSON OF INTEREST

I was lying next to Zena when the phone rang. She had cried herself to sleep after identifying John at the morgue. I was exhausted as well. The emotional blow was hard on both of us seeing John dead. And then there was that gentle old man who had been clearly tortured before someone broke his neck.

You didn't need to be a genius in sleuthing to see that there was a connection. But I couldn't figure out what it was. The house had to be the link, but fuck all if I knew what it was. The cops said it was a robbery that had gotten ugly, but there were too many things that didn't make sense. The one thing I learned at the academy was to trust your gut, especially when cops came up with a simple explanation of what they thought happened that was just too simple.

I studied Zena as she slept the sleep of the grieving and, once more, recognized that she was an illustration of the inconsistencies of how the *normals* regarded beauty and form. We were at the mercy of nature. Life is a genetic crap shoot. She came into this world, taking the helm of a leaky life boat that tested her resolve and ability to survive. My focus on her outer form was melting away; instead, I was drawn to her spirit, her inner beauty and courage, as corny as that sounded. Maybe a future writing schmaltzy Hallmark cards would be my next job if my relationship with Stan fizzled.

The phone continued to ring. I felt the dread of hearing more bad news.

"You gonna get that damn phone," she croaked, lifting an eyelid, her voice strained from too much sobbing.

I fumbled for the receiver. "Hello."

"This Cooper?"

"Yeah."

"Kapinski here. We need you to come downtown again."

I heard urgency. "Something come up?"

"We may have found the person who murdered your friend."

I was silent for some seconds, amazed that the cops had pegged someone for John's murder so quickly.

"Really?"

"Sometimes we get a lucky break."

"Maybe you and Zena could confirm if this suspect had a connection to Mr. Burke. He was one of the people you listed as possible suspects."

"Which one?"

"I'd rather do this in person."

"Give us half an hour."

The call got Zena's attention, and she sat up in bed. "Who was that?"

"Kapinski. He thinks they have a suspect for John's murder. Want us to come down to the station."

"They say who the suspect is?"

I shook my head.

She slipped out of bed, not a stitch of clothes on as was her usual get-into-bed attire for naps or bedtime snoozing. She smiled weakly at me. This wasn't a good time to gawk.

"I'll make us coffee while you get dressed," I offered, as she started to dress.

We got to the Ithaca police station on East Clinton Street, and the desk sergeant buzzed Detective Kapinski. His office was spare. Family photographs on his desk—kids, no wife. A few framed certificates on the wall, standard-issue file cabinets, and a wilted plant on a windowsill that was in dire need of water. I thought of Lilly and wondered if my plants and cat would be alive when I got back to the city.

"Thanks for coming down," Kapinski said and pointed to two seats in front of his desk. He reached into his desk drawer and took out a plastic bag. I recognized what it was: a bag from a crime scene with a label clearly marked *Evidence* and *Chain of Custody.*

Kapinski pointed to the bag, which had several pieces of jewelry inside. He pushed the bag toward us.

Zena gasped. "That's John's!"

"You sure?" he asked.

"Yes. Those are his," she asserted, fingering a few of them through the evidence bag. Then she instantly dropped them on the desk, noticing John's skin for the first time.

There was a folder on Kapinski's desk. He opened it and took out a stack of eight-by-ten photographs. He was hesitant.

"They're pretty graphic," he warned.

He slid the photos over to us, but I grabbed them first. I picked one up, looked it over, then studied another one. I handed one of them to Zena, one that was the least sickening.

"Pretty sure it's this guy Wally," she said. "He was the one who had a run-in with John." She stared at the photograph and grimaced. "His face is awful. Bad bar fight? He'd be someone to get into one."

"Not a bar fight," Kapinski said flatly.

She looked more closely at the photo. "He almost looks like he's dead."

Kapinski inhaled deeply, and when he exhaled, he said, "He is."

I looked through the first photograph again. Even though the photos were head shots, I could see stainless steel framing his head. Wally was laid out on one just as John had been. Ironically, the two were reunited in the cold confines of a morgue.

"Where did you find him?" I asked.

"In a creek," the detective replied. "A state trooper happened to spot a broken railing. He stopped and saw a pickup truck lying at the bottom of the creek."

I looked at the photos again.

"The trooper climbed down. Saw someone inside. Called an ambulance and had a tow truck pull the vehicle out. When the EMTs removed the man, the trooper found jewelry scattered all over the truck's cab. The vehicle was registered to Wallace Sullivan. I called

Wallace's residence and asked his girlfriend to come identify the body."

I saw Zena saddened, hearing that Wally's girlfriend would see what she had seen.

"So you're thinking that Wally robbed and killed him?" I asked. The detective heard my tone of incredulity.

"Evidence points that way." He gestured to the jewelry.

I closed my eyes, trying to picture how things played out. "You believe Wally managed to get John to go to those falls."

"Could be he followed Mr. Burke," Kapinski defended. "Ms. Zena said he liked going there. Not a stretch that Sullivan tracked him there."

"So John's trailer is torn apart, but he's not there at the time. He's supposed to be going to Gilmore's, only he never showed up. Strange that he and Gilmore are both dead," I said, trying to piece together the sequence of events.

"A coincidence."

"I don't believe in them."

"Are you playing detective now?"

"Humor me," I said.

"Okay, Columbo, keep going."

"Given the time frame, I don't put John at Gilmore's after he leaves the fairgrounds. I know that because I wished him luck when he headed back to his trailer. He had an appointment with the real estate agent. Sign papers to buy the house."

"You have a time for that."

I thought for a moment then said, "Around noon. And then maybe twenty minutes later, I get a call from Zena that John's trailer is ransacked. That's twelve-twenty. We checked the mess inside the trailer, asked around if anyone saw John. Nobody did, so we drove to Gilmore's house. Got there close to one o'clock and found the old man dead and no John there."

I then paused and asked, "When did we call 911?"

"Got a call from you at one-twenty according to our dispatcher," Kapinski said, looking at his notes.

"Can I use your wall, get some sticky notes and a pen?" I was thinking about what Lilly called my *crap board*. "Helps me visualize ideas that I get when I write articles."

"I seen that wall thing on that TV show *Person of Interest*," Kohl piped in like a kid who got the right answer in class.

I gave him an encouraging smile.

"This is out of normal protocol," said Kapinski.

"I know," I agreed.

Kapinski hesitated for a moment then handed me a stack of sticky notes and a pen. I gave them to Zena to hold, while I started to write and add them to the wall.

"What time did the hikers call in about finding John?" I asked.

Kapinski leafed through the pages in his notepad then said, "At two-ten." Zena handed me the first sticky note. I wrote, "Hikers find John, 2:10."

"When did the trooper call the accident in? Wally's truck?"

Kapinski looked at his notes again. "Two-thirty-three."

I added a second sticky to the wall.

"And the ME speculated due to a lack of rigor that John could have been killed two hours earlier," I continued. "That's a few minutes after noon."

I added another note and saw Kapinski do some mental math in his head.

I began thinking out loud. "If we use the ME's answer about rigor setting in, John might have been murdered around noon, and Wally is found around two-thirty. That's a two-and-a-half-hour window. How far is the creek where Wally was found from the falls?"

"Maybe thirty miles north from the state park."

"And where is Wally's place?" I asked. "Where he lives?"

"About five miles south of Ithaca."

"That would be thirty-five miles or so from Wally's place to Devil Falls."

I wrote this distance down on a new note. "And over sixty miles if you add the distance from Wally's residence to the falls and to where Wally crashed."

I added a new note for the mileage.

Zena was watching how I was approaching the timelines and said, "All of this doesn't include how long it takes to drive from Wally's house to Devils Falls and where his truck crashed. And the time to murder John and…" She hesitated. "And take his jewelry."

She had a good point, and I saw Kapinski see a glitch in the time frame and why Wally may not be John's killer.

I closed my eyes again, trying to put numbers and times together. "Is the creek where Wally crashed on the way back to town?"

Kapinski thought for a moment then said, "It's going away from town. North."

"What's north away from the falls?" I asked.

"Farms. Fields. More farms. Cortland and Syracuse. Maybe he thought he could hock the jewelry there."

"You know Wally's whereabouts today?" I asked Kapinski. "Before he was found."

"We'll talk to his girlfriend when she arrives." Kapinski knew something troubled me. "So you're thinking what?"

I pointed to my sticky notes, the times that were noted and the miles traveled. "We can't figure out if Wally broke into John's trailer. We can't figure out if or when he got to the falls. How he got to John. How he murdered him and then winds up at the bottom of a creek in the time frame here." I pointed to the wall of notes again.

I had a flashback standing in front of Kapinski, asking and answering questions as if I were back at the academy. It felt good. I would've been a good detective. Maybe I'd be a private investigator like Sam Spade. Not sure Lilly and Thelma would see this as a better career move.

Zena interrupted my flashback.

"John beat the shit out of this guy just a day ago. No way Wally could have gotten the jump on him," she said, invalidating Kapinski's hypothesis.

"Wally and your friend had a history," Kapinski said, flipping through the pages in notepad, defending his theory. "Maybe revenge was his motivation. You said he had a run-in with Mr. Burke at that restaurant. You told his girlfriend she was pregnant, and he came after you. Your friend intervened," he finished, looking at Zena for acknowledgment.

She didn't respond.

"He went at Mr. Burke again when he was doing his act. Tried stabbing him with one of the pins according to witnesses we interviewed. However, your friend basically kicked his ass when Sullivan tried that. Revenge can be a more tempting motivator."

"Okay, let's put the timing aside," I suggested, nodding to my wall of notes. "Why would Wally kill him? Why would he tear off cheap jewelry you could buy anywhere?"

"Payback, like I said."

"There's something else you're not telling us," Zena confronted. I could tell her "Liar, liar, pants on fire" radar had kicked in.

Kapinski hesitated.

"Come on, Detective, level with us."

"Wally may not have died from the crash itself," Kapinski said, almost reluctantly.

"If not, then what?" I said.

"Our ME, Dr. Bernstein, found quite a bit of heroin in his system."

Zena and I stood quiet as statues for a full minute.

"Enough to overdose?"

Kapinski shrugged and said, "A man smacked out on dope is not going to win a safe driver award. Maybe Sullivan was dumb enough to sell Maxwell's jewelry. A way to finance a fix and settle a score."

I wasn't convinced Kapinski's new theory had legs.

"It's a possibility," I said without enthusiasm.

"So glad you think so."

CHAPTER 87

COMPANY

They left the hot tub. Mona led Brinks into the bedroom, and her hands began wandering over his body. She undid his robe and then removed her own. She moved him to the bed and slid her body over him. He held her close, his hands on her buttocks, pressing them into his groin. She moved her stomach over him, feeling him getting aroused. Her hands moved below his stomach, and he groaned.

The doorbell rang.

"Shit," Brinks murmured. Mona took her hands away, the heat of the moment evaporating like a drop of water hitting a hot stone.

The doorbell rang again. He put his robe back on and walked to the hallway. There was a bank of security cameras positioned around his house. At the front door stood Tankowitz and the three Chinese accountants. Tankowitz held up a bottle of Cristal champagne waving it in front of the camera.

He returned to Mona and said, "I have visitors from work."

"I'll be in the bathroom." She blew him a kiss. This woman needed no tutoring as to what to do in a compromising situation.

Brinks waited until she was in the bathroom, hearing the door close. He turned to the front door, tied the sash to his bathrobe tight, and opened the door.

"Surprise!" the four men shouted at the same time.

"Oh my," Brinks said, doing his best to look surprised.

"I hope we aren't catching you at a bad time." He eyed Brinks's robe.

"No, no. Just came out of the shower."

"We wanted to have a goodbye commemoration drink," Wang explained. "Kung-fu movies never get old."

Tankowitz pushed past Brinks and the three accountants followed into the living room. They all stopped in the middle of the room. The Chinese men looked around, turning like a carousel.

"Nice digs," Qian admired.

"Real nice," Wang echoed.

"Job at Glowball been good to you," Zheng commented.

Tankowitz said nothing. He started pacing around, looking at the paintings, sculptures, sound system, furniture, and Persian rugs.

"You like art."

"I do."

"I know some of these names. Famous, right?"

"Some are, sure."

He brushed past Brinks, a frown deepening on his forehead.

It was too late for Brinks to stop Tankowitz as he wandered into the study. He spotted the stamp album and studied the page too long for Brinks's comfort.

"Quite a collection," he finally said.

Brinks did not respond.

"I knew a Wall Street guy once. Hedge funds. Made millions. I did an audit for him. One of investment fund managers. He thought the guy was shifting money into his own pockets. I came to his apartment. Real high-end apartment on Lexington Avenue. He liked stamps like you. Showed me ones he recently bought."

Brinks knew there was more to the story.

Tankowitz continued. "There was this auction in 2005. My guy bought one of these funny plane stamps like you have here. Paid a fortune."

"If mine was the real McCoy, it would be worth quite a lot." Brinks chuckled as he told this lie. "It's actually a fake. You can research it. A fake like this showed up in Florida on an absentee ballot that was sent to Broward County in 2006. You can check that out. Besides, people like me don't mind having reproductions of the original to fill in a collection."

"I guess," Tankowitz said warily.

Brinks studied Tankowitz's face to see if he bought his lie. He couldn't tell. Tankowitz would find that there was a fake stamp that surfaced just as he said. That, he hoped, would throw him off.

"I'm getting this itch under my *schmeklel*," Tankowitz said as he rubbed his crotch.

Brinks didn't know Yiddish slang, but an itch under his nemesis's dick was not good.

"I don't know much about art and stuff, but you seem to have really nice things."

"Thanks."

"Costs a lot, it looks like."

"Some of these do."

"Pretty good salary they give you." More of a statement than a question.

"I do okay at Glowball."

Tankowitz took out his iPhone and walked around the living room. He started taking photos of the art hanging on the wall, objects placed on shelves and tables, the rugs, and everything in sight.

"What are you doing?" Brinks protested.

"I admire good taste when I see it."

Brinks watched Tankowitz ricochet around his home from room to room like a pinball bouncing off rubber bumpers, snapping away at everything of value in sight.

"I always do a little background checking before I start a job. Your secretary mentioned that this man had called to confirm your employment. I wondered about that, so I paid a visit to the caller. Dapper Dan type, he was."

Brinks remembered when Tankowitz had chatted with Brandy when he first arrived. He hadn't thought about the call she had received from that jerk at Hammerstein's.

"There was a sculpture you liked. Seems you had a real boner for it according to this fellow."

Brinks felt his bowels go liquid.

Tankowitz waved his iPhone at him. "Pretty sure he can give me an idea about what these nice things would go for. I'm betting you're as crooked as an arthritic finger. I'm leaving the bottle with you, but don't pop the cork just yet. Maybe tell your boss to hold off on casting the flick."

Tankowitz ushered the three men out the door with him.

"Sleep tight," the big man said and closed the front door.

Mona slipped back into the room where Brinks was standing, looking as if he stepped on a snake, his face pale, a shiver running down his back.

"What was that all about?" Mona asked, coming up to him and wrapping her arms around his chest.

It took him a long moment to answer. "The best laid plans of mice and men…"

"Often go awry…" she completed.

He hugged her, feeling the warmth of her body pressed into his and the shivering abated. "I have to make a call."

"Should I go?"

"Yes. On an adventure with me. The white horse has arrived."

She gave him a quizzical look as he fetched his cell phone.

CHAPTER 88

BALLED UP

Detective Kapinski didn't particularly like the man. He was haughty, intrusive, and a smart aleck. The guy had made a fool out of him. Here came some writer from the big city who thought a year at the academy made him the be-all and end-all in investigative knowhow. A wannabe cop who couldn't hack it when it got tough but believed he was the sharpest knife in the drawer in town. His town.

Kapinski figured he had Burke's murder wrapped up nice and neat, and then *bang*, the wrapping came off faster than a stripper's clothes at a bachelor party. In less than an hour, Mr. Deducto's reasoning made Kapinski look like an amateur.

Although he hated to admit it, the asshole actually saved his bacon. Angie Bowers was all set to splash a front-page story about the murder. Kapinski was primed to point the finger at Burke whom, at the time, he thought was alive, off the grid, and breathing air, not underwater and dead. Fortunately, Cooper persuaded him to hold off.

He stared at his office wall with all the notes still in place. Cooper explained that the timeline for Burke's murder didn't jibe, and neither did pointing Sullivan for the murder. Cooper's theories of timing originally eluded him like solving a complex physics problem. If he felt like a fool in front of Kohl, imagine how a front-page story would have looked.

He looked at his watch. It was time to meet Wallace Sullivan's girlfriend. She was coming down to the morgue to identify the body. As he was about to leave, his phone rang.

"Kapinski."

"Hello, Detective. It's Dr. Bernstein."

"How's it going?"

"Fine," she answered, not one to be chatty.

"What can I do for you?"

"It's what I can do for you, Detective. I found something you'll be interested in."

"More on Sullivan's overdose?"

"No. You wanted to have my autopsy report on Mr. Burke."

"Right."

"The fall killed him." She paused. "What killed him was obvious. I mentioned some of that before. But what was of interest was that he had something lodged in his trachea."

"Like in his throat?"

"Yes. It would appear he swallowed this item just before he died. It was balled up."

"And this thing is what exactly?"

"Not sure, but your lab people can make more sense of it more than I can. We can discuss it when you arrive. Goodbye, Detective."

When the phone call ended, he left his office and took an unmarked car and headed to the Cayuga Medical Center. He started to think about what Maxwell could have swallowed. Probably not chewing gum since Bernstein made it a point to call him. Something so important that Burke didn't want his killer to have it. This case was becoming stranger by the minute.

CHAPTER 89

FIRE SALE

Brinks heard a truck pull up a few minutes after midnight. He looked at his security cameras. It was a truck idling in his driveway. No one else in sight. He took out his cell and dialed.

"Freddy, that you?"

"And a nice hello to you," Freddy replied.

"Sorry. I'm a bit jumpy, things the way they are."

"I told you that one day your very expensive habit would catch up with you."

"I'm not in the mood for a lecture."

"Just saying, buddy."

"Pull up to the back of the house."

He heard the trunk rumble past the side of the house and then stop in the back. He looked at the security cams again, and the street outside was quiet. Unlocking the door, he saw Freddy and three men who looked like Seal Team Six, muscles bulging out like a trio of steroid iron men.

Freddy held out his hand, and Brinks shook it.

"This is a new one for me. Like robbing a house with the owner helping."

Brinks cringed at the word *robbery*, but he knew Freddy well enough and that he was about to be fucked royally when it came down to it. It would be robbery.

Freddy started to wander around the house.

"Just give me a price. Everything you see. Paintings, prints, sculptures, in the house and out in my garden. If it's not nailed down, take it."

Freddy had his iPhone out and started taking photos of his artwork just as Tankowitz had done a few hours before. He noticed that Brinks was watching him. So he winked at him and touched the Send button on the phone.

"Gotta guy who can tell me what your artwork is worth."

"Not someone at Hammerstein's," Brinks said, thinking it would be totally creepy if it was.

"Nah. My pal used to work for Christies until he was pinched for putting shills in auctions and getting some under-the-table money from buyers who wanted to drive down the prices of what they were bidding on. Good for the buyers but bad for the auction house's reputation."

"Good to know if I ever go to auctions again."

"That'll be a change for you."

"Maybe a good thing," Brinks said, not really uncertain. "Like I said, take everything."

"We'll leave the toilet paper."

He didn't smile.

"Kinda funny in a way."

"What part of this nightmare is funny?"

"I know a bunch of what you have is stuff I sold to you. You buy, I sell, and now I get them back at a discount. I make money coming and going and coming again."

"Hilarious," Brinks said sourly.

Two hours later, Freddy approached Brinks, who sat on his sofa. He had a bottle of Scotch on the coffee table.

"You want a drink?"

"I'll pass," he said. "Booze makes me a soft touch, and we have to do this thing tonight. Your delicate business transaction."

"The bottom line, Freddy."

"I can give you twenty cents on the dollar," Freddy said, taking out his cell phone, pressing the calculator icon. He showed him a number.

"You're shitting me, right?" Brinks screamed, his face turning red with anger. "This is highway robbery."

"You can always find another buyer. The way I'm seeing this is that I'm doing you a favor."

"If getting fucked up the ass is a favor."

"Yeah, but you going to jail would be a real ass fucking. My fucking you, you walk away and disappear. Asshole intact. And you still walk away with a nice chunk of change. Four mil ain't bad, bucko. Find a place in a third-world country that still likes Americans, and you'll live like a king."

"Thanks for the travel agent advice." Brinks looked at Freddy's number. Not great but he would be comfortable enough. "And a new passport? Driver's license and bank account under my new name."

"Done and me being a great guy, I'll throw those in for free. Offshore bank account is all set. You take the deal and the money will be transferred tomorrow morning. I'll give you twenty thou in cash right now for candy and coke money. You can lie low in a cash-only motel until you and your girlfriend leave."

"And that woman I mentioned."

"Also done. Got plane ticket for both of you." Freddy paused. "She know about this sudden change of circumstances?"

"Not yet."

"You think she's gonna make a new life with you?"

"I'm hoping once she hears her white horse has arrived."

"Horse? If you got one, I ain't buying it."

"A metaphor."

Freddy shrugged and supervised his hulking crew of movers.

Brinks wandered into his garden. He remembered his conversation with Mona. It was a perfect night until Tankowitz had shown up. She had waited until Tankowitz left, and then she took off shortly thereafter. Before she went, he evaded her questions about being in trouble and asked her to wait for a call from him later. She smiled, saying this was mysterious and exciting and hoped he would call. It was time to see if she was just encouraging his hopeful thinking. He dialed her private number. After three rings, she picked up, sleep in her *hello.*

"Can you get away for a few weeks? Maybe longer?"

Brinks listened to a couple of questions.

"Someplace really nice. That adventure I talked to you about. I'll call you where to meet me. Pack light. And bring your passport."

She asked one more question, and he said, "I do love you. You must know that."

Mona said something, and a smile transformed his face.

CHAPTER 90

SIDE TRACKED

The ride to the morgue was somber. Kapinski said Wally's girlfriend would be there to confirm if the body was his. A few hours before, I had helped Zena pick out a funeral home that would take care of John's remains. He would be cremated. Zena already picked out a place where she would scatter his ashes, the same waterfalls where his body was found.

"Why the waterfalls?"

"It was special, he said."

"Even though that's where—"

"Even though. Maybe it's fitting. Bookends. I don't know. I'm sure you can come up some cycle of life wordy eulogy thing that makes sense about scattering him there."

I heard resentment and knew it wasn't directed at me as a personal swipe. She had a right to be pissed. She needed some way to vent. I was happy to be her emotional punching bag.

I spotted the same lab tech standing with a clipboard next to the body lockers. He pulled out one of the stainless-steel shelves, which had a body with a sheet covering it. Dr. Bernstein was there, wearing her professional persona. Clinical. Showing no evident emotions. This was the dead man protocol she followed.

There was a young woman crying silent sobs that made her chest heave. Detective Kapinski was next to her. Kohl stood behind them, taking in the morgue like a kid who has never been to a movie theater, his eyes wider than a Walter Keene waif.

Kapinski lifted the sheet, and the young woman looked down at the body, her sobs coming out even deeper, her hands fluttering to her face.

It only took me a second to place her as Wally's girlfriend. She seemed so happy just days before at Maxie's, wanting to share her good news with Zena. But then Wally came after Zena and John interceded, throwing the man to the ground.

The confluence of all these people in this room put the *a* in awkward.

The sobbing girlfriend spotted Zena and broke away from Kapinski. She zigzagged toward us, her legs wobbly as if she was on a boat that hit some chop. Kapinski followed.

"I know they think Wally killed your friend," she said in hiccupped words, pointing at Kapinski. "I just know he didn't. Just know it. I swear."

Kapinski took her elbow, trying to guide her away, but she resisted, wanting absolution for her dead boyfriend.

Zena looked at her. "I'm pretty sure he didn't."

Wally's girlfriend seemed stunned by Zena's proclamation. "You don't?"

Zena took her hand and patted it.

Kapinski's still-unproven theory was that a junkie killed a man twice as strong as him because he was strung out on dope and gained superhero strength. As fate would, his heroin-addled mind caused him to crash after leaving the scene of the murder. *Question the obvious*, ping-ponged around my skull. Sometimes, the obvious hid the truth.

I walked over to where Bernstein stood. "Can I ask you a question?"

Kapinski came over, seeing I was a loose cannon.

"I was told that Mr. Sullivan had a significant amount of heroin in his body."

Bernstein gave Kapinski the chilly look of someone who had breached the protocol of autopsy confidentiality. He shrugged, not appearing to be bothered by her unspoken condemnation.

Bernstein said nothing. As we stood around like gate posts, Wally's girlfriend came up to us, overhearing my question.

"Wouldn't surprise me," she said. She blew her nose and said, "Wally had a habit. No secret to people who knew him. I bet Detective Kapinski has his rap sheet. He did time at Elmira for possession and distribution."

Kapinski blinked a confirmation.

I looked at Wally's girlfriend. "Would you mind if I looked at him?" I gestured to Wally's corpse.

Bernstein and Kapinski looked at each other.

"I want to check out something. A belly button thing."

They raised their eyebrows. My navel intelligence was not something they were acquainted with.

"If you're okay with that," I asked, not waiting for Bernstein or Kapinski's procedural permission.

"Go ahead," she said through serious sniffling.

Bernstein gave me a dead-eye look of disapproval. Kapinski just looked bemused—me, this New York City smart aleck, thinking I had the keys to the magic kingdom of sleuthland.

The doc moved closer to the slab where Wally lay, and we all followed.

"He shot up mostly?" I asked the girlfriend.

"Mostly. Would smoke it sometimes or snort it. But he liked the needle. He liked the ritual. He'd get out all the paraphernalia. The alcohol swabs, syringe, spoon, lighter, cotton balls, rubber tube to tie himself off, and of course, his dope. He'd find a good vein. His face would go rubber like and get the smile of an idiot seeing God."

We all gathered closer around Wally. I turned to Bernstein.

"Can we see his arms?"

She sighed and pulled the sheet down to his hips.

"Can I take a look at them?"

The doc turned to the lab tech and said, "Gloves."

The lab tech reached into a box and pulled out a bunch of blue latex gloves.

I slipped a pair on with Kapinski eyeing me like a seagull at the beach waiting to snatch food. I lifted up his left arm first.

"Tracks," Kapinski observed.

"How old do you think these are?" I asked Bernstein.

She studied the arm. "Not new. A week or so old. Bruising is faded. Looks like an area he like to use."

"You said these tracks are old. You check other places?"

"Of course," the doc answered.

I waited for her to tell us what she found. She liked the tight-lipped approach.

"And?" I prompted.

"His right arm. Near the region anterior to the cubital fossa. Look at the bend at the elbow joint. There's a fresh puncture in the basilic vein."

Kapinski caught my eye, seeing where I was going. He turned to Wally's girlfriend. "Was Wally right-handed or a lefty?"

She didn't hesitate and said, "He was right-handed. Why?"

At that instant, the doc also caught on to what we were thinking. We circled around Wally's corpse like gatherers at an Irish wake and studied the needle mark in his right arm.

"How fresh is that puncture?" Kapinski asked.

Bernstein thought a moment then said, "Less than a day."

"Kinda odd for a righty to give himself a shot with his left hand," I offered.

Kapinski lifted his index finger to his upper lip, contemplating this idea.

"What if someone else gave him the juice?" I asked Kapinski.

Wally's girlfriend caught a breath in her throat. "So whaddya sayin'?"

"I'm not a real detective but—"

"You sayin' Wally was set up? Who'd wanna do that?"

Kapinski waited for my punch line.

"Could be the same guy who took out our friend."

He gave me a questioning squint, not wanting to make that leap so fast. I, on the other hand, tended to be a leaper. Never in doubt, many times wrong. The leaper motto.

"Let's put a pin in that idea," he said. "Let's see if it has legs."

The word *pin* and John was in bad taste, but I let it go. "Any more revelations before we go?" I asked Kapinski.

"Kinda," he said hesitantly.

"Kinda?" I repeated.

"Yeah. There's something Doctor Bernstein might want to disclose."

Bernstein blinked several times, her eyelids sending an approval like a signal lamp on a navy ship.

"I found something during the autopsy," Bernstein said matter-of-factly. "Something *in* Mr. Burke."

Zena and I shared the same frowning lines.

"It seems he swallowed something before he died," Bernstein explained.

"Something?" Zena questioned, the thought of her friend's last act before dying sounding more than bizarre.

"Not sure what," Dr. Bernstein reiterated.

Kapinski interjected himself, "The doc removed it. It was stuck in his throat."

"Pharynx," Bernstein corrected.

"Yeah, that. Forensics has it now."

"What was it?" I asked.

"We'll find out. My lab techs are working on it," Kapinski said.

Zena closed her eyes. I imagined she was replaying his death.

"Did he swallow it on purpose?" she asked, looking bewildered.

"Or something he gulped down that was in the pool," Kapinski conjectured.

"Or maybe it was something he was willing to die for, whatever it is."

If so, I wondered what it was.

CHAPTER 91

IN THE WIND

Leon dialed the burner phone. He had spent the night waiting to hear from Brinks, who had blown him off the day before. Typical LaLa land rude. He wanted to remind him about their deal, make sure Brinks didn't slimeball his way out of it. Yesterday, he said he had company and dismissed him like an uppity servant.

Brinks usually picked up in less than three rings. Now there was no answer. What was that all about? His thoughts drifted back to the fortune-teller. She would be his last stop on his way back to the west coast and the beginning of what he hoped would be a rewarding career on the silver screen.

He called again. No answer. There might be one person that could help him track him down. He dialed a new number.

"Hey, Freddy."

"I figured you'd call me," Freddy said as soon as he heard Leon's voice.

Leon's forehead crinkled. "Why's that?"

"You trying to get in touch with you-know-who, right?"

"Yeah. You have a message for me?"

"Not directly."

"I'm not following you, man."

"Your friend is in the wind."

"Still not following you," Leon said, his throat getting tight.

"Left for parts unknown." Freddy chuckled.

"You being funny?"

"Nope."

"Freddy. Stop screwing with me! Where's Brinks?"

"Splitsville."

"What?"

"Some shit blew up for him at work. He decided to run while the running was good."

Leon closed his eyelids so tight they hurt. "The accountants found something hinky?"

"They did. Dropped in on him unannounced and saw the very expense shit he likes to collect. One look as his crib and they saw he's livin' large. Too large for whatever he makes."

"So where did he go?"

"No idea," Freddy lied, which was almost true since all he did was get him passports and plane tickets as a jumping-off place to who knew where. "I did a midnight move for him. Took everything he owned except his dust."

"Fuck all." Leon let out a heavy sigh. "We had an arrangement. I had plans."

"Like they say, man plans. God laughs." Freddy waited, but Leon stayed silent. "So what, he left without paying you?"

"This wasn't about money. We had a deal."

"A Hollywood deal is like promising a broad you won't—"

"I gotta go," Leon said, cutting him off.

"Stay cool."

Leon hung up. His world was suddenly falling apart. All the shit he did. All the shit he put up with. The people he offed. Without warning, all his hard work went up in smoke. He realized that he could be the fall guy. He always thought he could hold whatever he did over Brinks's head if things went south. But Brinks was off the grid then.

Two thoughts collided inside his head. The first was how to salvage his career with Brinks gone. The second idea was more urgent: how to take care of the tiny tot. The longer he stayed here, his odds of making a quick exit would be like hopping over the La Brea Tar Pits.

Leon ran down several scenarios. He would have to stake out her place and gain entrance while she was there. The other issue was how he would take care of her. He had to be quick. It had to be quiet.

And then there was what to do with her body. Better she just vanish. No body ever found. That would throw the cops off for a while, looking for a missing person. The idea came to him. Her disappearing act. It was ironic in a way, but so what?

He surveyed his room and began packing. In the bathroom, he removed his toothbrush and toiletries. He wiped down all the surfaces that might contain his fingerprints. He pulled hair from the bathtub drain and wiped all surfaces clean.

His eyes swept the room and he picked up his luggage and disguise case. He left ten dollars for the maid who cleaned the room. Didn't want her to remember him as the stingy guy in 212. As he left the room, he felt the pressure of time.

He then did a quick exit to his car. Suitcase in the trunk. His disguise case by his side. He got back into his car and headed back to Ithaca. On the way, he started looking at stores. He reached the outskirts of Ithaca and saw a strip mall. He spotted the store he was looking for. Slipping into an open slot, he parked. His small case of disguises lay next to him. He picked out a new wig and changed into a blue work shirt. Perfect for what he needed.

Entering the hardware store, he roamed around, looking for what he wanted. He found a shelf of duct tape. He picked a large roll.

"Can I help?" a man said, his name sewn into the Kelly Hardware shirt he wore. Andy.

"Looking for chains," Leon reiterated, making his voice go basso.

"What kind, mister? Roller, transport, sash, link?"

"Heavy. For pulling stumps."

Andy pursed his lips. "What you need is half-inch. Proof coil chain. I'd recommend a grade 30. Galvanized. Cost you $5.45 a foot. Working load 4,500 pounds."

Leon nodded like he knew what the man was talking about.

"That'll do me. How about thirty feet. Six foot lengths."

"That'd be five of 'em, then."

Leon nodded. "And a satchel bag. Large. Put the chains in it."

"No problem."

"And I need locks. Five of them. Combination ones will do."

446

Andy gave him a thumbs-up. The hardware man went into the back of the store. Ten minutes later, a younger man followed him, carrying the lengths of chain.

"You have any burlap bags?" Leon asked.

"Sure. How many?"

"One will do."

The young man who carried the chain came back with a bag. Leon paid cash.

"You need help carrying all of this out?"

"No, but thanks."

He left with what he bought and headed to his car. He put all his items in the trunk. His next stop would be real interesting.

CHAPTER 92

REALITY CHECK

We sat around a desk in the incident room at the police station. Bernstein sat next to Kapinski, looking like she was sitting on a bed of nails. I sat next to Zena, holding her hand.

Kapinski looked around the room at each of us. "We've got a few facts but not enough to complete the picture. Three men are dead, and thanks to Mr. Cooper here, Mr. Sullivan may not be who I thought he was."

He paused and then continued, "What I'm doing is not following standard homicide protocol. But there is some urgency, and everyone here probably has ideas that may help us understand what happened to Mr. Burke, Mr. Sullivan and Ralph Gilmore."

I was impressed that Kapinski acknowledged that his assumption about Wally did not make as much sense as it did a few hours before. I was also surprised he acknowledged my input about why Wally couldn't have killed John.

"So is what we are doing a reality check?" I asked. "If so, I have some ideas."

"I figured you'd have more to say," Kapinski said flatly.

"Namaste," I said, using the Hindu version of thank-you.

He rolled his eyes.

"There's a technique I use when I have to write an article where it looks like a jigsaw puzzle and some of the pieces are missing."

All eyes were on me to explain.

"We share what we all know, what we don't know, and what we don't know what we don't know?"

448

I could see Kapinski followed my first two suppositions, but my last one about not knowing what we don't know stumped him.

He shrugged a go-ahead shrug, and so I continued.

"Aside from Mr. Sullivan, we have the Burke and Gilmore murders."

"Okay," he said halfheartedly to my first supposition.

"There's a connection to the house. But what?" I asked, posing a hypothetical question but knowing the answer.

Zena cleared her throat. "The man who lived in the house before Ralph Gilmore was John's uncle."

"You know this how?" Kapinski asked skeptically.

"John showed us a newspaper clipping when he returned to Ithaca from Nam. He's standing outside the College Street house with his uncle, Percy Maxwell. He was a director when silent movies were shot here years ago."

Kapinski pulled on his chin, trying to put this new connection together. "Wait a sec. Burke is Maxwell's nephew?

I nodded.

"So the nephew was buying his uncle's house."

"Right. Another thing we all know. The attic was tossed when we got there." I looked at Kapinski for confirmation.

Bernstein tapped on a manila file that was placed on the desk in front of her. "And we also know—or should I say the detective and I know—what Mr. Burke swallowed."

Zena's head practically snapped around as she looked at Bernstein and Kapinski.

"What Mr. Burke swallowed was a folded piece of paper," she explained directly.

"Our boys in the lab were able to make out what it is," Kapinski added.

Dr. Bernstein removed a copy of what they had removed from John's throat and pushed it to Zena and me.

We looked it over, and Zena said, "Oh my god! It's the contract John showed us. The one his uncle signed. The one he found in Gilmore's attic."

Kapinski had a Damascus moment and said, "You're thinking whoever killed Gilmore was looking for that contract."

"His trailer was tossed, right?" I pointed out. "And that hiding space we found in the attic looked like it was picked through."

"And you think…?" Kapinski prodded.

This was my "what we don't know what we don't know" moment to let us speculate.

"What if the guy who tossed the trailer and rummaged through Gilmore's attic was the same guy that set up Sullivan?"

"And killed Burke," Kapinski said, turning a question into a statement. "Your 'what we don't know what we don't know' link."

I nodded and looked at Kapinski. "Do you know Wally's whereabouts earlier today?"

"Yeah. His girlfriend said he went to a bar. The Black Cow. Said a guy had a cleanup job for him."

As soon as he said that, we had a good hunch that that guy was the setup man who killed Wally.

Another *aha* moment. "I'll take a ride over to the Cow," Kapinski said and stood. "Me and Boy Wonder will see if we can get an ID on the guy."

I assumed Boy Wonder was Officer Kohl.

Kapinski was about to leave when he came up to Zena and me. "Just one thing. Keep an eye out," he said.

Zena looked confused.

"There may be a bad guy still out there," Kapinski added.

She took my hand and squeezed.

"Sure," I said.

Zena and I then left the building and found my car. We got in and I drove. She stared blankly through the window, silent and sad. Driving back to the fairgrounds, I could feel that things would never be the same for her.

"You want company?"

"I won't be much."

"That's okay. How about we have a Scotch and raise a drink to John?"

"That would be nice," she replied in a soft voice.

"I'll park the car."

I saw Zena enter her trailer, and I gave her a little wave. The parking area for visitors was nearby. I found a spot and sat for a moment, thinking about the day. I gazed ahead, my eyes focused on the tree line that ringed the far side of the fairgrounds. The sun was crowning the tops of the maples and oaks. I couldn't hear the noise of the fairground where I parked. Peaceful silence for a change. My mind was at rest but tired. It had been a long day. And distressing. I felt drained. So much had happened since I first came to Ithaca. In just a few days, I had become close to two people, whom I never would have guessed would ever be in my life. If this were a movie, people would say it was too farfetched to be believable. A writer on a deadline hooks up with a dwarf and her best friend is murdered, a man who has pins pierced into his flesh for a living.

My Fellini-like thoughts about what might appear to be absurd or improbable were interrupted by my cell phone. I looked at the caller ID. Just what I needed, Stan calling me to give me shit.

CHAPTER 93

CURSE YOU FROM MY GRAVE

Zena entered the trailer, feeling like the walking dead. She was drained and too tired to grieve the way she wanted to grieve. She remembered when Pepe died. His wife, Bella, and Harry and Ethel and the other little people wailed, beating their fists against their chests like she saw in foreign movies. Greeks, Italians, Arabs. They did heartfelt grieving really well.

I will cry later, she told herself. *Right now, I have to keep it together.* There was John's funeral and then scattering his ashes at the falls. There was the contract he swallowed. And John's house, which was now my house. The house had a history and memories. Good ones for John. But not for her. Gilmore murdered in the attic. John's dream of living here dying with him.

And then there was Fenn. Where the hell was that going? He would leave soon, go back to his life, maybe suck up to that bitch of a girlfriend and try patching things up. Zena pretty much knew what they had was not a relationship with a future. She had seen that from the beginning. But a tiny piece of her hoped that maybe it was more than a nice interlude.

She decided to change her clothes, which had the sickly scent of the morgue. After a shower, she and Fenn would clink glasses and say a few kind words about John. She walked toward her bedroom and began to unbutton her shirt. A creak startled her, and she stopped halfway into the room. In the dim light, she saw the shadowy silhouette of a man standing against the wall.

"Fenn?"

"Nope."

She gasped and tried to close her bedroom door.

Leon quickly grabbed her. "Scream and you die," he said menacingly.

He came close, holding a knife, and took hold of her throat then forced her onto her bed. She quickly sat upright, clutching her open shirt together.

Leon stared at her chest, and his lips parted, showing white teeth. "Nice."

"My friend will be here any minute now," she said, forcing words through her constricted throat, trying to keep her words steady without panic.

"Then he'd be history too."

Zena looked hard at the man's face. The word *history* punctuated with a hiss. It clicked, and the words leaped out. "I know you."

"That's kinda why I'm here."

"You came to my booth."

"Yeah, I was afraid you'd remember me."

"You're the one that killed my friend and the old guy." She said this more like a question.

"Good thinking," Leon said smugly. "Too good for me, though."

"You fucking bastard!" Her eyes bored into him like a carbide-tipped drill.

He ignored her insults.

"One thing," she said.

"Yeah?"

Zena gave him a fearless stare that shot through him like an x-ray. "I will always know you. And I will curse you from my grave. I know how to do that."

Leon stiffened. "What the fuck does that supposed to mean?"

She sprung from the bed like a cougar, her hands claw-like, her finger nails diving for flesh. Her nails dug deep into his cheeks. He pushed her down, and as she fell back to the bed, her nails ripped downward, leaving lines of blood.

Leon reached for his face, felt the scratches, and then slapped her hard. She cried out and started to get up, and he hit her again, this time with a karate chop against her temple. Knocked out cold, her limp body slipped to the floor.

He held his hand to his cheeks. There was blood on his fingertips. The bitch had damaged his most valuable possession. He ran his fingers over the scratches. *They would heal,* he reassured himself. There would be no scars. A month and he'd be as handsome as ever again.

He turned his attention to the woman. She lay on top of a rug decorated with rose petals and unicorns. Convenient. He slipped out of the trailer, removed a few things from his car, then returned. He took out a roll of duct tape, tore a piece off, and taped it over her mouth. After that, he placed a burlap bag over her head and with more duct tape bound her feet. He did the same, putting her arms behind her back and taping her wrists together. Next, Leon shifted her to the middle of the rug and began to roll her over.

Leon opened the trailer door a crack, looking out to see who was nearby. It was clear of people. He scuttled back to Zena, still motionless inside the rug. He hoisted it over his shoulder. She hardly weighed a thing. She had figured out what he did. She could have been trouble. But not anymore.

He pushed the door open with his left foot and scouted the immediate area again for people. He saw a few carnies in the distance but none close enough to notice his exit. He went down the trailer's three steps and sprinted to his car. With his free hand, he took out the car keys and pressed the automatic trunk release button.

Less than a minute later, Zena was inside the trunk next to his satchel bag. He closed the trunk and got inside the car. He started it and drove toward the road. Leon was then on his way to take care of his last problem.

CHAPTER 94

KILLER ON THE ROAD

I sighed, looking at the caller ID and thought I might as well get this out of the way.

"Hi, Stan."

"You decide to join the circus?" he started. "You've been AWOL telephonically."

"Yeah. I've been practicing juggling with chainsaws."

"Try not to practice if you have a woody going. On the other hand, maybe a contralto chainsaw juggler would add to your carnival panache after I shit-can you."

"I really don't care."

"Ooo. The man is standing up to his meal ticket." Stan waited for a moment, processing what I said. "I'm no psychic like your pint-sized femme fatale, but I sense something's amiss with the miss."

"Wrong."

"Something else?"

"Yeah."

"Serious?"

"Very."

"Okay, Fenn, tell me what's wrong, and then I can stop our little I'm-the-boss-of-you dance in exchange for the I'm-your-friend dance."

I had to think about that for a second. My relationship with Stan had moments of levity, mentorship, and *bon mots*, but I wasn't sure that made us friends.

I decided to just tell him what was what. "Holey John was murdered. A.k.a. John Burke."

"The man with the piercings?"

"Him."

"No kidding. That's fucking awful."

Stan waited a time, and I knew what he was considering and didn't like it.

"I'm thinking that this can be a really big, kick-ass story after all," he said enthusiastically.

"No," I said with conviction. Stan was ever the news hound for what he determined was a good and juicy story. The story I hoped to write had morphed into the kind of story that made his editorial Johnson hard. It had a dwarf, a sideshow guy who had his flesh pierced, and now a murder. His self-promoted illusion that he was publishing a magazine that was far above the bilious gossip rags was Stan revealing what he really was: a publisher pandering for the salacious.

"Who killed your guy? How'd it happen?" I went on, ignoring my reply.

I could tell him about the people who were no longer among the living aside from John. Ralph. Wally. But that would just get Stan's tittle-tattle mojo going even stronger, and that meant a full court press about fame and fortune and keeping my job.

I made the mistake of answering him. "Haven't found him."

"Killer on the road."

Stan quoted a line from the last song that Jim Morrison had recorded before he died. I wondered if he knew that.

"This is real good. Amazing good kind of good." He stopped, and I felt his brain cells working out angles. "I should come up to… where are you again?"

"I need to go." Stan in the equation was not going to happen.

"Come on, Fenn. We can double-team this puppy. Make it the story of the year."

Again with delusions.

"New York City has more murders committed in one week than what happened here," I said.

"But not with a little person and a man who made a living get-ting skewered."

"Not going to happen."

"Think about it, Fenn. Think paycheck."

I ended the call and got out of the car, heading to Zena's trailer. I needed to comfort her. And maybe I needed her to comfort me.

I saw her trailer ahead. Her door suddenly opened when I was about one hundred yards away. I smiled, thinking about seeing her. Then out of the blue, a man burst out of her trailer, hauling a rolled-up rug over his shoulder. It took me a second to realize what the rug was, the one with rose petals and unicorns. The left side of my brain said she had hired some man to have it cleaned. Then the right side discarded that conclusion and knew exactly what was happening.

"Hey!" I yelled and started running after the man. He turned for a moment and ran even faster. He reached a car, the trunk popped open, and he dropped the rug in. The man then slammed the trunk closed and jumped into the car. The wheels of the car kicked up sod and fishtailed out of the fairgrounds, headed to the road.

I didn't bother checking her trailer. I knew who that man was. No belly button explanation needed. It had to be the guy. And I knew that that man had murder on his mind.

I ran as fast as I could to my car. It started right away, and I hauled ass to the road. Left or right? Right or left? Right would take me to town. Left would take me where? And then my gut reaction kicked in again because I needed to make a life-or-death decision. I had a feeling where Zena was probably headed, and it made my skin crawl.

CHAPTER 95

WRAPPED

It was dark as she came to. An odor of car exhaust filled the burlap bag that was pulled over her head. She felt something warm trickle down her cheek. Her skull hurt and head throbbed. Pain coming from where he hit her. Zena figured she was in a car. A trunk. The space was tight. She tried to move her legs, but they were bound together with something. Same with her hands and her mouth taped shut.

The car turned. She felt a smooth road became bumpy. Tires hit potholes, and she was jostled, her body tossed around, hitting metal and nameless things that filled the trunk.

The engine stopped. The car door opened and closed. Footsteps approached. The trunk opened. She felt fresh air sweep out the fumes replaced by a pine breeze. Her heart pounded inside her chest loud enough for people to hear. To rescue her. Silly thoughts. Zena was lifted and placed on the ground. There was a heavy fabric wrapped around her like a cocoon. A moment later, she was being rolled over and over, the material removed. She could make out a dim light filtering through the hood that covered her head. Sounds came to her. She focused on the scent and sounds to distract her terror.

She knew she would be killed, but it wasn't the idea of being killed that scared her. Make it fast and painless. It was about an ending not of her own choosing that made her mad. Her life, in many ways, had not been of her choosing. Born a dwarf. Born to parents who didn't want her. Having the world see her as other.

The man grunted. She could hear him rummage around the inside of the trunk. He grunted again, lifting something out of the trunk, making a jangling noise as he lowered it.

He grunted again as she was lifted up. He then placed her over his shoulder like a farmer heaving a sack of grain. They began walking. Uneven strides. She heard twigs breaking with each of his footsteps, the rustle of leaves being kicked as he strode. She tried kicking, but he just held her tighter, squeezing the breath out of her.

Zena felt the rustling of air. Wind whistling through trees. Where was she? A forest. This is where he planned to do it. Why a forest?

They walked for a while. Time seemed suddenly precious. She heard a new sound. The sound of water. It got louder as the man marched on, and then she understood where she was, where he was taking her.

Terrified thoughts rushed through her head, trying to imagine what he was going to do with her. She wouldn't see anything she realized. The bag over head would stay over her head. The tape over her mouth would stay over her mouth. There would be no pleas for her life. No bargains made with that man who had only one thought on his mind. Get rid of the one witness who could identify him.

The crushing sound of the waterfall filled her ears. He laid her down on the ground again, roughly without regard about hurting her. She tried to squirm away, and he kicked her hard against her ribs, knocking the air out of her. Something metallic thudded to the ground.

Zena then heard a zipper open. A grunt as he heaved whatever he had carried. It made clinking sounds.

He made her sit upright. She knew in an instant of horror what the jangling sound was. A chain was being wrapped around her waist and then crisscrossed over her chest. She heard a click and something being turned. It had to be a lock linking the ends of the chain. Another chain was wound around her neck. Another lock clicked. A third chain wrapped around her legs and feet.

She understood why he had chosen the waterfalls. The eeriness of her fate was darkly clear. The chains were heavy enough to hold her down, sink her fast. She would be like a mummy wrapped with metal. And like an unwanted kitten, she would be thrown into the water to drown. There would be no trace of her. She would sink quickly and rest on the bottom of the pool, where John had met a similar fate. Except she would never rise to the surface. No one would mourn over her, her body vanished forever.

CHAPTER 96

KALARIPPAYATTU

With one hand on the steering wheel and my other hand on my phone, I dialed Kapinski.

"Cooper," he said, reading the caller ID. "What's up?"

"Zena. He took her."

"Who took her?"

"Had to be the guy that offed John and old man Gilmore."

"He take her how?"

"Rolled up in a rug."

"A rug?" he repeated, clearly confused.

I took a breath and explained what I had seen.

"You in your car?"

"Yeah. I think I know where he's headed. It's crazy if I'm right. But maybe not that crazy."

"Where?" Kapinski asked.

"Back to the falls. Where he dumped John. I'm going there now."

"Slow down, pal," Kapinski said firmly. "I'll send the Staties for help."

"Right," I lied and pressed the pedal to the metal.

My heart pounded as fast as my thoughts reeled. Ralph, John, and Wally were pawns in a killer's chess game. And now he had Zena. Whoever that guy was had no compunction to kill.

I saw to the entrance to Taughannock State Park and turned sharply onto the entrance road. The parking area was just ahead. I scanned it as I drove in. There was only one car there. Its trunk had been left open.

I pulled up to the sedan and got out. The trunk was empty. Zena's rug lay on the ground. My eyes and ears were totally focused on the surrounding forest, trying to pick out any movement or sounds. There was a sign that had arrows next to trail names. The one that made my heart leap was the one that said *Devil Falls Trail*.

That had to be where he had taken her. *Follow my gut, my belly button.* I ran to the head of the trail and leapt over fallen branches, dodged thorny brushes, and ducked under low hanging limbs.

As I ran, I was about to yell Zena's name. But that might spook this fucker and make him hurry. Hurry to get rid of her. Hurry her to a most certain death. I heard water. A cascading sound. A pounding sound. The breaks between the trees got wider as I headed toward the falls. I slowed for a moment and checked the area to my right and then left. I moved more slowly, hoping to see movement or hear Zena screaming, pleading for her life.

I reached a path that forked right and left. *Shit! Which way should I go?* Then I remembered how Wally had died: a needle into his right arm instead of his left. The guy was a righty. A fifty-fifty chance. I went right and started to run again, more aware of where my feet were landing, trying to avoid making noise.

I saw a man through the trees. He was at the edge of the falls. He was doing something. Kept bending down then standing then bending over again. I caught my breath, taking in the woods around me. As I stepped closer, I could see he was totally absorbed. I crept a few more feet then stopped, pressing myself against a tree. I peered around and saw the man more clearly. It was him. The man who had run from Zena's trailer. But where was Zena?

I crouched down and moved toward him like a panther stalking its prey. I went about twenty feet, and I saw what he was doing. Zena was lying on the ground, desperately trying to wiggle away from the man. He kicked her in the ribs, and she stopped. He was wrapping chains all around her.

There was a single chain lying by a satchel bag. He picked it up, studying his handiwork as if deciding where to put it.

I had to move fast. I looked around for something that resembled a weapon. There were a few rocks. Too small. I spotted a broken branch. Then I caught sight of a stick a couple of feet away, its bark stripped off, a shaft of wood with its end splintered. I inched over and slowly pulled it toward me. The splintered end had something on it. Crusted, dried blood.

"Hey, asshole!" I screamed and ran toward him like a crazy meth head.

The man turned; his jaw dropped.

I stopped a few yards in front of him, and we stared at each other, waiting for someone to make the first move.

He moved backward and put his foot against Zena's side, pushing against her, making her roll closer to the edge of the waterfall. I heard a muffled cry coming from under the burlap bag that covered her head. The man gripped the chain he had been holding and pulled a knife out of his back pocket.

"Zena!" I yelled to let her know I was there.

"Ah, the boyfriend comes to the rescue," he laughed. He rolled Zena even closer to the edge, and my stomach tightened. I moved forward.

"And what? You're going to push her over, me standing here as a witness?"

"Something like that. Only a witness to be a witness has to be alive."

I wielded my stick in a parrying motion, trying to distract him.

"Skywalker shit don't work with me." He swung the chain around and over his head like a gladiator about to fight in the coliseum.

I changed my grip and held the stick with both my hands, moving my legs into a fighting stance. *Kalarippayattu.*

"What happened to your laser sword?" he taunted as he swung the chain at my head.

I ducked the chain and began leaping left then right.

He stepped away from Zena and took another swing at my head while thrusting his knife at me with his other hand.

"Who put the cat scratches on your pretty face?" I said and circled him.

For some reason, this threw his focus off for a second. He swung again, and I darted back. His balance shifted, and I came at him with a barrage of rhythmic strikes with my stick. He didn't expect that, and I clipped him on the shoulder and neck but not hard enough to stop his advance.

Before I could clip him again, he whipped the chain, this time hitting my chest. I stumbled and fell. He came at me, ready to bring the chain down to crush my head. I rolled away just as the heavy metal links smashed into the ground inches from my skull.

I grabbed my stick and jumped up. I began a combination of Chuvattadi and Kaithada—snakelike movements of defense and attack.

His chain whipped past me as I twirled away but not before he lunged with his knife. He caught my shoulder, and I felt a stinging slash, warm blood running down my arm. I ignored the pain and leapt back and forth again.

"Stand still like a fucking man!"

"Great idea," I said and stood still for a split second. He came at me, and I jumped left, striking him on the side of his forehead.

Like a picador stabbing a bull to make the animal more ferocious, he charged me with full-on rage, blood dripping into his eyes.

"You are so dead, motherfucker!"

I dodged again, the man's mouthy foam spitting out his ravings. Blood clouded his vision, and I hit him again, this time across his nose. It cracked, and he staggered back, but that only made him even more incensed.

"Oh, pretty face has a broken nose," I taunted.

He started toward me but then stopped. A thought entered his head. A crooked smile appeared as he backed away, moving toward Zena.

"Big mistake, pal," he said, putting his foot on her ribs.

Her muffled cries became louder than before.

With his right heel, he started rolling her to the edge of the waterfall's rim.

I screamed, "Stop!"

"Come any closer and she goes over."

I stood in place and tried to figure out my next move. His next move.

That's when he pushed her over the rim. I heard a muted scream. I ran at him as he knew I would and was ready for me, knowing that my focus would be elsewhere—on Zena, making me an easy target for his chained blow.

The chain grazed my shoulder where he cut me but not enough to stop me. He continued to take advantage of the momentum of his strike like a cowboy whipping a lasso around. Just as the metal links came at me again, I did what I was trained to do. Pure *Kalarippayattu* instinct. I blocked the chain with my stick, the chain whipping around it like a lasso. It was like slamming on the brakes, and the momentum of his body turned against him, knocking him off balance.

I yanked the stick, and the chain slipped out of his hand. Now it was attached to my stick. I whipped the chain at him, and it wrapped around his neck like a garrote. He tumbled backward, gripping the chain with his hands, trying to release its stranglehold. As he struggled to pull off the chain, he moved closer to the rim. The chain loosened, but it was too late. His feet skidded off the rim, his arms whirling around like helicopter blades desperately as he tried to regain his balance.

As he slipped backward, I saw his face, an unbelieving look of surprise, his eyes as large as a tarsier. In that instant, he vanished from my sight, no screaming, just the sound of the waterfalls.

I rushed to the rim and caught the last part of his fall, the chain flying off his body, his hand still gripping the knife, slashing it at the air. His body slammed against the side of the waterfall's ledges, his face smashing into them as well and then the spray of water as he hit the surface and sank like a cinder block, bubbles breaking the surface but nothing else.

Still looking down to where the guy hit the pool, an electric shock coursed up my spine. There was Zena, hanging precariously from an outcrop jutting from the rocky walls of the falls, one of the chains looped over a protrusion. I saw her wiggling.

"Stop that!" I screamed. "You're caught on a ledge. You move and you'll fall."

I heard sirens behind me as I stared helplessly at Zena. Kapinski and the Staties had arrived.

CHAPTER 97

IRONY

They got an emergency rescue crew out to the falls in less than fifteen minutes. I lay on the ground with my chest at the crest of the rim, talking to Zena, telling her help was on the way, to keep still, to keep calm. Everything was going to be okay.

As I talked to her, my eyes studied the pool of churning water near. There was no sign of the man who had tried to kill Zena and me. His body still hadn't surfaced. I presumed the force of the water crashing into the pool on top of the man with a chain around his neck could keep him submerged.

Kapinski and Kohl watched as a rescue team of four men connected descenders between a harness and rope line. One man on each side controlled their descent on the anchored ropes. They reached Zena. One man maneuvered her into harness, and the other unhooked the chain that had broken her fall from the outcrop.

Kapinski and Kohl approached me. "What happened?" the detective asked.

I explained how I had had a hunch that the man that kidnapped Zena would head there and the fight I had that ended with him falling off the waterfall's rim.

Kapinski shook his head, seeing the same irony that I had felt.

"The man was no Houdini," Kohl smirked, studying the water below. "And your stick fighting," he said in disbelief. The idea he had of me as a loose-wristed writer and now knowing that I knew exotic martial arts that killed a man was too much of a stretch for him.

"You need to book me?" I asked the detective.

Kapinski shook his head. "Not if it was self-defense. We need a body in any case."

I glanced over and saw Zena was safe on the ground. The EMTs carefully removed her burlap hood. Another EMT used a scalpel to slice through the duct tape that held her wrists and ankles together. Someone else took the tape off her mouth. She looked dazed and found my eyes. She teared up, and I blinked a relieved look at her. I watched as a cop used a bolt cutter to sever the locks that held the chains, and soon, she was free.

"Can you stand?" an EMT asked her.

She nodded, and he slipped a hand under her armpit to help her get up.

I walked over to her and cupped my hands around her cheeks. I bent over, and she put her arms around my neck, and I kissed her forehead.

"Oh, Fenn," she cried with relief.

"It's over," I said, feeling emotionally and physically exhausted.

She hugged me. "My knight in shining armor."

"In shiny undies."

She smiled, remembering what John had said about my chances on the midway.

Kapinski and Kohl approached us. Kapinski had a worried look on his face as he inspected Zena's face, her cuts and bruises.

"You okay?" he asked.

"I'll be all right."

"The man who did this—" Kapinski began.

"He was a guy I saw at my booth."

"He say anything to you?"

"Said it was too bad I recognized him. Said he killed Ralph too." She closed her eyes and said softly, "It was weird."

We waited for her to explain what part of her ordeal was weird.

"He actually came to my booth to get his fortune told. In a disguise. I see that now. He was trying to find out what trailer John lived in. I told him that wasn't allowed. He must've found John later. But there was something else."

We waited again.

"His speech. Very distinctive speech. And I'll never forget his face."

Kapinski said, "So you could remember him. His face?"

"Yes," she said.

"And of course you could too," Kapinski said to me. He looked at my bloody shirt where Zena's attacker had slashed me. "You better have them look at it." He called over an EMT. "You too, Ms. Zena."

I nodded.

"We'll have you look at mug shots when you both feel better."

I waited for a moment. "Your guys going to fish him out?" I pointed to the pool of water over two hundred feet below.

"We have divers coming."

An EMT came up to Zena and me. "We'll take you to the hospital."

I turned to Kohl. "Do me a favor."

"Sure."

I handed him my car keys and said, "Follow us to the hospital so I can get my car later."

Kapinski gave him a nod.

In the ambulance, I held Zena's hand. Tears came to her again, and her chest heaved sobs of relief. "I was so afraid," she said. "Not so much about dying. I mean I was scared about drowning, my lungs filling up with water, and choking to death. But what I was really afraid of was disappearing. That no one would find my body. No one would grieve me. No one would know I was taken. I would be invisible once more."

"But you didn't die."

"You saved my life," she said through sporadic sobs.

I didn't have a quippy response, and so I smiled weakly as if saving damsels in distress was an everyday kind of thing I did.

They took the gurney out of the ambulance with Zena strapped in and rushed her past the admission desk. I saw two uniformed cops at the desk, and they followed the EMTs and a nurse to an examination room.

Bernstein was at the door, and she held up her hand. "We'll take over from here," she said. "I'll come out and give you an update. Go get yourself patched up in the meantime."

Kapinski and Kohl showed up a few minutes later. Kohl gave back my car keys.

"What's with the escorts?" I asked Kapinski. I nodded toward the two cops standing guard at the door.

"Until we find the body."

A shudder ran through me. There was no "The End" to this story. No "happily ever after."

Bernstein came out of the exam room. "Cuts aren't too bad. Some bruises to her ribs. A concussion. I gave her a shot for the pain so she'll be a little woozy. We'll give her an MRI to be safe. She'll be here a day or two."

An orderly and a nurse wheeled her out of the exam room. Zena looked up at me and smiled. I thought she mouthed "I love you" as they wheeled her away.

I didn't say "I love you too." I just nodded, giving her my best shining-knight smile.

CHAPTER 98

NUMB

Back in my motel room, I pulled a chair to the window and cracked it open. I fired up my vape and held the smoke deep inside my lungs. I did this a couple more times and felt a mood change. I had been wrapped tighter than a Victorian corset, and I felt my body lose some of its tension.

I ran through the events of the last few hours. It was like watching a movie that jumped from one scene to another but in no logical order. The last frames were watching the man who had kidnapped Zena go tumbling backward. His eyes had caught mine for a split second. Was it disbelief? Or fear? Or the anger of someone who knew he would not write his own happy ending?

I had killed a man and still waited for a reaction. I understood what I had done but felt no regret. It was as if I was playing some video game where people never really die and reappear after you hit Reset.

I called home.

"You're calling," Selma said as soon as she picked up the phone. Caller ID was no stranger to her.

"Hi, Mom. Is Dad there?"

"You okay?"

"Fine. We can talk later. I need to speak to Dad."

"I can tell," she said.

"Tell what?"

"Something's wrong. I hear it in your voice."

"Nothing is wrong," I lied. If I told her what had happened, she would one—as a mother—become completely unhinged and two—as a therapist—insist on me going into trauma counseling. I wanted to avoid both.

"I know nothing, and this is not a *nothing* nothing."

"You're right. Is Dad there?"

"Okay. I'm not deaf. A son needs his father sometimes."

I could tell she was hurt that I didn't confide in her as to what my *nothing* nothing was.

"What's up, son?" my father said, getting on the phone.

I heard my mother in the background say to put my call on speaker.

"Not on speaker," I instructed my father.

"Right. So what's up?"

I came right out and said, "I think I killed a man today.'

He was quiet for a minute. "*Think?*"

I explained what had happened.

"No body yet," he asked as if he was back being a homicide detective.

"Nope."

He thought for a few moments. "That makes it difficult."

"But there's something else."

"What's that?"

"I don't feel anything."

"Numb."

"Yeah, numb. Not feeling guilty. No remorse."

"This guy a bad guy?"

"Very. Think he killed three people we know of. Then tried to get rid of Zena."

"The midget."

"Dwarf. Little person."

"Tried but failed?" he asked.

"Right."

"You the one that got in his way?"

"Yes."

"So he tried to kill your friend and kill you, right?"

"Yes."

My father took a few moments to organize his thoughts then said, "Look, son, there is evil in the world. Evil people. They are not candidates for therapy, rehab, or a 'Come to Jesus' moment. History is littered with millions of their victims."

"I guess."

"He was going to kill you," my father went on. "Remember that."

"I'll try."

"Happy to talk to you about this. Or anything. Okay? What you did won't be forgotten even if it was a righteous kill."

"Yeah," I said, trying to take his advice in.

I ended the call with Selma in the background, asking Marco what that was all about, and my father saying it was just a man-to-man thing. I heard her mutter something that sounded like "Yeah, yeah, right, guy talk." Better that she didn't know.

CHAPTER 99

FOLLOW THE MONEY

A week later, Zena was out of the hospital. We were gathered around the table in an incident room again at police headquarters.

"Thanks for coming today," Kapinski said.

He had gathered us together for the latest progress in what was called the incident room. I would have called it the catastrophe room since *incident* was a pretty weak way of describing what happened to Zena, John, Ralph, Wally, and me, but I let it go. He was running the show.

"The body," Zena said right off the bat. "I haven't heard shit from you about that."

He squirmed.

"The guy what, just evaporated?"

At the far end of the table, Zena spotted Stan and a second man.

"Who the hell are you?" she asked.

"Stan Blanker. Fenn's publisher. And my lawyer, Frank Connelly."

Her eyes shot back at me. "Tell him to go fuck himself if he's looking for a story."

"I did. He showed up here uninvited."

Stan offered a deferential look of guilt. "I'm here to help."

I cut him off. "You are not going to take this tragedy and give me thirty coins of silver to write a story."

My biblical reference of betrayal aimed at Stan seemed a bit over the top but needed to be said. I no longer cared about his threat about my job. My ethical compass had wandered into a shaky magnetic field, pointing me in the wrong direction for too long.

Clearly, Zena set the tone of the meeting. She was pissed and worried, having had two cops posted by her hospital room door "just in case," as Kapinski had explained.

Kapinski and Kohl sat opposite Zena and me. He also had two of his forensic people along. Bernstein sat next to me, coming from the hospital morgue with a stack of files. I assumed she had brought photos and notations from the Gilmore, John, and Wally's autopsies.

Zena stirred, waiting for Kapinski to move along.

I saw Stan giving her a pleading look, his raised eyebrows that signaled he wanted something. A quiet talk. A chance to persuade. Stan was like a hovering vulture, waiting for the right time to land on the carrion.

"No fucking way," she said, decoding his body language.

Stan gave her a contrite gesture and looked away.

Kapinski saw that Zena and Stan's exchange had played out. "If you all are finished with whatever has put a bee in your respective bonnets..."

Stan, Zena, and I nodded.

"I'd like to move on." He took out his worn notepad and flipped through it. "The elephant in the room is who is or was this guy. Our prime suspect is a big question mark."

I saw that Zena was fidgeting, and I knew why.

"So what's exactly happening with your search at the falls?" she asked.

"No luck with our divers. So we're dredging now."

Zena became more restless, sitting uneasily in her chair.

"If he's at the bottom of the falls, we'll find him," Kapinski said as assuringly as possible.

I frowned. A body should have been recovered by then. And there was no way that asshole could have survived the fall. I had seen him crash into the outcrop then slam repeatedly against the limestone walls that lined the waterfall.

Zena exhaled anxiously.

Kapinski heard it too and said, "Don't worry. He's not coming back either from hell or anywhere else."

"So what do we know about this guy?" I asked Kapinski.

One of the forensic men spoke. "Our perp is an unknown. We tried finding usable fingerprints. Dusted his car and the chains. Came up with zilch. The Gilmore attic. Sullivan's truck. They were all wiped down. Traces of blood on some leaves. All belonging to Mr. Burke and you."

Kapinski looked at another page of his notes. "We know our suspect was looking for something. So we checked around. Seems our local librarian and a woman who works in our county records office said there was a man looking for information about Percy Maxwell. Wanted to know where he might've lived. Said he was writing a story on Ithaca film history. Funny thing about that. Both gave two very different descriptions of what he looked like."

That caught my attention. "He was walking around in plain sight…"

"The Ghost Walker Murders," Stan said under his breath, thinking up a headline for the story he hoped would be written.

Zena closed her eyes, shaking her head.

"This man was a professional," Kapinski said with certainty. "Careful about not leaving traces. He's got the MO of a hit man."

"Hit men usually work for others," Stan interrupted. "The question is *who*."

Zena shot Stan a "Who the fuck asked you?" look.

"We all know the reason why Mr. Burke was murdered," Kapinski went on. "What he swallowed. The contract."

Kapinski pointed to the contract in an open file in front of him.

"Can I see it?" Connelly, the lawyer, asked.

Kapinski looked at Zena for permission.

She shrugged.

Connelly put on a pair on rimless eyeglasses as Kapinski handed him the copy.

"Mr. Connelly is no stranger to contracts," Stan said, having a chance to earn some Brownie points with Zena.

Connelly scrutinized the paper. "It's a contract as the detective indicated," he confirmed. He read it through. We waited then read it one more time.

"Anything special about it?" I asked.

Connelly jabbed a finger at the contract. "What's interesting is that the wording of the contract ensures perpetuity. In other words, the agreement with Mazer and Maxwell and these other men who signed this had to be honored if Mazer were ever to sell his company to another company. And if that company sells themselves to another entity, the clause is still in effect and so on and so on. Of course if the last company goes bust and is the last one holding this paper, the deal is dead."

"And if the last holder doesn't go bust?" Zena questioned, trying to understand the clause.

"It's an uninterrupted agreement."

"Like 'pay it forward forever,'" Kohl said brightly.

The lawyer half-nodded. "It would seem that if any holder existed, then any of the named DimaDozen people could have cashed out. Maybe none did for whatever reason. We don't know. But if they didn't, any holder has to honor the contract. Then we have motive."

"Motive," Zena repeated.

"*De lege lata.* Meaning 'of the law as it is' or, in this case, 'as the agreement stands.'"

"So if the agreement is binding and all the signatories are dead, then what?" I asked.

"Then any living relatives are entitled to the agreement."

"And John would've been entitled," Zena said.

"Of course," I said too loudly. Everyone looked at me. I looked at Zena. "He wanted *you* to find it. That's why he swallowed it."

Zena scrunched her eyebrows, visibly puzzled. "For what reason?"

I continued my line of reasoning. "Here's a guy willing to kill for it. John had to understand it must've had some value..."

I turned to the lawyer. "Somebody must have been afraid of what the contract would mean if it surfaced."

Connelly interjected his own assumption. "And of course, any payout might be an issue. The question would be how much it's worth."

"Follow the money," Stan said then looked at Zena. "The motive and the money and the murders. Mr. Connelly could help track that down. You find the money, you find the guy who hired him."

Kohl cleared his throat. "There is another possibility we didn't cover," he said uneasily. "Not about this contract you're all talking about."

We all looked at him.

"Devil Falls," he started.

"Go on," Kapinski said.

"Well, there's a creek."

Kapinski urged him to say what was on his mind with a bob of his head.

"Taughannock Creek is right by the falls. It empties into Cayuga Lake. If this guy didn't die and could manage to swim…"

Kohl left the rest of the sentence hanging.

We all sat still and silent.

Zena pushed her chair back and stood. "I don't believe this shit. You saying this asshole might still be alive."

"We can't say that for certain," Kapinski defended.

"I need certain," she insisted. "I don't want to be looking over my shoulder for the rest of my life."

"There's no reason you should," Kapinski replied. "If by any reason he's alive, which would be highly improbable, we know what he looks like. And he knows we know what he's done."

"In the meantime, I have a few ideas about how we can find who might be behind this," Connelly said.

"Like?" I asked.

"Assume this is a contract tied to an existing production studio. It makes sense that someone is sweating bullets if this contract turned up. If so, this was enough incentive…"

"To kill three people to find and destroy it," Zena added, completing his thought.

Connelly nodded. "People take dangerous risks if they have something to lose."

Zena studied Connelly. "John is dead."

"Yes, of course, and we are very sad for your loss."

"But he had a wife who may be alive," Zena said enthusiastically. "Maybe a daughter. They'd be entitled to whatever money came from this agreement."

Connelly saw where she was going with this. "Yes, assuming they are alive and can be located."

I could tell Zena considered what the lawyer said. "Located," she said softly.

A heavy silence fell over the room. There was nothing more to say.

"I'll have a squad car parked near your trailer just in case," Kapinski said to Zena. "You'll be safe."

Zena grimaced but said "Thank you" as we all got up.

Stan followed us. "Connelly will let you know what he turns up."

I nodded, knowing that Stan was trying to ingratiate himself to Zena. Always the charming bloodhound when it came to uncovering a juicy story.

CHAPTER 100

DEFACED

The man tugged at his necktie as he looked over the books of stamps. He put the loop to his eye to examine the Cape of Good Hope stamp. It was the first stamp issued in Africa and could fetch around $40,000 retail. He held his gaze on the stamp, admiring the design and the condition. An *ah* seeped through his open mouth. The man looked at another stamp then went to his well-thumbed edition of the *Stanley Burke Stamp Catalogue*. The stamp was the 1854 Half Anna from India, which he would sell for $20,000. This time an *ooh* made his mouth look like a donut hole, another rare collectible taking his breath away.

"You having a stamp-related orgasm?" Freddy teased.

The man removed the loop from this right eye and wiped sweat from his forehead with the back of his hand.

"Yes, Frederick, a philatelist's wet dream," the man agreed. "Dare I ask how you came across these fine specimens?"

"You know how this works, Mickey. Like before. No questions. Just give me a number to take these off my hands. And the coins. I came to you first, but I know other people that would be thrilled to see what I got."

"Fine, fine," Mickey relinquished. He then gave Freddy a number, and the latter smiled.

"Cash."

Mickey nodded, got up, and went to his safe. While he opened it, Freddy's cell phone rang.

"Yeah," he answered.

"You alone?" the man on the other end asked.

"Alone enough. Where you been?"

"Outta town."

"I figured. Still on that job with the movie guy?"

"Winding it down," Leon stammered.

"So what do I owe the pleasure to?" Freddy asked, feeling something amiss.

"I need you to pick me up. And I need a place where I can stay outta sight."

"The job go south on you or something?"

Freddy heard a painful groan.

"It is what it is." The man's breath came in short inhalations.

"You don't sound so good."

"I'm not."

"I don't recognize the number. Funny area code."

"Yeah. Borrowed the phone." Leon looked down at the motionless kid.

"Where are you?" Freddy asked.

He gave him a location.

Freddy listened for a minute then said, "In a fucking barn."

"Yeah. Ithaca." He paused then said, "And I need you fix me up with that doctor you know. No hospital. In her office is what I need. Bring drugs. Morphine. Plenty of it."

"Care to say what happened," Freddy probed, his anxiety rising.

"Bad fall. Real bad."

"What kind?"

"A run-in with a cliff. Doesn't matter how right now." A pause. "Brinks check in with you?"

"Like I said, he did the 'See ya later, boogie.'" Freddy half-smiled; Brinks's misfortune was his fortune.

"Another thing. The doc is gonna do some alterations."

"What kind?"

"Can't look like I did before."

"Shitting me right? A new face?"

Leon said nothing.

"That bad, huh?"

"Yeah," Leon said. "A different look that'll still get me in front of a camera."

"Without your buddy Brinks?"

"He was a flake. But I got a new angle."

"Without Brinks?"

"Hmm." Leon thought for another moment. "One more thing."

"Sure."

"I can't be Leon Schitke anymore. I need a new identity. Social number. License. Passport. The works."

"I can do that." Freddy waited, then asked, "What's your new name gonna be?"

Leon mulled that over. "Rowley Goodbody."

"Classy."

"Yeah. How soon can you get up here?"

Freddy turned to Mickey, who was at his safe, taking cash out. "Hey, Mickey," he shouted.

"What?"

"I need to borrow a vehicle."

"Why?"

"Better not know why?"

Leon heard Freddy talking to someone in the background again. He leaned against a bale of hay and began to puzzle out how much time he had. He figured the cops were still searching the pool. He had some time left but not much more before they figured out that there was no body. And that would get them thinking, and what he didn't need was cops thinking.

It was a miracle he had survived at all. His army days rappelling down walls were what saved him, using his arms and legs to break some of the impact as he smashed into the rocky face of the falls. He minimized the number of broken bones, although his ribs were cracked, and he was sure that his right ankle and left arm were broken. When he hit the water, the force of the falls pushed him down. Underwater, currents pushed him to a muddy bank with hanging bushes hiding him when he finally surfaced. He saw some kind of lake hearing police sirens get close. He knew he wouldn't be able to swim anywhere since his body was like a broken marionette.

That's when he spotted a barn at the edge of a clearing at the bank of the lake. The pain almost made him black out, but he crawled over rocks and thorny brambles, finding the barn door open. Using his elbows, he edged his way into the barn and found a dark corner and passed out.

He didn't know how long before a kid jabbed him in his thigh with his foot. Leon was still gripping the knife as if he was still in fight for his life. The kid held a fishing pole. He saw how bad he looked and offered to call an ambulance. He took out a cell phone, and before dialing 911, Leon threw his knife, the blade entering the kid's throat. He was dead before he hit the straw-strewn ground.

Freddy came back on the phone. "Gotta ride for you."

"How long before you get here?" Leon asked, his breathing hard.

Freddy saw Mickey had packed his gym bag with his payout. "Give me six hours."

Leon cut the connection. He rewound what had happened, and the last image he had before hitting the water was of Zena hanging from the outcrop. She could identify him same as her boyfriend. As before, she would be a problem. But a new face would take care of the problem. New face. New identify. New scheme.

He thought about the plastic surgery. His new face. He'd pick a look from one of the stars of the thirties. A winner back then could be a winner now.

He looked at the lifeless kid. He hoped no one would miss the youngster before Freddy came. He retrieved his knife but was too banged up to dig a grave with it. Maybe a barn fire just after Freddy picked him up. No need for any evidence that he escaped or even a dead witness. Just like Brinks, the old Leon would be dust in the wind. And then he would be back to Los Angeles and rise like the phoenix from the desert.

CHAPTER 101

LOOSE ENDS

I walked with Zena as we left the police conference room. "How about a drink?"

"Sure," she said vacantly, her spirit beaten down, her life force deflated. Her best friend's murder unsolved. Her attacker's whereabouts, if alive, unknown. Her future as empty as a politician's promises.

I headed back to where it all started. My first encounters with Zena and John. Bookends.

"Maxie's okay?" I asked.

"Sure."

We got a table. No fans asking for autographs. Just folks having a meal. We ordered drinks. Me a beer; she a Scotch.

She turned to me with a confused expression, light lines etched across her forehead as she questioned her situation.

"My world is so upside down," she started.

"How could it not be?"

"I used to feel I had a couple of anchors to hold me in place. They were make-believe but real at the same time. John always had my back. I felt safe from the world. And my Zena the Fortune-Teller routine gave me a purpose. I figured that in some way I actually helped people. And that helped me. I know I was living in a cocoon of my own making, but what's wrong with that? Don't we all do that? Make up a world that is tolerable to manage the chaos? Don't we all make believe that this job or that has some value even if it's just to pay our bills?"

Cocoon. Bubble. Dome. Comfortable routines. She was echoing my own life.

"We do." I reached out to hold her hand, small and dainty inside mine.

"I have to move on with my life. Right?"

She looked at me as if I could hand her a set of next life instructions.

"You have any ideas?" I asked.

She shrugged.

"Don't sell yourself short."

She gave me the finger.

A waiter came over, and I ordered another beer. Zena pointed to her empty glass for a second round. We sat without talking. She stared at the glass, her mind floating away to a place I did not want to intrude. Best to leave her be for now.

Her drink arrived, and she swallowed about half of it in one go. She made a face like you see when a movie cowboy downs a shot after a dusty trail ride.

"The G brothers?" I said, breaking the silence.

"Gave them notice. For once, they actually seemed to have some sympathy. Said they were sorry about John. Even said I'd be welcome to come back anytime."

"So there is a God," I said.

"Yeah, the god of taking a percentage of what you make."

"It's the G Brothers after all."

"Yeah."

"Well, at least that's one decision you've already made."

She nursed the rest of her drink, still thinking.

"What about the house?" I asked.

"I don't know. What happened there to Ralph creeps me out. Like living in a house that sits on an old Indian burial ground."

"Hard to pretend shit never happened."

"Yeah." She took a sip of her drink then set it down. "But I have this idea that I could try living there. Can't let this fucker and what he did win. It was John's wish. I should honor that. Get a shaman to burn sage and chase the bad juju out."

"Ithaca probably has a bunch of shamans."

"And I have another idea," she said, giving me a small smile. "I could be your sugar momma, you know." She smiled a bit wider now. "Now that you are jobless. Move in with me. See what happens."

Zena said that with a twinkle in her eye, but I thought she meant it.

I couldn't help to think about her offer. We had made a connection. But was there more to us than being FWB? It seemed clear she wanted it to be more than that. I loved her spirit, her directness, her courage. But I had only known her less than two weeks. I assumed she wanted to put me in the boyfriend category. I went inside my head, imagining being the boyfriend of a little person, handling the stares and comments that Zena had gotten all her life. The standard-issue guy with his dwarf companion. Was I still the jerk that I had always been and learned nothing from her?

I pushed that thought away and smiled back, taking a sip of my beer. "Really?"

"Hmm."

"Something to think about." I wasn't blowing her offer off, but I had too many loose ends in my life. There was Lilly. Did we still have a relationship worth pursuing? Did I want to? If not, I owed it to her to end it like a *mensch*. She would give me a fiery lecture about how I was a relationship coward. And I would agree. She would tell me that I had a closer, more committed relationship with my cat. I would agree again. She would accuse me of something going on with Zena, and I would probably sidestep that one since I had not figured out where Zena fit or did not fit into my life. And of course, there was leaving the city.

I looked at Zena as she studied me, she knowing that a million thoughts were banging around my head.

"No need to make a decision this second," she said, pretty sure that I wouldn't.

I nodded even though her eyes were trained on me like a doe not wanting the hunter to shoot.

She had another thought. "Are you uncomfortable being with me? Me being who and what I am."

"Of course not," I said too quickly.

Zena gave me an uncertain look.

More people came into Maxie's. A few did double-takes, seeing Zena and me sitting together. "There is something that you can do for me," she started.

"Okay."

"Something you could do if you want a new adventure with me."

I waited for a moment and gave her a "Go ahead" look.

"The contract. John wanted us to find it. He knew he'd die, and so protecting the contact would have value for someone else."

"You're thinking about his wife and kid."

She gave me a pleading look. "Stay here and help me find them. You told him you would try. You made a promise."

I had said that to him when he was alive, but I hesitated now. As with Zena, I didn't know what I wanted to do next.

"You know my dad already tracked down some information. No wife turning up."

"We need to try harder."

I looked at her, not knowing if I wanted to take this own as my new project.

"Maybe your dad could help again. We could go visit your folks. Tell them what happened to John. How we need to search for his family."

This was her new mission in life.

"It's an idea," I said. But the idea of Zena and Selma in the same room made me fidget.

"It's an idea," I repeated. *A really bad one*, I thought. With Selma, you needed to warm her up to the uncomfortable. Showing up with Zena might cause a heart attack. The last thing I wanted to convey to Zena was that I was uncomfortable bringing her to my folks. Having that thought, I wondered if I had evolved any with my time with her. Not as much as I had hoped. For the last few days, I had inhabited the same cocoon as Zena where the real world was outside of the G Brothers bubble. I caught myself struggling with the "what is normal and what is not" paradigm. Size may not matter much in bed as it does out of it.

Our drinks' glasses were empty, and more people entered. Our waitress came over.

"And another beer for me."

"Just water," Zena said and left.

"We could make a good team," she said, pressing me to make me agree. "Honoring John's wishes," she reminded me once again, donning the cloak of a little person guilt thrower.

I took a breath. A promise to a man who was now dead.

"We could go on a trip together."

"A trip?"

"Yeah. Vietnam. We go there, try and find Linh. And something else."

I waited for the *something else*.

"What happened to him."

"Those nightmares?"

"Yes."

"Why do you want to know about that? He may have done things that you don't want to know."

"Maybe but I knew his soul. He's not a killer. Wasn't a killer."

"But that's what soldiers do." I waited for a few seconds then said, "Something may have happened and that may explain why he spent years having people stab his flesh."

"For repentance?"

"Maybe."

"Well, I want closure."

"For who?"

"Me. For him. I'm sure his wife could tell us about his nightmares."

She tried a new approach, seeing I was hesitating. "You could write your own story. My story. John's. What happened here and then whatever unfolds over there. And fuck Stan. You could sell your story. Maybe to the *New Yorker*. They liked your kidnapping piece."

"Let me think about it."

"Okay."

I waited for a moment, postponing what I said next. "I'm going to head back to the city tomorrow."

"I figured you would. Clean up your messes with the misses." My little friend was beginning to sound like Selma.

"There's that."

"Can you do me a favor, assuming you survive your return?"

"Sure."

"Come back for John's memorial service. It would mean a lot to me."

I didn't hesitate this time. "I'd be happy to, sweetie."

"Sweetie is it now?"

"Always."

"And if you survive, you can tell me if you want to help me."

"I will seriously think it over."

I paid the bill, and we walked out into the evening air. It was still warm outside, a gentle summer breeze coming off the Cayuga Lake.

"You want to spend your last night with me?" she asked.

I wondered if this was a good idea.

"One quick roll in the hay before you go so you won't forget me."

"I will never forget you."

"Is that a yes or a no?"

I knew I would go back to a shit storm facing Lilly and Selma and whatever other things I had to figure out. So I had a "what the heck" moment as I often did, being a man who is not adverse to pleasure over pain. I reached for her hand and said softly, "I wanted dessert, you know."

"Now you can have it."

"Hmmm," I said. "How can a guy like me refuse that?"

"You can't, bucko."

CHAPTER 102

FACE THE MUSIC

We had a simple breakfast in her trailer the next morning. We were too edgy or uncertain about what to say to each other to have much of an appetite. The time we spent in bed the night before seemed frantic, like sex between a couple who thought that World War III was about to nuke everyone on the planet and we'd better get our last licks in—literally and figuratively.

We took a long shower together after breakfast. The shower was soothing, and when we were done, Zena put on her bathrobe and then wiped my body down with a soft, downy towel. She was gentle and hummed a song I did not know.

"Last night felt like a very special send-off," I said.

"You are special."

I got dressed and put my wallet and keys into my pocket.

"You have my cell," I said.

"And you have mine."

"Right," I said, feeling the awkwardness of leaving her.

"Call me when you get to the city."

"For sure."

"And think about helping me," she said, giving me a beseeching look.

"I will."

"Is that a wishy-washy 'I will' or a 'maybe I will'?"

"It's a real one."

"Okay then."

We held each other on the steps of her trailer. It would be her last day at the Giambolvo Brothers. She told me that people had planned a goodbye party for her when the circus and midway shut down for the night. I was happy for that. She needed closure there along with John. It also made me feel less guilty for leaving, knowing that she would be surrounded by her friends at least for that night.

I packed my things and moved out of the motel. Before I drove away, I took a few hits off my Special Queen. I held the smoke in and then blew it out slowly through the car window. *Goodbye, motel. Goodbye, Ithaca.* At least for now.

When I left the motel, I had noticed smoke coming from a barn in the distance. Two fire trucks were breaking the speed limit flying over a ridge of a hill, coming from the opposite direction as I got on Route 79.

I felt like my brain had been dropped into a blender, everything I had experienced in the last few days whirling around. To put a break on my jumbled thoughts, I turned on the radio. A Paul Simon song played: "Fifty Ways to Leave your Lover." I shook my head in disbelief. Is there such a thing as a radio life coincidence?

I sang along with Paul:

> Ooh, slip out the back, Jack
> Make a new plan, Stan
> You don't need to be coy, Roy
> Just listen to me

"Make a new plan, Stan" stuck in my head, echoing what Zena had said about ditching my boss. A few miles later, I came to a steep hill where a line of cars had slowed behind a tractor. A green van honked as it passed me, trying to get around the line of cars. I looked over and caught a glimpse of a man sitting in the passenger seat. His face was pretty banged up like he was on the losing side of a bare-knuckle cage fight.

The man with the smashed-up face traded a quick glance with me before turning away. The van swerved back into the lane ahead of the tractor. My first notion was why someone was in such a hurry.

My second thought drove a spiky chill down my back. Something about the man with the busted face. Something that familiar. The chill returned. My knuckles gripped the steering wheel, turning them chalk white.

"It couldn't be *him*," I said through the wind shield. "No fucking way."

I lost sight of the van, and my mind dwelled on the image of that banged-up face. I seesawed back and forth, wondering if that was the man I thought I'd killed. Maybe the weed was muddling up my mind. If I applied common sense logic, a man having his body smash all the way down a ragged cliff and landing under the crushing weight of a waterfall could not survive. If my logic was sound, then whom I had seen could not be the guy. But logic was not a reliable antidote against the inexplicable.

I called Kapinski and told him whom and what I had seen.

"Green van. On 79 heading toward Richford."

"Impossible, Cooper."

"Things can seem impossible until it isn't."

He mulled over what I had said. "Okay, I'll put out an APB. I sure hope you're not smoking dope here."

I figured the detective said that as a figure of speech.

"Let me know," I said and then thought for a moment. "Up to you if you want to tell Zena."

"I'll think on it. Maybe not worry her just yet."

He killed the connection, and I drove on.

Over the next hours, I talked myself out of the idea that that was the man who had killed three people and tried to do the same to Zena and me.

I hit the city midafternoon and drove down the West Side Highway, getting off at Twenty-Third Street. I found a space across the street from my apartment. I opened the trunk of my rented car and pulled out my luggage and laptop. When I looked up at my window on the fourth floor, I saw my cat staring down at me. He was smiling like the Cheshire Cat, knowing I was in a shit load of trouble.

CHAPTER 103

THE PITCH

Tankowitz picked up the call. The number was blocked, but many of his clients used that feature.

"Yes," he answered.

"Mr. Tankowitz."

"Speaking. And you are?"

"You don't need to know that right now. However, you will be interested in what I have to say."

"Really," he said doubtfully.

"It's about that money that went missing from your client?"

"What money?" Tankowitz said, becoming uneasy.

"Don't play cute," Leon said. "It's gone along with Brinks."

Tankowitz felt his neck muscles tighten.

Leon said, "I'm guessing you've been trying to find him. I'm guessing you keep running into dead ends."

"Let me guess," Tankowitz said guardedly. "You have information, and you want something in exchange."

"Smart man. There's a nice place we can meet. Have a nice chat. Give you a taste of what I know."

"A chat," Tankowitz repeated.

"And bring the big guy."

"Who might that be?"

"The man who wants you to find your pal as much as you. Brenner. Head of Glowball."

"I'm pretty sure that's not going to happen. And the more I talk to you, I'm hearing some guy sounding like he's got blackmail on his mind."

"Not a nice way to start a relationship. Call it what you want, but I'd hate to have what I know go any further than you and Brenner."

Tankowitz didn't need that extra bullshit on top of what he had already been trying to crisis manage. He called his bluff. "I think you need to fuck with someone who cares."

"Okay, but stockholders get hinky when certain information surfaces. Like cooked books and disappearing CFOs."

Tankowitz's jaw clenched. This guy knew more than he thought.

"So I talk and you and the big guy listen."

Silence.

"And tell Brenner I'll give him a peek at some old contracts that'll really fuck with his shit if they ever surfaced."

"What contracts?"

"A binding contract involving a huge Glowball payout that Brenner didn't know he had."

"This is bullshit."

"One way to find out is to meet me. If not…well, it's on you." Leon then gave Tankowitz the name of the bar if he wanted to meet. "I'll be easy to spot. Think of Karloff in *The Mummy*."

Tankowitz and Brenner passed midday drunks, nursing their drinks, staring like zombies at a baseball game on the bar's TV.

They headed to a dimly lit booth. The man said he would be hard to miss. He hadn't lied. His face was completely wrapped in bandages. His eyes were covered by a pair of sunglasses; a section of bandages were cut to expose his mouth. He was sipping a drink through a straw. When he saw the men approach, he stopped sipping and smiled.

"Gentlemen," Leon said pleasantly, "please have a seat."

Brenner frowned, seeing the man who looked like one of his studio extras. And Tankowitz was struck by the man's lisp, which almost made him chuckle coming from a mummy. He decided that would not be a good idea.

"I'm Rowley," Leon said, using his newly acquired name.

"Why are we here?" Brenner asked sternly. His face was stretched tight, his lips taut, his eyes like daggers puncturing Leon's wrapped-up skull.

"You have a problem," Leon started. "Brinks and what he did."

"This is not news to us," Brenner said indignantly.

"You missed something other than the shell game Brinks played on you."

"Ah. Some mysterious other thing," Brenner said, making the words sound frivolous. "You're wasting my time." With that, he began to stand.

"I suggest you sit." Leon slid a sheet of paper across the table to Tankowitz. "I believe you would not like to have this see the light of day."

"What is it?" Brenner asked.

"Read it, and then you tell me."

It took ten minutes for Tankowitz to understand the intent of the Mazer Maxwell deal. The blood vessels in his temples began to throb, and he muttered a few *fucks* as he read it.

He then looked at Tankowitz.

"It seems Glowball inherited this." Tankowitz gave the sheet of paper to Brenner. "Glowball inherited a contract attached to one of your acquired companies."

"Meaning what?"

"It's a binding contract that Glowball has to honor," Tankowitz said, pointing to the contact. "It was drawn up in 1926. It prescribes that the original signatories can cash out their shares at any time."

"Shares?"

"Shares which represent a percentage of the value for any company that holds the contract," Tankowitz explained. "A contract you now own."

The lines in Brenner's forehead creased. "But that was signed over ninety years ago. They'd be all dead by now. So why should I care?"

"Because any relatives who may still be alive inherit the same rights," Leon clarified.

"Why is this a problem?"

Tankowitz put in plain words what the contract stipulated.

"If that contract surfaced…"

"And there were five of them," Leon added smugly.

"The shares can be cashed in," Tankowitz said, spelling out the problem.

Brenner's face became a bloodless mask. "How much are we talking about?"

"It could be quite a lot," Tankowitz said. "Millions."

"How many?"

"Too many," Tankowitz answered.

Brenner scrutinized Leon and jabbed a finger at the sheet of paper. "Brinks hired you to find these."

"Actually you asked him to find any paper ghosts."

Leon saw recognition unfold on Brenner's face.

"And he hired you to find them." Brenner took a moment then said, "And you did."

"If I tell you more, it'd be like showing a poker hand before the last bet is made."

Tankowitz and Brenner were silent, but it was clear what Leon was saying. Not quite like being blackmailed but certainly skirting the edges.

"You want something," Brenner said.

Leon smirked and said, "That's why we're here. My guess is that you don't want those contracts left floating around."

"And what about any living heirs?"

"What can I say?" Leon said, lifting his hands upward. "They show up waving that paper and you'll have trucks of cash leaving the building."

"So your offer is what?" Tankowitz asked, getting to the point.

"I can tell you what happened to each one." Leon knew this was a total lie, but he said it so convincingly. Still the promising actor.

"And the relatives?" Brenner asked, looking for more information.

"Since this is still us playing poker, I won't show my cards just yet."

Tankowitz studied Leon. "And you want what for this? Money, I assume. So the question is, How much?"

"Oh, I want some money for sure. But I have another idea." He turned his attention to Brenner. "I always had this idea about becoming an actor."

Brenner frowned and said, "An actor. Really."

"As real as a morning boner."

After, he explained his terms, exactly the same ones he had laid out to Brinks about treating his speech impediment, having screen tests, and then given a few small roles to see where that could lead.

"Give us a moment," Brenner said. He and Tankowitz left the booth, left the bar, and went outside.

Leon watched them leave and had a moment of panic. Did they buy his pitch? He knew if they didn't return in the next few minutes, his spiel hadn't worked.

The door to the bar opened, and the sunlight outside silhouetted the two men who left a few minutes before. They were coming back. They were ready to deal.

After they had agreed to his terms, they left. There was an obligatory handshake. He felt like he was back in the saddle again. Almost. Sure, he would have a brand-new face. Handsome. Longer chin with a manly cleft like Kirk Douglas. A high forehead that blended handsome with intelligence. And full lips. Kissable.

The feeling of exhilaration did not last long. He Googled the Ithaca newspapers ever since he skipped town and read that the fucking midget survived. They ran her story for a couple of days. The newspapers had written him off for dead. The unknown killer. But there was the guy he passed when he and Freddy were driving. He saw the guy do a double-take.

As he finished his drink, he was sure that after his surgery, she would never recognize him. In any case, they would never cross paths again. Not in a million years. Yet in spite of this, he got the willies, the way she read his fortune; how she looked right through him. And when he tried to kill her, the words she said: *I will always know you.*

Then there was her Bruce Lee wannabe whatever boyfriend. The man who bested him. The man who thought he killed him.

The man who had seen him clearly when they fought to the death at Devil Falls. The man in the car he passed.

He made a decision. Once he was completely healed, he would track both of them down. It shouldn't be that hard. The Ithaca newspaper gave his name. How hard would it be to find that midget and her boyfriend? Research was his middle name.

Leon threw forty dollars on the table for the waitress and got up. It was a new day, a brave, new world, and in this new world, Leon concluded that both of them had to go. Just like Brinks had said, "Leave no trails."

EPILOGUE

WASHINGTON, DC

The obituary was short. He skimmed to the essentials.

> John Burke. A decorated war hero. Vietnam
> veteran. Bronze and Silver Stars. Purple Heart
> awarded for injuries sustained. Nephew of
> famed silent movie producer and director Percy
> Maxwell. Mr. Burke is preceded in death by
> his parents. Services will be private and held at
> Conklin's Funeral Home in Ithaca, New York.

The man felt an amazing sense of relief. He had waited for over forty years to find information about John Burke's whereabouts. In the years before the Internet, he had scoured newspapers, hunted down the smallest leads, combed microfiches, and always wound up with dead ends. The man that could ruin his life had disappeared.

When the Internet became a reliable tool for his mission to locate Burke, he would use search engines for any mention of John Burke with a filter focusing on Vietnam vets. And now the man he was looking for was found. Finally. He could breathe more easily after a lifetime of fearing ghosts. Actually, just one.

Senator Randall Stinger always had plans. Big plans. He was being considered as a pick for vice president in the upcoming election. As with any candidate for higher office, the press and especially members of the opposition would be hunting for skeletons in his closet. He admitted to a sexual indiscretion with an office worker twenty-five years before when he was single and was elected to the state assembly nevertheless. His *mea culpas* were duly made and forgiven. He made sure he went to church on a regular basis and even spoke at sponsored events by Women Against Violence that earned him praise. He was a decorated war hero. Promoted to lieutenant while on his second tour in Nam. Came home. Got married to a nice girl. Two kids, the obligatory golden retriever, and a promising future he had intentionally secured in one split second outside a village in the Central Highlands. With Burke gone, anybody searching his past for dirt would come up empty.

That had not been the case until that day. The one worrying act from his past was deliberate and criminal. It hung over him like the sword of Damocles those many years. If it ever came to light, what he had done, his career, and all the things he struggled to achieve to get this far would come to nothing. Shooting Burke was an act of perseverance to cover up the massacre he had initiated. If Burke had surfaced with his memory intact, the five-time elected congressman from Georgia and current US senator's career would go down in flames since there was no statute of limitations on war crimes.

He looked out his office window from the Hart Senate Office building. His memory from over forty years before about that day was as clear as the day it happened. When Burke realized what Stinger had done and would report the incident after his men left the ville, Stinger had shot him in the head. He called in a Huey to med-vac Burke out, assuming Burke would be sent home in a body bag. His bad luck was that the man survived. Stinger was quick to spin his fabricated version of what had happened; made Burke a hero by telling his manufactured account. There were no other witnesses to shooting Burke since the other grunts had beat feet back to base camp.

Even Duffy, the soldier that had nodded a "Do what needs to be done" nod, never saw what actually happened next. Besides, Duffy was dead, a victim of alcohol and drugs, according to his widow when Stinger came to the man's funeral.

Stinger remembered going to Walter Reed, the military's medical center for wounded vets when he was between tours. He saw Burke during visitor's hours for several weeks. The man was almost a vegetable. He came back for a visit around Thanksgiving to see what improvement his platoon leader had made if any. The bed was empty. The attending doc said that Burke had regained some of his brain functions and checked himself out. When he asked the doc where he had gone, the medical man just shrugged.

Once Stinger became a congressman, he was able to get into Burke's medical and VA history. The man he feared did not return to any VA hospitals or collect benefits in person. Monthly disability checks were sent to a bank account with offices around the country, and the bank refused to give him any information about activity. Stinger decided that probing too much might draw attention. He didn't need that, especially since the report that was written up by his CO concerning the massacre had been buried and heavily sanitized. They didn't need *My Lai*, version 2, on the six o'clock news.

The senator read the obit again. He decided to send flowers to the funeral home, have his campaign manager send out a press release, acknowledging a fallen comrade's death, about how he and Burke survived an ambush and the medals they had received. Reminding people about his military service was always a good thing for a candidate. He sat down and began to write an inscription for the card.

May he rest in peace at last.

He scribbled his signature and told his secretary to have it come from members of his former combat unit.

*****

I drove back to Ithaca to be with Zena to attend John's memorial service at Conklin's Funeral Home and accompany her when she would scatter John's ashes. A small crowd showed up to say their goodbyes and prayers for him. All the midway people came: Dolly Daggers the sword swallower, the armless artist, the remaining members of the Tom Thumbers, and Tillie, the tattooed lady, who found a new schtick by eating worms and other creepy-crawly things.

Zena stood at the front of the room where the service was held.

"He was my protector. He was my best friend. I will miss my friend, and if there is a place we go after we're done here, I know he will be at peace and maybe still keep an eye out for me."

After the service, we drove to Devil Falls with the urn that held John's cremains and a bottle of champagne.

Alone in the car, she began to question me.

"How did it go with *her*?" she started.

Her was Lilly, and I hadn't spoken to Zena about my return to the Big Apple.

"Rough."

"How rough?"

"She's-not-talking-to-me rough."

"I'm sorry."

I knew she wasn't.

"You mention me?"

"I did. That we became good friends, having survived all that had taken place."

Zena pressed he lips together. "Nothing more?"

I looked straight into her eyes and said, "Look, Zena. I've known you for what? Two weeks or so. We got close. Closer than most of the women I've been with. I really like you. You know that. We went through a harrowing experience that few have gone through. That is special and always will be."

"Special." She repeated my portrayal of what we experienced like a recipient of a dead mackerel.

"Yes."

"So what then? Are we just special friends?"

"More than just friends."

"Because we made love."

"We did."

"Were we an item?"

"Not in the way you want me to say."

I could tell that hurt her. That was the same question she had asked after we first made love. I knew she was ever hopeful about the *us* question. I thought she understood what we had. She had said we would be a temporary thing, a nice fling, and when I was gone,

I would be gone. Maybe she did not remember that conversation or did not want to.

"It didn't seem right to tell her that you and I shared a bed. Had sex. Made love. I think she suspected that anyway. But I didn't see the point of telling her more than I did. Whatever kind of jerk I may be, I don't try to intentionally hurt the people I care about. I cared about Lilly but couldn't give her what she wanted. In any case, she and I are no longer a couple. I imagine she will be collecting her things from my place as soon as I get back to the city."

Zena looked like she hoped that that was the case and said, "Because of me?"

I wondered why it was so important to Zena that she be the cause of my breakup.

"No, because of me," I said honestly. "I wasn't going to settle down, give up my life as journalist, make babies, and buy a house in Scarsdale. That was her dream. Not mine."

"Because…"

"Because there are things in my life that I haven't figured out. It wouldn't be fair to drag another person along while I do that. I'm a man dancing around a volcano."

Zena stared at me, hoping for more, but there was no more to give.

*****

I turned the rented car into the entrance of the state park. We went to the spot where Zena had almost died, where I had fought and seen my attacker fall into the pool of churning water at the bottom of the falls.

I popped the cork and poured the bubbly into two plastic cups. Zena opened the lid of the urn, and together, we poured John into the pounding torrent of water. She held a lovely arrangement of flowers and placed it next to a nearby tree.

"These are nice," she said, laying the flowers down.

"They are," I agreed.

"Funny about these flowers John got, sent to the funeral home."

"Why?"

"The card it came with," Zena said, puzzled. "No name that I could make out. More like a scribble. But it had an odd inscription." She read the card out loud. "*May he rest in peace at last.*"

"Maybe someone he served with over in Nam."

"Yes. It came from his old unit. But the *at last* wording seems strange, like whoever sent it knew what John went through."

I could see her figuring something out.

"Maybe whoever sent it could help us, you know?"

"*Us?*"

"Yeah. When we try to track down John's wife."

"Ah," I said. "There you go again with the *us* and the *we* and *the tracking down* thing."

She gave me a sweet smile and shrugged.

"You did say you'd consider it."

"*Consider* being the operative word here," I reminded her.

"I might change my mind about you writing a story about John and me."

"Is this a carrot you're dangling for me to come with you?"

"Can't blame a girl for trying. Just one more thing, Fenn."

"Which is what?"

"I'm not afraid of people dancing around volcanoes while sorting their shit out. We can still be a team even while you figure out whatever it is you're trying to figure out."

I gave her a look that acknowledged her offer.

We then turned to the rim of the falls and let the smell of pine trees and the cool mist of the falls soothe us, a peaceful feeling that we had not felt for too long a time.

Zena looked at the rock formation that sported a face. "When a devil falls, an angel rises." With that, she offered a toast and raised the cup of champagne. "To John and men who dance around volcanoes."

Zena put her hand into mine. I squeezed her hand and held it for a long while.

ACKNOWLEDGEMENTS

I would like to thank the following people for their support: Elisabeth Elo, author of *Finding Katarina M.* and *North of Boston* for her encouragement and support, Houston Police Department Commander, Zachary Becker for his help with police procedurals who is also the author of *Gun Shy*, Robert Ness who served in Viet Nam for sharing his experiences with me, Leslie Joseph and Emily Heill my first editors, and Robert Ducas, my first literary agent who sadly passed away.

The author also wants to acknowledge the following books that helped with my research: John H. Richardson's book about the world of little people, *In The Little World, A True Story of Dwarfs, Love and Trouble* (thank you Elisabeth), Carol Kammen whose book *Ithaca: A Brief History* and Janet O'Daniel's book *The Cliff Hangers* both of which gave me invaluable information about Ithaca's silent movie industry.

ABOUT THE AUTHOR

Jesse Kalfel is the author of *So You're Cremated, Now What?* His work includes a number of optioned screenplays along with stage plays, which have been performed in Boston and Manhattan. He is the recipient of two Hatch Awards and grants from the New York State Council on the Arts. He lives on the North Shore of Massachusetts with his wife and their adopted cats and dogs.

Printed in the USA
CPSIA information can be obtained
at www.ICGtesting.com
BVHW030321240823
668819BV00001B/1

9 781639 859009